Born and raised on the ̶ ̶ ̶ ̶ ̶ ̶ ̶ ̶ ̶ ̶ ̶ **Amy Ruttan** fled the ̶ ̶ ̶ ̶ country boy of her drea ̶ ̶ ̶ ̶ ̶ ̶ ̶ ̶ ̶ ̶ ̶ ̶ ̶ ̶now mum to three wonderful children, who have given her another job as a taxi driver. A voracious reader, she was given her first romance novel by her grandmother, who shared her penchant for a hot romance. From that moment Amy was hooked by the magical worlds, handsome heroes and sigh-worthy romances contained in the pages, and she knew what she wanted to be when she grew up.

Amy loves to hear from readers. It makes her day, in fact. You can find out more about Amy at her website: amyruttan.com

Carol Marinelli recently filled in a form asking for her job title. Thrilled to be able to put down her answer, she put writer. Then it asked what Carol did for relaxation and she put down the truth – writing. The third question asked for her hobbies. Well, not wanting to look obsessed she crossed the fingers on her hand and answered swimming but, given that the chlorine in the pool does terrible things to her highlights – I'm sure you can guess the real answer.

Emily Forbes is an award-winning author of Medical Romances for Mills & Boon. She has written over twenty-five books and has twice been a finalist in the Australian Romantic Book of the Year Award, won in 2013 for her novel *Sydney Harbour Hospital: Evie's Bombshell Wishlist*. You can get in touch with her at ̶ ̶ ̶ ̶ ̶ ̶ ̶ ̶ es@internode.on.net, or visit her

The Hot Docs on Call

COLLECTION

July 2019

August 2019

September 2019

October 2019

November 2019

December 2019

Hot Docs on Call: Surgeon's Seduction

AMY RUTTAN

CAROL MARINELLI

EMILY FORBES

MILLS & BOON

First Published in Great Britain 2019
By Mills & Boon, an imprint of HarperCollins *Publishers*
1 London Bridge Street, London, SE1 9GF

HOT DOCS ON CALL: SURGEON'S SEDUCTION
© 2019 Harlequin Books S.A.

One Night in New York © Amy Ruttan 2015
Seduced by the Heart Surgeon © Harlequin Books S.A. 2016
Falling for the Single Dad © Harlequin Books S.A. 2016

Special thanks and acknowledgement are given to
Carol Marinelli and Emily Forbes for their contribution
to *The Hollywood Hills Clinic* series.

ISBN: 978-0-263-27666-4

0819

MIX
Paper from
responsible sources
FSC™ C007454

This book is produced from independently certified FSC™ paper
to ensure responsible forest management.

For more information visit: www.harpercollins.co.uk/green

Printed and bound in Spain
by CPI, Barcelona

ONE NIGHT
IN NEW YORK

AMY RUTTAN

This book is dedicated to my fellow
quartet authors Tina Beckett,
Amalie Berlin and Lucy Ryder.

Thank you ladies for such an awesome experience.
I had so much fun creating an exciting world with
you and bringing West Manhattan Saints to life.

CHAPTER ONE

Manhattan, winter

THE BAR WASN'T particularly packed tonight, but that wasn't overly strange as it was the middle of the week. Still, as Sam Napier peered around the glitzy nightclub on the Upper West Side, far from his local watering hole in Brooklyn, there were a few glitterati mingling, drinks in their hands, trying to escape the wintry blast of cold air outside. It was a good night to people-watch and he had nothing else to do.

He leaned back against the bar, sipping his Scotch and people-watching. This was a place where he could just melt into the woodwork, if there was any wood in the chrome and glass bar, and no one knew who he was. It was nice.

The local watering hole in Brooklyn was great, but there would be a ninety-nine point nine percent chance that he would run into someone from work and/or one of his roommates and tonight he didn't want that. He didn't need to talk about how there was a new attending who could possibly mess with his future at West Manhattan Saints Hospital.

Besides, Enzo, his closest friend, had paired up with

Sam's roommate Kimberlyn and those two had recently moved to Tennessee. His other roommate, Tessa, had moved out and there was no way he could handle the *girl* talk with Holly his only current roommate, though some more were moving in. Just the thought of her chattering made him shudder.

There was no one to commiserate with. No close friends and those he was close to wouldn't expect him to open up anyway. He kept most things to himself, but tonight he really needed to drown his sorrows. No one would understand that one of the department heads who had a say in his appointment as a pediatric fellow had retired and a new replacement surgeon had been appointed. And apparently the surgeon replacing Dr. Powers, the former Head of Obstetrics and Maternal-Fetal Medicine, was one of the top surgeons in the field and a slave-driver.

But Sam didn't see the need for maternal-fetal medicine at West Manhattan Saints. Dr. Amelia Chang, Head of Pediatrics, could handle most issues in utero with the OB/GYN, and even then they could send the patient on to a larger hospital if necessary.

In all Sam's years at West Manhattan Saints he'd barely seen Dr. Powers in surgery. So why did she need a replacement for such a small department? The obstetrics department at West Manhattan Saints was not large. The hospital was known for trauma, with Dr. Ootaka at the helm, and Pediatrics.

This new attending was a waste of money as far as Sam was concerned. But not surprising, given who the chief of surgery was. This new attending was probably BFFs with Professor Gareth Langley.

Great. Just what he needed: another egotistical, maniacal surgeon like the chief of surgery at West Manhattan Saints or, worse, like his mother...

At least he'd learned one thing from her numerous failed relationships and dalliances: successful surgeons couldn't have a family.

"You need to find someone, Sam. You're lonely." Kimberlyn's plea popped into his mind. *I know some nice girls,"* she had said repeatedly.

Sam had always rebuffed her. The last thing he wanted was a relationship. He didn't have time for one. Still, he kind of wished sometimes he had someone, even if just for a moment.

Sam was knocked out of his reverie and his drink was splashed down the front of his sweater when he was whacked by an icy wet scarf.

"Holy crackers! It's cold out there," a big puffy yeti said, sitting down on the bar stool next to him as it began to pull off its layers.

"Bloody hell..."

"Oh, my God. I'm so sorry." As the last layer came off a beautiful redheaded vixen reached for a napkin and began to dab at his sweater in a futile attempt to soak up the expensive Scotch that had seeped into the fibers. "I can't believe I did that. I didn't see you there."

"Obviously not." Sam wiped away the chunk of snow that was melting in his eye. "Then again, I don't how much you could see with that many layers on. It's not that cold outside, lass."

Her brown eyes widened. "You're Scottish."

"Half," he mumbled, snatching the napkin from her hand and trying to fix the damage to his sweater himself. When he got agitated his accent came out thicker. His mother was American, but since his father had mostly raised him in the Highlands he had more Scot in him than Yankee, though he had been born in Manhattan at the hospital he was currently completing his residency in.

"I hope it's not designer," she said with concern.

"What's not?" Sam asked confused.

"The sweater."

He chuckled. "Hardly. No, it's not designer. I just like it, that's all."

And he did. His gran had knitted it for him. It was a blue-gray V-neck sweater, which had seen better days, but it gave him a sense of home.

She smiled, a lovely warm one that made his heart skip a beat. There was something about red-haired women that made him melt just a bit. Maybe it was something about gingers sticking together, even though his hair was more auburn and hers was a bit more mahogany than the classic ginger.

Bloody hell. Why am I analyzing hair color? How many drinks have I had?

Then he remembered the Scotch currently soaked into his sweater had been his first and he'd only had a taste of it.

"I'm really sorry. Can I replace the drink I spilled?" she asked.

"That you can do."

"I have to say I'm disappointed."

"How so?" he asked.

"I thought you were going to answer me with 'Aye.'"

Sam laughed. "No, I only save that for when I'm really tetchy. My name is Sam, by the way."

"Mindy." She held out her hand and he took it in

his, brushing a quick kiss across her knuckles, which made her gasp.

He heard it and it pleased him to know he'd gotten that response out of her. Something his dear old dad had taught him.

"A pleasure to meet you, Mindy." Sam was still holding her hand as she stared up at him for a moment, her eyes wide, her pink lips open, but only for a moment then pink tinged her cheeks and she took back her hand.

"It's a pleasure to meet you." She cleared her throat and turned to the barkeeper. "One Merlot and a...?"

"Scotch."

The barkeep nodded and moved away. Sam took the bar stool next to her. "So, I take it you're not from around these parts."

"What makes you say that?" she asked.

"You were bundled up enough to make a trek to the South Pole."

Mindy chuckled. "I'm really not used to the cold."

"I gathered that."

The barkeeper returned with their drinks and Mindy slid him some money. He could just say thanks for the drink and move on, really he should, but she was just the kind of distraction from his own problems that he was looking for. It had been some time since he'd indulged, he'd been so focused on his residency. He never entered into one-night situations, because he refused to follow in the same footsteps as his mother, but maybe tonight if Mindy was interested he could relent, just a bit.

"Where are you from?" Sam asked.

"California. Born and raised. And where are you from?"

"Here," Sam replied, winking at her.

"Oh, come on. I told you mine, now tell me yours."

"Well, I was born in Manhattan, but I was raised in the Highlands by my father."

"How interesting." She took a sip of her wine. "Was he a laird?"

It was meant as a tease. He knew it. It always was.

"Aye, he is."

Mindy choked on her wine. "You're not serious?"

"I am. Very. Did you not hear my 'Aye'?"

"I thought that was only saved for when you were tetchy?"

"Or when I'm *very* serious." He winked at her.

"He's a laird?"

"It's not as romantic as you're thinking it is. It just means he owns a large bit of land in the Highlands. He doesn't serve out justice to his lowly tenants. He's not nobility."

"So what does that make you?"

"Make me?"

"Or are there other heirs apparent?" She winked as she took a sip of her Merlot.

Sam laughed. "I'm the eldest, but really it doesn't make me anything other than what you see here."

Mindy cocked her head to one side. "And here I thought I was talking to royalty."

Sam chuckled. "Hardly. So what brought you from the warm confines of California to the harsh and bitter environment of Manhattan?"

"You're mocking me, aren't you?"

"Just a wee bit."

Mindy sighed and tucked a long strand of mahogany hair behind her ear. "A new job and a new...start."

"I can tell from your tone that you wanted to get as far away from California as possible."

"How can you tell that from my tone?"

"It was tight, like you were in pain."

What are you doing?

As Mindy glanced over at the devilishly handsome man, warmth spread through her, a zing of something she hadn't felt in quite some time.

Maybe it's the wine?

No, not the wine. Even when she'd still been with Dean, the last few years of their marriage had been detached and they had just been going through the motions. Of course, she'd thought it was their careers that had kept them apart, she'd never suspected someone else and she had certainly never expected that someone else to be her best friend and colleague. Dean and Owen's betrayal cut her to the quick. She'd trusted Dean. He had been her husband and he betrayed her.

Trust was something she never gave freely. She'd been burned so many times by so-called friends. She'd thought she'd been able to trust her husband. The one person who'd held her heart. So when he'd done the unthinkable she'd had a hard time believing in any one else, in trusting another person. Intimacy was a huge leap of faith, letting someone see that vulnerable side to you.

So, yeah, it had been a long time since she'd even contemplated thinking about a man in a sexual way. It had been a while since a tingle of excitement at the possibility of something more had revved her motor, but when his lips brushed against her knuckles suddenly the cold winter temperatures had no longer bothered her.

Sam's blue eyes were twinkling mischievously. He was a bad boy. There was no mistaking it, but the way he leaned against the bar, the emotional walls he had in place, the devilry in those blue, blue eyes. Sam was the kind of man her mother had always warned her to steer clear of. Yet it had been the *nice* man, the respectable one, whom her mother had approved of, who had betrayed her trust.

Besides, she was just flirting with this handsome heir of a Scottish laird in an upscale Manhattan bar. It didn't have to go any further than this.

Why not?

It might be nice to cut loose and celebrate a new life, at a new hospital. Tonight she didn't have to be a world-renowned maternal-fetal surgeon. Tonight she just had to be Mindy. She'd never see this guy again. He wouldn't use her or hurt her.

She could just be Mindy. Lonely and scared out of her mind Mindy, but still…

What was he saying? Oh, yes, he thought she sounded in pain. Great.

She giggled nervously.

Maybe he sensed she needed a change of topic because he asked, "So, what makes me so funny, then? Is it the accent that amuses you so much? Or is it my boyish charm?" He waggled his eyebrows suggestively, making her melt just a bit.

"Boyish charm for sure." She smiled at him, which was easy to do. She couldn't recall ever smiling and flirting with Dean, but, then, she had always been a wallflower. Shy and meek. This was new, it felt good. She picked up her drink and took a sip, wincing at the burn of alcohol. Honestly, she didn't know why she'd ordered wine, she wasn't much of a drinker.

"Something wrong with your wine?" Sam asked.

"No, nothing. It's fine. I don't usually go to bars."

"Then can I ask why you wanted to brave the harsh, bitter environment of winter to come to a bar and suffer through what looks to be a very painful glass of wine."

Mindy shrugged. "As I said, I'm new here. I wanted to meet people."

Sam leaned over. "*Well*, you've met me."

"You're laying it on very thick now."

"It amuses me to do so." He cleared his throat and then swigged down the last of his Scotch. "There, that's better. My mellow American accent is back. What do you think?"

"I prefer the Scottish one." Then she giggled.

It was pathetic that she was giggling. It had been a while since she'd dated or flirted, but when you spent your whole career operating on such delicate humans as fetuses you didn't really have much of a life. Not when their tiny little lives were in your hands. Not when their mothers' lives were in your hands. She spent a lot of time in research, in ORs, sitting by patients' bedsides.

Too many happy families depended on her and being one of the top surgeons in her field meant she was in high demand.

There was no time for socializing or anything else. She'd met Dean when they had both been interns, learning under the same surgeon. They'd both been maternal-fetal specialists. They'd both been on the same trajectory.

Or so she'd thought.

"Dean, don't you want to have kids? I'm ready. I think we're ready."

"We're not ready, Mindy. You just think you're ready. You work around kids and babies all day long. We have to focus on our careers now. Once we're both really settled and in the top of our chosen fields, then we'll settle down. We'll have a couple of kids."

And then that had never happened and now it wouldn't happen because, number one, she was no longer Dean's wife, number two, he was still in California, and, number three, Dean was gay.

There had been a lot of sniggers in the private practice she'd worked at in Los Angeles with Dean about how she'd found out he'd been cheating on her. Mindy had known Owen was gay, he had been her best friend. She didn't care that Dean was gay, it was the fact that he'd gone behind her back and cheated on her with Owen and that the two of them had been carrying on for over a year and hadn't told her. She'd shared her insecurities with Owen about her marriage. She'd trusted him too and he'd used those secret hurts and concerns against her.

That's what had hurt the most. Dean knew everything she'd told Owen.

"You look angry all of a sudden. Are you okay?" Sam asked, breaking her out of her thoughts.

"I'm fine." Well, she wasn't. Not really. She was still letting Dean and Owen get to her. Even though it had been a year since her divorce had been finalized.

Dean and Owen had moved on and were in the process of adopting a child.

A child. Mindy had wanted a child for five years,

but Dean had never been ready and Owen had told her not to push Dean on the matter.

"I'm fine," she said again, and swigged back the last of her Merlot. "Just. Fine."

So many years of her life wasted. Too many.

"I don't think you are." Sam got up. "Do you want me to walk you home?"

"You can do more than walk me home." She wasn't sure if it was the wine or what, but she grabbed the collar of Sam's sweater, or where there would've been a collar if he wasn't wearing a V-neck, and pulled him close to her, planting a kiss on his lips because she had to see for herself if those lips against hers would be just as thrilling as when they'd brushed against her knuckles.

And God help her. They were.

Stop. Stop. Stop.

Only she couldn't. His arms went around her, his strong hands on her back as their bodies pressed together. The kiss deepened, so even if she wanted to turn back now she couldn't. It had been so long since she'd had this kind of human contact.

So long that she'd forgotten what it was like and maybe even forgotten that she craved it, to have a man be aroused by *her* and not by her best friend.

Just her.

Sam broke off the kiss. "If you continue to do that I don't think I'll be able to stop."

"What if I don't want you to stop?"

Sam's blue eyes twinkled. "Well, then, that's a whole different story."

"My apartment is next door."

He grinned. "Oh, aye?"

"Yeah." Mindy grabbed her copious layers and took his hand, leading him out of the bar. She was going to be impulsive. *Even if it was just this once in her life.* She was going to live a little and she was going to do it with this dishy Scottish laird heir, or whoever he claimed to be.

She just needed this.

She badly needed to wipe the slate clean.

"Hold on. I just need to get my jacket. I may be more used to the winters than you, but I don't want to freeze out there."

"Sorry, I wasn't thinking."

He grinned and winked at her. "It's okay. For a moment I wasn't thinking either. I was just thinking about kissing you again." Then he leaned in, brushing his knuckles down the side of her face, which made her knees go weak, just before he kissed her. A light kiss that made her whole body tingle with anticipation.

Mindy watched the dishy Scot go to the coat check and slip on his jacket.

She couldn't believe that she was actually doing this, that she was taking a strange man home to her apartment to have sex with. A younger man to boot.

In all her thirty-seven years she'd never done anything like this. She'd never lived dangerously. She was always too afraid to take the chance, to take the risk. Except when it came to surgery. When she was in the OR it gave her a whole different kind of rush. When she was in the OR and a mother and her baby's lives were in jeopardy she went with her gut instinct. It was the same instinct she was using now.

Mindy was trying to listen to her gut more often, especially about non-medical situations. She'd been terrified about leaving California, which was safe and what she knew, but she'd listened to her gut and made the decision to travel across country.

So when she'd seen Sam and spoken with him, her gut had told her to take a chance, to live a little. She hadn't been with anyone since Dean and even then that had been some time ago.

It was time to start afresh.

She could do this and, more importantly, she wanted to do this.

He joined her. "Lead the way."

Mindy's cheeks flushed with heat and she knew she was blushing, but she didn't care as she took his hand. They walked across the street to her condo. The doorman let her in and didn't even bat an eyelash over the fact that she had gone to the bar alone less than an hour ago and was returning with a man.

They got into the elevator and she hit the button to her floor.

"Penthouse?" he remarked.

"It's the best."

The elevator stopped and they walked down the hall to her apartment. She was shaking. She was very nervous about what was going to happen, but she wanted it to happen.

"Here it is," she said, hoping that her voice didn't wobble too much.

Get a grip on yourself, Mindy! You're not some inexperienced virgin. You've done this before.

"Are you nervous, Mindy?" he asked.

"A bit."

"Look, we don't have to do this. I won't be mad."

He was being a gentleman. He was giving her a

way out, but she didn't want a way out. She wanted this. She needed this night. Tomorrow she was going to start her new job and she wouldn't have time for moments like this.

As of tomorrow she planned to focus solely on building her career and her patient list at West Manhattan Saints. There would be no time for dating, gorgeous men or trysts. It was now or never.

"No, I want this. It's just that I've…I've never done this before."

He smiled at her tenderly, stroking her face. "I have a confession."

"Oh, yes?"

"I haven't done this for a very long time, and if you want to stop at any moment, I'll stop. I won't force you, I won't pressure you."

Mindy smiled and then kissed him, just like she had in the bar. His arms came around her, their bodies pressed together.

"I want this." She unlocked the door to her apartment and pulled him inside.

There was no turning back now for her.

CHAPTER TWO

SAM HURRIED DOWN the hall of West Manhattan Saints at a quick pace, but considering he was late it was a pace that wasn't quick enough for his liking. He'd been reluctant to leave that temptress's bed this morning, but he had and before she'd woken up.

Which was good. He didn't want to deal with any aftermath. At least her apartment was close to the hospital, but he was still late. He was never late and people would notice. It wasn't good.

Not when today was the day the new head of maternal-fetal medicine was being introduced to the peds floor. He'd barely made it to the hospital in time for a shower and a fresh set of scrubs. His sweater, currently hanging in his locker, still smelled strongly of Scotch. He straightened the collar of his white lab coat and slung his stethoscope around his neck without missing a beat.

"Holly said you didn't make it home last night," Rebecca, their new roommate, teased as she fell into step beside him.

"Since when did you become my keeper?"

"You're tetchy this morning. What happened last night?"

"Nothing. Look, shouldn't you be on the trauma floor?" Sam asked, trying to get rid of Rebecca before she pried too much deeper. His roommate didn't need to know that he'd had a one-night stand. He didn't know her well enough yet and she seemed to report everything back to Holly, Tessa or Kimberlyn. And those three were always purporting to know nice girls to set him up with. The three of them were in cahoots.

Sam figured it had something to do with the fact that he had been the only male in the brownstone for some time. Not to mention that they were all loved up themselves and seemed determined to push soulmatedom on everyone else.

"Heading there now. Just wanted to wish you good luck with the new head. I hear she's tough."

Sam grunted his thanks as Rebecca headed down another hallway that led back to Trauma and he kept on his course to Peds. Before he pushed open the rainbow-colored double doors that led into the pediatric department, he straightened his hair in the reflection of the mirror.

There was already a crowd gathering in the main thoroughfare of the department, right in front of the main charge desk. Sam could see Dr. Amelia Chang talking calmly to the group of surgeons who were all vying for the two coveted fellowship positions in Peds.

As he moved into the group he caught Dr. Chang's gaze and could see she was quite aware that he was late. Her quiet disapproval and disappointment was hard to miss.

Mother would not be impressed.

At least Dr. Chang wouldn't humiliate him and call him out on the carpet for being late. His mother's way of teaching her residents was shaming them so they didn't do it again. Dr. Chang would probably put him on scut duty. Labs and charting he could deal with.

"Now that we're all here, we can finally get down to business. As you are all aware, this pediatric fellowship is one of the top five on the eastern seaboard, and we can only open this fellowship to two worthy residents. Because of that, the hospital has always felt that those two positions should not be decided solely by the pediatric head. That's why the head of Neonatology, Dr. Hall, taking over from Dr. Powers, the head of Obstetrics, Dr. Finn, and also the new head of Maternal-Fetal Medicine will *all* have a say in who gets those two spots." Dr. Chang leaned against the charge desk, her eyes scanning the crowd, silently assessing them in that unnerving way she had before continuing.

"I know some of you have questioned the need for Maternal-Fetal Medicine to have an impact on your career as a pediatric fellow at West Manhattan Saints. We don't see a lot of births that require a need for that, but that is changing. West Manhattan Saints hopes to become an innovative leader in maternal-fetal medicine and high-risk pregnancies. We will be expanding our birthing center to accommodate high-risk pregnancies."

Sam was stunned, but pleased that this new head wasn't a waste of resources and he could see the potential of Labor and Delivery, Neonatology and Pediatrics hand in hand to become one of the best hospitals on the eastern seaboard. Still, how many high-risk pregnancies could they possibly see?

"As you know, Dr. Powers retired, and after many years of excellent service we wish her the best. Thankfully, Professor Langley was able to find a replacement for the maternal-fetal role, which means the selection for fellowship won't be delayed any longer. Dr. Walker is one of the top maternal-fetal surgeons from California."

A knot of dread formed in Sam's stomach and he quickly scanned the room and then saw Dr. Walker approaching the group. He couldn't believe what he was seeing.

Mindy.

The vixen from last night, the bumbling yeti who had spilled his Scotch and then seduced him, was walking with Dr. Finn. She looked so different from last night. All that glorious, silken mahogany hair was tied back and she wore black square glasses with only light lip gloss. Her look was demure, professional, but as Sam let his gaze rove over her, her appearance didn't fool him. He knew what was lurking under the surface and just the thought of her in his arms and under him caused his blood to boil.

This was *not* good. Not the sex, that had been beyond good, but the fact that it had been with one of his new bosses was *not good*. If he had known that, he would've walked away from her. He refused to follow the same path as his mother. She'd used sex to get what she wanted when she'd been a young surgeon and he'd seen how that had broken his father's heart.

He wanted to get the fellowship on his own merits, because he had talent. He wanted to prove to his mother that he had what it took to be the very best, to get where he was without sleeping his way there. He'd show her.

Mindy's appearance was bad.

Very bad.

He tried to move to the back of the crowd, but it was too late. She looked out over the crowd, and that bright smile faded, wavering slightly as their gazes locked.

"Without further ado I would like to introduce the new head of Maternal-Fetal Medicine, Dr. Mindy Walker."

Mindy blushed slightly and broke the visual connection as she came up beside Dr. Chang, shaking her hand as everyone applauded her politely.

Sam tried to swallow the lump in his throat as he pretended that he didn't know her. Even though no one else had seemed to notice the interplay between the two of them, he felt singled out.

Why did it have to be her? Why did his only one-night stand in the last three years have to be someone who was responsible for the fate of his career?

Bloody fates.

He slid his attention back to Mindy, who was now addressing the crowd.

"I want to thank everyone here. I'm a perfectionist when it comes to my specialty. I don't tolerate a lot of things when it comes to my surgical practice. Fragile lives are in our hands. There is no time for mistakes and because I'm new to this hospital and have yet to get to know all of you, I'll be requesting each one of you to work on my rotation for at least a week or more before I make any decisions about who will be getting a fellowship. My department is not large by any means yet. I'm also one of the top IVF and fertility doctors in the country. I'm a board certified OB/GYN. Pregnancy and the safe of arrival of babies and their mothers are my passion. One I take seriously." She paused, her gaze penetrating him, and it was then Sam knew he was in trouble. Deep trouble.

"I look forward to working with all of you." She turned and began to chat with Dr. Chang and the other heads.

Everyone clapped politely as the crowd dispersed to start their rounds. What else could they do? The committee had the control over the fellowship. He just had to make sure he kept his nose down and worked hard.

And keep his distance.

Sam tried to slip away with the crowd.

"Dr. Napier, could you come here a moment, please?" Dr. Chang called out.

So much for slinking off and going unnoticed today.

He turned around and walked over to Dr. Chang and Dr. Walker. Mindy's face was expressionless as he approached them.

"Yes, Dr. Chang?" He said his words carefully, because he didn't want his Scottish accent to bubble up. He'd told Mindy that it surfaced when his emotions weren't in check.

"You were late this morning. Are you okay?" Dr. Chang asked.

"I…" He tried not to make eye contact with Mindy, who had a pink tinge to her cheeks. "I overslept, that's all. It won't happen again."

Dr. Chang nodded, assessing him. He hated disappointing her. She embodied everything great in pediatric surgery and he wanted one of the fellowship spots. It's why he had been willing to come to West Manhattan Saints and work in a hospital that had ties to his mother and ties to Professor Langley, who was the first man his mother had had an affair with.

Sam detested Langley, but having a chance to work and learn beside Dr. Amelia Chang? He could put aside all his animosity for that.

"See that it doesn't," Dr. Chang said.

"I'll make sure of it, Dr. Chang."

"Dr. Walker has requested you join her service for the first rotation."

Sam cringed inwardly. "Of course."

"It's a great honor to learn from her. The skills you'll learn from her will be invaluable." Dr. Chang didn't say any more as she walked away, presumably to start her rounds. The only people around the charge station now were him and Mindy.

No. Not Mindy. Dr. Walker.

Well, whoever she was. She looked none too pleased to see him.

"Dr. Napier?" Her eyes were positively flinty, her arms crossed and her lips pursed together in a thin line. Sam wasn't exactly sure how she got the words out.

"Dr. Walker," he acknowledged. He wanted to ask her why she hadn't told him what her job was, but, then, the conversation last night had never really stretched to that.

"Well, I hope you have a good understanding of high-risk pregnancies and have clocked some hours in OB/GYN and genetics. My caseload here is heavy. I have mothers coming in from a lot of different hospitals, some as far west as California, to seek my professional help. I don't want an inept surgeon bumbling around in my OR."

She was clearly angry.

"I can assure you I'm one of the top residents in this program, Dr. Walker."

Mindy snorted. "That remains to be seen."

"What do you mean by that?" Sam asked.

"You know what I mean," she snapped under her breath. "Don't think sleeping with me gains you any extra footing here, Dr. Napier. In fact, it's detrimental to your position in this program. I don't play favorites."

Sam vibrated with anger and without thinking he grabbed Mindy by her arm and dragged her to the nearest empty exam room, not caring who saw them. Which was saying a whole lot. He hated drawing attention to himself, but suggesting he'd slept with her to get ahead? That was taking it too far.

He was here to work hard for himself. He needed to nip this in the bud. He didn't want any rumors flying around.

And he wasn't going to allow a rumor to destroy his career, his reputation.

He pushed her into the exam room, flicked on the light, shut the door and stood in front of it, stopping her only means of escape.

"Do you think I slept with you to *gain footing*? If that's what you think, you had better change your opinion right now." His brogue was coming out very thickly, but he couldn't control it.

He was angry.

Very angry.

Mindy was shaking with a mixture of anger and betrayal.

Dammit.

Of course the one time she had a one-night stand it had to be with a surgical resident and one she was going to have direct involvement with. The day before she'd slept with Sam, she'd been going over the residents' files, reading over notes from other attendings, reports from other doctors and patients.

Dr. Samuel Napier was well respected, admired and most if not all of the surgeons who worked with him commented on his bedside manner with pediatric patients and his skill in the operating room. Though he dealt more with older children than babies.

She'd earmarked him as one to watch, but hadn't intended to choose him as her first resident. Her process was to weed out the weaker members of the herd. Mindy had had another resident in mind, but when she'd walked into that meeting and learned that her hot, brooding one-night stand was none other than Dr. Samuel Napier she had been absolutely furious.

No wonder he got good reports.

He probably slept with all his attendings. Not a hard thing to do when most of the surgeons in Pediatrics at this hospital were female. He'd used her. She knew she shouldn't have let her guard down, because she couldn't trust anyone.

And now he'd frog-marched her into this exam room to give her a talking-to? And she was his superior? No, this wasn't happening. Mindy refused to be pushed around again.

"I'm not changing my opinion of you just because you say that I should. Why should I trust you? You didn't even tell me you worked at the hospital, that you were a surgical resident."

Sam's eyes narrowed, those delectable lips which she could still feel imprinted against her body, were pursed together.

"You *didn't* tell me *you* were a surgeon either."

"I did too."

A diabolical grin spread across Sam's face. "No, you didn't."

Mindy opened her mouth to argue further and realized through those hazy, jangled memories of their meeting in the bar that all she'd told him had been her first name and that she'd moved to New York to start a new job, but not what that job was.

"You know that I'm right." His grin turned smug and he leaned against the door.

"You could've still looked up my CV online once you learned about the new head of Maternal-Fetal Medicine and our meeting was just an opportune moment."

The grin disappeared. "I did not sleep with you for personal gain. I'm extremely good at my job, so if you need to test me, so be it. I will take whatever challenge you have for me, and gladly. Though it's a waste of time."

Mindy snorted. "You think that maternal-fetal medicine and working on my service is a waste of time?"

"I do. My plan is to work with Dr. Chang and become a pediatric surgeon. Infants go to the NICU or the neonatologist. You're just a glorified obstetrician."

Mindy shook her head. "You're a bit arrogant, aren't you?"

"You have to be in this line of work. You have to be tough for the patients, for the parents and you have to be that tough to swim in this shark tank."

"You think surgery is a shark tank?"

"I do. Don't you?"

Mindy couldn't argue with him on that. It was. She'd learned the hard way that you couldn't trust other surgeons, especially not when you had ten or more residents competing for OR time, competing for attendings' attention and competing for only a couple of spots in a small fellowship pool.

When she'd entered surgery she hadn't been a shark. Dean and Owen had been sharks, but she hadn't. All she'd had had been raw talent. It used to infuriate Dean when she was chosen over him when they'd been residents. That should've been a clue.

Well, now she was one and she wasn't going to let an arrogant resident think that she wasn't. She needed to be tough. When she'd taken this job and uprooted her life to start fresh in New York City, she'd known she was going to have to be a shark from the get-go.

"Well, I guess I'll be wasting your time, but know this, some of those pediatric patients' problems start in utero. You think my specialty is a waste of time? Let me tell you something. The more my specialty advances, the more genetics advances and the more likely your job as a pediatric surgeon will become obsolete. Operating and taking care of those issues while the baby is still in utero will save them countless surgeries later in life. Dr. Chang is an excellent pediatric surgeon, but she doesn't have the skill to operate in utero. If people like me have our way, all pediatric problems will be taken care of while still in the protective walls of the womb and there will be less children on the pediatric floor." She moved closer to him. "Soon pediatric surgeons will be like the dinosaurs. Extinct."

Sam didn't say anything. In fact, for a moment he looked at bit shocked.

"So you think my specialty, my service is a waste of time? Well, I won't hold you to your rotation on my service, but I can tell you, Dr. Napier, that I won't be basing my vote on a resident who isn't willing to graciously learn all the specialties that are involved with taking care of children."

Mindy tried to move past him, still shaking.

"Wait." Sam grabbed her arm to stop her.

He was so close. Only a couple of hours ago he'd been in her bed. When she'd woken up and he'd been gone, it had stung, but she had been almost euphoric and definitely relaxed when she'd got into work. Until she'd seen him standing with the residents.

It had been like a slap to the face.

Just reaffirming to her that she couldn't trust men. They were all users.

"I'm sorry, Dr. Walker."

Mindy was stunned. "Thank you, Dr. Napier."

"I'll gladly work on your service and I'll prove to you my merit as a surgeon, but please know that I didn't sleep with you because you were my attending. Had I known, I would've kept as far away from you as possible. Nothing will taint my career at this hospital, or my chance to become a fellow in Dr. Chang's program. Nothing."

As Mindy looked up at Sam she wanted to believe him, but couldn't. "Okay. I'll give you a fair chance, Dr. Napier, but one toe out of line…"

"The implication is clear." He let go of her arm and stepped away from the door. "I look forward to learning from you, Dr. Walker."

Mindy nodded. She was pleased that she'd gotten through to him, but she could see the barriers, ones that had come down just a teeny bit last night, were building again. Walls that were meant to keep people out, from knowing the true Sam.

She didn't know the true version of him. Maybe if circumstances had been different, if something more could've stemmed from their night of passion, she might know the real Sam who remained locked behind those protective walls.

There could've been something more there.

Whatever he was protecting, it ran deep and Mindy would never know.

It was for the best.

She was his boss; he was a resident. That's all it could ever be, but she couldn't help but feel an inkling of regret.

"I'll see you at rounds in thirty minutes." Mindy didn't look at him, but he didn't stop her from leaving this time, which was good, because she had to distance herself from him emotionally.

Dr. Samuel Napier was off-limits, even if she didn't want him to be.

CHAPTER THREE

Sam stood back because the ER was absolutely packed full of casualties from a multi-car pile-up. Usually, he'd be right into the fray, helping, but Mindy didn't want him to so much as touch a patient.

There were more than enough trauma residents and general surgeon residents to lend a helping hand.

Mindy wanted him watching as she assessed an injured pregnant mother. One who was only twenty-six weeks. Mindy and neonatologist Dr. Hall were assessing the mother in a trauma pod and Sam was watching them.

Which kind of annoyed him. Greatly. He wanted to be in the throng, helping the wounded. This was going against the grain for him.

As he scanned the medical staff out on the floor he could see at least two residents he knew doing what they did best. Practicing medicine.

Rebecca looked up from where he was working and shot him a look of *What gives?* And all Sam could do was shrug. He had his orders. He was to observe. Very similar to his mother's methods.

Don't think about her now.

"Get out of the way!" Dr. Chang's voice was shrill above the din and he watched as she ran beside a gurney, a little body wrapped up and bagged, as they pushed through the crowds toward the surgical floor.

Sam's gut instinct was to run after Dr. Chang and that child. Every fiber of his being screamed at him to go.

"Dr. Napier?"

Sam cursed under his breath as he turned around.

"Distracted?" Mindy asked, slinging her stethoscope around her neck.

"No."

Her eyes narrowed. "Well, Ms. Bayberry is your responsibility. Get her up to Ultrasound and monitor her contractions. She's pregnant with twins and was involved in the collision. We're looking for signs of pre-term labor. Also contact her current practitioner. I'd like her updated files about her pregnancy."

"Isn't that best left to an intern?" he asked, annoyed that he wasn't with Dr. Chang.

Mindy crossed her arms. "I asked you to do it, Dr. Napier. Do you have a problem with that?"

"No. Of course not." Sam moved passed Mindy toward Ms. Bayberry's bed. Dr. Hall ignored him as she conferred with Mindy about the treatment should poor Ms. Bayberry go into labor.

"Will my babies be okay?" Ms. Bayberry asked nervously, her eyes wide with fear. This was the part of the job he hated the most, when he couldn't answer the patient's questions.

"Will this treatment help my son?"

"Will this cure him?"

It tugged at his heartstrings. It ate him up inside and he didn't know where the parents found strength. He'd talked to his father about that once, after watching children struggle with life-threatening conditions.

It scared him, bringing a child into the world, and for one moment, when he had first been starting his residency and focusing on pediatrics, he'd thought about leaving and following in his mother's footsteps.

"I don't know how you do it. How do you find the strength when your child is sick?"

"You just do. What else can you do? You give them everything. That's what being a parent is," his father had said. *"I would do anything for you and your brothers. I don't care what happens to me. Only my children matter."*

And as Ms. Bayberry looked up at him, fear in her eyes, it affected him. Only he couldn't let her see it. For her, he had to be strong so that she could be strong for her babies, but he couldn't promise her anything.

That was something he learned from his mother.

Never promise a patient something you couldn't deliver with one hundred percent certainty. Even though Ms. Bayberry was in the best hands with Mindy, of that he was sure, he didn't know the future so he could only offer her what he could to ease her mind.

"You're in the best hands, Ms. Bayberry. Let's get you upstairs for some scans." And he smiled at her and she relaxed. Though she was still terrified, he could see a bit of that fear dissipating and the goal was to keep her calm.

He was taking some vitals and making sure the machines monitoring her contractions were ready to transport when he glanced up.

Mindy was watching him. She wasn't listening to Dr. Hall her gaze was focused on him. He wasn't sure if it was with admiration or surprise, but whatever it was it made his heart beat just a bit faster and he looked away as he worked with the nurse to get Ms. Bayberry to transport.

Mindy made it clear that he was to stick by his patient's side and make sure that she didn't go into preterm labor. He had to stay focused. He was already in Mindy's bad books, even though he'd made it clear to her that it had been a mistake.

And it had been. A huge mistake.

If only Mindy hadn't been his new boss.

If only what?

Could he honestly tell himself that he wouldn't have pursued her? No, he wouldn't have, because right now he didn't have time for that sort of thing. The only thing about their one night together was he wouldn't have thought it a mistake. Never a mistake.

He wheeled Ms. Bayberry out of the emergency department, with only one glance back to see residents in his class darting through Trauma after their attending, getting their hands dirty, wishing he was working with Dr. Chang on the child she'd been wheeling up to surgery.

A touch from Ms. Bayberry brought him back to the present. The gauze on her forehead was soaked and as they waited on for the elevator to come, he reached down and gingerly touched her forehead.

"Has anyone seen to that?"

"It's just a scratch," she said, but wincing as she did so.

"Let me take a look." As he peeled back the bandages, he could see a large gash. One that would leave a nasty scar but wasn't life-threatening. "That's not pleasant."

"I'm sure it's not," Ms. Bayberry said, her voice rising. "I was more concerned about getting my babies checked out than having them attend to my cut."

"Of course, but I think we'll have someone with real talent stitch that up for you, okay?"

She smiled. "You?"

"No, not me. I'm a pediatric surgeon, I deal with delicate stitches, but we're very fortunate to have a former plastic surgeon to the *stars* on staff."

Ms. Bayberry chuckled and the doors to the elevator opened. Sam stopped an intern who was getting off the elevator.

"Page Dr. Alexander in Plastics to come to the fourth floor OB/GYN ultrasound room. Stat."

The intern looked confused, but nodded.

"You don't have to page a special plastic surgeon to stitch me up, Doctor. I'm sure you can do a fine job."

Sam smiled down at her. "I could do an okay job but, come on, we have to have you looking spiffy when those babies come out and you have your first photographs with them. Wash away any reminder of today."

Ms. Bayberry grinned and leaned back against the pillows as the elevator headed up to the fourth floor. He'd take care of her scars. He just wished all scars were all that easy to wash away.

"Dr. Napier, what is going on in there?" Mindy stood in the doorway of the ultrasound room, watching as a tanned, blond-haired Adonis from the plastic surgical ward was bent over her patient, working on her forehead.

"I'm trying to concentrate here," Dr. Alexander said over his shoulder in an annoyed tone.

Sam rolled his eyes and Mindy could tell there was

tension between the two of them. Who *wasn't* Sam fighting with at this hospital? *Sheesh*. She had been hearing some tales about the so-called lone wolf of the residency program.

After her lengthy discussion with Dr. Hall, Mindy got called to assess on another small case, one that wasn't urgent, but as Sam hadn't paged her that Ms. Bayberry had gone into pre-term labor or that there were unusual findings with her ultrasound, Mindy foolishly trusted Sam was okay.

She did not expect to walk in on one of the top plastic surgeons, working on her patient and in the ultrasound room.

"What is going here, Dr. Napier?" Mindy asked again in hushed undertones as Sam shut the door. "You were supposed to report back to me with the results of Ms. Bayberry's ultrasound."

"You told me not to leave her side. You told me to monitor her for pre-term labor."

Mindy crossed her arms. "Why the heck is Dr. Alexander in there, stitching up her forehead? I thought her wound was shut with skin glue?"

Sam winced. "I know, but it was going to leave a nasty scar."

"So you thought that putting her through more stress of unnecessary stitching would be better for her? What if she goes into pre-term labor?"

"She won't. The babies are fine and she hasn't been having any contractions or bleeding. I checked her myself."

Mindy cocked an eyebrow. "You checked her yourself?"

"I have done that kind of procedure before."

"Do you really think her having the stitches is a top priority?"

"I do. The babies are stable, for now, but there was an irregularity I need you to look at. I had you paged ten minutes ago, but figured you were with another patient."

Mindy pulled out her pager. "I wasn't paged…" And then trailed off when she saw that she had indeed been paged over ten minutes ago by Sam, but the darned thing was on silent mode.

Dammit.

When she had her private practice, she was only dealing with her patients. She wasn't on a rotation at a hospital. She wasn't called in to deal with traumatic events to pregnant mothers. When she was needed in the hospital it was because she scheduled her time there. She was not used to working in a busy hospital, not used to dealing with trauma patients or residents who were in her service.

She was not off to a good start.

"My apologies, Dr. Napier." The blood rushed to her cheeks.

"There's no need to apologize, Dr. Walker. Now that you're here I'd like to show you the results of Ms. Bayberry's ultrasound."

"Of course." Mindy followed him into the consult room, where they sat down in front of the computer.

Sam brought up the ultrasounds of the twins. "As you can see, there is no fluid or blood pooling any-where. The placenta is attached and no obvious tears."

"She's lucky. When she was rammed by the car behind her and pushed into the car in front of her the steering-wheel pushed into her abdomen."

"Well, that's it exactly. I know it's not your field of surgery." Sam did some more clicks. "But there's lots of blood in her spleen. I think she's damaged her spleen and it could rupture."

Mindy leaned forward. "I think you're right, Dr. Napier."

Dammit.

Taking a ruptured spleen out of a woman who was not so far into her pregnancy was going to be tricky. Not impossible, but tricky. It could send her patient into pre-term labor and that's not something she wanted.

They needed to keep those babies in utero for as long as possible.

"We're going to need a consult from someone who is used to repairing and or removing spleens in high-pressure situations. Page Dr. Ootaka for a consult."

Sam nodded. "Of course, Dr. Walker."

"Good catch, Sam. Thanks for looking at the bigger picture."

Sam shrugged. "In pediatrics we sometimes have to look at the bigger picture when it comes to kids."

He left the consult room and Mindy leaned back in her chair, but only for a moment. She got up and entered the exam room where Dr. Alexander was just dressing his handiwork.

"There, all done." He grinned down at Ms. Bayberry. "Now, when those babies are born, there won't be any sign of a scar."

"Thank you, Dr. Alexander," Mindy said.

Dr. Alexander shrugged. "Sam's my girlfriend's roommate. It was the least I could do." He collected up his things and left.

Mindy turned to her patient. "Your babies are fine,

Ms. Bayberry. There is no sign of injury to your uterus or your placenta. Things with the babies look stable. However, your spleen was damaged in the accident."

"What does that mean?" Ms. Bayberry asked, her voice rising an octave. The monitors on her alerted Mindy to the up-kick in blood pressure.

"It means we have to go in and repair your spleen." Mindy moved toward the bed. "May I look?"

Ms. Bayberry nodded and Mindy lifted the blanket, to see the bruising on the left side of her abdomen. The patient winced.

"Yes, we need to go and repair the damage," Mindy said gently.

"How are you going to do that?"

"Laparoscopically," Dr. Ootaka said, coming into the room, trailed by two of his residents. "I'm Dr. Takeo Ootaka. I have done this procedure countless times. You are in good hands."

"What about my babies?" Ms. Bayberry asked nervously, her eyes instantly darting to Sam, who stood by the door. She'd obviously latched onto Sam as a bit of a safety blanket, which often happened in traumatic situations.

"Dr. Napier and I will be in the OR the entire time. We'll monitor your babies and make sure they stay right where they belong."

Dr. Ootaka grunted in approval and then turned to the male resident with him. "Prep this woman for a CT and then surgery. May I look?"

Dr. Ootaka didn't wait for permission as he leaned over Ms. Bayberry's left side.

"Yes. Yes. We'll take care of this, Ms. Bayberry," Dr. Ootaka said.

Mindy gave her a reassuring squeeze on the shoulder as Dr. Ootaka's residents began to prep Ms. Bayberry and Mindy walked with Dr. Ootaka to the hall, with Sam trailing behind.

"I plan to have your patient down to the OR in the next hour, maybe less. I don't need to tell you that massive internal bleeding will put those babies in jeopardy."

Mindy nodded. "My resident and I will be ready, scrubbed in and waiting."

Dr. Ootaka nodded. "Good."

"Let's go, Dr. Napier."

"I thought you wanted me to stay with Ms. Bayberry?" Sam asked.

"She's in good hands with Dr. Ootaka's residents. They can monitor her. Right now we have to get a neonatal team ready and on standby in case Ms. Bayberry goes into premature labor."

"You think that will happen?"

"I hope it won't," Mindy said quickly as they moved down the hall to gather their team and ready them for surgery. She stopped and stretched her back, groaning.

"What's wrong?" Sam asked.

"Just a sore spot. It's been a while since I've been on a long rotation in a hospital."

Sam grunted. "What, they don't have long rotations at the hospitals in California?"

"For your information, Dr. Napier, I had a private practice, or did you not hear a word Dr. Chang said when she introduced me?"

"You told me in no uncertain terms that your personal life was not my concern. I'm just your resident." There was a devilish twinkle to his eyes as he said it.

Darn him.

He was proving to be a challenge.

"You're right. I did. So why don't you go back to Ms. Bayberry and continue to monitor her until she's brought down to the OR. Also, make sure her next of kin is updated on the situation."

"Of course, Dr. Walker." Then he did a little bow of his head and headed back to the exam room where Ms. Bayberry was.

Mindy sighed. He was a pain, but he was a good physician. The way he was with Ms. Bayberry, reassuring her, taking care of her.

She'd seen the look of longing when he'd been watching Dr. Chang working on patients. The drive, that look of ambition, she knew it well. When she had been in her obstetrics fellowship she and Dean had worked side by side to gain the attention of one the most noted maternal-fetal specialists on the West Coast, Dr. Guild.

The spark of competition and rivalry. That's what had driven her and Dean closer together, why the attraction had grown. At least, that's what she'd thought. Now she wasn't so sure.

It wasn't competition or rivalry with Sam, but he was trying to show his self-worth. He was trying to prove to her that he was tough, that he didn't have a soft underbelly when it came to his patients.

Or to her.

And then an image of their night together flashed through her mind. Of Sam and her together, his arms around her, his hands in her hair and his lips against her skin. It caused her blood to burn.

Mindy took a deep, calming breath. She couldn't

think of Sam that way. He was a resident. She wasn't looking for a relationship. She didn't want one. They were too much trouble.

Sam was here to learn from her. That's all.

And Mindy had to keep telling herself that to get through the rotation, heck, the next week while he was on her service. When he was off her service and back in Peds then there would be a safe, comfortable distance between the two of them.

He was after a pediatric fellowship, not OB/GYN, and she didn't have any room to mentor a fellow. OB/GYN fellows went through Dr. Finn. All she was here for was maternal-fetal medicine and infertility issues. She was here to bring in big cases, to bring in money for West Manhattan Saints.

She was here to rebuild her life and that life didn't include Dr. Sam Napier.

It couldn't.

CHAPTER FOUR

Sam shook his head at the nurse in the OR, who was holding up his cellphone again so he could see that it was buzzing. Sam mouthed the words "Not important" and "Scrubbing in" to the nurse, who was annoyed that his phone on the sterile tray was the only one giving her an issue.

He cursed under his breath as the water washed over his arms. He knew exactly what those texts were about.

Darn Langley.

"What's with all the texts? Is it from the woman you slept with last night?" Rebecca asked, as she came up beside him to scrub in.

"What?" Sam snapped.

Rebecca smirked. "Oh, come on. I'm not an idiot. Holly told me all about you. So who is the woman?"

"I don't know what Holly has been telling you. Whatever it is, it's not true. No one and it's not her."

"Aha, so you admit you got some action."

Sam cursed under his breath. "Would you stop concerning yourself in my personal life?"

"Okay, I didn't mean to tick you off."

Sam rolled his eyes and lathered the soap over his hands. "If you must know, it's my mother. She got wind that I'm on an OB/GYN service this week as a sort of a punishment."

Rebecca frowned. "I wouldn't call working with Dr. Walker a punishment. Have you read some of her papers? She's a big deal."

"I didn't say it was punishment." In fact, it wasn't. He was enjoying his time on Dr. Walker's service, but he knew his mother. Nothing was as worthy or extraordinary as neuro.

Sam rinsed and then shook his hands over the sink. He headed into the OR and was helped into a gown and gloves. He was hoping that they were just a precaution, that they wouldn't have to be used to deliver the twins.

Out of the corner of his eyes he could see the neonatologist team, ready and waiting. Then he saw Mindy, attaching the monitors and watching as the babies' heartbeats came online.

Please, let them stay in.

He knew the survival rate for infants so young was low.

"Dr. Napier?" a small voice called out to him.

Sam went over to Ms. Bayberry's side. She was trembling, waiting for anesthesia, her arms strapped down.

"I'm here," he said.

There was relief. "I'm glad you're here."

"Of course. Where else would I be?"

Ms. Bayberry smiled. "How are the babies?"

Sam glanced over at Mindy and the monitors. Mindy nodded and gave a thumbs-up.

"They're doing really good, Ms. Bayberry."

"Please, just call me Linda. I feel like an old lady when you call me that."

Sam chuckled. "Deal. As long as you call me Sam, then."

"Sam?" she said. "I would've never pegged you for a Sam. I thought you were Scottish."

"I'm American too." He winked.

"Is my husband on his way?" she asked.

"He's in the waiting room. I'll give him regular updates, I promise." Sam glanced up as Dr. Ootaka entered the OR, with Rebecca trailing him. "I think they're going to get started soon. I'm going to watch those babies like a hawk. I won't let them out of my sight."

Linda sighed and nodded, staring back up at the ceiling.

Sam stepped out of the way of the anesthesiologist and glanced up in the gallery. He could see Holly amongst the crowd of eager onlookers. Whenever Dr. Ootaka did a surgery he always garnered a lot of attention. Enzo and Kimberlyn would've been all over this. He missed them.

The room was filled with some of West Manhattan Saints' finest surgeons.

His mother should be pleased with that, instead of harassing him with endless texts about wasting his time when he should be focusing on pediatrics. And if he'd changed his mind about pediatrics then he shouldn't be *slumming* in OB/GYN when he could switch over to neuro. She could pull some strings.

Even though he hadn't read the texts, he knew exactly what they said, because they were always the same.

Always. It annoyed him. As if he wanted her help. Sam didn't want anything from her.

At least that was one thing his mother had going for her; she was a creature of habit.

Sam moved toward Mindy as Linda drifted off and they put the tube down her throat. Sam watched the monitor closely, keeping his distance.

"She can't be under too long, Dr. Ootaka," Mindy piped up as she took her seat next to the fetal monitor. The steady sound of the two heartbeats beat in time with his own.

"I'm well aware of that, Dr. Walker. Ten blade."

The surgery began as laparoscopic incisions were made and the camera inserted to get a better look at the damage done to the spleen.

"You should really move closer," Mindy whispered. "You could learn a lot from Dr. Ootaka."

"I'm fine right here, Dr. Walker." Sam eyed the monitor as the heartbeat of twin A began to rise, but just slightly.

"Are you sure?" Mindy asked.

"I promised her that I wouldn't take my eyes off the babies. Even if it means they're still inside her."

"Okay, then." There was a hint of admiration in her voice and it secretly pleased him that he had impressed her.

Don't think about that.

All eyes in the gallery were focused on Dr. Ootaka and his team.

"Do you know what injection I gave Ms. Bayberry before we came in here?" Mindy asked casually.

"Is this a test?" Sam asked confused.

"Sort of. Just passing some time. So do you?"

"Since the risk of pre-term labor is high I would

hope that you injected some corticosteroids into her, thus speeding along lung development of the babies."

"Correct, Dr. Napier."

"I've dealt with preemies before, Dr. Walker. I do work in pediatrics."

"What about a micro-preemie? Have you ever delivered or worked on a micro-preemie before?"

Sam grinned behind his mask. He could never forget Maya, who was Enzo's niece. He had been there when she'd come in. She had been his charge and he'd made it his personal mission to take care of her. Maya was alive because of him. "I have. In my first year."

"You've seen a lot, then," Mindy remarked.

"I have, and I hope to see more when I gain a fellowship spot with Dr. Chang."

"No disrespect to Dr. Chang, but she's not a neonatologist. If you want to work with preemies you should be working with Dr. Hall in the NICU."

"Dr. Hall is a great surgeon, but I need a peds fellowship before I move into neonatology. Like you, I want many feathers in my cap."

"You're very sure of yourself."

Sam didn't respond. They'd had this discussion before and it didn't bother him that she thought of him that way. In surgery that was a compliment. Suddenly an alarm went off and Mindy leapt to her feet.

"Dr. Walker, what is going on down there?" Dr. Ootaka demanded. "This is a delicate procedure."

"I am well aware of that, Dr. Ootaka," Mindy snapped. "One of the twins is distressed."

"Is she in labor?"

Mindy shook her head. "No. Just the baby being active and jostling around."

The general surgical team had stopped what they were doing so as not cause any more damage by the moving baby and because of that Linda's blood pressure went down.

"Dammit," Mindy cursed under her breath. "We have to get that baby to calm down. If it doesn't, I'll have to deliver or risk the mother bleeding out because they can't repair her spleen."

Sam thought back to when his stepmother had been pregnant with twins. The boys had been active and the only way his father had been able to get them to settle down had been to talk to them softly, in a deep, even voice.

"Let me try." Sam stepped forward and placed his hands on Linda's belly. Leaning over, he began to recite an old Gaelic song his father used to sing to his brothers. He was very aware that all eyes were on him and that everyone was listening to him sing, but he didn't care.

He'd made a promise to Linda Bayberry. It was better if the babies stayed in utero.

The alarms disappeared, the jostling settled and the babies were no longer a threat to their mother's spleen removal.

"Whatever you're doing, Dr. Napier, keep it up," Dr. Ootaka said. "It's unconventional, but it works and that's the most important thing."

It was a compliment and Sam took it and continued singing, his hands on the side of Linda's abdomen where the more restless twin was. As if in appreciation of his singing, a gentle kick nudged his palm, reminding him why he did what he did in the first place.

* * *

Mindy smiled as she watched Mr. Bayberry lean over and kiss the top of Linda's head, his hand on her belly. Linda was still groggy and missing her spleen, but the babies were okay, though Mindy had every intention of keeping Linda in the hospital for some time to monitor her, especially since she'd had a major organ removed.

It was touch and go, especially when that one twin had started acting up and then Sam had stepped up and calmed the fetus down. As if the fetus had known the mother trusted him.

He'd sung to the babies. Calming them and melting her heart.

Would Dean ever have done that? She seriously doubted it.

Sam might put up barriers to keep people out, but he had such a soft spot, especially when it came to children, and for her that was something that was highly attractive in a man.

Dammit.

Mindy shook her head and headed down to the cafeteria to get something to eat. It was late at night so really she should just head for home, but she wanted to stay and monitor Ms. Bayberry through the night.

The cafeteria had limited service so late, but at least she could get a sandwich from a machine and coffee. When she entered the dimly lit cafeteria there was one other soul there, hunched over a table, eating a pathetic-looking sandwich and nursing what looked like a generic can of diet soda.

Walk away.

Only she couldn't, because she was a weak fool. "You did good in there today."

Sam looked up. "Dr. Walker? I thought your shift was over?"

"I could say the same thing about yours as well, Dr. Napier."

Sam shrugged. "I made a promise. I'm going to stay here and monitor her for the night."

"Funny, that's what I thought I was going to do."

Sam cocked an eyebrow. "An attending? Usually attendings fob those kinds of jobs off on us lowly residents or even lower interns."

Mindy chuckled. "Mind if I join you?"

"No, not at all."

Mindy sank down into the hard plastic chair and let out a sigh of relief. She hadn't realized how long she'd been standing.

"Is the patient's husband with her?"

Mindy nodded. "He is. She's still quite groggy, but in stable condition."

"Good. Are you planning on keeping her in the hospital for a while?"

"Yep. She needs to heal. She's had major surgery and is pregnant with twins, which adds an extra burden on the body. I'll probably keep her here until those babies are ready to be born."

"That's a long time."

Mindy shrugged. "The protein in her blood was a little high for my liking and as I gave her an injection of cortocosteriods the chances that she could develop pre-eclampsia are slightly higher now. I'd rather have her here, where I can watch her."

"Now, that I didn't know," Sam remarked, as he slid the uneaten half of his sandwich toward her.

"What?" Mindy asked, gladly taking the sandwich.

"The risk of pre-eclampsia and the ACS."

"Any time you give a pregnant woman a drug it's risky. When you add the stress of twins, well…" Mindy trailed off. "We'll keep an eye on her."

"I will. You should go home and sleep. You look like you didn't get much sleep last night." And then he winked, causing her to blush.

"That was inappropriate, Dr. Napier."

"I'm sorry. I couldn't resist. When I get tired I get a little punchy and, besides, you're eating my sandwich."

Mindy chuckled. "It's terrible."

Sam shrugged. "It's nutrition, sort of. I lived off vending-machine sandwiches as a kid."

"Really? How random."

Sam shrugged. "It is what it is."

"You should go home, Sam. That's an order."

He cocked an eyebrow. "Are we on a first-name basis now?"

No, they weren't. Not since they'd spent the night together, which had been last night. She'd made it clear that she didn't trust him, that their one night of passion was to be forgotten. It had never happened.

Yet, sitting here with him in an empty cafeteria after a stressful surgery, worrying about whether or not they would have to deliver two babies who probably wouldn't make it, caused her to let her guard down.

"What was that song you were singing?" she asked, changing the subject.

Sam chuckled and then ran his fingers through his hair. "It was *'Huis, Huis air an Each'*. Just a simple song my father would sing to my twin brothers. It used to calm them, thought I would give it a shot. I'm actually surprised I remembered the words."

"It was beautiful. Wish I knew the words."

Sam smiled, those blue eyes twinkling in the dim light, and then the smile faded and he looked away. "Well, I'm glad it worked."

"Me too." Mindy swallowed the last of the sandwich, which stuck in her throat as silence descended between them. "Well, I'd better go check on Ms. Bayberry."

Sam shook his head. "Go home. I'll round on her tonight."

"Don't you have a home to go to?"

"It's just a flat in a brownstone overrun by other surgeons. Most will be here tonight anyhow, and I don't fancy riding the subway back to Brooklyn tonight."

Mindy nodded. "Well, make sure you get some sleep tonight. I'll be starting my rounds at six in the morning."

Sam nodded. "I'll be there. Goodnight, Dr. Walker."

"Goodnight, Dr. Napier."

Mindy got up and hurried out of the cafeteria, not looking back even though she could feel his gaze on her, watching her walk away.

This was going to be difficult. Everything about him drew her in—the compassion he had for his patients, his talent, the air of mystery about him.

He's off-limits.

And she had to keep telling herself that. She had to keep reminding herself that Sam was off-limits. She was his teacher.

Not that there was a specific rule about attendings, residents and interns, but it would be detrimental to Sam's career if people thought he was sleeping his way to the top. She should know, rumors had spread about her. After word had got out about Dean and Owen, the two people she'd trusted and worked in partnership with, it had destroyed her reputation in one fell swoop.

How could a patient put faith in someone who had put their faith in the hands of people who had duped her for so long?

Words and knowledge had power. If used by the wrong people, it could destroy everything Sam had worked for and she didn't want that for him. If today was any indication Mindy had no doubt that Sam was going to be a brilliant pediatric surgeon and she wasn't going to let a rumor about the two of them destroy that.

So she had to be careful about how she addressed him.

She couldn't let herself slip into familiarity.

She had to keep her distance from him and not get sucked in by the spell he seemed to be able to cast over her. She was made of stronger stuff than that; at least she thought she was. Although Dean and Owen had lied to her for so long, so what did she know?

Mindy stopped and glanced back over her shoulder down the hall toward the cafeteria, but Sam had disappeared. Probably he was on his way to check on Ms. Bayberry.

Go home before you do or say something you'll regret.

Mindy sighed and headed toward the attendings' lounge to change into her street clothes. It had been her first major rotation since starting at West Manhattan Saints. She was exhausted, but she also didn't want to go home. Her apartment was empty, lonely and memories of Sam were everywhere.

Don't chicken out. Go home.

Mindy groaned and tried not to think about what had taken place at her apartment last night, in her bed, because those thoughts, though pleasant, were very unwelcome and for a moment she was terrified she wasn't going to be able to succeed in keeping her distance from him.

She was pretty darned sure that she was going to fail miserably, but what a way to fail.

CHAPTER FIVE

SAM HAD BEEN off Mindy's rotation for two weeks and he found he missed it, but she had to give a fair shake to other residents applying for the fellowship. His first week back on the peds round he happened upon Dr. Snow, who was currently on rotation with Mindy, and all she was doing was whining about how nasty and how hard it was.

How the patients whined and complained constantly. As if kids didn't whine?

Sam laughed to himself as he thought of that. When he'd worked his full week with Mindy he'd learned so much. She'd kept her distance since she'd accidentally called him Sam after Ms. Bayberry's surgery, but that was fine by him.

He didn't want rumors starting.

It was bad enough having a famous mother, one who had slept with the current chief of surgery, albeit twenty years ago. He'd told Enzo about it when they'd got to know each other, but he was the only other person who knew, besides Dr. Chang, who knew his mother as well from medical school. And Sam didn't have to worry about anyone accusing him of favoritism when it came to his mother and Dr. Amelia Chang.

It was no secret that his mother and Dr. Chang did not see eye to eye. Sam had actually been concerned when he'd first been accepted into the surgical residency program. He'd known that he'd always wanted to be a pediatric surgeon. He loved working with kids, but when he'd heard the head of Pediatrics was his mother's "nemesis" of sorts, he had been worried that he wouldn't have a shot in heck of getting into the program, but he'd applied anyway.

And had been accepted.

Dr. Chang had known exactly who he was. She had told him as much on the first day he'd become a resident and had started clocking hours on the peds floor.

He'd been charting when she'd come up beside him.

"You have your mother's eyes."

"Pardon me?"

She stared at him, those thoughtful obsidian eyes boring right through him. "You have your father's soul. Let's hope you have your mother's talent. If you do, you'll be brilliant."

That was all she'd said. She would request him at odd intervals and always with the most delicate situations or the toughest cases.

Dr. Chang would observe him.

It's why he and Enzo had become more than just competition in their first year of residency. They'd moved beyond the macho chest-thrusting and territory-marking in the game of surgery and had become friends, because Sam had been there when Enzo's niece Maya had been born.

Dr. Chang had put Maya, a fragile preemie with a low expectation to survive, in his charge. And Maya had thrived because Sam had known that a way to help regulate a heartbeat was to place the baby against a bare chest. It was called kangaroo care. Maya hadn't been able to feed and Enzo's sister had been unable at that point to provide skin to skin contact, so during a long shift at night Sam had sat down in a rocking chair in the NICU and had done just that for little Maya. Wrapping her up against his chest, upright and prone, cradled on the inside of his scrubs, a blanket over them while he'd charted, very poorly.

Enzo had caught him, pausing slightly in the doorway of the NICU. He hadn't teased him, hadn't said anything. A look had been all that was needed to understand what was happening.

It was because of that he'd had a permanent spot at Enzo's family home for dinner and when he hadn't shown up, plates of food had been sent to him.

Sam chuckled and leaned over his chart. He missed Enzo. Missed seeing him in the halls of West Manhattan Saint. He missed the food. Darn him for falling in love with Kimberlyn and them moving away.

It had gotten him through some lonely patches when he'd first moved to New York. His mother didn't have much to do with him and the rest of his close family was in Scotland. His dad, his brothers and stepmother, as well as various aunts, uncles, cousins and one venerable grandmother.

Even though he'd been born in New York and had spent some time on this side of the pond, he was alone. When he'd been with his mother, he'd been alone. She had always been working and he'd spent a lot of his childhood, when he'd been with her, in the hallways of the hospital or in the observation room while she'd been in surgery.

He glanced up from his charting and saw Mindy in the NICU, bending over a tiny micro-preemie in an incubator. Mindy was in her scrubs and updating the neonatologist so it appeared that the baby had just been born.

She's alone.

Mindy had said she'd grown up on the west coast, a native to California. Though she hadn't moved an ocean away from her family, she'd moved clear across the country to start a new life. It must've been something drastic that had chased her away. To isolate herself.

He didn't know about isolating oneself on purpose, but he did get loneliness. Even living in a house full of other surgeons. Tessa had moved out and was starting a family, Kimberlyn and Enzo were together and gone, even Holly had moved on with Dr. Alexander and she had family around. Sure, there was the new roommate, Rebecca, but he didn't really know her yet and wasn't sure he wanted to. She was too chatty.

He had no one. Just like Mindy didn't have anyone and he felt sorry for her. She deserved better and though he shouldn't approach her, he should just keep his distance from her, he closed his chart and headed toward the NICU.

Mindy was standing next to the incubator, staring down at the small preemie inside, but he could tell by her expression that she really wasn't watching the preemie. She had a far-off expression on her face.

"Boy or girl?" Sam asked, as he came up beside her and peered down at the bundle, hooked up to wires but alive.

"Boy," Mindy said offhandedly. She set down the

chart she was holding. "I delivered him about an hour ago after I repaired his CPAM."

"Congenital pulmonary airway malformation?"

"Yes. I usually try to keep the fetus inside after I do the repair, but Mom had the beginning stages of pre-eclampsia. With the extra stressors of surgery, I delivered the baby."

"Wish I could have seen that procedure in action."

Mindy cocked any eyebrow. "I thought that maternal-fetal medicine wasn't your intended specialty, that your main focus was pediatrics?"

"It is, but it doesn't mean I don't appreciate complex surgeries. Especially when those complex surgeries involve children. Perhaps I judged maternal-fetal medicine too harshly."

"Really now?" she asked, obviously humored.

Sam leaned over and gazed at the lad through the glass. "Poor mite."

"Yes, it was unfortunate, but now that it's repaired he has a shot of growing up normally. Of surviving. Twenty or thirty years ago he wouldn't have survived his birth."

"Is this where you're going to start spouting off at me about how my chosen specialty is for dinosaurs?" Sam teased. "That there will be no need for pediatric surgeons or neonatologists?"

Mindy laughed. "I'm sorry, Dr. Napier. As I said, I was quite annoyed to see you as a resident."

"I know. I know. Trust me, I felt the same."

"You were annoyed I was an attending?"

Sam nodded. "Of course. A woman I'd had an amazing night with was now off-limits."

Mindy snorted. "Like you had every intention of

calling me again." She walked out of the NICU and Sam trailed after her.

"You don't know that," Sam protested. Though she was right. At the time he hadn't had any intention of calling her again, but spending a week with her on her service had made him think differently about her. He'd seen her in a new light. If it wasn't a bad idea, if he had more time to commit to a relationship instead of being tied to the hospital, he would pursue a woman like Mindy Walker.

"We didn't exchange numbers," Mindy said.

"Ah, but I know where you live. I could've found out if I chose too."

Mindy chuckled. "That sounds mighty stalkerish, Dr. Napier. Mighty stalkerish indeed."

Sam groaned. "Oh, come on. It's not stalkerish at all." He leaned over the charge desk as she pulled a chart from behind the counter. "How is the new resident on your service going?"

"That's not any of your business," Mindy said, not looking at him.

"I'm just curious, that's all."

"No, you're not. You're competitive, you shark." It wasn't said in an accusatory tone, there was a twinkle to her eyes.

"I swear, it's not competitive in nature. Just curious. I heard some…complaints."

Mindy's mouth dropped open. "Complaints? What do you mean, complaints? From who?"

Sam grinned. "I can't say, unless I want to get attacked by a pod of sharks. Do sharks come in pods, I wonder?"

Mindy frowned and then playfully pushed. "Jerk!"

"What was that for?"

"What complaints?" Mindy demanded. "As your superior, I demand you tell me."

Sam cocked an eyebrow. "As my superior, you demand I tell you? I don't think so." He turned to leave but she grabbed his arm.

"Come on, tell me. This is my first job in a teaching hospital and I want to make sure that I'm imparting my wisdom on the residents well."

"You're doing a fine job. Really, the complaints were that you were a bit demanding and a workhorse."

Mindy smiled then, but then cleared her throat. "Is that all?"

"It pleases you to know you're being tough."

"It does. I want them to be afraid of me and my service."

"You want to be like the Godzilla of the OB/GYN floor?" Sam asked.

"If you can survive my toughness then you can make it in my field."

"Ah, but there's a problem. The residents currently rotating on your service aren't OB/GYN residents. You have a whole smackerel of them who are chomping at the bit to work with you. You're working with residents who are eyeing a pediatric fellowship with Dr. Chang. So it might be lost on them."

Mindy smiled smugly. "That may be, Dr. Napier, but I deal with kids when they're still developing. I have to be hard on all residents who have any kind of inkling of wanting to work with children. They're a precious commodity. If you can't stand the heat…"

"Get out of the oven?"

Mindy laughed. "Kitchen, Dr. Napier."

"So, I have to ask, did Dr. Snow do well in the procedure?"

"I wouldn't know. She never did make it to surgery."

Sam was confused. "I can't see her missing something like that. She'd as soon as skin me than let me have a shot at any specialized procedure. Of all the sharks, she's the nastiest."

"You think highly of her," Mindy teased, and then she sighed. "Actually, I didn't let her into my OR and she's effectively off my service."

Now he was intrigued. "And you're not going to elaborate any further."

"It's not prudent. You are her competition."

Sam didn't say anything further as Mindy finished her charting and set the binder back in its place. The only thing that would have kept Dr. Snow out of surgery was if she'd done something really bad to anger her attending. In their first days, Dr. Snow had been a bit pompous, but she was a talented surgeon and Sam couldn't help but wonder what Dr. Snow had done. Well, whatever it was, it wasn't his business to know.

Mindy was right. Dr. Snow was his competition and he didn't want to have any unfair advantages.

"That's foolish, Samuel! Take whatever advantages you can get. Given the chance, another surgeon will stab you in the back to take your spot."

His mother's cutthroat attitude had never sat well with him.

It was his father's gentle soul which always seemed to win out. His mother's downfall was that sometimes she acted before she thought and Sam was a bit more methodical. He didn't gossip; he didn't jump into the fray unless it was during a medical emergency.

"I'm going to go grab a coffee. I still have a few more hours left on my shift. I'll see you around." Mindy moved around to the other side of the charge desk and headed down the hall.

"Dr. Walker…Mindy, wait."

Mindy spun around, stunned, but she didn't chastise him for using her first name.

"Would you like to get a cup of coffee with me? I'm on call, but I thought you might like some company."

What are you doing?

He didn't know. He never acted this spontaneously, but he couldn't help himself. All he knew was he was probably setting himself up for something he wasn't sure he was ready for.

Mindy stood there for a few moments, absolutely dumbfounded. It felt like she was standing there for hours, but of course that was foolish.

She was surprised that Sam had asked her to have coffee with him.

Say no. You can't trust him. He's just using you.

"Sure." She couldn't believe the words that were coming out of her mouth.

What're you doing? She didn't know at that moment. She was actually surprised at herself, but she was lonely. She knew hardly anyone in New York. There was no harm in getting a cup of coffee.

Sam smiled the grin that melted her heart. *Darn him.*

"Good. I have to get my post-op notes off to Dr. Chang. I'll meet you in the cafeteria in thirty minutes?"

"No, not the cafeteria." If she was going to go

through with this then she was going to do it outside the hospital.

"Where, then? I'm on call and I can't go far."

"There's a coffee shop next to the hospital. You'll be close enough to run back if you get called in."

"Okay." Sam picked up his notes. "I'll see you there in half an hour."

"Sure," she said nervously, and then quickly walked away before she did something ridiculous like blush.

This was not going according to plan. Her plan had been to swear off Sam, even though she knew that was going to be a hard thing to do. There were so many things about him that she liked and admired. She also had a hard time forgetting about the way he kissed, even though that had been nearly a month ago.

Sam was also the only person she'd really connected with in New York. She'd spoken to other attendings, her patients, nurses, but there wasn't a connection. Mindy had been so busy she hadn't had the time to form any friendships or to get to know anyone. And she had a hard time opening up.

Perhaps she was blocking them out because she was scared of trusting people. Especially after what had happened in California.

She'd been deceived and she'd had no idea. Instead she'd lived in this oblivious little bubble, thinking that her marriage was okay, that her best friend wasn't betraying her. All the things she'd told Owen made her stomach knot. She'd been such a fool.

After it had all gone down it had been the pitying looks she'd been unable to handle. The "Poor Mindy"'s. She hadn't liked being pitied. When she'd been an in-

tern she'd struggled that first year and had been pitied.
She'd been the underdog and scared of her own shadow.

When Dr. Guild had taken her under her wing
Mindy had blossomed. That shy girl who had domi-
nated her life had disappeared and all of those who had
dubbed her the runt of the surgical litter had been left
behind as she'd become a surgical star.

It was hard for Mindy to make friends. She just
didn't want to open herself up to any more hurt.

With Sam it was totally different. She was just at
ease around him. She liked to talk to him and she kept
forgetting that she shouldn't be so relaxed around him,
because Sam was off-limits and because she refused to
open her heart again. It just wasn't worth it.

She found herself in the coffee shop next to the
hospital, still in a bit of daze, with a latte in her hand.
One of those limited edition spiced ones.

Mindy took a seat in the corner, waiting with anticipation for Sam to come. Though part of her hoped
he wouldn't. It would be easier if he didn't show and
she was hoping that he would be called to something.

The chime over the door tingled and Sam walked
in. He didn't see her at first, so she watched as every
female in the coffee shop turned their appreciative gaze
on him and she had to admit she couldn't blame them.
He was tall, broad-shouldered, with dark reddish hair,
ridiculously gorgeous features and eyes that had no
business being on a man who wasn't going to be an
actor or a model.

Mindy could almost see him in a kilt with a big
giant sword. What do the Highlanders call their big
giant swords?

Why the heck are you thinking about big giant swords at this moment?

Mindy shook her head and rubbed her eyes. She needed to get some more sleep. He ordered a small coffee and headed over to her. All eyes followed the handsome doctor as he slid into the booth across from her.

Sam frowned. "What?"

"What?" Mindy asked, confused.

"You're staring at me like I have horns growing out of my head or something."

"Sorry, I was just watching all your admirers give me the look of death."

Sam glanced over his shoulder and a few female patrons who were still looking in their direction looked away quickly.

Sam chuckled and smiled with smug satisfaction. "Oh, that. I'm used to that."

Mindy snorted. "I'm sure you are. What're you drinking?"

"Black coffee with a shot of espresso. Dr. Chang paged me just as I was leaving. There's a surgery in about thirty minutes."

"Oh?"

Sam nodded. "Not pleasant, I'm afraid, but it needs to be done and once it's done the child will be better off for it."

Mindy was just about to ask what surgery when she got a page herself. She frowned when she saw it was from the OB/GYN department.

It was in regard to Ms. Bayberry. She was over the crucial twenty-five weeks, but the babies needed longer in utero.

"What's wrong?" Sam asked, as they both stood up together.

"It's Ms. Bayberry." Mindy slipped her phone back into her pocket.

"Is she in labor?" He was concerned. She could tell. Mindy knew he still checked on Linda. It was sweet.

It wasn't just sweet, it was the mark of a caring surgeon. One who was looking beyond being just a surgical god and being an actual *good* doctor. Even if Sam didn't want to admit it. To admit something like that, to admit to caring while in competition with other interns could be a sign of weakness. She should know. Mindy had felt that bite, that sting against her jugular when she cared too deeply, but once she'd realized it didn't matter she no longer cared.

She was going to be the physician she wanted to be and that was all that mattered. Sam was just starting a surgical career. He'd learn it soon enough, but then again maybe he already had and if he did it was commendable. Being a surgical resident was tough. It was supposed to be tough and it was a phase in her life she was glad was over.

"No, she's not in labor." Mindy finished the rest of her latte and crumpled the cup, tossing it into the garbage. "The neonatologist called me. There's something on the ultrasound she wants me to take a look at."

Sam frowned. "Can I come?"

"Don't you have a surgery with Dr. Chang?"

"Not for thirty minutes. If she needs me before then, she can page me. I would really like to be there when you look over the ultrasound."

Mindy grinned. "Changing your mind about maternal-fetal medicine?"

"No." Sam downed the rest of his coffee. "I still want to be a pediatric surgeon, but perhaps after completing my fellowship with Dr. Chang I'll be looking to add maternal-fetal medicine to my résumé. Really specialize."

Mindy cocked an eyebrow. "Wow. You have mighty big aspirations and you're cocky. What makes you think you have a shot at that pediatric fellowship?"

Sam shrugged as they walked out of the coffee house together. "Because I want it and because I'm going to earn it all on my own merit. You said so yourself, I'm a fine surgeon."

"Hmm. That remains to be seen. I haven't actually seen you in any complicated procedure yet."

"That's true. The week I was on your rotation all I did was observe and calm down a set of twins during a splenectomy."

"Maybe I'll have to observe your surgery later with Dr. Chang."

"Or, if there is something that has to be done surgically to Ms. Bayberry's twins, I can be on the case."

"You're pushy," Mindy teased.

"It's only natural. I was the first doctor on her case and she likes me. We have a rapport."

"That's true. I'll think about it."

"It makes the most sense since you've banished Dr. Snow from your service."

Mindy shook her head and they headed to meet Dr. Hall, the neonatologist, in an exam room. When they got there Dr. Hall was frowning as she leaned over the ultrasound image on the computer. She barely glanced over her shoulder to acknowledge them as they walked into the room.

"What seems to be the trouble?" Mindy asked, as

she took a seat next to Dr. Hall. Sam stood behind her, leaning over so he could look at the screen as well. She was very aware that he was so close. The heat of his body permeated her scrubs, causing her blood to sing.

"Take a look. It was missed in the ultrasound done by her regular OB/GYN, but now that she's almost thirty weeks you can see it clearly as the twins are in a different position."

Mindy's heart skipped a beat when she saw one of the most rare pregnancy conditions.

"Is that the same amniotic sac?" Sam asked, his breath on her neck.

Mindy moved close to the computer, more to get away from Sam being so close to her. "Yes, it's a mono-amniotic pregnancy."

"Why was this missed earlier, Dr. Walker?" Sam asked.

"It's sometimes hard to see, depending on where the babies lie." Mindy clicked on a file and brought up an earlier ultrasound, zooming in. "See this line. It looks like it was a membrane dividing the fetuses, but it clearly is not. As they've moved and grown, you can clearly see that no membrane divides the amniotic sac."

"And you can see here, the cords are starting to tangle," Dr. Hall remarked.

Mindy pinched the bridge of her nose. "That's not good."

"No, the babies are at risk of cutting off their blood supply now. Is that correct, Dr. Walker?" Sam asked.

"Yes." Mindy stood. "Ms. Bayberry is thirty weeks tomorrow. We'll have to keep a close eye on her. Let's try to get her to thirty weeks and then we'll deliver the babies."

Dr. Hall nodded. "I'll prep my neonatology staff."

Mindy turned to Sam. "Can you inform Dr. Chang for me, Dr. Napier? I would like her present at the surgery."

"Of course, Dr. Walker." Sam left the room to track down Dr. Chang before she got prepped for surgery.

Dr. Hall left the exam room to prep her team and now Mindy was faced with breaking the news to Ms. Bayberry. As if the poor woman hadn't been under enough stress. Now Mindy had to break the news to her that her twins' lives were in danger. At least when she'd had the splenectomy they'd given Ms. Bayberry a shot of corticosteroids to help strengthen the babies' lungs. She'd be given another shot tonight.

Any little bit helped.

At least the babies were almost thirty weeks.

At least their cords weren't tangling at twenty weeks, when there would be nothing they could do to save them.

Being thirty weeks along, at least the babies had a chance.

And Mindy was going to make sure they got the chance they deserved.

CHAPTER SIX

SAM STOOD NEXT to Dr. Chang as she scrubbed in. He was annoyed that he wasn't going to be allowed into the OR while they delivered Ms. Bayberry's twins.

"There will be too many people in there. It's a delicate surgery, and we have Neonatology, Pediatrics and OB/GYN. You can watch from the gallery, like the other residents."

That command had come down from Professor Langley, but he didn't actually have the guts to come down and tell him in person. He'd sent his lackey to tell him. Langley never really dealt with him. He always seemed to avoid him.

He must feel guilty and that pleased Sam to no end.

Good. Langley's affair with his mother had torn his family apart. Crushed his father. It was best Langley keep his distance from him.

"You're scowling," Dr. Chang remarked, as she scrubbed her arms and hands.

"I think I should be in there. I was on this case since day one," Sam snapped.

"Professor Langley has a point. There will be a lot of people in there."

"I calmed the patient."

"Yes, when her husband was absent, and she'll be under general anesthesia again. This is a delicate procedure. We can't have the cords continue to tangle. If they tangle before the babies are ready to be born, it could kill both of them."

Sam grunted in response. He got that, but he still wanted to be in there. Mono-amniotic twins was such a rare occurrence he doubted he'd ever get to see another case like this in the near future. In fact, it was Dr. Chang's first time to see such a case. Even she'd never seen mono-amniotic twins.

And it wasn't just the rarity of the case he was moaning about. He cared for the patient. Linda Bayberry and her husband Frank were two of the nicest native New Yorkers he'd ever met, besides Enzo's family, though he wouldn't let anyone else know that.

He'd been following the case since day one and he wanted to see it through. He wanted to make sure those babies were okay.

"I heard from your mother today," Dr. Chang said, with a note of derision in her tone.

Oh, bloody hell.

"Aye, and what did she want?" His brogue was slipping out in his annoyance.

Dr. Chang smiled at him. "Oh, she wanted to tell me that I'm wasting her son's talent and surgical skill by having him work in OB/GYN. She didn't pay for your education and pull strings for you to be delivering babies like some glorified midwife."

Sam cursed under his breath. "And what would she know about that? I'm sorry she laid into you like that, Dr. Chang. I hope you know that I don't think that way."

Dr. Chang shook off her hands. "I know and I know your mother."

"What did you say to her?"

"Nothing. I hung up on her." There was an evil grin on Dr. Chang's face as she walked into the OR.

Sam chuckled to himself. He was glad that Dr. Chang didn't put up with his mother's ridiculous behavior. He was also angry that his mother had done that. She was bound and determined to ruin his career as a pediatric surgeon.

His mother wouldn't be happy unless he was a bloody neurosurgeon. Not that there was anything wrong with neurosurgeons. On the contrary, he respected many of them—the brain was a delicate organ.

It took such precision to operate on it and the nervous system, but was it any more difficult or delicate than when you were dealing with a heart no bigger than a grape or veins the size of a human hair?

No. It wasn't, but then kids had never really mattered to his mother.

Sam knew all about that.

Disgusted with her behavior, he headed up to the gallery and pushed his way to the front through the throng of eager observers so he could watch Mindy in action.

He was surprised that none of his other roommates were in the room, but they were probably off doing surgeries, while he was stuck up in the gallery like a first-year intern. Observing, rather than helping.

"Did you hear that Dr. Monica Hanley is coming to West Manhattan Saints?"

"No, I hadn't. Get out of town. *The* Dr. Hanley is coming here. When?"

Sam perked up at the mention of his mother's name and when he glanced around he could see it was two young interns on the other side of the gallery who were talking about it.

"She's coming in a couple of weeks. Apparently there's a kid with some kind of inoperable brain tumor, but she's going to be testing her new surgical procedure to remove the tumor and she's going to do her ground-breaking surgery here."

"That's amazing."

Sam groaned inwardly.

Great. Just what he needed to hear. His mother was coming to West Manhattan Saints to flaunt neurosurgery in his face once again and he was ticked off. Why did she have to come here to do the surgery? Why hadn't Dr. Chang told him his mother was coming? Did Dr. Chang even know? Perhaps she didn't as she'd hung up on her.

Even then, he wouldn't put it past his mother to go over the head of the Pediatrics attending to Professor Langley to get permission to do the surgery here.

Why here?

"I hear her son works at West Manhattan Saints and that's why she's coming." This was said in a hushed undertone.

"Her son? She has a son and he works here? Who is he?"

"I don't know, but I'm sure he's going to get picked to assist. I mean, come on, the son of Dr. Hanley. I'm sure she pulled strings to get him into the program. He's probably riding on her coattails and doesn't have to lift a finger. Just has all the most awesome surgeries handed to him."

"I hate him on principle," the other intern griped.

Sam's stomach knotted, his worst fears about being his mother's son realized. It was a good thing they had different surnames. This was why he didn't want people to know who his mother was. They would stop looking at him as a surgeon and only see him as someone who'd got to where he was because of his mother.

He wanted to get up and leave, or confront the two gossiping fools as they continued to gossip about Dr. Hanley's son and how crummy a surgeon he was, but instead he blocked them out. He was safe behind his walls.

Sam was here to learn. He was here to observe a once-in-a-lifetime surgery. He was here to advance his career because he was a surgeon. A good surgeon.

He knew one thing—he was *not* going to be around when his mother was here. He wasn't going to allow that can of worms to taint his surgical career in the hospital where he planned to spend many years becoming one of the best pediatric surgeons. If she was going to be here, he wasn't.

Mindy was still on a high after safely delivering the mono-amniotic twins. This was her third delivery of mono-amniotic twins and thankfully the second successful delivery. In the first year of her fellowship Dr. Guild had delivered a pair, but sadly the cord restriction had been so bad that one twin hadn't made it.

It had crushed Mindy, breaking her heart. She'd almost walked away from maternal-fetal medicine. Who needed that kind of heartbreak every day? But Dr. Guild had talked some sense into her.

"Next time we catch it sooner. Next time we perfect

the skill, so that next time we save a life before the life needs to be saved."

Mindy hadn't been able to walk away from her specialty then. She'd thrown herself into it, because the more she'd learned, the better she'd got and the more lives she'd saved.

Life was short sometimes and it sucked, but that's what drove Mindy to rise above that. To find another way to save more lives.

It's why she had one of the lowest mortality rates for a surgeon who was so young.

Saving lives. Precious lives.

"I saw Dr. Napier scowling in the gallery. I'm surprised you didn't have him in the OR with you, Dr. Chang," Mindy remarked as they scrubbed out. The neonatologists had whisked the babies off to the NICU in stable condition and Mindy had finished with Ms. Bayberry and she was in Recovery and stable as well.

Dr. Chang had stayed until the end, asking questions about the procedure.

Dr. Guild had always said it was a mark of a good surgeon to never stop learning and Mindy was a big believer in the Socratic method of teaching. Even if she was teaching a world-renowned and respected pediatric surgeon such as Dr. Amelia Chang.

"Professor Langley didn't want him in the OR, so I told him that there were too many people in the OR."

Mindy was confused. "Why would he not want Dr. Napier in the OR?"

Dr. Chang snorted. "Probably because Dr. Napier's mother complained to him about how many hours her son was getting in OB/GYN, seeing how she finds both our practices of medicine to be a waste of talent."

"Who is his mother?"

"Another surgeon. He doesn't like to say and I'm not in a position to divulge her name. Dr. Napier is pretty private."

"I get that. We all have secrets."

Dr. Chang cocked an eyebrow. "Yes."

"Does his mother have the same last name?"

"No, he has his father's name. His parents were married for a short while. I knew Dr. Napier's mother when she married Frasier Napier. I really liked Dr. Napier's father, never cared for his mother too much."

"I don't blame you. She sounds like a real…"

"Pain?" Dr. Chang laughed. "Yeah, she is."

"I'm surprised that Dr. Napier never told me who his mother is."

"Now, that you'll have to ask Dr. Napier about. I doubt you'll get any answers from him, though. He's a private person. I don't even know why he keeps it to himself, but I respect his wishes." Dr. Chang finished scrubbing up and then left the scrub room, tossing her surgical cap in a receptacle on the way out.

Mindy finished her scrubbing and headed out too.

There were many more layers to Dr. Samuel Napier than met the eye. In the course of her career she'd met other physicians who'd had famous parents in the medical field and they had been quite proud to boast about that. Yet Sam didn't really talk about his mother much. He'd mentioned his father and family in Scotland with fondness, but nothing about his mother.

Don't pry.

She didn't want people to know about her humiliation in California.

That was her business and apparently Sam wanted

to keep his secret about his mother private too and she respected that.

Besides, who was she to go prying? She was just an attending at the hospital he worked at and she was just someone he'd slept with once.

They weren't friends; they were no longer lovers. If he'd wanted to tell her about his mother, he would've.

Mindy scrubbed her hand over her face and headed toward her office, where she could dictate a report of the successful delivery of Ms. Bayberry's mono-amniotic twins while it was still fresh in her mind.

As she passed the skills lab, she could see someone hunched over a simulated womb, trying to insert a needle through to the fetus. Of course he was failing, because the sensors were going off and Sam was cursing in a very thick Scottish brogue.

Just leave him.

Only she couldn't. She was his teacher after all.

"Bloody hell."

"Is something wrong?" Mindy asked, as she shut the door to the skills lab behind her.

Sam glanced up. "Sorry, Dr. Walker. Did you need the skills lab?"

"No, no. I just happened to be walking by after Ms. Bayberry's surgery and saw you in here. Is everything okay? You didn't stay for the whole surgery."

"I'm fine. Once I saw the twins were going to make it, I left. My shift was over."

"Why didn't you go home?"

Sam shrugged. "It's lonely at home and I thought I would practice some other skills."

Mindy nodded and headed over to him. "Is there a particular reason you're cursing at this simulation?"

"Just a wee bit frustrated."

"Here, I can help." Mindy placed her hand over his and then paused, removing her hand. "How about I show you?"

"Aye, that would be good." Sam handed her the catheter and needle and stood, moving out of the way so she had access to the simulation on the table.

Once again Mindy was very aware that Sam was standing very close to her. Why did she keep putting herself in the way of temptation?

Because you're weak.

"It requires a certain bit of skill to do this. The womb is strong but fragile, as is the life it holds inside. Are you watching?"

"Aye." Sam leaned in closer.

"Good." Mindy cleared her throat and then proceeded to show Sam how to do the procedure. "Keep your hands steady but firm. One wrong move…"

"I know. Can you do that again?" he asked.

"Of course." She removed the needle and reset the simulation. As she prepared to show him again, his hands slipped over hers, causing a zing of excitement to course through her as she recalled the way those strong hands had felt on her body, in her hair. "What're you doing?"

"I want to feel. Do you mind?"

Yes.

"No." Mindy's voice caught in her throat as the words came out. "Not at all."

His touch made her tremble slightly but she regained control of herself. The last thing she wanted to do was mess up the procedure or let Sam know how he affected her.

"Amazing," Sam whispered, his hot breath fanning her neck, causing gooseflesh to break out on her skin and down her back.

"It is. Do you want to try again?"

"Yes." He moved away from her and she got up. Sam took her place and she reset the simulation.

"You can do it." Mindy stood back and watched the monitors as Sam expertly copied the procedure. "See, I knew you could do it."

Sam nodded. "Thanks for your help, Mindy."

She frowned. "I don't think—"

"I know. You don't think I should be using your first name, but in the last month you're the person I've talked to most and I believe I am your only friend in New York."

"We're friends?" Mindy asked.

Sam smiled, his blue eyes twinkling. "I'd like to think so. We can be friends, can't we? Coworkers can be friends. Just as long as you don't show me favoritism, we're okay."

Mindy chuckled. "Yeah, I think we can be friends, Dr. Napier."

"Sam."

"Sam." It felt right to say it again, but also wrong. She couldn't let him in. She was afraid.

"I'd just ask when we're on duty for you to call me Dr. Napier. The whole favoritism thing."

"That really bothers you."

"What does?" he asked.

"People thinking you're getting preferential treatment."

"Aye. It does."

"I know it does. Your accent thickens."

He grinned. "You are getting to know me well."

I tried not to. Only she didn't say that thought out loud.

"Well, that's what friends are for. Though I'm surprised you don't have many friends who are residents."

"I do, but they're not in my specialty and some have moved away."

"Oh, really? I never see them around."

Sam shrugged. "They're all busy with their own lives. I live with several of them in Brooklyn. I see them when I head back to my flat."

"I'm surprised you leave the hospital. I swear you live here."

"I could say the same for you, except I have seen your apartment." Then he frowned. "Sorry, Mindy. I didn't mean…"

Heat flushed her cheeks at the reminder that he'd been to her place. Slept in her bed…well, not exactly slept in her bed.

"I've been busy here. Consults, surgeries. I can't really set my own hours, like I did in my private practice."

Sam nodded. "When are you off next?"

"Tomorrow."

"Me too." Sam stood. "As a thank-you for helping me in the simulation lab I'd like to take you on a little tourist jaunt of New York City."

"A jaunt?" She asked. "Why?"

"You say that like I'm offering you a big bowl of the plague or something."

"I don't do jaunts," Mindy said.

"Oh, come on. Who doesn't do jaunts?"

"Me." Mindy chuckled.

"Well, you're going to go on one tomorrow," Sam said with finality.

"Fine. So where will this *jaunt* take us?"

"Have you seen all the touristy sights yet?"

"No. I haven't had time."

"Then it's settled. I'll pick you up tomorrow at nine a.m. sharp and we'll see all the sights of New York City."

"What? It's the middle of winter. It's cold out there."

Sam chuckled and headed toward the lab door. "I won't take no for an answer. You can dress in layers to fend off the cold, like any good New Yorker would do. Besides, it's time to get you got acclimatized to the cold weather if you aim to remain in New York."

Mindy scowled. "What if I don't come downstairs at nine a.m.?"

"Then you'll leave me standing in the cold in front of your apartment, shouting your name."

Mindy gasped. "You wouldn't do that."

He cocked an eyebrow. "Oh, wouldn't I?"

"I wouldn't hear you high up in my penthouse."

"I don't care. I'll still do it."

"Fine," Mindy agreed grudgingly. "I'll dress in layers, but you'd better take me to all the really famous landmarks. Not the landmarks a native New Yorker *thinks* are famous. Like some weird house or building that was in some obscure movie in the eighties."

He laughed. "Agreed. I'll see you tomorrow, then."

Mindy's heart skipped a beat as he left the simulation lab, whistling something. What had she just done? This was not keeping her distance. This was the opposite.

She tried to tell herself that they were just friends.

That this outing would be innocent. Nothing had to happen. Nothing needed to be said. They were just friends.

Yeah, keep telling yourself that.

CHAPTER SEVEN

I HOPE HE's not down there, shouting.

Mindy was running late, though only by about five minutes. Still, she darted from the elevator and past the doorman out onto the street. She was terrified that Sam was going to make good on his promise and begin to shout her name.

When she rushed outside he was standing in front of her building, his hands deep in a black peacoat, looking up toward the sky. Then he looked at her and grinned, that cocky, devilish smile that made her weak in the knees.

"I thought you'd be out here, screaming my name," Mindy said as she walked over to him.

"Well, I was contemplating it but I remembered that your place is a penthouse and that's a bloody tall building."

Mindy chuckled. "It's the best."

He cocked an eyebrow. "You really think so? I prefer the brownstone myself. That's why I live in one."

"I thought you lived in an apartment with a bunch of other residents?"

"Aye, but the flats are in a brownstone. It's kind of

just a bedroom really. Though one of my roommates moved in with her boyfriend recently."

"You live with girls. Why does that not surprise me?" she teased.

"There is one other man in the house."

"Sure, sure."

"There is. I don't know why you don't believe me. What have I got to hide?"

"A harem."

Sam snorted. "Oh, aye, a harem of surgical residents."

Mindy rolled her eyes and then laughed. "So, what do you have planned for us today since you were so insistent that I spend my day off touring New York City in the freezing cold temperatures."

"This *isn't* cold."

"It is when you're from California."

"Aye, well. Yes, I guess so."

"How do the Scots keep warm? Especially when wearing kilts?"

Sam groaned. "I'm not wearing a kilt. Why are you bringing up kilts now?"

"Because you're making fun of the fact that I'm from California and I hate the cold."

"I had porridge this morning."

Mindy wrinkled his nose. "Ugh."

"It keeps you warm. It's hearty."

"No, thanks," Mindy said.

"You need to toughen up, Mindy." Then he slipped his arm through hers. "And we'll start by dragging you out on a ferry to visit one of my favorite ladies."

"You told me that we were going to see traditional

tourist attractions. I don't want to visit one of your girl-friends on some obscure island."

He looked at her like she was crazy. "I was talking about the Statue of Liberty, you daft hen."

She glared at him.

"What's that look for?" he asked.

"For calling me a daft hen!"

"I'm sorry."

"Oh, well, that's okay."

Sam chuckled as they walked toward the subway station. "You were a wee bit jealous when you thought I was going to drag you to meet a girlfriend."

"Hardly."

"Aye, you were." His eyes were twinkling. "Admit it."

"I'm not going to admit to anything and you can't make me. So how are we going to get to the Statue of Liberty?" she asked, changing the subject of jealously and girlfriends, because he was right, the thought of him with another woman drove her a bit bonkers. It made her see green, though it shouldn't. She didn't have a claim on him.

"We're going to take the Number One train down to the South Ferry Station."

Mindy dug in her heels. "We're taking the subway?"

"What're you worrying about? There's nothing wrong with taking the subway."

"I've never taken public transportation before."

"Never?"

She shook her head. "In Los Angeles it wasn't safe."

"Well, it would take you all day in this kind of traf-fic to get down to the South Ferry Station and even then it would be almost impossible and probably expensive to find parking. I also don't have a car. Do you?"

"No. I've been meaning to go and look…"

Sam *tsked* under his breath. "Trust me. Don't waste your money. If you want to leave the city for some reason, rent a car. Trust me, the subway train will not bite you."

He took her gloved hand and squeezed it. "Do you trust me?" he asked.

"I have no choice."

Sam laughed. "Aye, that's true. Come on. I swear it will be fun."

Mindy let him lead her down the steps of the Eighty-Sixth Street Station into the underground of New York City. The first thing she noticed was that it was warm but the air was dank and smelled stale. She wrinkled her nose but followed him through the turnstiles as he paid their fare and he led her to the platform.

She gripped his arm, holding on to him for dear life, and he teased her.

"Do you think I'm going to push you off to meet your maker?"

"If you do, I'm taking you with me," she said.

He laughed again. She liked the way he laughed, it always made her smile.

"Deal," he said. "But I promise you I won't be throwing you over the edge. It would be a waste of a beautiful woman."

Heat bloomed in Mindy's cheeks. She wanted to chastise him for saying that, but they were alone. They weren't on duty. They were just two friends exploring the city and she didn't have a problem with him telling her she was beautiful.

There was a rumbling sound and she peeked down the dark tunnel to see two headlights in the distance.

"Come on, we have to move to the front of the train and get one of the first five compartments."

"Why?" Mindy asked, as Sam guided her down to the other end of the platform.

"They only allow the first five compartments of the train to exit at the South Ferry Station. I don't know why, but that's just the way it is."

The train slowed and stopped, the breeze blowing her loose hair into her face as it pulled into the station. The doors opened and a few people got off. Once the way was clear Sam pushed his way on, dragging her with him.

Surprisingly, there was a seat and he sat her down and stood in front of her. The doors dinged shut and the train pulled out of the station and down the dark tunnel.

"I feel bad with you standing there."

"Don't feel bad. I don't think you should be standing on your first ride on the subway. Maybe when we head back up to the Upper West Side." He winked at her, holding tight to the handhold above him, his body swaying back and forth with the train.

They chatted the best they could during their subway ride to the South Street Ferry. It was hard, with the constant jolting coupled with the loading and unloading of people.

"Come on. Up you get." He held out his free hand and helped her to her feet.

"Why?" she asked, as she held on for dear life.

"The next stop is ours and we have to get off as quickly as we can before people start pushing to get on."

Sam gripped her hand tight as the train came to

a stop and the doors opened. He led her through the throng of people and out onto the platform. He guided her through the crowd and up to street level, where they headed to the Battery to catch the ferry to take them to Liberty Park.

Mindy shivered in the cold wind. "Do they operate on bitter days like today?"

"The only day they don't run is December twenty-fifth and this is not bitter, you big wimp."

She punched him in the arm but didn't let go of his hand as they walked to the ferries. As they approached the depot she could see signs about pre-booking to enter the pedestal and the crown of the Statue of Liberty.

"You have to reserve your tickets in advance."

"Don't worry. I booked them last night. Got the last two tickets for this morning." He glanced at her briefly as they waited in line. "You're trying to figure out a way out of this. Why?"

"Why? Because it's freaking cold. What if the boat sinks and we're eaten by sharks?"

Sam cocked an eyebrow. "Are you afraid of the water?"

"I'm not afraid of water. I'm afraid of sharks and drowning. Oh, and hypothermia."

He laughed. "You're a strange duck, Mindy Walker."

"I'm going to take that as a compliment."

"As you should." Sam winked and they boarded the ferry, which would take them on a short ride out on said frigid waters toward Lady Liberty, who faced southeast, greeting all newcomers to the U.S.A. Even though it was cold outside, it was sunny. A brilliant sunny day that reflected off the patina of the statue and her torch, making her seem to glow. Mindy had seen so many pictures of her but hadn't really paid attention to this famous landmark when she'd arrived in New York just over a month ago. Now close up to her she could see why people loved her. Mindy leaned over the rail, smiling.

"When you smile like that, you're really quite stunning," Sam said.

"You really shouldn't flatter me like that."

"Why?" he asked.

"I might let it go to my head and forget myself." Then she blushed, the heat rushing to her cheeks, even though it was cold. Why was she flirting with him? He was off-limits. Only she couldn't help herself. It was easy around him.

Too easy.

Sam's eyes twinkled, but he didn't respond. Instead, he leaned over the railing beside her and though she was kind of hoping he would say something, she was glad that he didn't. She hadn't meant to say what she had, but she really had forgotten herself for a moment and who she was with. It was nice.

It had been so long since she'd been at ease around a man.

She'd forgotten how good it felt to have that kind of intimacy with someone and she really missed it.

Sam was surprised by what she'd said.

"I might let it go to my head and forget myself."

He'd momentarily forgotten who he was with, but when she'd said those words his blood had heated with desire. Mindy looked so delectable all bundled up. Her soft purple knitted hat and infinity scarf set off the color of her eyes against her dark, rich red hair and he fought the desire to pull her up against him and kiss her, because at this moment all he could remember was the taste of her lips.

They had been so sweet.

All he could think about was her body naked with his. His lips on her ivory throat, his hands in her silky hair.

Get a grip on yourself, man.

So he didn't say anything in response to her, just leaned over the railing and tried to focus on their approach to Liberty Island. He was hoping the cold wind biting at his cheeks would take away the lust singing in his blood.

He couldn't remember the last time he'd wanted a woman like this. Other than the first night they'd met, but even then if she hadn't initiated the kiss, if she hadn't asked him back to her apartment, he probably would've done nothing.

Vixen that she was, he was absolutely lost to her and he knew he was so weak that if she asked him now to take her in his arms, he would without hesitation.

She's off-limits.

And he had to keep reminding himself of that fact.

They were friends and nothing more. He wouldn't walk down the same path his mother had. He wouldn't sleep or have a relationship with a doctor who was his attending before he was. If she was still available when his fellowship was over, and he was an attending in his own right, then perhaps they could revisit their night of passion.

But, really, who was he kidding? He still had a couple years of working in the pediatric field before he became an attending. By then she would have moved on. A beautiful, funny, compassionate and talented surgeon like Mindy would have no problem finding someone. If only she would open up.

There were a few walls she'd carefully constructed around her.

It's why he had a feeling she didn't have many friends and he couldn't figure out why she was keeping people out of her life. Why she was so closed off.

Any time they had come close to talking about something personal her walls had gone up. Of course, the same applied to him. His personal life was just that. Personal, and very few people knew his secrets. He preferred it that way. Fewer rumors that way.

"You hear about Dr. Hanley? The only reason she got that spot was because she slept with her attending, Dr. Langley."

"Yes, and it totally destroyed her marriage. I feel bad. She has a son. Poor kid."

The problem was the "poor kid" had been him, and he'd heard every word those other surgeons had said about his mother. It still stung to this day and he refused to be lumped in with his mother, even though he seriously doubted Mindy was as much of a jerk as the professor was. If it hadn't been for the fact that Dr. Chang was at West Manhattan Saints he would never have applied to the surgical program.

He avoided Langley as much as he could, because he was one of the reasons his parents had split up. Why his mother had a reputation that followed her brilliance. Why people admired her, lauded her, but talked behind her back.

Sam didn't want that.

"Thank goodness!" Mindy exclaimed, breaking through his morose thoughts. "We're finally going to be on dry land."

Sam chuckled. "There, now the sharks can't get you. Unless I push you off the island."

Mindy turned toward him. "You do that and, like at the subway station, I'm going to take you with me. You're bigger, they'll eat you first."

Sam grinned but didn't respond as he took her outstretched arm and they headed down to the lower deck to get off the boat and check out the Statue of Liberty.

He tried to keep his mind off the fact he was with one of the most beautiful women he'd seen for a long time and instead focus on the interesting museum in the pedestal of the Statue of Liberty.

Okay, the museum was not that interesting and he'd been to it before, but Mindy seemed engrossed in looking over everything.

"You're absolutely and utterly bored, aren't you?" Mindy asked, peering over a display, not looking at him.

"How can you possibly know that? You're not paying attention to me at all."

She smiled to herself. "I know when someone is bored. You've been shifting your weight on the balls of your feet, whistling and just trailing behind me."

"Okay, the museum isn't my cup of tea. I've been here before."

"I figured as much," she said. "I do appreciate you bringing me."

"Not a problem."

"Should we race to the top?" she teased.

"Are you kidding? It's like over two hundred stairs to the top."

"It's three hundred and fifty-four, to be precise, but of course you would've known that had you read what I just read." And for good measure she made a superior face.

"Why, you little…"

Mindy laughed and raced to the stairwell, taking the stairs quickly while Sam chased her. They didn't run the whole way, they took breaks and stopped their mad chase when they came across others who were tackling the spiral staircase at a more leisurely pace and probably thought they were out of their gourds, racing around a national monument.

When they got to the top Sam leaned against the wall to catch his breath for a moment, so he didn't sound too winded in front of her.

"You're such an old man," Mindy teased.

"I'm younger than you."

"Low blow, old man Napier. Very low blow indeed."

Sam grinned and came up beside her so they could look out over the water. Even though it was chilly out, the brilliant morning sun reflected against the water like diamonds.

"It is beautiful," Mindy admitted. "I'm glad you brought me out here to see this. Even if it's cold."

"You're welcome." He glanced at her, actually he couldn't take his eyes off of her, watching her delight in their trip. "Well, we'd better head down if we're going to get to our next destination in time."

Mindy cocked an eyebrow. "Next destination. No, we don't need to go anywhere else. This was great."

"I won't hear any arguments. We're going to the Empire State Building."

"What is with your obsession with tall buildings today?"

"I'm taking you to all the touristy spots, like I said I would. I can't help it that a lot of touristy spots are tall buildings. Well, two are for sure." And he winked at her. "You're at my mercy today, Mindy."

Mindy just rolled her eyes and then laughed. "Whatever you say."

Sam chuckled as he followed her down the endless steps back to the pedestal of the Statue of Liberty. He kept his hands firmly jammed in his pockets so as not to reach out and pull her into his arms.

The idea of having her at his mercy excited him.

Stop thinking that way or you'll be in trouble.

It seemed to him that he had to keep reminding himself of this fact.

Frequently.

It was hard not to, though. There were so many things he liked about Mindy. Even though she seemed to have her own walls firmly in place, keeping him out, she still was this bright, shiny and happy person. Her brilliance, her enthusiasm for everything she put herself into appealed to him.

She had fire in her. When residents or interns displeased her, especially when working on a fragile case, when a mother and her unborn baby's lives were at stake, she was a fierce protector of her patients.

Dr. Mindy Walker was someone you didn't want to cross professionally, but sometimes he got the feeling that she wasn't always like that. That the fierceness was a defense mechanism, part of the walls.

He'd done a bit of research about her, read some of her papers. She'd had a very lucrative practice in California. What would make her sell it, pack up her life and move to a place where the air hurt her face?

Sam chuckled again to himself as he thought of her saying that a couple times since they'd left her apartment.

"Why am I living where the air hurts my face?"

And then she would make a pouty face.

"Ugh," she groaned, as they stepped outside and headed toward the dock to pick up their ferry back to Battery Park.

"Yeah, yeah, the air. It hurts."

Mindy punched him in the arm. "Smart aleck."

They boarded the ferry and soon they were pushing off away from the Statue of Liberty. This time they sat on the benches inside. He leaned back against the bench, his arms spread, and she leaned back into his arm. She didn't snuggle in but she didn't move away either.

It was nice.

"So, why did you move here again?"

Mindy cleared her throat. "I told you. It was an opportunity I couldn't pass up. Professor Langley made me an offer I couldn't refuse."

Sam snorted at the mention of the chief of surgery. "I see."

"You don't really like Professor Langley, do you?"

"What do you mean?" Sam straightened up and crossed his arms.

"Aha, so you have some secrets too."

Sam shrugged. "We just don't get on, that's all."

"That's funny, because I could've sworn that he

mentioned to me that you were one of the residents to watch."

The compliment just slid off of him. He didn't care if Langley thought highly of him. If it had been Dr. Chang that would've been different. He respected Dr. Chang. In fact, he respected most of the surgeons as West Manhattan Saints except Langley, because he'd ruined his parents' marriage.

"Was it worth it, Monica? The promotion meant so much to you, you felt it necessary to throw our marriage away?"

"You don't understand me, Frasier. You don't understand what it's like being a surgeon. Being the best. Langley understands my needs. You don't. You just want me to be a mother, a housewife, grubbing around on your land in the Highlands. That's not what I want. That's not what I deserve. I never wanted to be a mother!"

His parents' last fight haunted him.

The heartbreak in his father's voice because his father had truly loved his mother. Sam's father had been blinded by love to the point that he had fallen in love with someone who didn't value love and family the same way he did.

It had nearly destroyed his father and it cut Sam to the quick when she hadn't wanted full custody of him. That he'd moved from New York to Scotland. In the end, living with his father and being raised in the Highlands had given him a happy childhood, but it was the rejection of the woman he called Mother that still hurt.

When he had visited her, she'd barely spent any time with him unless he'd been in the hospital with her and he'd got to watch her and Langley together.

It was when she'd taken her posting at Harvard and left West Manhattan Saints that he'd stopped visiting her as often, because she hadn't had time for him.

"What's wrong?" Mindy asked. "You just totally closed off."

"Just thinking." Sam gave her a half-smile. "We're here. You ready for your next adventure?"

"And if I say no?"

"You don't have a choice, remember? I'm in charge today." He held his hand out and she took it as they disembarked from the ferry and moved through the crowds heading to the subway station so they could catch the next ride up to the Empire State Building.

Sam shook the thoughts of his mother from his head.

His mother was not allowed in today. She wasn't going to ruin this day. This day was all about him and Mindy.

Today he was going to have fun too, because he couldn't remember the last time he'd had this much fun.

CHAPTER EIGHT

MINDY PEERED THROUGH the binoculars on the top of the Empire State Building. Usually she wasn't one for heights—she wasn't afraid of them, but she didn't go out of her way to visit tall buildings and ride an elevator to the top of one.

At least the Statue of Liberty had stairs, but the Empire State Building had an elevator and she didn't really like elevators or their enclosed spaces too much, but she just squeezed Sam's hand tight.

He gave her an encouraging smile and squeezed her hand back, but once they were at the top it was fine and she was glad she was able to have a nice vantage point of the city. It was truly beautiful.

She could only imagine what it would be like to be at the top of the Empire State Building as the sun was setting. From her penthouse apartment, when she actually looked out her window at night, she would stare at this building all lit up. Another true icon of the city she was slowly growing to love.

And she was.

She may not be used to the winters yet, but she could see the appeal of living and *making* it in New York.

Sam shivered beside her.

"Now who's cold?" she teased, as she focused the viewfinder on him. The money had run out so she couldn't see anything anymore, but he didn't know that.

He tutted under his breath. "Well, it's a bit windy up here. At least when we were at the top of the Statue of Liberty we were in an enclosed space. This is out in the open."

"Okay, well, how about we head down? I'm a bit hungry. Do you want to grab a slice of pizza? Isn't that the traditional thing to do in New York City?"

"We're not going for a slice."

"We're not?" She was a bit disappointed.

"No, I have somewhere better we can go."

"But you're not going to tell me, are you?"

He shook his head and grinned in that annoying but sexy way of his.

"Did anyone mention that you're a pain, Dr. Napier?"

"Aye, several times. Especially my roommates. Remember, most of them are female."

"Right. You did mention that. Oh, didn't I see one of your former roommates on the OB/GYN list for an appointment? Uh, Dr. Camara?"

Sam frowned. "Yes, she's pregnant, but she's seeing you? Is something wrong?" There was genuine concern in his voice.

"No, nothing is wrong. I happened to be a licensed OB/GYN as well. I was covering for another doctor. There's nothing wrong there." She smiled. "It's nice, you know?"

"What is?" he asked, as they stood in line, waiting for the elevator to go down.

"That you care about your friends so much, but I don't think you show it much."

Sam snorted. "Of course I care. She's pregnant. I wouldn't want anything to happen to her or the baby."

"Okay, now you're putting the accent on thick, and as you're not annoyed you're doing it on purpose."

"Does that bother you?" he asked, a twinkle of devilment in his eyes.

Yes. It turns me on.

And Mindy could distinctly remember the last time his thick accent had turned her on. She'd jumped into his arms when he'd been a perfect stranger and had begged him to go home with her. When they'd been at her apartment his brogue had been thick the more aroused he'd become, and just thinking about it made her hot under the collar.

"No, it doesn't bother me in the least."

Liar.

"Then why even bring it up?" Sam teased.

"If you don't shut it soon I'm going to…"

Sam leaned over to whisper in her ear. "You're going to what, Dr. Walker?"

Mindy was going to retaliate but the doors to the elevator opened and they shuffled on and were surrounded by other people. So she kept her mouth shut, but she could see Sam smirking to himself, because he knew she wouldn't continue the conversation on an elevator crammed full of people.

He was such a pain in the butt.

At least it was a fast ride down. Once they were out on the street and the crowd of people leaving the lobby of the Empire State Building dispersed she turned to him.

"What now?"

"Now I'm going to take you for lunch," he said with a wink.

"How do I even know I'm going to like this lunch? I mean, you won't tell me where we're going," Mindy groused.

"You'll like it. Well, maybe you won't. I don't know what kind of food you like. Perhaps I should've asked you that before I made reservations."

"I like pizza."

Sam winced. "Sorry, no pizza where we're going."

"Am I dressed okay, then? You said you made reservations." She was dressed casually. She wasn't dressed in her yoga attire, but still it wasn't business casual. "Will jeans and a nice sweater do for wherever it is you're taking me?"

He stood back and rubbed his chin while she spun around. "Well, I don't know. I guess you'll do."

Mindy punched him playfully in the arm. "I'm *so* putting you on scut duty for a month."

He laughed out loud and grabbed her mittened hand. "You can't do that, Dr. Walker. I'm not on your service."

"Oh, I can. I can have a few choice words with Dr. Chang…"

"Blackmail. I see."

They both laughed and Mindy let Sam lead her wherever he was planning on taking her. Not that she was too impressed they were walking but, then, she found the wind wasn't biting as much anymore.

Maybe she was really getting acclimatized, which was a scary thought. She'd never thought she would ever get used to winter.

"You're frowning," Sam remarked.

"The cold isn't bothering me."

He chuckled. "I knew you'd get used to it."

"Well, just because I'm used to it doesn't mean I like it. Why couldn't we have taken a cab?"

"It's not that far away." Sam pointed. "See, it's just across the street."

Mindy looked to where he was pointing and saw the red canopied entranceway to The Russian Tea Room.

"Oh!"

"I take it that meets your approval?" Sam asked.

"It does."

"Come on or we'll be late for our reservations."

They dashed across West Fifty-Seventh Street, dodging cars and taxi cabs. The door was opened for them by the doorman, who doffed his hat as they entered the exquisite entrance of the world-famous Russian Tea Room.

"Wow," Mindy whispered, as she pulled off her knitted hat. She'd seen pictures of it, heard about it and knew it was featured in several famous television shows, but standing in the lushly red decorated Russian Tea Room in person, well, she realized pictures and television didn't do it justice. The dark green walls, with gold imperial eagles emblazoned on them, gave the room a vibe of decadence and mystery.

Sam spoke to the host and they were escorted to a corner booth, which was offset and away from some other afternoon diners. They settled into the booth.

"I thought it would be busier," Mindy said, shrugging out of her jacket.

"We missed the lunch crowd, it's time for early tea."

"Tea?"

"Well, I do come from Scotland. We do have tea and I frankly haven't had a proper tea in a long time."

Mindy leaned on her elbow. "You know, the more you use the word 'tea,' the more it loses its meaning."

"Tea, tea, tea." Sam opened the menu. "How adventurous are you when it comes to cuisine? I mean, you did tell me your favorite food was pizza."

"I think I'm pretty adventurous, but I draw the line at blood sausage. I know exactly what that is and I'm not interested."

"Oh, come on, it's not that…you're right, but it sounds worse than it is. Black pudding is more English than Russian, though."

"So what do you want me to try?"

"How about caviar?" Sam asked. "It's been a while since I had some."

"Are you serious?"

"Very." He cocked his head to one side. "Does the idea of caviar gross you out?"

"No it doesn't gross me out. I'm willing to try anything. Once."

Sam grinned and when the waiter came he ordered a royal afternoon tea for two. When Mindy glanced at the menu she had no idea where she was going to put all that food. She was hungry, but blinis, assorted sandwiches and caviar sounded a little rich.

As she watched Sam conversing in a friendly way with the waiter, she smiled. She couldn't help herself. When she and Dean had gone out to dinner, he had treated the wait staff, or anyone in the service industry, with disdain, like they were beneath him, no better than the dirt under his shoe. It had got to the stage that Mindy hadn't actually liked going out with Dean half the time. Even after the awkward relationship with their waiter there hadn't been much to talk about. They'd just eaten, possibly talked about cases.

There had been no spark.

She was spending the day with Sam and not once had she thought about when it would end. It was easy being with him. So easy.

Too easy.

No, she'd sworn now was the time she was going to focus on herself. She was going to find herself again.

They could only be friends. Nothing more.

It was a nice thought to entertain, because that's all it could be. Just a fantasy.

Sam was totally relaxed for the first time in…well, he couldn't remember when. Mindy, when she wasn't Dr. Walker, was a vivacious and funny woman to be around. The more time he spent with her the more he wanted to be with her.

"You're lonely. You need to find someone."

Kimberlyn's words seemed to strike a chord with him once again. Maybe she was right after all. Settling down, having someone had never been on his radar. At least, not until after he had his career set, but even then he wasn't sure if he could give his all to his career and a family.

He hadn't had the best role model when it came to surgeons and families.

Then again, he knew colleagues who made it work.

All he had to do was start by looking at his roommates. Especially Enzo and Kimberlyn. A relationship that had started with them being competitors. Then they'd both turned down a fellowship with Dr. Ootaka in favor of the other getting it. Now, that was love. And those two were joined at the hip.

Maybe I can have it all?

He shook that thought out of his head as fast as he could.

No. He couldn't have it all. At least, not with Mindy. It was bad enough that his mother's reputation could ruin him if people found out he was her son, but to start up a relationship with an attending when that surgeon was responsible for deciding if he got a fellowship or not could not happen.

He would not have that haunting his career.

The waiter brought their tea and set down two glass tea cups that had ornate pewter handles and delicate pewter carving wrapped all around them.

"Oh! So pretty," Mindy gushed, and then set the cup down to let the waiter pour her tea.

Sam couldn't help but smile as he watched her.

Dammit. Why her?

Why had she had to walk into that bar that night? Why had he gone with her back up to her apartment? Why did he have to want the one woman he couldn't have?

"You never do things the easy way, son. You always take the hardest road to hoe."

Sam took a sip of his tea, mulling over his father's words. It was true. Nothing ever came very easily for him. He had to work hard for things, but it made him appreciate it all the more when he achieved his goal.

Sure, he could've done his fellowship at his mother's hospital. He could've had his surgical training handed to him on a silver platter. Lord knew, he knew enough children of physicians who did just that, but he hadn't wanted his training to be handed to him.

And he most definitely didn't want to work with his mother or be under her thumb.

"This is really great," Mindy said with a contented sigh. "It almost makes me not want to go into work tomorrow. Almost."

"Really? I didn't think tea would have that effect on you."

"I have a busy caseload tomorrow. I have a mother being transported in from upstate. She's pregnant with quintuplets."

Sam raised his eyebrows. "Quints? Do you need a resident tomorrow?"

"I thought you had tomorrow off as well?" Mindy teased.

"I can also switch a shift. How often do you come across quints?"

"In my line of work, often enough." Mindy leaned back against the booth. "Those mono-amniotic twins, however, those are rare."

"I'd like to assist if I may."

Mindy grinned at him. "When the time comes. I am trying to keep those babies inside her for a bit longer. I don't want them to be born too premature."

"So the quints are the only thing on your docket tomorrow?" he asked.

"No, not the only thing. I have a few client consultations. I'm considered one of the top infertility doctors in the country, so it keeps me pretty busy."

"You're a surgeon of many talents."

"I should hope so. I spent enough time in my fellowships." She looked a little wistful. "Missed out a bit on things."

"Aye, but it must've been worth it."

"Oh, yes, it was. I wouldn't change my education for anything."

Sam leaned across the table. "You studied at Stanford?"

Mindy nodded. "Like I said before, I'm a native Californian. Never really traveled much. I liked the west coast too much."

"Which begs the question again, why did you leave?" He knew he'd touched a part that was hidden behind one of her walls. The sparkle in her eye disappeared and her spine stiffened. She wouldn't look him in the eye either, just traced her long, delicate fingers over the filigree on her cup.

"I told you, the chief made me an offer I couldn't refuse."

Sam knew better than to press the subject. He didn't want this day to end on a sour note. If he couldn't have her the way he wanted her, he wanted them to remain friends. He wanted to continue to work with her, learn from her because she was a brilliant surgeon.

"Right. I forgot."

The waiter brought a tray of assorted sandwiches and blinis with caviar. Sam thanked the waiter and then held out a blini with caviar on it.

"So, you said you were how adventurous when it comes to your food?"

The smile returned to Mindy's face. "No way out of this, is there?"

"Nope."

She held out her plate and he gave her one. The rest

of the tea went well. They talked about the hospital, about cases, about New York, and neither of them pried further into the other's personal life.

It was a nice, friendly tea.

When it was over he hailed a cab and they took a taxi back to her apartment. He walked her to the door and stood under the canopy with her, not wanting their day to end but knowing that it must.

"I had a great time today, Sam. Thank you for showing this California girl around New York."

"It was no problem. I'd been meaning to revisit some of those spots myself. I hadn't been to the Statue of Liberty since I was a young boy."

"Well, I'm glad you took me."

"Me too."

An awkward silence fell between them. They just stood there. He wanted to reach out, run his hands over her cheek and pull her into a kiss. That's usually how he ended dates when he was dating.

Only he couldn't with her.

"I'll see you in the morning, Sam." Mindy turned and disappeared inside.

Sam sighed, jammed his hands into his pockets and left to catch the subway back to his lonely flat in Brooklyn.

Not that he'd be alone as most of his roommates were off tonight, but without Mindy the world seemed like a pretty hollow, lonely and empty place.

It was the same world he woke up in every day, but after spending one day with Mindy he realized just how lonely he was.

CHAPTER NINE

MINDY TRIED NOT to let her gaze wander to Sam as she walked into the boardroom. It had been a week since their day in New York together. When he'd walked her to the door of her apartment she'd lingered.

She didn't know why. Perhaps it had been habit. She had been waiting for him to kiss her, even though kissing him again wouldn't have been wise.

Yet she'd waited there and he hadn't done anything. Just stood with her, his blue eyes dark, his face unreadable.

She actually didn't know why he'd waited there either, but the more he'd lingered the more she'd fought herself over inviting him up to her apartment. Of course, the last time she'd done that they'd slept together and she couldn't do that again.

Though she'd wanted to.

Being with Sam was so easy. She admired and respected him as a surgeon; he was fun, sexy, intelligent. Sexy.

Stop thinking about sex and his sexiness.

Only she couldn't when she was around him.

Focus.

Right now she had in front of her a skilled team of

pediatricians, neonatologists, nurse practitioners, residents, anesthesiologists, just about anyone who could possibly help with her quint case. Mindy had been keeping an eye on Mrs. Jameson for about a week, but it was apparent to Mindy that with Mrs. Jameson's condition they would have to prepare an elite team of practitioners in preparation for the quints' birth.

It was coming sooner rather than later.

She glanced up quickly to see that Sam was sitting next to Dr. Chang, leaning back in the chair, focused on her intently. When their gazes met he smiled, just briefly.

It sent a zing through her.

Before she could get started, though, there was a knock and Professor Langley stepped into the room.

"My apologies, Dr. Walker. I hope I haven't missed anything."

"No, of course not. Come in."

He nodded and then waved to someone else who was standing just outside the door. "I hope you don't mind, but I read the case file on the quints. I noticed one of them had a brain bleed that might need to be addressed."

"Yes. I was about to talk about the medical conditions of the babies."

"I thought you might want the help of one of the finest neurosurgeons. So I brought in Dr. Hanley." He stepped aside and Dr. Hanley stepped into the room.

Mindy's eyes widened. There was a collective gasp. Everyone knew who Dr. Hanley was. Who didn't? She was one of the most renowned and respected neurosurgeons.

"Thank you for allowing me to join you." Dr. Hanley's gaze fell on Dr. Chang and Sam. "Dr. Chang."

There was an odd tone to Dr. Hanley's greeting and as Mindy glanced at Sam she could see he was not happy. His lips were pressed together in a firm line of annoyance.

Mindy knew he had issues with Professor Langley, but open hostility wouldn't be good for his career and could impede his fellowship.

"You can proceed now, Dr. Walker," Professor Langley, the chief of surgery, said, taking a seat next to Dr. Hanley.

"Thank you." Mindy turned to the computer and brought up an ultrasound and Mrs. Jameson's medical records. "As you can see, Mrs. Jameson is a thirty-four-year-old female whose LMP was approximately thirty weeks ago today. She is Gravida One and Parity X. That pregnancy resulted in a forty-week-term delivery of a healthy baby boy who weighed approximately eight pounds seven ounces. There were no complications."

Mindy went on with her presentation, explaining about the different quints, and began to set out the teams that would be responsible for each baby. Most of the babies didn't seem to have a whole lot of medical problems. The fact that Mrs. Jameson had gotten to thirty weeks was a blessing, but she was starting to have frequent contractions and Mindy knew she had to get the teams prepared now, because once one of the waters broke that was it. It was time to get those babies out.

"As you can see, it's baby C that has fluid buildup around his brain and baby C is the one we're most concerned with." Mindy clicked on a close-up of baby C.

Dr. Hanley got up and walked over to the screen. "Hmm, I would need some more comprehensive films, but it looks like a simple shunt would take care of that. We should closely monitor that buildup of fluid, Dr. Walker. If it continues, we shouldn't delay in delivering the babies."

"I agree, Dr. Hanley," Mindy said. "I'll have that set up for you right away."

"Do." Dr. Hanley didn't even really acknowledge her as she headed back to her seat beside Professor Langley.

She'd heard rumors that Dr. Hanley was a piece of work. She could see why. Unfazed, Mindy went on with her presentation and went on to assign the teams that were responsible for each baby.

As she was about to assign Sam to Dr. Chang's team, Dr. Hanley stood up.

"If you don't mind, Dr. Walker, I would request that Dr. Napier be on my team for Baby C. I would like him to work on the shunt with me."

Sam's eyes narrowed and he scowled, not at all impressed.

"I think Dr. Chang requires Dr. Napier's assistance," Mindy said, and then regretted it. She didn't want anyone to think she was playing favorites.

Dr. Hanley glared at her now. "Nonsense, he's a resident and I require his assistance."

"Dr. Napier can work with Dr. Hanley," the chief of surgery said, standing up. "I trust there were will be no further discussions. Keep us updated on the patient, Dr. Walker."

He excused himself and Dr. Hanley followed him.

Mindy was absolutely confused. She knew that Dr.

Hanley was a brilliant surgeon but so was she. Yet they were bending over backwards to accommodate Dr. Hanley.

As people began to disperse Dr. Chang leaned over to a visibly angry Sam and whispered a few words, but he rebuffed her, stood and stormed out of the room.

What in the world?

She knew Sam didn't like orders from Chief Langley and didn't like time taken from pediatrics, but he was having a shot at working with Dr. Hanley. He shouldn't look a gift horse in the mouth.

Dr. Chang sent her a furtive glance but didn't say anything else. She just left the room quietly. Mindy couldn't help but wonder what was up between Dr. Hanley, the chief and Sam. Any time Professor Langley was mentioned Sam would tense up.

What did he have against him?

Curiosity killed the cat.

Even though she really wanted to know what was going on, she knew it wasn't her business. She wasn't going to pry or push. When Sam was ready to tell her, he'd tell her, though she was really dying to know. Besides, she didn't exactly open up to him and she wouldn't. There had to be a good reason Sam kept it secret and she'd respect his wishes. Some things could destroy a career very fast.

Mindy sighed and cleaned up her presentation. She shouldn't be fussing over why Sam was upset. The teams had been set up. Her focus should be on her patient. On those babies. That's why she'd come to West Manhattan Saints. She'd come to provide the best medical care, to focus on her career.

Let Dr. Chang, the chief and Dr. Hanley deal with fighting over Sam.

She couldn't worry about it.

Sam had to deal with his own problems.

Sam was furious. What the heck was his mother doing here? He was also so angry that she'd called him out like that, requesting him and taking him off Dr. Chang's service. He was sure the surgery his mother wanted him to work on, placing a shunt on Baby C, would be exciting, but he'd rather learn the procedure from anyone but his mother.

Not that he'd have an actual chance to participate in the surgery. His mother didn't really involve her residents. She didn't let them get their hands dirty. Sam knew his mother well. She liked to hog all the glory.

His mother was speaking to Langley at the end of the hallway. She was touching his arm and laughing in an intimate way. It made Sam's teeth grind, seeing them together, because it instantly brought back the memory of his father holding his hand almost twenty years ago and the look of heartache on his father's face as he'd realized his wife was cheating on him.

They finished talking and Langley walked away. His mother turned around and smiled, briefly. Not in a warm compassionate way, or in a way that showed she was glad to see him. It was polite.

"Well, I can tell by your expression you're not exactly happy to see me, Dr. Napier."

Sam was pleased that at least he was keeping his anonymity.

"Perhaps we should take this somewhere more private."

His mother smirked. "Of course. My temporary office is down the hall."

Sam nodded and followed behind his mother as she led him to the office she was using. His stomach knotted when he saw all the boxes. How long was temporary?

She shut the door and Sam crossed his arms.

"I know that look," his mother said. "You're not happy that I'm here."

"Aye."

She chuckled. "So like your father."

"What are you doing here?" Sam asked, not wanting her to talk about his father with him. She had no right.

"That's the way you talk to your mother after not seeing her for five years?"

"I didn't think you cared particularly."

She shrugged and then tossed her blonde hair over her shoulder. "I kept busy."

So like his mother. She didn't admit to caring. It infuriated him.

"What're you doing here, Mother?"

"Saving a life?"

Sam glanced around at the boxes. "Dr. Walker requested your presence? I thought she only just discovered the issue with Baby C in the last week."

"No Dr. Walker did not request my presence. Gareth did."

Sam cringed inwardly at his mother's familiarity with Langley. It was another kick in the pants to him. A reminder about how she and Langley had broken his family apart.

"Again. Why?"

"There's a patient here in your pediatric ward. One with an inoperable brain tumor."

"Janie?" Sam asked.

His mother nodded. "Her parents have agreed to allow me to try and resect it using a new technique. That's why I'm here for some time. If the surgery is successful then I'll publish a paper and credit Gareth and West Manhattan Saints."

"How generous of you." Sam was very familiar with Janie and her family. Janie was one of his special patients and it broke his heart that she had a tumor that was ending her life. He didn't particularly like the fact that his mother was here and was planning on using poor Janie as a guinea pig to further her research.

"You're mad that I requested you," his mother said.

"I don't want anyone to know that you're my mother. You know that and you agreed to those conditions if you were to ever come here."

His mother snorted. "I really don't know why."

"I want to earn this fellowship on my own."

His mother snorted again and moved to sit behind her desk. "Really a waste."

"Pediatrics is a waste?"

"No."

"Then a waste of my talent?"

His mother shrugged. "I wouldn't know. I've never seen you operate, but given that you're my child I would assume that you have decent surgical abilities."

Sam rolled his eyes. "How generous of you to compliment me."

"You're being immature."

"Why did you request me?"

"To test your surgical abilities. Chief Langley

speaks very highly of you and I want to see if you live up to his praise."

"I don't need to live up to anyone's expectations. I came here to learn under Dr. Chang."

His mother snorted. "You could be extraordinary. Brain surgery is cutting edge. If your abilities are as good as Gareth says they are then you're just wasting your talent in pediatrics. Do you want to settle for the ordinary?"

"Aye. I do."

His mother shook her head and then picked up a file, effectively dismissing him as she opened it up and began to read. "You're on my service. There's no point in arguing about it."

"I would rather not be."

"If you raise a stink don't you think people will question why you don't want to work with me?"

She had a point.

"Fine," he agreed grudgingly, but he was not happy. Not that she cared. His mother only cared about herself.

"Good. Well, if we're done talking I'd rather like to get to work."

"Of course, *Mother*." Sam opened the door and barged out, slamming it behind him. As he turned around he crashed right into Mindy.

"Dr. Napier!" She gasped in surprise.

"I'm sorry, Dr. Walker. What're you doing here?"

"Bringing Dr. Hanley the information she requested on Baby C. Is she busy?"

"Yes, but I'm sure she'll want to see the file."

Mindy glanced up at him and frowned. "Are you okay, Sam?"

He frowned. "Perfectly."

He wanted to tell her he wasn't fine. That he was annoyed, but if he did then he would have to tell her that Dr. Hanley was his mother and then the whole story about his mother and Langley would come out.

The only people at West Manhattan Saints that knew about his situation were Langley and Dr. Chang. Sam knew that Dr. Chang wouldn't say anything and he thought Langley had enough couth not to say anything either.

After all, his mother had eventually made him a cuckold as well. Still, there was no reason to take it out on Mindy, but he really didn't want to get into it right now. He just had to go somewhere and calm down. Maybe do some charting in a broom closet.

"Are you sure you're okay?"

"I'm fine. Good day, Dr. Walker." He walked away from her, brushing her off. It hurt him to do it, but it was for the best.

This kind of situation was why he didn't want to get involved with anyone he worked with. Messes like this. Rumors and secrets. He was here to practice medicine, not fall in love.

Who said anything about love?

Sam cursed under his breath.

He knew he had to get out of there and put some distance between him and his mother.

CHAPTER TEN

MINDY COULD FEEL all eyes on her as she carefully made an incision in her patient's uterus. Baby B's amniotic sac had broken and it was time to deliver the quintuplets. They had managed to last until thirty-two weeks.

Two weeks longer than when they'd had the meeting in the boardroom. Which was great, and the fluid around Baby C's brain remained stable, though he would still need a shunt. There were teams of neonatologists and pediatric doctors waiting to take the babies as she delivered them. She could see Sam standing there, waiting for Baby C. Once Baby C was delivered Sam was going to take him into the next OR where a shunt would be placed by Dr. Hanley.

Even though Dr. Hanley was a brilliant neurosurgeon, she was a bit of a narcissist.

Mindy took a deep calming breath as she continued to work. There were a lot of lives at stake and she didn't have time to worry about anyone else in this room.

"Delivering Baby A," she announced out loud, as she made the cut and gently removed Baby A from the uterus. She cut the cord and handed the baby to the waiting team. As Mindy focused on the next baby, she could hear the healthy scream of Baby A, who was being assessed under an islet table by Team A.

Mindy smiled, though no one could tell she was smiling under her surgical mask. She did love the sound of healthy lungs.

"Delivering Baby B."

The resident on Dr. Chang's team stepped forward with a blanket and Mindy cut the cord and placed the baby in team B's care. Then headed to her problem baby.

"Delivering Baby C."

Sam stepped forward, waiting to take his charge. He winked at her from behind the mask in an encouraging way as she quickly delivered Baby C.

Sam took the little guy and whisked him off to a warming table to check his vitals before they took him into surgery.

Mindy stopped for a moment. Just a moment, but didn't hear a cry from Baby C.

Come on, little guy. Come on.

Then there was a weak wail from across the OR.

"How is he, Dr. Napier?" Mindy called out, as she cauterized a bleeder quickly so she could move on to the other babies.

"Weak. His vitals aren't good and he has some apparent hydrocephalus. Taking Baby C to OR two."

Mindy glanced up briefly to see Baby C being hooked up to monitors and ventilators, prepping him for his immediate surgery. Such a hard start to life.

"Delivering Baby D," she called out, as she removed the tiny baby. Baby D had some breathing issues, but Mindy couldn't worry about that as she finished up and moved on to Baby E. The final baby.

As much as she was thinking about the babies and all those fragile little lives in different teams' hands, she couldn't think about them. She had to focus on the mom's health, so that she could recover and take care of all those babies.

She'd controlled the whole procedure as far as she could by setting the teams. As much as she wanted to hover over all those precious lives, she had to step back and let go. She had to let the teams she'd picked take over.

It was a perk of having her practice in a hospital setting that she knew the surgeons and could hand-pick them. When her practice was private and out of the office, she left that decision up to the neonatologist team, which stressed her out.

This way was better.

"Delivering Baby E." She handed the little girl to team E and now she had to make sure Mom was okay and stitched up. "Add Syntocinon to her IV."

"Yes, Dr. Walker." The anesthesiologist added the meds.

Mindy went to work on repairing bleeders and then finally was able to remove the placentas. Once they were gone she could work on closing up the uterus. "Good work, Dr. Walker."

Mindy glanced up to see Dr. Chang standing beside her.

"Is everything okay with your team?"

"Perfect. My team can handle Baby B. She's on her way to the NICU. I wanted to observe, if that's okay?"

"Of course."

Mindy worked diligently to check the uterus, to make sure nothing of the five separate placentas had been left behind. If anything remained it could pose a serious infection risk to the mother.

Once she'd checked and made sure everything was intact and healthy, she began to close up the uterus.

"Dr. Chang, they need you in OR two. It's Baby C."

Dr. Chang glanced back at the nurse who had come in. "Can't Dr. Hanley handle a shunt?"

"There are some more complications to Baby C and Dr. Hall is dealing with Baby E."

Mindy glanced up and Dr. Chang nodded to the nurse.

"I'll be there in a moment." Dr. Chang turned to Mindy. "Don't worry, we'll take care of him. Dr. Napier is in there."

"I know the baby is in good hands."

Dr. Chang nodded and left.

Focus.

Sam and Amelia were more than capable of helping Baby C. Both of them were brilliant surgeons. Baby C was in good hands.

Still, a sense of dread settled over her and she glanced at the mother, who was still under general anesthesia, and she felt a pang of heartache for her. When Mrs. Jameson woke up she wasn't going to be able to hold her babies and then she would have to tell her that one of those babies needed a bit more medical care.

It was the least favorite part of her job.

Mindy sighed and continued closing up Mrs. Jameson so they could get her into Recovery.

After her job was done she could check on the babies.

She could see a long night in her future but she didn't mind in the least.

* * *

Sam stood in the critical level of the NICU. Baby C, who had been named Michael, was critically ill.

The shunt placement had gone fine, but then he developed pulmonary hypertension and was currently on a ventilator, helping him to breathe.

Last night his bowel had perforated, which was common with premature babies.

Sam hadn't left Michael's side. He felt responsible for him. Sam was the resident on his case and Dr. Chang, Dr. Hall and his mother had many other patients they had to deal with so they couldn't hang about.

Really, he shouldn't be either, but he couldn't help himself. When it came to babies who were so ill... At least Maya hadn't been this ill when he'd dealt with her.

Michael, on the other hand...

Sam glanced furtively at the monitor, watching Michael's vitals, which told him that the poor little guy was struggling.

"Come on, buddy," he mumbled under his breath.

"Why are you still here?"

Sam spun around to see his mother enter Michael's private room. "I'm monitoring my patient."

"There are capable NICU nurses who can do that." His mother moved around to the incubator.

"I'm very well aware of that." Sam stepped back to allow his mother to open the incubator and examine the baby.

"Incisions look good."

"Aye," Sam remarked. "There's nothing wrong with the shunt placement."

His mother smiled. "Of course there isn't."

Sam rolled his eyes.

"You did good in my OR," his mother said. "I'd like you to aid in my surgery with Janie."

"Why?"

"I'm offering you a chance at something brilliant, rather than standing here staring at a monitor."

"I'm monitoring my patient," he said through gritted teeth.

His mother shook her head. "Call it what you will, but I don't think you'll be standing here much longer."

"What's that supposed to mean?"

"Samuel, I raised you better than that. Look at the vitals. Baby C won't make it through the night."

It was like a slap across the cheek.

"You're wasting your time in pediatrics. Switch to neurosurgery. I didn't pay for your education to waste it on children."

"You're not a pediatric surgeon," Sam snapped.

"See the facts, Sam."

"Michael, not Baby C, will do just fine."

His mother shook his head. "You're throwing away your talent, wasting your time here."

"Neurosurgery has a high mortality rate as well," Sam snapped.

"What does that have to do with anything?"

"You seem to be implying that I'm wasting my time with children who are just going to die anyway."

"That's not what I was implying. Honestly, Samuel, what I meant was what can you do to prevent his death by standing here, staring at a monitor? You should be working on your surgical skills. Not standing here."

"So you've mentioned."

"So?" his mother asked.

"What?"

"Are you going to continue to stand here?"

"Aye," Sam snapped.

His mother shook her head again and left the NICU room. Sam cursed under his breath. His mother was absolutely impossible. She wasn't much of an optimist, but when he stared at the monitors again he knew that his mother was probably right.

He clenched his fists and wanted to hit something, wanted to scream.

"Dr. Napier, what're you still doing here?" Dr. Chang asked as she walked into the room.

"I… I don't know." Sam ran his fingers through his hair. "What's his prognosis?"

Dr. Chang sighed. "It's not good. He's got a lot of cards stacked against him."

Sam stared down at the little baby, struggling to live. "He can turn a corner. I've seen worse."

"I know. He can, but…I don't think so," Dr. Chang sighed. "There's nothing more you can do here. The parents will be coming up soon. I'm going to talk about options."

"Can I stay?"

"No. Go home, Sam. You've done all you can do."

Sam nodded, even though he didn't want to leave. For some reason he felt responsible for this child. Like if he was more extraordinary he could've saved the child's life, but his mother had made it clear that he wasn't. He was only ordinary.

His mother had made that clear.

As he stood in the hall Michael's mother, Mrs. Jameson, was wheeled past him. She didn't notice him there, but the look on her face spoke volumes. Mrs. Jameson already knew what was going on. She knew why Dr. Chang was calling her into Michael's room.

Sam hovered, watching through the window as Dr. Chang knelt down, placing a hand on Mrs. Jameson's knee as she broke the news.

Mrs. Jameson hunched over, her face in her hands, her shoulders shaking. Sam's heart clenched and he could feel tears sting his own eyes. How did parents deal with it? It was something he had never understood, but he admired them for it.

Admired the hours spent by bedsides. The hope, then watching hope dashed and seeing sorrow replace it was too much for him. Especially today.

I want to save them all.

He'd been pushed to his breaking point and he began to question himself. Could he handle this?

He used to be able to handle this. So what had changed?

Mindy.

Before she'd come along he'd managed to keep his emotions in check. Nothing had fazed him. He hated to see children suffer and when they died it hurt him, but none had affected him like this one and it was all Mindy's fault.

Somehow, some way she'd got him to open up and he didn't like it one bit.

He had to get out of there.

Sam left West Manhattan Saints as fast as he could, but instead of taking the subway back to his flat in Brooklyn he walked toward her apartment.

The doorman wasn't on duty and he slipped in after holding the door open for an elderly man exiting.

Sam was on autopilot as he hit the button to the

penthouse floor and in what seemed like a New York minute he was standing in front of her door, knocking.

Mindy opened the door. "Sam? What're you doing here?"

"Don't speak."

"What—?" He cut her off by taking her in his arms and kissing her.

Mindy was shocked that Sam had shown up at her door. The last time she'd seen him had been in Michael's room in the NICU. He'd been staring down into the incubator, looking heartbroken.

She wanted to reach out to him, because it was obvious that he was hurting. Ever since the surgery three days ago he'd been different. Withdrawn, almost downtrodden, and she didn't know why.

So, instead of going to him, she'd walked away. Besides, it was better that way. He wouldn't have appreciated her consoling him at work and it wouldn't have been good for her either. She couldn't let him into her heart and if she'd gone to him in that NICU he would've broken down all the careful walls protecting her. So she had let him be.

Now she was wrapped up in his arms and he was kissing her. A kiss that made her knees knock together.

The kiss ended and she had to lean against his chest for a moment to get her bearings. Right now it felt like the world was spinning off kilter a bit.

"Can I come inside?"

Turn him away. Say no.

As she glanced up into those blue eyes, which were glazed over in lust, tenderness and pain, she found she couldn't resist him. She was so weak. And though her common sense told her not to, she wanted to trust him. She wanted him to fill that empty, raw spot in her heart. She wasn't sure she could, but she could have tonight.

And she wanted tonight.

So badly.

"Yes," she whispered.

He grinned, relieved. "Good."

Mindy tried to step to the side to let him in but instead he scooped her up in his arms and kicked her door shut with the heel of his shoe.

"Sam!" she gasped.

"I'm sorry. I can't help myself." He headed off in the direction of the bedroom.

"Sam," she whispered, as he nuzzled her neck.

"Do you want me to stop?"

"No."

"Good." He set her down on the bed, joining her. He leaned over her and a shiver of anticipation coursed through her.

This was wrong. So wrong.

And she didn't care one bit, because right here and now it was just the two of them. There was no one else. Here they were just Sam and Mindy.

He brushed his knuckles down the side of her face, his blue eyes twinkling in the dim light that filtered in through the crack in her drapes, just a bit of the city creeping in on them.

"You're so beautiful." Then he leaned down and pressed another kiss against her lips, light at first and then more urgent, as if he couldn't get enough of her. His body was pressed against hers and she was glad she wasn't wearing one of her skirts, so she could open her legs and let his weight settle between her thighs.

Mindy arched her hips. She wanted him closer and she didn't want anything between them.

No clothes, no walls. Nothing. Just them.

Sam moaned. "Mindy, I want you."

"How much?"

Sam kissed her again, his tongue pushing past her lips, entwining with hers, making her blood sing with need.

"So much." He ran his hand over her body, but clothes were in the way. She wanted his hands on her bare flesh.

Mindy pushed him away.

"Have you changed your mind?" he asked.

"No." She sat up and took off her baggy T-shirt. "I want you naked." And she reached for the belt on his trousers, undoing it and slowly pulling it out of the belt loops. She then went for the button at the top of his pants. Sam moaned as her hand slipped underneath to touch him, just for a moment.

They made quick work of their clothes, until they were both naked. Nothing between them.

"I've tried so hard to resist you," Sam whispered against her neck. "But I can't. I need you again."

"I want you too, Sam."

She wanted him to erase her past. She wanted him to help her forget. When she was in his arms she wasn't that meek wallflower she had been in California and she wasn't a surgeon. She was just Mindy. Sexy, desirable Mindy, and she loved that he made her feel that way. No man had ever made her feel that way before.

"I want you so badly."

His lips captured hers in a kiss, silencing any more words between them. Mindy pulled him down. His body pressed against hers. It was just them, exposed and vulnerable to each other. His hands slipped down her sides, trailing over her flesh in little circles.

"So beautiful," he murmured.

It drove her wild and made her blood heat. His fingers found their way up to her breast, circling around her nipple, teasing. She sighed.

"So beautiful," he said again. "You drive me wild."

She ran her fingers through his hair as he began to kiss her again, but just light kisses starting at the lips and training lower, down over her neck. Lingering at her breasts, he used his tongue to tease her. She arched her back as pleasure shot through her again.

"I love it when you moan like that."

"Do you?" Mindy asked dreamily.

"Aye."

"Why?"

"Because when you moan like that I know you want me just as much as I want you." He took one nipple in his mouth and gently sucked for a moment. "Tell me how much you want me."

"So bad," she whispered.

His hand moved between her legs and he began to stroke her. Mindy cried out and then, when his hand was replaced by his mouth and tongue, it made her topple over the edge. She tried to stop herself from coming, but she couldn't. It was too much. It was a pleasure she'd never experienced before.

As she came down from her climax Sam moved away.

"Where are you going?" There was a definite shake to her voice.

"Hold on." He searched his trouser pocket and

pulled a condom out. "I didn't think you wanted me to continue without this."

"Good call." Mindy sat up, even though her legs felt a bit boneless. She took the condom packet from his hand.

"What're you doing?" Sam asked.

She pushed him down and straddled his legs. "Let me help you."

"I don't think that's…" He trailed off as she opened the wrapper and rolled it down over his shaft. Sam uttered a few choice Gaelic words as she stroked him.

"I love having you under me," she teased him, leaning over him and nibbling on his ear lobe.

"I'd rather have you under me." And before she knew what was happening he'd flipped her and was pressing her back down against the mattress, covering her with his body, spreading her legs and thrusting into her.

Mindy bit her lip to stop from crying out. She dug her nails into his shoulder as Sam filled her completely.

"You feel so good," he moaned. "So good."

She moved her hips, encouraging him to move, but he just chuckled.

"Why are you teasing me?" she asked.

"I want you to beg." He began to nibble her neck. "Beg for it."

"Please."

"Please, what?"

"I want you, Sam. Please, make love to me."

He moaned. "As you wish."

Sam moved slowly at first, taking his time, but she wanted so much more of him she urged him to go faster until he lost control and was thrusting against her hard and fast. Soon another coil of heat unfurled deep within her, pleasure overtaking her as he brought her to another climax. Only this time they were joined as one. This time when she came it would be around him, it would be with him, and that's what she wanted most.

She wrapped her legs around him, holding him tight against her, urging him on. Sam cried out as he came and she held him until he collapsed against her. Mindy ran her hand down his neck, his pulse racing under her fingertips.

What have I done?

She knew and she didn't care. She wanted Sam. She wanted him to make her forget about the pain and humiliation she'd endured in California.

She wanted to feel again. Mindy had thought that their one-night stand would make her feel again and though it had been good, it hadn't changed her. Not the way tonight had. There had been more to tonight. A connection she couldn't quite explain, or perhaps she didn't want to explain because she wasn't ready to admit it to herself.

Either way, tonight when Sam had come to her, so vulnerable and full of emotion, she'd felt alive again. Like she wasn't just a spent force. She'd felt desirable. Sexy. Dean had never made her feel that way before he'd admitted to himself that he was gay.

In fact, no other man had made her feel like Sam did.

She wished they could stay like this forever, but they couldn't. Tears stung her eyes, but only for a moment, and she got them under control. Mindy wasn't ready for Sam to see her cry yet. She wasn't ready to show that weakness, that flaw in her.

Right now she just wanted to savor the moment of being with him. Their bodies pressed together, limbs entwined, hearts racing.

It felt so good, being with him. Too good almost and that was a dangerous thing. Sam was supposed to be off-limits and it was obvious that she couldn't resist him.

She'd tried and failed.

Sam kissed her gently on the lips, his fingers stroking her face as she ran her hands down over his back. He rolled away from her and propped himself up on one elbow, those blue eyes twinkling with tenderness.

"Don't go yet."

A sly smile played on his lips. "What makes you think I was going somewhere?"

"The last time you moved away I fell asleep and when I woke up you were gone. I want you right here."

"The last time we were together it was a one-night stand between strangers." He leaned over and kissed her again. "You taste so good."

"Stay. Please."

"I'm not going anywhere yet."

She rolled over on her side and touched his face. She didn't want him to go. She didn't want this stolen moment to end. Not yet. She just wanted to remain here in this cocoon of happiness, where the outside world couldn't intrude. Where there were no nasty rumors, no sick people, no surgeries. Nothing. Just them. Just two people together.

"I want you again, Sam. I need you again."

He grinned lazily. "Let me catch my breath."

She cocked an eyebrow. "Oh, yes?"

"Yes, because I'm not done with you yet. Not by a long shot."

A zing coursed through her. *Oh, yes.* This was all so wrong, wanting him. So wrong that it felt so right.

CHAPTER ELEVEN

MINDY COULDN'T HELP but blush as Sam stroked her cheek. The last time they'd slept together she hadn't really known him so there had been no awkward moment afterwards. It had saved a bit of embarrassment, a bit of giggling, and then she did grin, because she was glad he was still here. She was glad it had happened.

This time it had been so much better because she liked Sam. She knew Sam. He was more than eye candy. More than just a one-night stand she'd picked up in a bar. She admired him. Respected him. He was her friend.

More than a friend.

She was falling for him. It thrilled and terrified her.

"You look quite pleased with yourself," Sam said.

"A bit." She tucked her arm under her pillow and rolled onto her side. "So, what brought you to my door tonight?"

Sam grinned. "You need a justification?"

"I thought we were just going to be friends."

"I needed to see you. I just didn't know how much until you opened the door."

Mindy smiled. She knew he'd been stressed about Michael. For some reason Sam was taking Michael's medical condition very hard. Everyone had noticed by the way he'd hovered over the incubator for the first forty-eight hours of Michael's life. It was dedication, but Mindy had an inkling that it was something more.

"I'm glad you came to see me."

"Are you?"

"I am."

Sam rolled over and sat up, running his fingers through his hair. "This has been one heck of a week."

"What's going on? Something is bothering you and I think it's more than just an ill patient."

He sighed again. "It's hard for me to say. I don't tell many people."

He was hiding something from her and it made her nervous.

He's not Dean. Besides, she had her own secrets. "I get it."

He cocked an eyebrow. "You get what?"

"I get secrets and not wanting to share them."

"Do you?" he asked.

"Of course."

"You have secrets?"

Mindy shrugged. "There's not much to tell. I left California and an ex-husband behind."

"An ex-husband?" Sam asked.

"Yes." Her cheeks flushed with warmth and she couldn't believe she was actually telling Sam about Dean. "He cheated on me. I trusted him and he destroyed that trust." It was so hard to say the words. She didn't tell him that Dean had cheated on her with her best friend, but Sam was the first person in New York she'd told about Dean. She was trying so hard to hide that part of her life. It was so good to finally tell someone the hurt she'd buried for over a year.

Sam looked thoughtful and she worried it was too much information. That he'd leave or be embarrassed. Instead, he sighed wearily, "Dr. Hanley is my mother."

"Your mother?"

"Aye. She's my mother."

Now she was really shocked. Dr. Hanley was his mother? She didn't see a resemblance and she would've had no idea by the way they dealt with each other. She knew there was a vague disdain on Dr. Hanley's side, not unusual for a world-class surgeon who thought highly of herself, but a mother-son connection? That she would never have guessed. She'd known Sam's mother was a doctor, but Dr. Hanley? She hadn't pegged Dr. Hanley for the maternal type.

"You look like you've gone into shock."

"I guess I have a bit. Why were you keeping it a secret?" Mindy asked.

Sam sighed. "I'm not as extraordinary as her. Just ask her yourself."

"What?" Mindy asked confused. "Since when is she the expert on that?"

"I didn't want any favors in my career. I wanted to earn my place," Sam said. "I'm Dr. Napier. Not Dr. Hanley's son. Well, I am, but I'm not."

"You have something to prove. I get that. I respect it."

Sam smiled. "Aye, but do you really get it? You're a top-notch surgeon too."

"I do get it. It's why I left California."

"Because you got divorced?"

"Yes," Mindy said. "He was my partner in my practice. I trusted him, but after his betrayal came out I couldn't trust him. Not his opinions on patients, not in the OR. It would've been detrimental to my patients to continue on in that environment. It would've been detrimental to me to continue second-guessing myself."

"Your career means a lot to you."

Mindy nodded. "It does. Though I'm hardly a tough surgeon like your mom. I tend to wear my heart on my sleeve."

"That's not necessarily a bad quality. And you are tough. You demand excellence and perfection."

"I do. I came here to do serious work."

"Are you implying I'm not serious work?"

Mindy laughed. "No."

"Am I a mistake?" he asked, running his hand over her cheek.

"I haven't figured that out yet."

Sam chuckled and then sobered up. "I promise you I'm not trying to sleep my way to the top."

Mindy's spine stiffened. "What're you talking about?"

"My mother. She slept her way to the top, breaking my father's heart. See, surgery and her career were more important than her marriage and me."

"I know you're not sleeping your way to the top, but what are we doing?"

Sam sighed. "I don't know."

"I don't think a relationship is on the cards."

Because she couldn't let it be. No matter how much she wanted it.

"I can't promise you anything."

It stung, but she'd known that all along. She knew that he couldn't offer her anything and she really couldn't offer him anything either. She was still finding herself, still rebuilding her life after what had happened with Dean.

This time was for her.

"I don't expect anything." She leaned over and kissed him on the lips. "I'm glad you came over tonight, though."

"Me too. Though I wish…"

"What?"

"Maybe my mother is right. Maybe if I was more extraordinary like her I could do more for Michael. His siblings are thriving; it makes no sense that he's not."

"You care for your patients. That's an extraordinary quality."

"Caring is not good enough." He rolled out of bed and started pulling on his clothes.

"Where are you going?" she asked.

"Back to the hospital."

"Sam, there's nothing more you can do. Standing over Michael's incubator won't do anything to help him. Stay here. Rest."

He smiled at her. "It's best I leave. Besides, if I get back into that bed I'm not going to rest."

A zing shot through her body and she blushed again at his suggestion. He was right. He couldn't spend the night here. What had happened here between them tonight was a secret. No one else could know because it could ruin both of their reputations.

"You'd better go, but promise me you won't go back to the hospital." She knew it was futile. She knew he was going back to the hospital. He was dedicated. It was another thing she loved about him.

Loved?

No, that couldn't be. She wasn't ready and he was off limits, but Sam was so easy to be with and it scared her to death.

What am I doing? She didn't know.

"What's wrong?" Sam asked, as he finished buttoning his shirt.

"What do you mean?" Mindy asked.

"Something changed. Your demeanor."

"Nothing," she said.

"No, it's something."

"It's nothing." Who was she kidding? It was. It was turning into something fast and she was scared.

Sam knew it was something, even though she was denying it. Something had changed. They'd been having an easy conversation and then her walls had gone up again. Maybe it was something he'd done, but then when he'd told her he couldn't promise her any more than what had happened between them she had still been amiable.

"Well, I think I'll head out."

Mindy nodded, but would barely look at him. "I'll see you in the morning. You're on my service again."

"Unless I'm forced to work on my mother's."

Mindy's head snapped up. "What?"

Sam sighed and sat down on the edge of the bed. "She's demanding that I join her in the OR for her experimental surgery on one of Dr. Chang's patients."

"The brain surgery."

"Yes."

"Well, are you familiar with the patient?" Mindy asked.

"Yes. Very."

"Then it makes sense."

He frowned. "You're taking her side?"

"No, but I do see why she would want you on the case if you're familiar with the patient and she's not."

Sam snorted. "That's never stopped her before and, besides, I won't do much in her OR. She never allows her residents to get their hands dirty."

"Are you trying to tell me to keep you busy so you don't end up in her OR?"

Sam snorted again. "I doubt you can stop her."

"Why? I'm an attending as well."

"Because she'll go to Langley." And he would grant his mother her wish because he was wrapped around his mother's little finger. *Don't think about it.*

"Ah," Mindy said, nodding. "Yes, he'll likely cave to a well-known surgeon over me."

Or cave to a woman he slept with.

Only he didn't say that thought out loud. Mindy didn't need to know that. It was embarrassing. Shameful. And he was doing the same here with Mindy. Though he tried to tell himself otherwise. He cared for Mindy and his mother didn't seem to care about anyone but herself.

They were different.

Were they?

That thought made his stomach twist.

"Well, I'd better go."

Mindy nodded. "Okay. I'll see you tomorrow."

"Right." Sam lingered, wondering if she'd lean over and kiss him, but she didn't and maybe that was for the best. He saw himself out of her penthouse and headed out onto the street. He had every good intention of heading back to Brooklyn, just like when he'd originally left the hospital and instead had ended up at Mindy's place and in her arms.

Her warm, soft arms.

He fought the urge to turn back. He couldn't go back, because he didn't want to hurt her, because he didn't want to promise her something that he couldn't give her.

He never wanted to hurt her. He didn't want to be like his mother.

Instead, he headed back to the hospital to torture himself further. He wanted to be there by Michael's bedside if he passed on. Sam felt it was his duty to be by his patient's side. Although it pained him to watch a child lose the battle for life, he wanted to be there. To say goodbye.

When he walked into the residents' locker room his phone rang. It was Kimberlyn.

"You know what time it is?" Sam teased, as he answered the call from his former roommate.

"Why are you answering, then?" she teased.

"Why not?"

"Where are you?" she asked.

"I went back home to sleep and now I'm back at the hospital."

Kimberlyn snorted. "I don't believe that for a second."

"Why? You're how many miles away? You don't know what I'm doing."

"There's no way you could've caught a subway, slept and come back in the amount of time you were gone."

"Fine. I didn't go home." Sam put his phone on

hands-free and pulled off his shirt, then pulled on his scrubs.

"Where are you? You're all echoey."

"That's none of your business, Mother."

Kimberlyn snorted. "Great. You're in the locker room and probably getting naked. Nasty. I thought you were off? You should go home and sleep."

"I've been busy. So you've called to nag me. I have to say I've missed it."

Kimberlyn chuckled. "Me too. I called because I felt like I should and I'll be up your way in a few days. We're visiting Enzo's parents."

"Good." Sam was pleased. "I have to go."

"So do I. I'm headed home, though not to get hot and heavy with Enzo, who is on duty tonight. Where are you headed?"

"Back up to the NICU."

"I miss nagging you," she sighed. "I'll talk to you later."

"Yes." They said a few more words and he hung up. He pulled on his lab coat, shut his locker and then made his way to the NICU. The NICU was still dark, just a few nurses and a neonatologist fellow going from room to room, but it was quiet.

He liked the NICU. He liked the quiet, except for tonight. It was too quiet. He headed into Michael's room and over to the incubator, peering down at the little guy struggling to live.

Live.

Sam sighed and pulled up a chair, grabbing Michael's chart. "Well, I hope you don't mind the company tonight, buddy."

He flipped open the chart, read the last stats and

smiled. They'd improved. Michael's stats had actually improved.

"You're back?"

Sam looked up and saw Dr. Chang. "You're still here?"

"It's my night to do a twenty-four-hour shift. You haven't answered why you've come back. I thought you left?"

"I did for a bit. Just walked around. His stats are better."

Dr. Chang smiled. "They are. He's still in danger but he's turned a bit of a corner."

"What did you tell the parents?"

"I gave them options, they're still thinking about them. Of course, if Michael is getting stronger they probably won't have to worry about them." Dr. Chang stood on the other side of the incubator and smiled down at the little baby. "Dr. Walker is an excellent surgeon."

Sam's stomach flipped over. Did she know? "Yes, she is. I've learned a lot from her."

Dr. Chang glanced up at him. "I'm sure you have."

"What's that supposed to mean?"

Dr. Chang cocked an eyebrow. "What are you implying? I mean you must've learned a lot from such a skilled surgeon. Nothing more. Should I be concerned?"

"No. I just…with my mother being here…"

Dr. Chang snorted. "Enough said."

"How do you feel about her working on Janie?"

He could tell by Dr. Chang's expression, her furrowed brow and the tense way she stood that she wasn't too keen on it. "Janie's parents approved of the surgery.

They weren't coerced. Janie is terminal. If the procedure works then Janie may get more time."

Sam nodded. He'd expected that answer from Dr. Chang. She was quite diplomatic. He admired that about her.

"Are you going to stay here?" Dr. Chang asked.

"I think so."

"Catch up on your filing, then. I'll send an intern in with your charts. Print neatly, your writing is atrocious." She winked and then left the NICU.

Sam laughed and set Michael's file back, before leaning back in the rocking chair. He hoped that his mother didn't force him to work on her surgery. He hoped she picked another resident so rumors wouldn't begin to fly.

He'd rather work with Mindy on her service. His blood heated as he thought of Mindy and the fact he'd left her again, naked in bed. At least this time he hadn't had to sneak off. They had talked, laughed, until she'd closed herself off again. Of course, he'd thrown up his own walls too.

It was for the best.

CHAPTER TWELVE

MINDY FINISHED ROUNDING on her patients in the maternity ward and sent off the two interns she'd been assigned to do various labs and tests. She was surprised that Sam hadn't shown up for his rounding. It wasn't like him.

Maybe he's avoiding me.

And she hated thinking that. Sam wasn't Dean.

Perhaps his mother got hold of him?

It was clear from their conversation that Sam and his mother didn't have the best relationship, but there was more to it than that. Then again, she hadn't told him everything. She'd just glossed over why she didn't want a relationship.

It was a pathetic excuse now that she thought about it.

Still, it was for the best. She knew the other attendings were all going to vote that Sam get one of the pediatric fellowships. He'd proved his worth to them long before she'd shown up, but she didn't feel like she could cast a vote.

Not after last night.

Mindy bit her lip, nervous about how to approach it

because she didn't want rumors to start flying around about her and Sam.

That would ruin her reputation here and could really mess up Sam's career.

I don't want to leave and find a new place.

Dean had called her a coward the day before she'd left for New York because she'd felt too embarrassed to face her problems, and maybe he was right.

Being bullied as a young girl and pushed around on her residency, well, she didn't really have a thick skin. Or not as thick as some others did.

She couldn't have a vote on the fellowship. It wouldn't be right.

Mindy put the chart of her last patient away behind the nursing station on the OB/GYN floor and headed over to Pediatrics. She had to speak to Dr. Chang and then Professor Langley. She wouldn't tell them why she was withdrawing her vote, only that she couldn't make a proper decision because she hadn't been here long enough.

Hopefully they would understand, without asking her to explain too much.

She was glad about what had happened between her and Sam; she cared about him a great deal and she didn't want to ruin his career. He was going to make a fine pediatric surgeon.

As she crossed through the NICU she paused to check on the progress of the quints, speaking briefly with the neonatologist nurses before heading to the level three NICU, where Michael was being cared for.

She swiped her identification card and entered the critical care NICU. Michael's room was the first room in that area of the NICU. She peered through the glass and saw Sam fast asleep in the rocking chair next to the incubator.

So that's why he hadn't answered his page or made rounds.

Mindy smiled as she watched him, her heart melting a bit to see his dedication to children, to his patient. Why couldn't they have met at a different time? Why couldn't she have met him first instead of Dean? Why did she have to be his boss?

Life wasn't fair.

Look at poor Michael struggling to live while his four other siblings did well. That wasn't fair. She turned to leave but then went into the room to wake Sam. They may not ever have a relationship but she couldn't let him sleep the day away. He was late for rounds.

"Rise and shine," she called out, as she shut the door behind her.

Sam jumped up. "What time is it?"

"Nine o'clock in the morning."

Sam cursed under his breath. "I'm sorry. I can't believe I completely missed rounds like that."

"Your interns were wondering what happened when they showed up and you didn't."

"Great, they're going to think I'm a slacker." Sam stood and stretched. "I'm sorry for missing rounds, Dr. Walker."

"It's fine, Sam."

"No, it's not fine. The decision is coming soon about the fellowship. I can't be slacking off now."

"It's not like you were in an on-call room or at your apartment. You were with a patient," Mindy offered.

"You're being too easy on me, Dr. Walker." Sam

sighed. "I don't want you to be easy on me just because…"

"Don't finish that sentence," Mindy said. "I'm not being easy on you just because of what happened last night. Last night was a mistake."

Sam frowned. "Right. Well, I'm sorry nonetheless."

Mindy nodded. "Besides, I'm withdrawing my vote."

He cocked an eyebrow. "Why would you be doing that, then?"

"I don't think it's really fair of me to give an opinion now. If someone found out then it would have bad repercussions. Surgery is a very competitive career."

"Aye, I know. Why don't you vote for someone else, then?"

"Besides all that we've been through, you're the best and you deserve it."

Sam's cheeks tinged red. "Thank you, but there are two positions."

"I can't vote for someone I don't have confidence in. I can make one vote for the other spot, but I can't for the spot that's rightfully yours. So I won't vote for either."

"How are you going to get out of that?" He asked.

"I have my ways."

Sam nodded. "I appreciate it."

Mindy smiled. "I don't regret what happened between us, but I don't want it to ruin our careers. I really don't want to leave another practice."

"I don't know why you ran from California. You weren't in the wrong. Your ex is the one who wronged you."

"It was just easier," Mindy said quickly, because

she didn't want to talk about it. Yeah, maybe she had been a bit of a coward for running away. She was the surgeon who'd made the most money in the practice, she was the one who'd brought in the most clients, but she'd been unable to stay in California. She couldn't be around Dean and Owen. Most of all, she didn't like that people saw her differently. New York was a clean slate and that's the way it was going to stay.

"Straighten yourself out and report to the OB/GYN floor. Your interns are currently running amok down there."

Sam nodded. "I will and thank you, Mindy."

She smiled and left the NICU.

Mindy eventually found Dr. Chang in her office. She gently rapped on the door.

"Can I speak to you for a moment?" she asked.

Dr. Chang looked up. "Of course, Dr. Walker. Come in."

Mindy shut the door and sat down in a chair. "I want to talk to you about my vote."

"Ah, yes, I was hoping you would come by and let me know. I'm hoping to announce my decision next week to the board of directors."

"I want to withdraw."

Dr. Chang looked confused. "Withdraw?"

Mindy nodded. "I haven't worked here long enough to determine who would be most deserving of the fellowship spots. I know that Dr. Powers made her recommendations before she left, but I don't think I can really give one."

Dr. Chang tented her fingers and leaned back in her chair. "I understand that. Thank you for coming to me with your concerns. Most surgeons wouldn't; they would be arrogant enough to think they can vote."

"I'm not that arrogant, I'm afraid," Mindy said.

"I know." Dr. Chang smiled. "It's one of the reasons I like you. My dealings with most OB/GYNs who specialize in the field of maternal-fetal medicine think they are God's gift to surgeons."

Mindy chuckled. "That sounds about right."

"Don't get me wrong. They have every right to. I do know it's a fairly new field of medicine and each advancement saves lives. By all rights, you have the right to swagger a bit."

"Perhaps, but that's not my style. I keep a fairly low profile and do my duty to my patients."

Dr. Chang smiled. "As do I. Which is why I like you."

"Thank you. The feeling is mutual."

"So. How long have you and Sam been involved?"

The question caught Mindy completely off guard. She was going to deny it, but what was the point? "How did you know?"

"I read people. I can tell when people lie to me, but I also know when people are sneaking about."

"I can tell you we're not involved."

Dr. Chang nodded. "But...?"

"Before I started work here I went to a bar. Picked up a man and had a one-night stand. I had no idea it was Sam and he had no idea who I was."

"Ah, that makes sense."

"There's nothing more to tell. Nothing further will happen. I don't want to risk his career, he's a brilliant surgeon."

"He is." Dr. Chang smiled. "Thank you for being

so honest. It won't leave these walls. I like Sam and I want him to work with me. He has so much potential."

"In spite of what his mother thinks?"

Dr. Chang chuckled. "Agreed. So he told you. Well, that's good. Honestly, I don't know how much longer he'll be able to keep that secret from the rest of the hospital. That woman may be a brilliant neurosurgeon but she has no couth when it comes to name-dropping."

"I noticed. I take it you don't like *that* woman much either."

Dr. Chang grinned. "Ah, yes. Well, we were residents together. I found her quite annoying and what she did to her husband and Sam… There's no excuse for that. No excuse for cheating and breaking apart your family in such a callous way, but you didn't hear that from me."

"I won't say a word."

"He doesn't like it brought up. I admire him for not seeking favors or using his mother's name to gain footing. He may be a bit of a lone wolf here but everything he gets, every advance, every surgery he earns on his own merit."

"He told me as much," Mindy said.

Only Mindy wasn't sure that Sam quite believed that. His mother's shadow loomed over him. Even if people didn't know that Sam and Dr. Hanley were related, there was something holding him back, even if he didn't want to admit it.

Of course, there were things she didn't want to admit either. There were things she wanted to remain locked away. Everyone had their secrets, but relationships didn't work when there were secrets.

Mindy stood up. "Thank you for understanding, Dr. Chang, and I appreciate your discretion."

"Thank you for your honesty, Dr. Walker. You know the hospital doesn't frown on relationships between attendings?"

"I'm afraid I do, and it's for personal reasons."

Dr. Chang nodded. "I respect that." She reached across the desk and Mindy shook her hand. She left Dr. Chang's office but didn't feel any better. She was glad that she didn't have to have a say in the fellowship this time around and she was glad to get the truth out in the open with a colleague she admired. One who respected Sam as well, one who wouldn't do any damage to his career. It felt like a huge weight had been lifted off her shoulders and even though the stress of being discovered was gone, something still didn't feel quite right because even though she wouldn't date Sam, even though nothing could go any further, she wanted it to.

Try as she may, Mindy had fallen in love with Sam and it made her sad that nothing could happen between them.

Sam gritted his teeth as he made his way to the OR floor. He was on the pediatric floor when he saw that they were prepping Janie for surgery and then he got the page to head down to OR three. He'd managed to avoid his mother for two days, but now, with them prepping Janie, he knew she'd be paging him.

When he got down there he was going to pass on the surgery. Even though it was Janie and he liked the family, he wasn't going to work with his mother. He just didn't have the patience to be in her presence today.

When he got down to the surgical floor, his mother was already in the OR.

Of course. Now I have to scrub in.

It was one of her little tricks. She was avoiding him, ignoring his texts about wanting to talk about the upcoming surgery because she knew he was going to turn her down. It was a game his mother liked to play. It was immature and Sam hated it, but he was used to it.

He entered the scrub room and glanced through the window into the OR to see his mother speaking to a few reporters, who were garbed and waiting anxiously for the surgery to start. At least poor Janie wasn't lying there while all this nonsense was going on. It just seemed to be the surgical team prepping for surgery, while his mother and Langley spoke to the press.

Great. Just what I need.

Both the people responsible for breaking his father's heart in the same OR and they wanted him to assist? Well, he would assist. He would just stand by and maybe suction the odd bleeder.

He finished scrubbing and headed into the OR, staying back near the doors waiting until his mother saw that he was there, but instead of her coming over Langley headed over to him.

"Why aren't you gowned, Dr. Napier?"

"I'm not planning on staying."

"Dr. Hanley requested your assistance."

"I'm well aware of that," Sam snapped.

"I would watch your tone with me. Now, go get gowned properly. The patient will be coming down soon."

He hated it when the man ordered him about like he was a child.

Don't let him get to you. That's what he kept telling himself, but he was losing the battle fast.

"I'm on Dr. Walker's rotation and I would prefer to stay there."

"I'm sure Dr. Walker won't mind you attending this surgery."

"I'm sure she wouldn't, but I would prefer to sit out all the same." Sam turned to leave, but Langley stepped in front of him.

"You're staying here."

White-hot rage bubbled up in Sam. He didn't like the tone Langley was taking with him, as if he was a child. As if he was his father. Sam lost all rational thought at that moment and the dam burst.

"You're not my father! You may have slept with my mother when I was a child, but you don't have any right to order me about and I won't stand for hours in an OR with my mother." Then he realized what he'd said out loud to Langley. He was the chief of surgery. The room had gone quiet and then he saw the gallery was full. It was full of his fellow residents, who had heard him shouting.

Kimberlyn, who had come up to visit Enzo's family, was in the gallery, in shock, and Holly's mouth was hanging open pretty wide, and standing in the back row was Mindy. She looked heartbroken for him, she was pitying him. He didn't want her pity. It tore out of his heart.

"I'm sorry. I don't know—"

"What do you think you're doing?" his mother shrieked. Professor Langley stepped back, still in shock himself at what had happened.

"I don't..." Sam didn't know what to say, because

right now, at this instant, his reputation was ruined. It was absolutely shattered.

"You're an ungrateful son. How dare you humiliate and attack the chief of surgery in my OR? How dare you turn down this opportunity from me? Do you know how many strings I had to pull to get you into this surgical program and to get you into the pediatric program with Dr. Chang? In case you weren't aware, you're not *that* extraordinary."

"No. I guess I'm not," Sam shouted. "I never asked you to assist me. I didn't want your help. I didn't want to earn my accolades the way you did. Sleeping your way to the top."

"Get out of my OR," she shouted.

"With pleasure."

Sam marched through the scrub room, ripping off his surgical mask and scrubbing out quickly. Langley followed him out into the hallway.

"Dr. Napier, wait!" It was Langley who had followed him out. He didn't know why and he wasn't too impressed that he had.

Sam stopped and turned. "You'll have to scrub in again."

"I am aware of that."

"What do you want?" Sam demanded.

"What was that about?" Langley asked.

"I think it's obvious."

"Why did you apply for the surgical program here?" he asked. "You clearly loathe me."

"Because of Dr. Chang. I knew she was the best in pediatrics. If it wasn't for her, I wouldn't have touched West Manhattan Saints with a ten-foot pole."

Langley crossed his arms. "Because of me?"

"Yes. You ruined my parents' marriage."

The older man shook his head. "Your parents' marriage was ruined long before I hit the scene."

"Why did you sleep with her?" Sam asked.

"Should you really be prying into your mother's private life like that? Isn't that inappropriate?"

"Tell me. Why did you sleep with her? Why did you break up a marriage? You could've had anyone, but you decided to pursue a married woman."

"I loved her." There was sadness on Gareth Langley's face. It was apparent that his mother had hurt more than his father, but at this moment Sam didn't have any sympathy for Langley. He could've walked away.

Mother could've walked away too.

"So did my father," Sam snapped. "So did a lot of men."

Langley winced at that statement, because he knew it to be true. "Yes, and I do regret what happened."

"That's not good enough."

"She broke my heart too," Langley said.

"I don't care. And in case it's not clear for you, I'm tendering my resignation from the surgical program and West Manhattan Saints." He turned around and didn't wait for the professor to say anything further.

The word was out that Dr. Hanley was his mother, that she'd pulled strings to get him into the program. He hadn't got where he was on his own merit. It had all been his mother, begging people to take him.

Well, he could take a hint.

He didn't know exactly where he'd go. Perhaps back home to Scotland. He didn't know, he just knew that his time at West Manhattan Saints was at an end.

"Sam!"

He whipped around and saw Mindy chasing after him. He didn't want to see her, he didn't want her to see him like this, and he didn't need her pity. So he turned back around and kept on, but she caught up with him and grabbed his arm, stopping him.

"Sam, didn't you hear me?"

"Aye," he said tersely, not looking her in the eye. "What do you want? Are you coming to shatter the rest of my tattered reputation by calling me by my first name in the halls?"

Mindy let go of his arm. "Why are you angry with me?"

"I don't have time for this."

"You stood up to your mother. That's a good thing."

Sam snorted. "Is it really?"

"It is. Don't listen to her. You're an extraordinary surgeon in your own right. You deserve to be here."

"No. I don't. I got here on her ticket. That much was made clear."

"You're a fool to believe that!"

"A fool?" He shook his head. "I'm done with this conversation. I have my locker to clean out."

Mindy blocked his escape route and stood in front of him. "What?"

"I resigned."

"You did what?" she asked, shocked.

"I quit."

Her brow furrowed. "That's a foolish thing to do."

He snorted. "Look who's talking."

Mindy's eyes narrowed. "What is that supposed to mean?"

"You know what I mean."

"No, but I do know that running away from this is a coward's way out. So everyone knows now that Dr. Hanley is your mother and slept with the chief. Who cares? It's their problem. You're a fine surgeon. You shouldn't quit."

"Why not? You ran away from California when your husband cheated on you. I'm doing the same. I'm running away."

"I—I didn't run."

He'd hurt her. It killed him, but it was for the best. Love was too hard and uncertain and he wanted nothing to do with it, even though he did. It was just that he had nothing to give her.

Nothing, so it was best to cut the strings. Let her go.

Besides, she'd made it clear she couldn't give him anything and he didn't want to end up with someone who would hurt him like his mother had hurt his father, or do the same to her.

"You did. So I am. I don't need any favors or forgiveness," Sam snapped.

"Well, you won't be getting any forgiveness, if that's what you want." Mindy turned on her heel and marched in the other direction.

Sam's heart twisted and he hated himself for doing that, because he loved her even though he didn't really know what love was himself. He just knew he'd fallen in love with Mindy, but there was no way he'd win her back now.

It was for the best this way.

Go after her.

Only he didn't chase after her, because he didn't deserve her.

He didn't deserve any of this.

CHAPTER THIRTEEN

Three days later

"GO AWAY! I don't want to talk." Sam was tired of the incessant knocking. Every one of his roommates had come by his door in the last three days to try and talk him into coming back because the cat was out of the bag. Even Kimberlyn and Enzo had dropped by to talk some sense into him.

Everyone was interested in the fact that Dr. Hanley was his mother and that his mother and Langley had once been an item.

All he wanted was to be left in peace to pack. He was going to head back home to Scotland, set up a family practice. He was licensed for that at least.

That's not what you wanted to do.

No, it wasn't the dream when he'd been becoming a doctor. He'd wanted to be a pediatric surgeon. He loved working with kids, saving their lives. That was his joy, but that was never going to happen.

At least he would be an ocean apart from his mother and Mindy.

His heart ached as he thought of Mindy again.

Well, at least with him gone she could practice her medicine in a relatively peaceful environment.

The knocking continued and Sam cursed under his breath. He set down the stack of books he was going through and crossed his small apartment, flinging open the door. He was expecting it to be Kimberlyn or Holly, since they were the most insistent door-knockers.

"What do you want?" He was stunned to see Dr. Chang standing in the hallway, in street clothes. "Dr. Chang?"

"I'm aware that you're busy, Dr. Napier, but can I come in?"

"Sure." Sam stepped to the side and Dr. Chang walked into his apartment.

"Nice place."

"Thanks." Sam was still stunned. "Why are you here, Dr. Chang?"

Dr. Chang set her purse down on his bed and then took a seat in one of the battered old leather wing chairs he had in his small makeshift sitting room.

"This is a comfortable chair." Then she crossed her arms and leaned back. "You're heading back to Scotland, I hear?"

"How did you hear that?"

"Your father called me."

Now it was Sam's turn to be stunned. "My dad called you?"

"Yes, he and my husband were friends when he was married to your mother back in the mists of time."

Sam perched on the edge of the other wing chair. "I didn't know that."

Dr. Chang shrugged. "Well, you do know that your

mother and I were in the same resident program. Along with Chief Langley."

Sam grumbled under his breath. "I'd rather you not bring up his name."

"I know he did something horrible. He pursued a married woman and broke up a family, but he did love her and he thought she loved him too."

Sam snorted. "My mother doesn't love anyone."

Dr. Chang smiled. "No, and Chief Langley found that out soon enough."

"I know my mother cheated on Langley, but I don't have much sympathy for him. After all, he was just doing a favor for my mother by accepting me into the program. I don't need his pity or her favors."

"You're stubborn, like her."

"I'm nothing like her," Sam snapped.

"You are, in some ways. Look, your mother in her eccentric, egotistical way may *think* that she pulled strings to get you into this program, but it wasn't Chief Langley who helped pick the interns for the program the year you entered. It was me."

"You?"

Dr. Chang nodded. "Me. The board trusts me more than Langley when it comes to West Manhattan Saints' surgical program. I'm the one who had the final say and what I saw in your application was high grades and glowing reference letters. There was no hesitation on my part to accept you into the surgical program. Despite what your mother says, you're far from ordinary. She's just too stubborn to see what a brilliant surgeon you are."

Sam didn't know what to say. He was stunned. From the moment he'd decided to pursue a career in medicine he'd thrown his whole self into practicing medicine, while his mother had watched from afar and nitpicked over his skills.

Perhaps she'd been worried that if Sam didn't make it, it would somehow look bad on her, and by controlling his specialty she would be able to keep him under her thumb. Only he hadn't chosen her specialty. So she'd gone about knocking his confidence, so that he would turn to neurosurgery and she would dazzle him with her surgical prowess.

"I've made a right mess of things."

"In your words, aye, you have."

"I don't think I can go back."

Dr. Chang's eyes narrowed as she frowned. "You really have no choice. I don't accept your resignation."

"You really don't have a choice. The chief of surgery…Langley makes that call."

"No, *you* don't have a choice." Dr. Chang stood and stared him down, though she was much shorter than him. "*I* chose you when you were an intern, Sam. I've been grooming you."

Sam was stunned. "Pardon?"

"I think you heard me. You have earned one of the fellowship spots. It was a no-brainer and since I really don't want to go back to the drawing board you really have no choice."

"Did Mindy vote for me?"

"No. She withdrew her consideration after she told me what had transpired between the two of you."

Sam was shocked. "She told you?"

"She did and told me that what happened was unintentional. So even though she felt you were an extraordinary surgeon, she couldn't rightfully vote for anyone. Maternal-Fetal Medicine's vote for fellowship was based on Dr. Powers's notes before she retired."

Sam was still stunned. Mindy knew that he didn't like favors and she'd done the best thing she could for him and told her colleague that she'd slept with a resident. She'd put her own career and reputation in jeopardy, by telling Dr. Chang that their one-night stand had been just a coincidence.

You're an idiot.

Sam sank back down in his wing chair and scrubbed a hand over his face. "I've made a right *bourach* of this whole thing."

"I agree."

Sam glanced up at Dr. Chang. "I have to talk to Langley and my mother."

Dr. Chang nodded. "I would also talk to Dr. Walker, but I don't think I have to tell you that."

"No, you don't."

"So you'll be coming back to West Manhattan Saints?"

Sam grinned. "Aye."

"Good." She picked up her purse and went to leave, but turned. "Look, your mother does care for you in her own way. She never wanted to be a mother, but your father wanted you and kind of pressed his case. I'm sorry that your father was hurt and that you think that maybe a family doesn't work if you're a surgeon, but it can. As long as both parties are willing."

"So you think maybe if my father hadn't made my mother have me, their marriage might've worked?"

"No, they were two different people. What I was saying wasn't implying that you should blame yourself for their break-up. I think they would've eventually gone their separate ways anyway. What I was trying to say was that your mother cares in her own way. She just doesn't know how to apologize. She doesn't know how to love."

Sam nodded. "I get it."

"I'm glad you do." Dr. Chang left his apartment, closing the door behind her.

Sam got up and stared out the window, watching Dr. Chang as she left the brownstone and headed to her car parked on the street.

He'd been so influenced by his parents' failed marriage, only seeing the one side because he had been there the day his father's heart had been crushed. All he'd seen had been the evil man who had stolen his mother away.

Sam had never once thought that his mother had been at fault for it all or that his dad had caused undue strain and hurt his mother as well by trying to make her something she wasn't.

He'd never wanted to hurt Mindy, but he had by implying that she was a coward for running away, and yet he'd planned to do the same thing.

He was the coward.

Mindy had risked her reputation to make sure that he got what he deserved, and he'd thrown it all away.

Dr. Chang had a successful marriage and children. One day he could as well. He didn't have to be alone to be successful. For his mother, yes, but him? No, he didn't need to sentence himself to that lifestyle.

He'd make it right with Mindy and if she didn't want his heart then he deserved it, but he was going to make sure that she knew he was staying at West Manhattan Saints and she was going to stay as well. He wasn't going to let her run because he would make sure everyone knew that what had happened had been his fault.

There was a knock at the door and Kimberlyn poked her head in and Enzo was loitering in the hall. "Hey, I take it you're staying?"

Sam glanced over his shoulder. "Aye."

"Good." She smiled. "Because if you hadn't listened to Dr. Chang and changed your mind we were going to hog-tie you to make you stay."

Sam chuckled. "No need for hog-tying. I'm staying and I think I'll head over to the hospital now and rectify that."

Rectify it all.

It took Sam over an hour to get to the hospital. He wasn't even sure if Mindy was on duty, but right now he was going to confront his mother and he owed the professor an apology. He headed up to the floor where his mother's office was.

He could see her shadow through the blinds.

Sam took a deep calming breath and knocked.

"Come."

He opened the door and shut it behind him.

"Well, I didn't expect to see you again, to be honest," his mother said casually.

"I know."

"I thought you were going to Scotland?"

"I changed my mind. How did you know about Scotland?"

"Your father."

Sam cocked an eyebrow. "You talked to Dad?"

"Yes." She tented her fingers and leaned back in her chair. "Is there something you want to say to me?"

"I'm sorry that you felt the need to pull strings for me, to watch out for me, but really I'm not a failure. I won't bring shame to you."

His mother was visibly stunned. "Oh."

"I *am* an extraordinary surgeon. Professor Langley didn't pick me for this program. Dr. Chang did, and it was based on my own merits. I will make a fine pediatric surgeon."

"Are you looking for me to apologize?"

Sam shook his head. "No. I'm not. I don't need your validation and you don't need to apologize for my life. I may have been angry with you for a long time about Dad, but I can tell it was for the best. For all parties."

"Are you looking for my approval, then?" she asked, confused.

"No. I'm not. I'm not looking for something you can't give."

She nodded and turned back to her work. "Good. Well, I'm glad that's all sorted. Your patient Janie came through her surgery. She's post-op day three and she's doing remarkably well. I think my surgical technique was a complete success. Of course, we'll have to continue to monitor her, but barring any complications I think her prognosis is certainly better than it was."

Sam rolled his eyes as she launched into talking about the procedure and the interviews. As well as all the nitty-gritty medical information that was going to go into the paper she was going to publish in a distinguished medical journal.

He'd never get an apology from his mother because she wasn't wired that way, and he was fine with that now. He hadn't been before and even though he'd prided himself on his mother not influencing him in his career, she had, in a different way.

Now he could move away.

His mother would never change, but at least he understood that now.

Now he had closure.

So he let her talk and just listened.

"Did you get the fellowship you were after?" she finally asked, breaking his chain of thought.

"Yes. I did."

His mother nodded. "Good, but I still think neurosurgery would be a better choice."

"For you, but not for me. I like working with children."

"I never did."

"What?"

"Like working with children. I'm not good with children." A blush tinged her cheek. It was her roundabout way of apologizing to him, without apologizing to him. In her own awkward way she was apologizing for what had happened years ago, for all those nights he'd sat in an OR gallery, reading or playing with his toys by himself, while she'd worked. For eating sandwiches from a vending machine instead of having a home-cooked meal.

When his dad had taken him to Scotland she could've walked away and forgotten about him, but she hadn't. Every summer he'd come to New York and spent time with her, even though he hadn't been with her, but to her, his sitting in the gallery, watching her perform surgery, had been a way for them to connect, and maybe that's why she'd wanted him in neurosurgery as well. As a way to find some common ground, as a way to spend time with him.

And even though it had been a less-than-ideal childhood, spending his summers playing in the hallways of a hospital, at least it had been an attempt.

She hadn't forgotten about him. His mother had just tried the best she could.

Sam grinned. "That's nothing to be ashamed about. We can't all be extraordinary when it comes to pediatrics."

CHAPTER FOURTEEN

MINDY ROLLED HER shoulders. She'd been hunched over her charting for some time. She took off her glasses and set them on her desk, rubbing the bridge of her nose where they'd pinched most, and she tried not to think about Sam.

Of course, that was an exercise in futility, because she couldn't get him out of her mind. Even though the words he'd said had stung, he'd been right.

She was a coward. Instead of facing the supposed rumors, the pitying looks and the laughter, she'd turned tail and run. She could've stayed in Los Angeles and really stuck it to Dean because she was what had made the practice so affluent.

Mindy was tired of running and even though now everyone knew about the dalliance between Sam and her, she wasn't going to leave.

She was here for the long haul.

Of course, she'd heard that he was running away. He was going back to Scotland.

Maybe it's for the best.

Really, what kind of future did they have together? She was older than him, more accomplished, and that might lead to professional jealousy and resentment. Besides Dean being gay, that's also what had happened with their friendship. They'd no longer trusted each other or respected each other.

If he had just come out as gay, that wouldn't have been as bad as the cruel way he'd thrown it in her face. But as she thought back to their relationship, he always had been a bit put out when she'd been given the better surgeries and the attention from their attending.

She'd just been so enamored with the thought of love and marriage that she'd replaced the idea of what love actually was.

But love meant being happy for each other, not trying to bring the other person down.

Love meant being friends. Love meant fighting and making up.

It meant remembering why you were together and sticking it out because, like oxygen, you couldn't live without the other person.

And that's not what she'd had with Dean.

The only person she could think of who fit all those criteria in her head was Sam. Tears stung her eyes, but she wiped them away quickly. She was not going to cry over Sam. He'd made it clear that he didn't want to be with her. He'd go to Scotland and move on.

And so would she. Though it would take some time, she would heal.

There was a knock at the door. She got up, stretching, and opened the door.

"Yes, how can I...?" She trailed off as she looked up to see a six-foot burly Scotsman standing in her doorway. "Dr. Napier, I'm surprised to see you."

"Aye, I can tell by the look on your face. Can I come in?"

Mindy moved to the side and let him into her office.
She shut the door, keeping her back to it just in case
she needed to make a quick retreat, and stood there,
crossing her arms over her chest. "I thought you were
in Scotland?"

"My plane was supposed to leave tonight."

"Supposed? Was it delayed?"

"No. I'm not getting on that plane."

"Well, what are you doing? Attacking me some
more? After the way you treated me when I was just
making sure you were okay, that was uncalled for."

"Aye, it was."

Mindy was stunned, but then shook her head. No,
she wasn't going to fall into his charming trap. She
wasn't going to let him off so easily, but that was a
harder thing to say than to do. "You hurt me."

"I know."

"I don't think I can forgive you or trust you."

"I understand, but I have something important I
need to tell you." Sam took a step toward her. "I'm
not going to Scotland. I'm staying at West Manhattan Saints."

"You are?"

"Aye."

"And what, you expect me to leave? I can tell you,
you have another thing coming if you think that I'm
leaving. I'm not going to turn tail. I'm not a coward."

"No, I know you're not. That was bad form on my
part and I don't want you to leave."

"You don't?" she asked, confused.

"No. I've come here to apologize. I was a fool. A
pigheaded fool."

"Yes, you were." Mindy relaxed. "So that's all you've come here for? To apologize and tell me you're staying."

"Sort of." His eyes were twinkling. "There was one more thing."

"One more thing?" Her heart began to race and her knees began to shake as he came closer to her, his blue eyes dark and sparkling with tenderness. Just like they'd been when they'd made love. When he'd taken her in his arms and they'd become one.

"Aye," he said, his voice turning husky as he moved in closer, making her press against the door. "I love you and I aim to earn back your trust. Whatever it takes. I want you, Mindy. Only you."

The words stunned her, to the point she wasn't sure if she'd heard them right. "Sorry, what?"

"I love you. I know I did wrong by you and there is no excuse I can offer you to make that better. I understand if you can't or won't return those feelings, but I wanted you to know that I do love you. I will always love you."

Tears stung Mindy's eyes. She couldn't believe what he was saying. "I thought you didn't want any rumors about dating an attending."

"It doesn't matter now. I know my own worth and let the others talk. I'm not going to be miserable because of what someone else thinks. I love you, Mindy Walker. I will always love you."

Mindy melted. She couldn't deny what she felt and she couldn't stay mad at him any longer. She'd always been afraid of things but she wasn't going to run away from this. "I love you too, but if you ever push me away like that again I'm going to kick you."

"I swear. I never want to hurt you, Mindy. Never

again. I can't promise I won't make a *bourach* out of things, but if I do make a mess I promise that I will make it right."

Mindy laughed. "Deal."

Sam grinned. "Good. I'm glad. I think I'm going to kiss you now—that okay?"

"Aye," she said, tears rolling down her cheeks.

Sam laughed and then pulled her into his arms and kissed her, like it was the first time all over again. Like the slate had been wiped clean and there was nothing between them now. The ghosts of their pasts were wiped clean; it was just the two of them.

Two fools in love.

His hands were wrapped around her, holding her close and making her feel safe. This was what love was and Mindy didn't want to let it go. She was never going to let this go.

When the kiss ended she smiled up at him. "Just one condition."

Sam cocked an eyebrow. "There are conditions now?"

"Just one. I'm not traveling to Brooklyn to stay in an apartment in a house full of residents and fellows."

"What're you suggesting, then?"

"That you take all those boxes you packed and move into a certain penthouse apartment down the street."

Sam laughed. "Well, my roommates might not be happy about me vacating but, aye, I'll agree to your term as long as you agree to mine."

"You think you're in a position to bargain?"

"Aye."

"So what is your term?"

"That you shut up and kiss me again."

"I can agree to that term." And she fulfilled her end of the bargain promptly.

EPILOGUE

Three months later

MINDY WALKED ALONG the halls of West Manhattan Saints toward the NICU. She was grinning ear to ear. It was spring and she loved days like this. Mostly she was glad the cold, sucktacular winter was over.

As she walked down the hall Sam came up beside her, and he was grinning as well.

"You're very happy today," Mindy teased.

"So are you!"

"It's spring." She took a sip of her coffee. "I love spring."

"Come on, you survived your first New York winter. You should be proud of that."

"I am proud of that! Who said I wasn't?"

"No one." Sam chuckled. "Are you ready for the big day?"

"Of course I'm ready for this day. This day is another reason why today is my favorite day. It's spring and the quints are going home."

Sam chuckled. "Yeah, today is a good day."

He reached down and grabbed her hand, squeezing it, making her blush. She was so happy with Sam.

They'd been together three months, but it felt like longer than that. His roommates had grumbled about him leaving, but it had only been half-hearted. They'd been happy for him.

It had been a huge step, asking him to move in with her. She usually didn't move so fast with relationships, but then again this was different from her relationship with Dean. It was right to move it along so fast.

There was surprisingly no animosity at the hospital, because Chief Langley made sure that everyone knew she had nothing to do with Sam getting one of the pediatric fellowship spots and Mindy was able to be open about her relationship with Sam.

They weren't trying to hide anything.

She was positive there were still rumors floating around about them, but frankly she didn't care anymore. There were always going to be gossips.

Even Sam had come to terms with the fact that everyone knew his mother was Dr. Monica Hanley. Some doctors still referred to him as Dr. Hanley's son, which vexed him no end, but you couldn't change people and Mindy learned you can't live your life worrying about what other people thought of you, because that was no life worth living at all.

Mindy had let go of her anger toward Dean and Owen, and in her heart she forgave them. Sam had taught her to trust again and that was worth moving on for.

Once their busy period was over and they both had some vacation time, Sam promised to take her to Scotland to meet his father and the rest of his family. Although he warned her that his gran wouldn't be pleased that she'd ruined the sweater she'd knitted for him.

"Gran is a teetotaler. She won't be happy you ruined the sweater by spilling Scotch all over me."

"Are you going to tell her you were the one drinking said Scotch?"

"No. I'm not a fool."

Sam brought her out of her reverie. "I love you." He bent down and kissed her on the lips in the middle of the busy hall of the hospital.

"Dr. Napier, I can't go into that press conference with you holding my hand and kissing me like that."

"Of course you can." He pulled her to a side hallway. "Have you reconsidered my question?"

Mindy shook her head. "I'm not answering that question right now."

"Oh, aye?"

"Aye. I have to concentrate on this press conference. I'm not used to press conferences."

"You'll be fine."

"We should call your mother in from Harvard to do this. After all, she did take care of Michael Jameson's shunt."

Sam groaned. "It took three months to get her to go back to Harvard. Haven't I suffered enough?"

"No." Mindy kissed him on the cheek.

"Thanks."

"At least you have to go up there and talk about Michael. Since you were his primary pediatrician."

"Dr. Chang is, I'm just a fellow."

"Dr. Chang is on vacation and as her fellow you have to fill in for her."

"You're enjoying this, aren't you?" Sam asked.

"I am." Mindy grinned and then swiped her card to open the NICU. "Come on, then."

Sam followed her into the NICU, into a private room

where Mr. and Mrs. Jameson were waiting with five very special bundles of joy.

"Dr. Napier, Dr. Walker!" Mrs. Jameson exclaimed.

"Good morning," Mindy said. "Have they photographed the babies yet?"

Mrs. Jameson nodded. "They have. Does that mean we can go?"

"Yes, you can go," Sam said. "All the babies are healthy; they've all passed their car-seat tests with flying colors. You can take them home."

"So you don't need them for that press conference that's gathered downstairs?" Mr. Jameson asked.

"No. You're not needed for that," Mindy said. "Take your babies home. It's been a long time coming."

Mrs. Jameson's eyes filled with tears. "Thank you both. And give my thanks to Dr. Hanley and Dr. Chang as well. Actually…I think there are too many people to thank."

"We know. You don't need to thank us. It was our pleasure." Mindy gave Mrs. Jameson a hug.

"Keep us posted with pictures."

"I will." Mrs. Jameson was beaming as she and Mr. Jameson loaded five car-seat carriers into a large stroller that had been specially fashioned for them.

Mindy and Sam left the NICU and headed toward the conference room. As they got closer they could hear the buzz of a crowd. Journalists were waiting to hear about West Manhattan Saints' first quintuplet delivery and she knew they were also waiting to see the quints. Too bad they would be disappointed.

She was about to open the door, but Sam stopped her.

"No, this isn't happening."

Mindy was shocked as he grabbed her by the arm

and frog-marched her once again into a private room, shutting the door behind him.

"What are you doing?"

"I'm not letting you out of this room until you answer the question I asked you this morning."

"Sam, aren't we rushing things?"

He cocked an eyebrow. "How are we rushing things? Three months ago I moved in with you and now you're telling me that soon I'm going to be a father, so me asking you to marry me is rushing things?"

Mindy sighed. "I was married once before."

"I swear I won't cheat on you with your best friend."

"You're my best friend."

"Aye, well, if you become my wife then I won't have to cheat on you with myself."

Mindy laughed. "That makes no sense."

"Well, you not giving me an answer to my proposal makes no sense either."

She smiled. "Why don't we have the baby first and then talk marriage."

He shook his head. "That's backwards. We have to do this the traditional way."

"What has been traditional about this?"

"Nothing, but I aim to rectify that." He took a step toward her and cupped her face in his hands. "I love you, Mindy. That's never going to change."

Her heart skipped a beat. "I love you too."

"So?"

Tears filled her eyes and this time she couldn't stop them. Usually she was quite good at it, but she was blaming it on the pregnancy hormones. "Yes. I'll marry you."

Sam pulled her into his arms and kissed her, making

her knees go weak. When he pulled away she moaned in protest.

"You have a press conference, remember?"

"Do we have to go?" she whined.

"You're the one who said we did." Sam kissed her again. "Come on. You can do this. I have a feeling with the reputation you're getting here at West Manhattan Saints that this won't be the last. I think it's the first of many."

Mindy took his hand. "I'm ready."

And she was. She was ready to face just about anything, as long as she had Sam.

* * * * *

SEDUCED BY
THE HEART
SURGEON

CAROL MARINELLI

CHAPTER ONE

'YOU ALREADY KNOW, don't you, Freya?'

'Know what?' Freya frowned as she attempted to pull up the zipper on her friend Beth's wedding dress. It had slipped up easily at the final fitting just last week so Freya gave it another tug but it refused to budge. 'Have you…?'

Freya stopped herself from continuing with the question. She, more than most, knew just how much damage that a throwaway comment about weight could cause and she certainly didn't want to inflict that pain on Beth. Especially not on her wedding day, but, hell, the dress was tight.

Then it dawned on Freya why she was having so much trouble getting Beth into her wedding dress. Beth had declined Freya's offer of champagne as they prepared for her late afternoon wedding and the girls' night in at Freya's apartment last week had been a very tame affair.

Freya worked it out just a split second before her friend said it.

'I'm pregnant!'

Oh, Freya was very grateful for that split second because her eyes had screwed closed as yet another friend revealed their happy news, but by the time Beth had turned around, Freya had composed herself and was smiling.

'That's fantastic news, Beth.'

'Don't pretend that you didn't know.'

'I honestly had no idea,' Freya admitted.

'I didn't have even one of the cocktails you'd made!'

'I thought it was a bit odd,' Freya admitted, because Beth loved a drink. 'I just believed you when you said that you were detoxing for the wedding.'

Oh, it had been a tame night. Two of the women were pregnant, one was breastfeeding and now Freya understood why Beth had also declined the cocktails that Freya had prepared. For Freya, it had been a long night of being told, *It will be your turn soon,* and asked, *Are you still not seeing anyone?* Her friends didn't know about her fertility issues, so they hadn't been deliberately insensitive. She could have told them that day that she'd had blood work done and when Hilary was back from her trip she would be having some further tests to see if she might be a candidate for IVF through an egg donor.

Freya didn't really open up to anyone, though, not fully.

'So when did you find out?' Freya asked Beth.

'Two weeks ago. I was devastated at first, I have to admit.'

'Devastated?' Freya checked. She knew very well that Beth and Neil both wanted a family and so she wondered if they had found out that there was something wrong with the baby.

'Well, I was very upset,' Beth clarified. 'We've been saving up for the honeymoon for ages and had paid for all drinks to be included...' Beth rolled her eyes at the perceived inconvenience. 'I'm fine about it now.'

Fine!

Freya did her best not to dwell on that word.

Finally the zip was up and she arranged the huge bow on Beth's dress.

Freya knew that she overthought everything but, really, to use the word *fine* to describe the news that you were pregnant irked her!

'Have you told your parents?' Freya asked once she had unclenched her jaw.

'Not yet. Neil's going to reveal the news during the speeches, so we can capture everyone's expressions. Can you warn the cameraman?'

'Sure.'

'You won't forget?'

'I never forget,' Freya said. 'That's why you've got me planning your wedding, remember!'

Oh, Freya was on edge and trying not to be but Beth really was a bridezilla.

'Okay, done. Wow. You look amazing!' Freya said. 'Simply stunning.'

No one could ever tell when Freya was lying. It was why she was so successful in PR.

The dress that Beth had chosen was a long sheath of ivory tulle, tied in the middle with a huge satin bow.

Like an oddly wrapped parcel, Freya thought.

Worse, Beth had chosen similar for Freya to wear. Hers was knee-length, though, and the shade of Freya's dress was Antique White. Freya felt as if she was wearing an old teabag. Her brunette hair had been teased into curls and Beth had insisted on red lips for them both. The only saving grace was that the bow on Freya's dress was smaller.

They looked like two poodles who'd been badly clipped, Freya thought as she stared at their reflections.

'Are you wearing a bra?' Beth checked.

'It didn't work with the dress,' Freya said.

'Well, put some plasters on them,' Beth said. 'I don't want *your* nipples in *my* photos.'

There was a knock at the door and, of course, brides didn't answer doors, so Freya opened it and smiled when she saw Beth's father, realising it was time for her to head down and check the last-minute details.

'Right, I'm going to go down and make sure everything is in place,' Freya said. 'Enjoy every moment and leave all the worrying to me.'

'I shall.' Beth nodded. 'It's all set for midnight?'

'It is.'

'I want everyone watching us kiss as we ring in the New Year.'

'They shall be.'

'Thanks for organising everything.'

'Well, it's been a lot more fun sorting out flowers and table plans than getting everyone at The Hills to glam up for the new brochure…'

'They're already a glam lot.'

'I know they are.' That hadn't been what Freya had meant but there wasn't time for all that now. 'I'll see you down in the hotel chapel.'

'Don't forget the plasters,' Beth reminded her. Freya smiled and picked up her posy of red flowers to match her red lips then stepped out of the room and let out a very long breath.

Again she had lied. This wedding had been *hell* to organise.

Two of the hotels that Beth and Neil had chosen as potential venues had explained that their stairways and escalators were for all of their guests, especially on New Year's Eve. It had been difficult to find somewhere to accommodate all their demands but Freya had achieved it.

The wedding was at five, then dinner and speeches,

but instead of being able to relax afterwards she had to keep the cameraman and photographer sober, as well as get two hundred guests out of the ballroom and onto the main staircase. Oh, and her ex, Edward, was going to be there.

As he had been at three other weddings she'd attended this year.

Freya was so over weddings!

She knew that her PR skills were a very large reason that Beth had chosen her to be bridesmaid.

It didn't offend Freya.

To survive as top PR consultant in LA, you needed to keep in with your contacts. Beth was a journalist, and the many hours that Freya had spent organising the wedding would be returned in kind.

It was called networking and Freya was very good at that.

Freya got to her hotel room to freshen up. She checked her make-up and wished she hadn't—it was far too much.

She really didn't like this dress and how *much* it revealed of her shoulders. Her upper back was bare too and she felt exposed. Freya turned and craned her neck and told herself that everyone in the chapel would be looking at the bride rather than the bridesmaid's spinal column.

As always, she checked her phone and saw that there were several messages and missed calls from her brother, James.

Work.

Freya knew that it would be.

James Rothsberg was *the* cosmetic surgeon in LA and for the past six years he had poured everything into The Hollywood Hills Medical Center. It was an amazing facility frequented by the rich and famous. Affectionately known as The Hills, it had everything from obstetrics to intensive care and was the top tier of health care. Two years ago James had asked Freya to come on board and she had put her PR skills to excellent commercial use.

Till now.

It was time to give back, she had told James.

And he'd listened.

Which was why, instead of rolling her eyes at being called late afternoon on New Year's Eve, Freya called her brother.

'Hi, James,' Freya said. 'You've been trying to get hold of me.'

'I have,' James said. 'Freya, I need you at The Hills tomorrow at nine.'

'On New Year's Day?' Freya checked.

'I've just taken a call from Geoff, and Paulo's condition has deteriorated. I've just spoken with Zackary and he's agreed to come in and be interviewed tomorrow instead of waiting till Monday.'

Freya's eyes screwed closed as James carried on talking.

'I need you to be at the interview.'

'Me?' Freya tried to keep the quake from her voice. 'Since when did I sit in on the hiring of medical personnel?'

'Since you talked me into taking on charitable cases,' James answered tartly. 'And, given we're going to be asking him to donate his skills for nothing...'

'He already knows that he'll be doing some pro bono work.'

'Freya?'

She could hear the question in her brother's voice at her reluctance to sit in on the interview. After all, Freya had been the one pushing for The Hills to embrace this. Freya had been the one looking into a suitable charity to properly support and now things were finally moving along. But what James didn't understand was that the very seemingly together, always-very-much-in-control Freya had got herself into a little pickle that her older brother didn't know about.

There was a big pickle her brother didn't know about either, namely that the charity she'd found was headed by his ex, Mila Brightman, but it was the other pickle in the jar that Freya was wrestling with now.

She had already been dreading meeting the hotshot cardiac surgeon Zackary Carlton.

Or Zack, as she'd found out he'd prefer to be known.

They had flirted via emails.

Not much.

It felt massive to Freya, though.

'I need you there tomorrow at nine,' James said. 'I'm sure he's going to have questions about the promotional side of things and I want a press release out saying that we have Zackary on board.'

'Zack!' Freya said. 'He prefers to be called Zack.'

'Noted,' James responded. 'I'll see you tomorrow at nine. I'll flick over some details tonight.'

'Thanks.'

Oh, God.

After the tame girls' night with her smug married friends, Freya had poured another cocktail and opened up her laptop and located a certain series of emails.

She never got involved with people she worked with. Actually, Freya really didn't get too involved full stop. But this teeny tiny flirt had been fun and Zack had out-right asked if she was single.

Several daiquiris later, when Freya, who took her health seriously and didn't often drink, had decided to embrace the merits of *not* being married, she had typed her response back.

Very single. (Don't tell James.)

And now, tomorrow, she had to face him.

His response had made her blush and it was making her blush now.

I never kiss and tell.

Hopefully he wouldn't get the role, Freya thought, but who was she kidding? James wanted Zack Carlton on board, so much so that he had him currently housed in a luxury apartment that The Hills owned and was interviewing him on New Year's Day.

It had been a stupid flirt, a tiny one, but it had been completely out of character for her, and not just professionally. Freya wasn't a flirty person at all, she was far too controlled for that.

Blame it on the daiquiris.

Actually, she couldn't because the flirt had started a couple of emails prior to that.

She sighed. He was probably fifty and married with sixteen children. She'd blush about it tomorrow, but right now she had to deal with the wedding.

First, though, she texted her neighbour Red. Freya had a late checkout but hadn't been intending to use it as she wanted to get home to her little dog, Cleo. Instead, she asked Red if he would let her out and feed her in the morning.

With that sorted she went to go but then Freya caught sight of her bare shoulders; she turned and looked again at her spine.

It had been that sight that had terrified James. Freya could still remember his shocked reaction as he had sat her up so that the doctor could listen to her chest.

'Freya!'

She had always kept this part of her body covered, hiding her secret, denying to everyone she had a problem, partying her way through her parents' appalling divorce and pretending she didn't care.

It was hard enough having high-profile actors as parents and wearing the Rothsberg name, but when that marriage had ended, to have it played out over the media had been agony.

And when a journalist had pointed out that Freya was just a little bit younger than her father's latest girlfriend, a magazine had taken it one nasty step further and pointed out that Freya was also considerably larger.

Her comfort during the very public break-up had, till then, been food and she'd had to endure the spotlight that had shone on her parents suddenly widening to accommodate both herself and James.

She had rigorously denied herself the comfort of food. Very rigorously!

And she had also partied hard.

James had hauled her out of a nightclub and, too weak to row with her brother, Freya had collapsed and been rushed to hospital.

There she had been stripped and put into a gown and then James had been allowed back in, and that was when he had seen her spine and the true extent of her problem had been exposed.

Now, fourteen years later, she would stand today with the most loathed part of her body on show and, joy of joys, eat at the top table.

Freya was better now—so, so much better.

Recovered, healed, whatever the best word was, but there were still hurts and repercussions that she had to deal with, and one of the big ones was that she rarely had a period.

Seriously rarely.

Once, maybe twice a year.

'It's your own fault,' Freya told her reflection, and then came away from the mirror and headed out to the elevator.

She got in and closed her eyes, resting against the wall as she angled her neck to release tension. When she opened them, instead of being on the mezzanine level, she was on the ground floor, and looking into the eyes of Him!

'Well, you prove my theory,' he said in a deep, sexy voice.

It was Him!

The man she had seen a few days ago.

Freya had been speaking with the hotel's events co-ordinator and working out how long they would need to freeze the escalators for, when they'd both stopped talking as the sound of Cuban heels had rung out on the marble floor. And they had stopped talking with good reason. Tall, tanned, with shaggy, curly black hair, he had walked past them in dark jeans and tight T-shirt, carrying a large backpack. He had been just so sexy that he'd simply stopped conversations. Both women had watched him go up to the desk to check in and then shared a guilty smile once they'd finished checking him out.

And now Freya was in the lift with Him.

'And your theory is?' Freya asked.

'That all the good girls are taken.' He asked her which floor she wanted. 'I've already pressed...' Actually, no, her selection had been erased. 'The mezzanine level.' She watched as long suntanned fingers pressed said level and then he pressed for floor twenty-eight and she wished, how she wished, she had given the thirtieth floor as her choice of destination, just for a minute or two more alone with him.

'Shouldn't brides be smiling on their wedding day?' he asked, and Freya tried to place his accent.

'Believe me, the bride is smiling,' Freya said in a dry voice. 'I'm the bridesmaid.'

'Did I hear the word *maid*?'

Freya laughed at the cheeky inference and the slow smile he gave in return had her stomach tighten. Sexy green eyes were looking right at her, and he didn't make her feel like an old maid in the least…

Freya blinked at her own thought process.

The hotel events coordinator had, when they'd been watching him, sighed that he was probably gay and Freya had said if that were the case, *again*, then she really had to get out of LA.

Oh, he was so not gay. His eyes might as well be blow-torches because he had her face just turn to fire.

Sadly the doors pinged open.

'Enjoy the wedding…' he said.

'Oh, I shan't, it's going to be a very long evening,' Freya replied, peeling herself from the wall, when she really didn't want to get out.

'Yeah, I get it.' he said. 'I do my best to avoid weddings.' He met her eyes. 'Especially my own.'

Was he telling her that he was single?

She thought back to the flirty emails that she would live to regret tomorrow, but flirting was kind of fun, Freya was finding out, and she was *very* single.

'And me,' Freya said.

The elevator doors were open but the conversation

wasn't closed and he put one big boot out to keep them open as he asked Freya a question. 'Why did she want a big white wedding on a Thursday?'

'Because it's New Year's Eve.'

'So it is! Well, thanks for reminding me, I'd be in trouble if I didn't call home.'

'You're Australian?' Freya asked, now that she'd placed his accent.

He nodded.

'LA's a long way from home.'

'It is,' he answered. 'And I'm suddenly lonely.'

He didn't look lonely in the least, not with that smile.

'Poor you,' Freya replied, and met his smouldering gaze. His deep green eyes were thickly lashed and she looked down to a dark red mouth and stubbled jaw.

He was so hot, so direct, so bad, so sexy and her reaction to him so acute that Freya could possibly have forgiven herself if she'd hit the button to close the doors and leapt up onto those lean hips.

'I'd better go,' she said, because, yes, she'd better. 'It was nice to meet you…' Freya fished for his name.

'We don't need names, do we?'

She ought to have been offended, Freya thought. She ought to be very, very offended and yet she wasn't.

'Enjoy the wedding,' he offered, 'and thanks for messing up my theory.'

'But I haven't,' Freya said, simply unable to resist prolonging this delicious, rare flirt and, just when she had hit 'send' on that blasted email, she offered a verbal response that would be just as hard to retract. 'I'm not a good girl.'

'It would seem that you are,' he answered smoothly, 'given that you're about to get out.'

The bow around her middle was killing Freya. She

wanted to tear it off, and the dress too, and stamp on them. Instead she stood as his eyes performed a long and slow perusal of her aroused body and Beth would be furious because her nipples were throbbing. They needed his mouth. Oh, yes, they did.

Oh, she was in no position to take offence as his gaze lingered and lingered, because Freya was doing the exact same thing to him. Down that wide chest her eyes went. He was wearing a silver-grey T-shirt and he too had two nipples, she knew that because she counted them slowly and carefully. Then she looked down to his flat stomach. His T-shirt was half-tucked in and she fought not to lift it free. He had on a heavy leather belt that made her thighs want to press together. She looked at the thick bulge in his jeans and was frustrated by the button-up flies, because she'd break her nails tearing at them just to get to him. What the hell was happening? Freya wondered. Because she completely wanted to sink to her knees and to do just that.

It was, for Freya, the oddest feeling. She wasn't very free in bed and she wasn't the most generous lover. She just hoped to have her needs met. 'One for you, one for me' type of thing, and if her needs weren't met then she'd lie twitching with resentment. Actually, even if they were met, it was so underwhelming that she lay twitching anyway, wondering why she couldn't enjoy it. Freya controlled everything that went in her mouth and what she was looking at now wasn't one of them.

Freya licked her lips, not deliberately but very provocatively, it would seem, because he just grew before her eyes. She watched as that lovely hand that had earlier pressed the button had no choice but to make a little room and he rearranged himself to her eyes.

Freya tore them from his bulging crotch and he gave

her a slow, appreciative smile in reward for her lovely effort to get him so hard and so soon.

'I'm impressed,' he said.

'With what?' Freya breathed. She could hardly speak.

'It takes great skill to be such a turn-on in that dress.'

And Freya had more than seen just how turned on he was. 'I have to go.'

'Then go.'

He didn't remove his boot from the door, and Freya could either step over his leg or walk around him. The scent of him mingled with her arousal and Freya had this terrifying moment of absolute conviction that she wasn't going to make it to the chapel in time.

He was sex.

And suddenly, for the first time in her life, so was she.

Freya didn't walk around him, she put one high-heeled foot over his calf and proceeded to step over the hurdle.

She'd never gotten over them at school and was having the same trouble now.

He was terribly polite, for such a filthy animal he really was extremely polite, because his hand settled on her arm to help her over.

Oh, she needed help because the feel of his warm fingers on her bare skin had Freya wanting to straddle his calf and she knew that the bastard knew it.

'Do you want to come up for a drink?' he offered in that low, sexy, deep voice but, really, why bother attempting to be polite? Freya thought. A drink was the very last thing on either of their minds.

'I have a wedding to get to,' Freya croaked. 'I really do.'

'Then you'd better go, or you're going to be extremely unpresentable very soon.'

Oh, those eyes, Freya thought, unwilling to leave the

heat of his gaze, but then she looked at his mouth as he stated what he'd already achieved.

'I want to mess you up,' he said. 'I want you dishevelled.'

She deserved a gold medal and the national anthem sung in her honour because she had made it over his leg. Freya tried to walk off, she really did, but her muscles were protesting and her damp knickers were demanding that she take them off.

'Hey,' he called to her blushing shoulders. She could feel his eyes on her spine and it didn't make her feel ill, instead it made Freya, foolishly, dangerously, turn around. 'If the wedding gets to be a bit...' He shrugged. And then, with utter and no doubt practised ease, he gave her a free pass to heaven. 'Room 2812.'

CHAPTER TWO

'FREYA?' THE HOTEL'S events coordinator prompted when Freya didn't answer her question.

'I was just taking it all in,' Freya said, rather than admit her mind was still back in the elevator. She looked around the ballroom. 'Yes, Beth's going to be very pleased.'

The tables were dressed in red but instead of having flowers as centrepieces Beth had decided on huge bows. There were bows on the chairs too. Freya's carefully worded response told the hotel events coordinator that she had done an amazing job with terrible directions.

They shared another small smile and Freya nearly burst out laughing, a part of her wanting to tell the other woman about her little…er…encounter with the man they'd been admiring a few days ago. Instead, she headed off to the chapel where guests were starting to arrive, hugging the memory to herself and smiling. It had been fun and Freya had never had fun like that.

Freya knew that she was a private, prickly person.

She was, thanks to her psychology degree that lay languishing unused on her résumé, very self-aware. And her very self-aware self knew why she didn't let her guard down.

Freya didn't trust anyone with her feelings.

And walking towards her was yet another reason why. Edward!

'Freya, we have to stop meeting like this.' He smiled.

'Well, now that all our friends are married, we shall,' Freya answered coolly.

'Won't I be getting an invite to yours?' Edward asked.

'That would be a no,' Freya said.

'Are you here with anyone?'

Freya was not going to prolong this conversation so she gave him a very tight smile and walked off.

Oh, how she loathed him.

He was married now and had twins but that hadn't stopped him from trying to chat her up at the last wedding they'd been at. Freya knew, because she'd been dealing with the RSVPs, that Cathy, his wife, wasn't attending tonight as one of their children was unwell.

Oh, a come-on from Edward she so did not need.

Not when she had Mr Room 2812, Freya thought with a sudden smile.

Of course she wouldn't be taking him up on his offer but it had been such, *such* a nice offer to have that it got her through the wedding and then the meal.

The endless five-course meal at the top table.

It was hard to explain, even to herself, but set menus were for Freya the hardest.

Chicken or beef was served alternatively and Freya let out a small breath of relief that she was given chicken, which would have been her choice.

'Would you mind…?' Beth's mother said. 'I don't like red meat.'

'Of course.' Freya smiled, to show that it didn't matter in the least to her, and they swapped plates.

She had been worried about the meal at the wedding and had thought about talking to her friend, Mila, about it. She sometimes discussed her eating disorder with Mila, because Mila didn't treat Freya as if she had two heads and tiptoe around her. But weddings were a bit of a touchy subject between Freya and Mila, given James had jilted her friend at the altar. Also, she was avoiding Mila a bit at the moment, because Freya still hadn't told James that the Bright Hope Clinic charity was run by his ex-fiancée.

James didn't even know they'd remained friends.

Oh, it was a long dinner and then came the speeches.

Freya glared at the cameraman, who was getting stuck into the champagne. She would have preferred Beth to have chosen someone else, but the wedding budget was getting tight, Beth had said. Freya had gently suggested losing a few bows but that hadn't gone down well.

'My wife and I have an extra surprise for you all,' Neil said. 'You'll be thrilled to know that the stork arrived early....'

The whole room melted and clapped and the cameraman must have seen Freya's stern glare because he panned to the guests and then back to the happy couple. Neil made a joke about more free cocktails for him on their cruise. This had Freya's jaw tense.

Then the dancing started but Freya still couldn't relax as Beth had yet more requests.

'I want him to film messages for us from all the guests.'

'I know that you do.'

'But I don't want the messages to just be about the baby,' Beth said. 'I want them mainly to be about me.'

Me, me, me, me, me, Freya thought as she nodded and smiled.

Freya took a glass of champagne from a passing waiter

and then Edward came over. 'You're looking gorgeous, Freya,' he said.

She looked terrible, as Mr Room 2812 had so sexily pointed out!

'Can I get you another drink?' Edward offered.

'No, thank you.'

'You were blonde last time I saw you,' he said. 'You've gone back to brunette.'

'Really?' Freya's response was sarcastic. 'Thanks for letting me know.'

'I'm actually staying here tonight,' Edward said. 'How about a dance for old times' sake?'

'How about I throw this champagne in your face?'

Freya walked off with her drink and headed outside to drag the cool night air into her lungs. She loved LA in winter and she promised to take herself riding some time soon. It was her best method for relaxing and she had been introduced to it when she had been in rehab.

Freya never cried.

Not even in rehab had she let them break her but tonight she suddenly felt close.

It wasn't Edward, she harboured no hidden feelings for him—well, no nice ones.

It was how they'd ended things that still stung, all these years on.

Her long stint in rehab had been spread far and wide across the media and everyone had thought she'd been on drugs. At the age of twenty-three, when they'd started dating, he'd asked about it and Freya had told him about her eating disorder.

It had been hard to reveal but she'd pushed on and had told him she was recovered, or healed, or whatever the best word was. But when she'd told him that she probably couldn't have children he had, on the spot, dumped her and accused her of stringing him along. It had felt as if Edward had only been dating her on the assumption that one day she'd be pregnant.

'I thought we were enjoying each other's company,' Freya had said. 'Not looking for future mating partners.'

'Well, it's preferable to have that option,' had been his callous response.

It had hurt, it had been such a horrible blow to her recovering self, but she had refused to let it plunge her back into hell.

Freya knew she should go back inside but she could not face Edward.

Did he think she'd have an affair, that married men were all that was left? Oh, no, she would rather, far rather, get in that elevator and…

Why not? Freya thought.

They'd both, in that brief exchange, stated that they were single.

And she'd promised this coming year to do more of the things she liked and to try new things.

No.

Freya simply couldn't see it.

Going up and knocking on Sexy Bastard's door just for sex.

Or maybe he'd left it open and she would just slip in.

Actually, Freya could see it.

And she *had* promised to keep her New Year's resolutions…

New Year.

Yikes! Freya remembered a little too late that she had to get everyone out for the photo shoot and the next twenty minutes were frantic indeed.

It had been a long and difficult night, Freya thought,

and a part of her longed to just head upstairs and to find out what simply letting go and having fun actually meant.

An aching part of Zack had really wished she would head up!

He'd arrived back in his room so turned on and waiting.

Come on, he'd thought.

God knew, he'd needed the distraction.

He'd unlatched the door and lain on the bed, hands behind his head.

She was stunning.

Dark eyes, dark hair and that mouth… She'd looked a little familiar but all he had ever seen of LA till now had been the airport so Zack had shrugged that thought off. It would come to him overnight.

Would she?

Of course she would. The attraction had been through the roof but by ten he'd downgraded his expectations because the speeches were surely well over with.

By eleven-thirty he'd woken from a doze and stared out to the LA night.

Not at the city but at the mountains beyond and he knew he had to ring his parents before the lines got busy. He got up and took out his cellphone and took a steadying breath before he made the call.

Zack was thirty-three and the last time he'd been home, a couple of years ago, he'd been the same age as his brother Toby had been when he had died.

Except Toby had been married and working in the family practice and his wife, Alice, had wanted to start a family.

Whereas Zack, as his parents had constantly pointed out, was a drifter.

He was a highly skilled paediatric cardiac surgeon, Zack had riposted, but that was just boasting, he was told. And what good were his skills when they were so badly needed in Kurranda, the remote outback town where he and Toby had been raised.

He could picture the phone ringing in the hall. Reception was haphazard there and the landline to the family doctor really was a lifeline for the community.

His mother answered on the third ring.

'Hey, Mum,' Zack said. 'Happy New Year.'

'I'm sure it is where you are.'

Zack closed his eyes, it was just more of the same.

'How's Nepal?'

'I'm in LA,' Zack answered.

'I thought you *had* to be in Nepal.'

'I did have to be there for Christmas,' Zack answered. 'There was an operation I wanted to do before I left but we had to wait for some equipment to arrive. I would have been home if I could.'

'Well, why aren't you now?'

'Because I've got an interview tomorrow.'

'In LA?'

'It's a top medical centre. They've got some of the most amazing equipment and facilities and I don't want to let that side of things slide…' Zack stopped even attempting to explain. He did not want to argue with his mother. Judy Carlton simply could not, would not, get it, and Zack was over trying to explain. 'Is Dad there?'

'You just missed him. He got called out for Tara. Do you remember her?'

Of course he damn well remembered, they'd been friends. What his mother didn't know was that they had been each other's first. Zack had fought to stop that getting out as Tara's father was very religious.

Zack stayed silent.

'She married Jed.'

'Yep.'

'Well, the baby's not due till the end of January but it looks as if she might deliver early and it's breech. I can't talk for long, they might need the air ambulance...'

'I get it.' Zack said. 'Will you wish Dad a happy New Year for me and could you—?'

'Zack,' his mum broke in, 'you should be here to say it to him for yourself. Even if you'd just come home on a stopover it would have been something.'

'I would have but this interview is being slotted in, they need me to start straight away. There's a very sick child—'

'Oh, I don't have time for your fancy position,' Judy said. 'I'll pass on to Tara and her husband how well you're doing, shall I?'

Zack knew that translated to, *You should be back here, scrubbing in with your father, rather than Tara having to be airlifted.* 'That was a low blow.'

'I know.' His mother didn't quite apologise. 'I'm tired, Zack, and your dad is too. He didn't get any break over Christmas and the place just seems to be getting busier. So much for retiring.'

Zack closed his eyes. Sometimes he wished he could just give up on his own dreams and give them the solution they wanted.

'By now you and Toby...' Judy swallowed and Zack then heard his mother, a very strong woman, give way to tears. New Year always did that to her and this coming year marked another difficult milestone. 'It will be ten years soon.'

'I know it will.'

At the beginning of February it would be ten years since Toby had died.

He and Zack had been on a weekend away. Both had been good horsemen but a snake had spooked Toby's horse and thrown him off.

Zack looked out of the hotel window again and out towards the dark shadows of the hills and thought of the red earth of home. Even if he didn't want to be there for ever he missed it at times and now was one of those times. As he stood there he remembered too the agony of hours spent with his brother, waiting for help to arrive while knowing there was none to be had.

At the age of thirty-one Toby had died in his younger brother's arms.

Zack knew his mother needed to talk and so he forgot about the sniping and let her.

'Things would be so different if he was still alive. He loved the clinic. Toby and your father had such plans for it. Alice is pregnant again by her new husband.'

He was hardly her new husband, Zack thought. Alice had been remarried for seven years.

'Mum, she's allowed to be happy.'

'She and Toby were so happy, though,' Judy said. 'I wanted grandchildren.'

'I know.'

'And that's not going to happen, is it?'

'No.'

'Are you seeing someone?'

She asked him the same question every time they spoke and it was always the same answer he gave. 'No one serious.'

'Zack…?'

'What?' Zack said, and when there was silence he

told her the truth. 'Mum, I won't be giving you grand-children.'

Zack was direct, yes. There was no point giving her false hope. The life his parents had planned for him wasn't the one he wanted. He never wanted to be tied down, not to one person and not to one place.

Zack wasn't cruel, though.

What he didn't tell his mother was that Toby had been far from happy with his life.

That was the reason Toby had called him up and asked if he'd join him on a weekend away. There, in the out-back, lying by a fire, looking up at the stars, Toby had told him the truth—that he felt stifled, and wanted away, not just from Kurranda and the medical practice but also from his marriage.

Zack had been stunned. He'd thought that Alice and Toby, childhood sweethearts, had been so happy but Toby had told him that, no, things hadn't been good for a very long while.

It had been a long night spent talking, sometimes seri-ously, but also they'd shared laughter, not knowing what was to come the very next day.

Toby hadn't quite taken that secret to his grave, it had been left with Zack. He'd never shared it with anyone and it weighed heavily inside.

'I really do have to go,' Judy said. 'I'd better head over there now in case your dad needs help to organ-ise the air ambulance and things…' His mother wasn't a doctor or nurse but she was a huge part of the fabric of the town. She would liaise with the air ambulance and locals and make sure the transfer was seamless. Then she'd have Tara's parents over for coffee and a meal as they awaited news.

That was who his mother was.

'Happy New Year,' Zack said.

Judy made a small huffing noise.

His parents had decided, on Toby's death and Zack's failure to settle, that there could be no more happy years.

'Happy New Year, Zack,' Judy said, but even that came out with a slight edge. Zack made sure he was happy, that he lived, that he grabbed this rare gift by the throat and got every bit of life out of it.

He'd promised his brother he would.

'Mum,' Zack suddenly said. 'I'll come home for a visit in April. Tell Dad that.'

'For how long?'

'I'm not sure, but I'll be back to see you both then.'

He ended the call and though he could not stand the thought of living back there, and being in a place where everyone knew your business, it didn't mean he didn't love nature and space and the people.

And, though things were strained, he loved his family.

Zack lay on the bed and closed his eyes but he couldn't unwind. Speaking with his parents always left him feeling like that. The plans his parents had had for him had been set in stone from the day he was born. They just hadn't thought to consult the baby they had made.

He was to study medicine in Melbourne as his father and brother had done, but even before he had left for the city Zack had known in his heart that he wasn't coming back.

Tara had known it too.

Of course he remembered Tara.

Not just the hot, sexy kisses behind a barn and sultry outback nights, more he remembered a conversation that had taken place the night before he'd left as they'd lain in each other's arms. 'You're not coming back, are you?' Tara had asked.

'You talk as if I'm leaving the country. I'm only going to Melbourne. I'll be back for the summer breaks.' Even at eighteen he'd been direct. 'But, no, I can't see myself here, Tara.'

'And I don't want to be there,' Tara said. She was a country girl and loved it and neither wanted to change or to change the other.

'Have you told your parents?' she asked.

'I've tried,' Zack said. 'They don't understand.'

He was still trying.

And all these years later they still didn't understand.

Zack went to pour a drink but the half-bottle of wine was empty and he wasn't a big fan of American beer.

He was about to ring for room service but, still churned up from the conversation with his mother, he pulled on his boots again and took the elevator down, but it only took him to the mezzanine level and he decided to take the escalator down to the bar.

There were people everywhere, all standing on the stairs, and then he found out why.

The wedding.

'You'll have to use the elevators if you want to get to the ground floor,' someone told him, and they sounded annoyed. 'The escalators and stairs are in use.'

And there was the woman from said elevator, organising the wedding party, telling people to step back or to stand a fraction more to the left.

Zack watched as a gentleman came over to her and whatever she said had him step abruptly back.

Oh, she was a snappy, bossy little thing, Zack thought.

Not with him, though.

And then she looked up.

Oh, my... Freya thought, and another of Edward's sleazy come-ons left her mind.

If Mr 2812 had been sexy before, he was sinfully so now—dishevelled and just raw male, he made her toes curl in her very painful shoes. His hair was messy, his T-shirt was all crumpled and, alongside all the suits and formal clothes, in those dark jeans and tight T-shirt he stood out, deliciously so.

Freya dragged her mind away from rude thoughts. This shot was important and the countdown had started. Beth and Neil were in position and everyone was in place and she should be able to relax soon. All she had to do was wave the happy couple off and the rest of the night was hers.

Concentrate, Freya.

She couldn't.

There was just this prickling awareness all over her as she recalled his scent and the feel of his hand on her arm.

Oh, God. She gazed up at him and hoped her eyes weren't frantic, but that was how she suddenly felt— frantic for him.

'Ten!' everybody shouted. 'Nine!'

They could not stop staring and, as the countdown drew to its conclusion, as everyone started cheering and kissing, Beth's carefully organised photos were ruined by a tall guy bursting through and dashing down the stairs.

'Auld Lang Syne' was being sung out around them as his hands took her by the upper arms. Briefly she wondered why, instead of kissing her as she badly needed him to do, he was moving her away. But then Freya found out exactly why.

This wasn't a kiss suitable for public exposure.

They were in a small booth to the side of the hotel's reception when his mouth first met hers. They came together so hard that their teeth met and his tongue was strong and thick and very indecent. Her hips were held by him, and animal passion, which had never taken up resi-dence in Freya before, rapidly made itself right at home.

Her hands were pressing into his chest, not to push him away, just to feel him, to rub those solid muscles beneath greedy palms. Then they went up to his head and her fingers dug into his hair. She kissed him back on tiptoe, so that her heels lifted up out of her shoes in an attempt to scale him.

He pulled back and gave her an intense look and there was no mention of going up for a drink.

'I have to get back…' It was a feeble protest she made. 'I just need ten more minutes to sort the wedding party out.'

'We can't wait.'

His erection was in her groin and Freya herself was pressing hard into him.

'I have to make sure that they get off okay…'

He peered out.

'They're waving and the bride is about to throw the bouquet. Do you want to go and try to catch it?'

The question was a loaded one.

What was she looking for—an amazing night with no names, or to dash off and catch the bouquet and the dream that it might one day be her?

'God, no,' Freya said. She was more than happy with being a third-time bridesmaid and so she took his head in her hands and got back to that mouth for one more deep kiss before they hit the elevators.

Freya pressed the button for the twenty-eighth floor.

'You remembered,' he said.

'Oh, yes!'

CHAPTER THREE

SADLY FOR THEM the elevator was full.

The wedding guests were dispersing and either heading to their rooms or to the bars. There were many, many opportunities for Freya to change her mind on the long and frustrating ride to the twenty-eighth floor and say that this was a terrible idea and so not like her.

It never entered Freya's head to do so.

Her rigid, controlled life was in desperate need of fun and adventure, and he offered that and more.

He was beautiful.

Even with her back to him she could feel the energy between them, it was utter attraction and arousal at its most basic and Freya could not wait to indulge.

'What floor are you on?' he asked, running a finger over her bare shoulder as they crawled towards her floor. His touch was electric and, yes, it was terribly tempting to get off at the tenth floor, but there might be a problem as she hadn't packed her toiletry bag with a wild night in mind.

She gave a small shake of her head and then turned and looked him right in the eye as the elevator came to her floor and a couple got out.

'I haven't got...' she mouthed.

'I have,' he mouthed back. Of course he did, Freya

thought. This guy had nearly had her at five p.m. after all—no doubt he came prepared for women dropping their knickers on sight—but they were already past her floor and so they waited—oh, how they waited—for them to hit his floor.

As the crowd thinned out there was a bit more space but they didn't utilise it. She could feel his eyes on her shoulder, on her spine, and then she got the bliss of his mouth on the part of her she hated the most.

She leant back into him even as the doors opened.

'Thank God,' Zack said, and he took her hand and they just about ran the length of the corridor.

He opened up the door and they fell into the room. Their mouths locked and they didn't bother with the lights. Just hot, hard kisses as Freya kissed him with abandon up against the wall.

He more than partook because he tore that dress off and the sound of it ripping was as delicious as the feel of his hands on her bare skin.

'Oh, God,' he said as he played with her breasts and tweaked her nipples as if he'd been waiting for them all night.

He had been.

Freya had never been more grateful for ignoring the bride's plea because, unable to resist a taste, he lowered his head and took one nipple into his hungry mouth.

'She wanted me to wear sticking plasters over them.'

'We don't like the bride,' he said as he withdrew his mouth, and it made her laugh. It was just such a relief after a very long and difficult day to laugh and vent to someone who got her. He took the other breast in his mouth and sucked hard. Freya pushed him off, only because it was her turn to taste *his* salty chest. Oh, he tasted amazing, like he'd been swimming in the ocean and had then showered in ice. Salty, refreshing and so firm.

Freya dealt with his heavy leather belt as best she could with her mouth on his chest, licking him, tasting him and then moaning her frustration.

'Why button-ups…?' Freya whimpered.

'So I can picture your fingers undoing them and getting it out.' She was doing just that and Freya herself wasn't gentle. He was so thick and long and already there was a silver drizzle that trickled onto her fingers as she explored him.

'Get naked,' he told her, and he went into his pocket. He wished he'd kicked off his boots so he could do the same but there really wasn't time. As she shed her knickers he dressed his erection and Freya toppled a little as she took off her shoes.

'Come here,' he said, and she just stepped to him and he lifted her to where she'd wanted to be all along.

'Oh…' He didn't guide her on, he held her hips as her hands went behind his neck.

'Lean back,' he told her, and as he held her by the hips he rubbed her wet sex over his stomach and scented himself with her.

'I'm going to come…' Freya was, the feel of the hairs on his stomach, the rough guide of his hands, the way he was holding her, and she couldn't hold on.

'That's the intention,' Sexy Bastard said.

She had kind of got this wasn't going to be like anything she'd experienced before but she found out for certain then. As her body arched, as she let out a building moan, he took her coming. He just drove into her tight and twitching and moaned at the pleasure.

'Oh, yeah,' he said.

Oh, yes, Freya thought.

He just parted her orgasm, it was like being a virgin all over again, or not, Freya thought because that had been *such* an underwhelming encounter.

This wasn't.

She went limp for a moment and he took full advantage, grinding her down to meet his thrusts. Her hands took in his muscled shoulders and she dug her nails in, and then she just had to taste that shoulder, sucking it as her hands explored his broad upper back.

Her nails dug in again, deeper, and he took her a bit slower but with measured tension. It was an odd consent but she read it—he wanted more of the same so she scratched him hard.

'Careful,' he warned as her mouth sucked skin, but he wasn't telling her to stop, she knew that. 'You'll pay for each bruise.'

Oh, she would gladly pay.

He took her to the desk, or she guessed that's what it was, because it was cold and hard on her back. Freya went to wrap her legs around him but his hand pressed her thighs apart and he took her hard and so deep that she just about performed a sit-up as her entire lower abdomen contracted.

'Come on,' he said, and she opened her eyes to his gruff command but then her eyes met his and he smiled down at her.

'Nice,' he said, bucking into her.

'So…' Freya couldn't finish. She had never known anything like it. His face tensed and then he released into her, and she met the impact with a deep force of her own. Her orgasm just rolled through her like thunder and then lightning clapped her tight with no pause in between. It just dissolved her from the inside out, and as it left she quivered and then he collapsed onto her.

He was so heavy, and breathless, but then his mouth was an unexpected soft caress. Even as he came out of her he kissed her. Even as he unsheathed he kissed her back to earth, and as he stripped off his boots and jeans, his mouth never left her skin. Naked now, he picked her up from the hard desk and carried her to the bed.

He got in beside her and scooped her into his body. His hand stroked her breast and he kissed her shoulder as she lay feeling bewildered yet drowsy and sedated.

'Go to sleep,' he said.

He seemed to know just what she needed and yet they didn't even know each other's names.

'How…?' She attempted to gather a thought into a sentence.

'Chemistry,' he answered.

And to sleep they went.

CHAPTER FOUR

'I SHOULD HAVE paid way more attention in science class,' Freya said a few hours later as she woke to the thought of his last word and the feel of her loose, relaxed body in his arms as he spooned in behind her.

'Oh, I'll make you pay attention,' he said low and deep into her ear. 'Happy New Year.'

'And you,' Freya said.

'It already is.'

Last night he'd barely been able to get the words out to his mother, knowing how pointless they were, but now Zack was happy, indulging in one of his passions.

The other was work and that was so intense that he lived for escapes like this.

'Were you going to come to my room?' he asked. 'Honest answer.'

'I was thinking about it,' Freya said. 'I wasn't having the best night.'

'What did you say to that guy?'

Freya frowned.

'The one who walked off just before you saw me…'

'Oh, that was Edward—'

'No names,' he interrupted, and Freya lay there, feeling his fingers gently kneading her stomach.

Freya wanted to know his name, she wanted to know

more about him, and yet he'd reminded her that there would be no exchange of names. But as she lay there, enjoying the gentle massage of his fingers, and thought about it, she realised that it was actually quite freeing. There would be no *I'm Freya Rothsberg. Yes, Aubrey St Claire and Michael Rothsberg are indeed my parents.* And if he recognised the name, then he'd know about their messy divorce. And there would be no *I'm thirty-one, single, perfectionist, infertile but trying not to be, recovered anorexic.* She didn't have to say she was a big shot in PR. Or that she was stressing about taking on the charity side of her brother's medical centre. Or that, though she'd pushed James to let her, really she wanted to use her psychology degree.

No names didn't mean no past but it meant she didn't have to reveal anything that she didn't want to.

Who was she without all of that? Freya lay there and pondered.

She.

The woman in his arms, and that was enough for him.

He.

Freya understood now the bliss of no names.

'He's an ex.' Freya answered the question after a very long pause. 'And he tried it on last night. Several times.'

'I'd try it on again with you…'

'He's married.'

'Bastard,' Zack said. 'Did you know that he was when you were together?'

'He wasn't married then,' Freya said. 'From the way we broke up it would seem he wanted a wife and children. He's got what he wanted but his wife wasn't there last night. He said he wanted to bring in the New Year with me up in his room.'

'What did you say to him?'

'I told him I hadn't enjoyed sex with him the first time around and that I felt sorry for his short-suffering wife.'

He laughed.

'You're not married, are you?' Freya checked.

He could lie, she guessed, but she felt he wouldn't.

There was no point in lying.

'Oh, no,' Zack said. 'And I have no intention to ever be. This is absolutely guilt-free sex, baby…'

Freya doubted this encounter would be entirely guilt free, no doubt she'd be crawling with shame a few hours from now, but that was her.

'Do you have any New Year's resolutions?' he asked.

'Many,' Freya said. She had pored over them for hours and had them all written out.

'Such as?'

They were mostly the same as every other year—unlike other people, who seemed to swear to go on a diet or exercise, Freya's resolution was to not embark on a sudden diet or obsess over exercise. Not that she told him that.

Neither did she tell him about the baby she wanted and her dream of having her own little family.

Nor did she tell him that she was over men. Though perhaps not completely over them, given where she was.

So she just lay there, overthinking but oddly lulled by the soothing stroke of his hands and the nudge of his erection behind her. No, there was no need to tell him about the career she wanted to tackle but had been avoiding doing so.

'I made my list of resolutions yesterday after my run,' Freya said.

'Do you run a lot?' he asked, his fingers examining her slim, toned body.

'On alternate days,' Freya said.

'And what do you do on the other one?'

'I go for a walk,' Freya said, and the threat of tears was back but she held them in, although she did admit a truth she would never dare to another. 'And I try not to run.' She was more honest with a stranger than the people closest to her and his response was kind.

He gave a light kiss to her shoulder.

'It's okay.'

He could feel her near to tears and he got that.

Anonymity at times came with deep trust, for you were at your most bare.

'I ran,' Zack said. 'Well, I'm not a runner but I ran from all that was expected of me and I'm still running.'

She couldn't imagine him running from anything.

He was so confrontational to all of her senses she could not imagine there were things he might not be able to face.

'So what list of resolutions did you make?' he asked.

She smiled as he ran a lazy hand down her body and pulled her into him.

'Making more time for the things I like.'

'And me,' Zack said, and he started to kiss her neck.

'Try new things...' Freya said, and the arm under her moved and fingers came to her small breast and stroked it.

'I like that one too.'

He pinched her nipple and she properly understood what he'd meant about him picturing her undoing his button flies because in her mind's eye she could see those brown fingers squeezing her hard. Instead of slapping him away, she took a shaky breath as he squeezed it tight again and she felt like a bud bursting.

He took her hand and put it between her legs and then,

still tweaking her breasts, his other hand met hers between her legs and *they* explored her.

'Not that one,' Freya said, and he laughed into her shoulder.

'I'm just feeling you all over,' Zack said. Working out boundaries had never been more fun. 'I want to taste you all over.'

'I don't like oral,' Freya said.

God, this was freeing, just to say it outright! To declare her needs and to state what she didn't want.

'You would.'

'No, thank you.'

He took himself in his hand and aimed the head at her fingers and moistened them as she brought herself, with a very nice lot of help from him, right to the edge.

'Not yet…' he said.

'You don't dictate my orgasm,' Freya responded in a brittle voice, trying to remember how *she* dictated her world.

'Oh, but I do.'

He went against everything she believed in the bedroom but fantastically so.

He was right at her entrance and she refused to beg, she just lay on her side, hot with anticipation. The easiest thing to do would be to not play safe but he rolled away from her and she heard the tear of foil. Freya loathed the intrusion but then he was back, lifting her hair and warming up her neck again with his mouth.

'Watch my neck,' Freya warned.

'Wear your hair down.'

'Okay.'

They both smiled at the ease of the solution.

He was making a terrible mess, she was sure, and she was doing all she could not to beg when finally he slid in and she moaned because she was swollen from last night, and it hurt quite a bit.

His large thigh came over her and he took her very slowly, painstakingly so, and she pressed back, trying to hurry him.

'What would you have done if you'd come to my room?' he asked.

'Guess,' Freya said through gritted teeth. It was obvious to her they would have had sex, only he wasn't letting her get away with that.

'Would you have knocked?'

'I don't know…' She was frantic, wanting to close her eyes and just focus on her building orgasm—not be dragged into conversation.

'I'd left the door open,' he said.

'Faster…' she begged.

'Would you have knocked?' he persisted, taking her at a slow, leisurely pace.

'No.' He gave it to her faster as a reward for her answer and then slowed when she didn't elaborate.

'I'd have come in,' Freya said as he dragged out her fantasy, as he made her reveal her thoughts.

'I might have been asleep.'

He rolled her onto her stomach and crushed her with his weight and the angle had him stroke her to the edge of bliss but he refused to push her over.

'What if I'd been asleep?' he asked.

'I'd have woken you with my mouth,' Freya said because, though she loathed the thought of it, she wanted to be the woman who could do that. 'More…' she now begged. It was like he had unbuttoned her.

'More?' Zack checked, and pulled out of her. She let out a sob of frustration.

He knelt up, pulled up her hips and Freya told him exactly where her thoughts last night had been.

'I'd have got you hard with my mouth and climbed on.'

'Dirty girl.'

'Yes,' Freya said. 'I am.'

She could hear his ragged breathing and his hand hovering over her bare cheek before he gave her a light spank.

'Yes…' Freya whimpered, and she did not recognise her own voice, or her own requests. He spanked her harder and she just about came and as her hand shot between her legs to ensure she did just that, Zack spanked her again.

'More,' Freya said.

Oh, he would have loved to carry on with the spanking, but the sound of her moans and the sight of her meant he had to be inside her.

She asked for more but he told her to be quiet, disobeying her plea to spank her again as he took her.

He seared inside her and not gently.

God, she always held back now but she was asking for more, for rougher…

He just took over and she pressed her face into the mattress.

Freya came, choking out her sobs as she pulsed around him, but he did not relent and he did not come.

There was a slight curse from him and the condom was gone, she knew, it had to be. She had never had sex without one and this was amazing.

For Zack too.

The feel of her hot and swollen was more acute and the sound of her moaning. Her hand came back and she dug her nails into his thighs. He scooped an arm under her stomach and drove in harder.

She felt like a rag doll, limp everywhere except on the inside, where she was pulled taut by him.

Freya had never completely let go in sex, she had tried to and had thought she had in those little slivers of orgasm in days gone by, but she knew now she hadn't.

Rude words were uttered and her head felt as if it had turned red as he swelled and shot into her.

Her orgasm was so sexy, a clutch of muscle that drew him in, and his warm come felt like ice seeping over her hot, swollen tightness.

And he pushed and groaned and let go deep into her until they were spent.

She listened to his long, pleasured sigh as he pulled out and then another sigh as he slipped back in to where it was warm and then out he went.

He joined her and they lay on their stomachs, facing each other, sleepy, satisfied smiles on their faces.

Freya had never had this moment where nothing else mattered than this bliss.

Soon other things would but for now nothing did.

God, she had spent most of her life trying to stay in control, only to find in some things she didn't want to.

And for Zack, who, as fleeting as his relationships were, did his best to be considerate and hold back, now looked into the eyes of someone who didn't need him to.

'Sore?' he asked, running a hand over where he had spanked her.

'I'm still high.'

They lay there and Zack said something that he usually wouldn't. 'I wish I could be your alternate day...' But that sounded way too much like making plans for Zack so he made light of what he'd just said. 'Nope, you'd be hanging up your running shoes for good.'

And Freya too kept it light. 'I don't think I could deal with you even on alternate days.' She smiled.

Freya actually meant it.

He had changed everything in her very ordered world and had awoken a side to her that she hadn't been aware existed.

They were touching down on their real worlds, and, on a very clear day, flight-wise, it was a surprisingly bumpy landing that was to come.

Maybe paradise *was* hard to leave because, as it turned out, they did it terribly.

The buzz of her phone as a seven a.m. alarm went off was equalled by the chime of his and they both groaned.

'I have to go…' Freya said.

'We need to talk.'

They really did, Zack had realised.

No names definitely didn't mean no condoms.

'Look, you don't have anything to worry about from my end.' Zack had his doctor's voice on, not that she knew it. 'I'm always careful and I've just had some health checks.' He dealt with all this in a very practical, forthright way. He was completely in work mode now, and what Freya couldn't know was that at work Zack was a very different man.

'You don't have to worry about me getting pregnant.' Freya wasn't going to go into detail about her fertility issues so she let him assume she was on the Pill, but his expression remained serious, even as they lay on their stomachs facing each other. 'I had some blood work done this week,' Freya said. 'It was all fine.' His expression was still grim and she was starting to get annoyed. 'I can go and get my computer if you don't believe me.' Her voice was rising. 'It was a torn condom, for God's sake.'

Accidents happened!

Just never to her.

Freya made sure of it.

She sat up, not liking all she had told him.

This man knew more about her than she'd told anyone and it was getting harder and harder to look him in the eye.

Zack sat up, knowing he hadn't handled that well. He tried to improve the sudden drop in atmosphere. 'Let's get some breakfast…' He'd made her feel bad and that hadn't been his intention, but in his line of work Zack had to be sure.

The snooze alarm went off and he swiped it and then picked up the hotel phone and ordered breakfast for two.

'Coffee?' he checked.

Freya shook her head. 'I'll have a green tea.'

He ordered and then climbed from the bed. 'I'll just have a shower…' Zack said, and threw her one of the robes. 'In case breakfast arrives while I'm in there.'

He turned on the cold tap and, apart from the issue that needed to be discussed, Zack felt amazing. So much so that he was considering not just explaining that his career was the reason he needed more information but breaking their game and finding out names.

Seeing her again.

Freya.

Just as he'd predicted it would, overnight her name had come to him.

It couldn't be!

Zack turned off the shower and stepped into the bedroom, and saw that she had gone. The robe lay on the bed and her clothes and shoes were gone, and Zack let out a breath for his poor handling of things. He went into his laptop and pulled up the glossy brochure that had been sent along with the forms he'd had to fill in.

There was a photograph of the luxurious Hollywood Hills Medical Center, where he was to be interviewed this morning. He scrolled through several photographs of the doctors and nurses who practised there but Zack bypassed them and went to the section near the end.

He had already looked her up.

A few flirty emails had had him curious as to what Freya Rothsberg looked like.

Zack looked at the photo and remembered being in Nepal and checking out who the woman at the end of the emails was. It was a head shot and her long hair was blonde and straight in this image, unlike the curly brunette of last night. Here it was sleek and worn up and her make-up was neutral and she was wearing a dark grey dress with a high neck and capped sleeves.

She looked corporate and elegant and almost unrecognisable from the sultry beauty of last night.

Still, it explained better to Zack why they'd ignited on sight—for a couple of weeks up till Christmas they'd been flirting!

CHAPTER FIVE

ZACK READ THROUGH their email exchanges in the taxi on the way to The Hills.

At first it had been a semi-formal 'Dear Zackary' type of exchange.

Zack had been head-hunted by James Rothsberg and he'd had some questions about the charitable side of things so James had flicked over to Freya some of the questions that he had raised.

To: ZCarlton@ZackaryCarlton.com
From: Freya.Rothsberg@TheHollywoodHillsClinic.com
Dear Zackary,
James has passed your concerns on to me and I hope I can address them.

For some time The Hollywood Hills has been looking into a suitable charity to partner and support.

The highly regarded Bright Hope Clinic was chosen. The clinic treats underprivileged children and is situated in the south of LA, where its services are desperately needed in the densely populated area. As a result their facilities and equipment are severely stretched.

The partnership of the Bright Hope Clinic with The Hollywood Hills aims to increase the number and scope of cases that can be treated. We are lucky to have world-class facilities and can also allow for easy transfer of emergency or overseas patients using the Hills' helicopter or ambulance transport system. The Bright Hope Clinic in South LA will still run as usual, with cases requiring more complex care being referred to the Bright Hope at The Hollywood Hills.

Sincerely,
Freya Rothsberg
Public Relations Consultant

To: Freya.Rothsberg@TheHollywoodHillsClinic.com
From: ZCarlton@ZackaryCarlton.com
All good. I'll take a look into the Bright Hope Clinic and get back to you with any questions.
Zack

To: ZCarlton@ZackaryCarlton.com
From: Freya.Rothsberg@TheHollywoodHillsClinic.com
Dear Zackary,
I have attached some further information on the Bright Hope Clinic as well as the names of some contacts I have there, who would be happy to answer any of your questions.
Sincerely,
Freya Rothsberg

To: Freya.Rothsberg@TheHollywoodHillsClinic.com
From: ZCarlton@ZackaryCarlton.com
Zack!
Please can you email the forms and brochures on The Hills, the postal service is a bit slow in Nepal. Also, I note

that you have the same surname as James and wondered if The Hills is a family-led clinic?

Zack loathed the politics of work and the thought of butting up against husband and wife with their own agendas held no appeal.

To: ZCarlton@ZackaryCarlton.com
From:Freya.Rothsberg@TheHollywoodHillsClinic.com
Dear Zack!
Please find attached the brochure that will better explain the clinic structure.
   To address your concern—James is my brother. So, no, there aren't twenty Rothsbergs or husband-and-wife teams :-)
Freya!

He grinned that she'd read between the lines and understood his concerns.

To: Freya.Rothsberg@TheHollywoodHillsClinic.com
From: ZCarlton@ZackaryCarlton.com
Good to know!
Zack!

Flicking through the brochure, he had smiled again when he'd seen who he was dealing with and on a rather long night in Nepal he'd responded again.

To: Freya.Rothsberg@TheHollywoodHillsClinic.com
From: ZCarlton@ZackaryCarlton.com
I meant good to know that there aren't hundreds of you, as opposed to your marital status.
Zack!

He'd regretted sending it, because Zack never flirted or got involved with anyone at work, but it had been such a subtle flirt that she probably hadn't got it.

Two days had passed and he'd actually forgotten when her response had come back.

Oh, she'd got it.

To: ZCarlton@ZackaryCarlton.com
From: Freya.Rothsberg@TheHollywoodHillsClinic.com
Zack!
Is there a question mark missing in the previous email?
Freya!

No he never got involved with people at work, but a quickie with the PR rep surely didn't count, Zack had thought, and there were slim pickings where he'd been that night and it was nice to dream.

To: Freya.Rothsberg@TheHollywoodHillsClinic.com
From: ZCarlton@ZackaryCarlton.com
?

Her response?

There hadn't been one.

His next email, after a long day of surgery followed by a very long night in Nepal:

To: Freya.Rothsberg@TheHollywoodHillsClinic.com
From: ZCarlton@ZackaryCarlton.com
??

To: ZCarlton@ZackaryCarlton.com
From: Freya.Rothsberg@TheHollywoodHillsClinic.com
Very single. (Don't tell James.)

To: Freya.Rothsburg@TheHollywoodHillsClinic.com
From: ZCarlton@ZackaryCarlton.com
I never kiss and tell.

He smiled as he finished reading and did a quick search on her name, and suddenly Zack wasn't smiling.

There was an article on Freya, accompanied by a picture of her collapsed and being taken out of a nightclub and he read about her drug habit. There was a quote from her mother, stating that Freya was finally getting the help she needed and was in rehab.

He thought of the woman who had slunk out of his hotel room rather than face the music.

Oh, yes, they needed to talk!

Freya wasn't proud that she had dressed and left but she hadn't wanted last night to dissolve into a terse exchange.

And neither had she liked how one minute they'd been so, so intimate and the next he had reduced it to a lab-report exchange. She'd heard the shower being turned on and had gone red in the face as she'd recalled her pleas and her demands, and what had felt fine—in fact, amazing—just a short while ago had then felt like an embarrassing mistake.

She'd pulled on her dress and slipped out of his suite, taking the walk of shame back to her own room. Once in there she had surprised herself by letting out a shocked burst of laughter.

Who knew?

Not she.

Freya showered and massaged loads of conditioner into her hair and then as she dried herself off she looked at her body, turning to see her red butt cheeks. God, she felt better for it. And, now that she thought about it more calmly, Freya liked the head-on way he had tackled the awkward subject.

She'd print off her results, Freya decided. She would cross out her name and other details and put the relevant part in an envelope and leave it at Reception to be delivered to his room.

Freya got ready and dried her hair so that it was its usual straight self, and was about to put it up when she remembered why she couldn't.

The memory of them had her wanting more. Freya did her best to quell a building want and she pulled out of her wardrobe the dress she had worn before the bridesmaid outfit.

It had been a one-off, a little sexual adventure and one that was never to be repeated again, Freya told herself.

She pulled on a neutral linen shift that she wore with flat ballet pumps and she carefully did her very neutral make-up then gave a sigh of relief when she finally recognised herself in the mirror.

Freya.

She called down to Reception and asked for her car to be brought around and decided that, given she had late check-out and Red was feeding Cleo, she would come back after the interview to pack. She took the elevator and went to one of the juice bars in the foyer and ordered her regular blend along with a nutrition bar and she was back in control.

Freya headed over to the business centre and printed the necessary form off, blacked out all details except the relevant part and lined up at Reception. The want and desire for him wasn't diminishing in the way she'd hoped.

It was building.

If anything, the thought of never seeing him again, of

it really having been just one night had her hesitate when the receptionist asked if she could help her.

'Could I check in for another night?' Freya asked.

'Sure.' The receptionist smiled. 'I'll just check that we don't have anyone incoming for your room. No, that's fine. Is there anything else I can do for you?'

'Yes,' Freya said. 'Could I have another card for my room, please?'

'Of course.'

It took just a few seconds but Freya knew what a monumental few seconds they were. The receptionist popped the card into a little wallet with Freya's room number on it, but instead of putting it in her bag Freya put it in the envelope along with her blood results.

'Could you please deliver this to room 2812?' Freya asked, determinedly not blushing, telling herself that the receptionist would not care or even guess what she was up to.

'Sure.' The receptionist smiled. 'I'll make sure that's done for you. Is there anything else I can help you with?'

'That's it, thanks.'

Oh, my!

Freya was all flustered as she drove to work and then parked in her reserved spot at The Hills.

It really was stunning. James had put everything into the place and the patient list read like a who's who of the film industry. They did a lot more than just cosmetic procedures here, though. From obstetrics to intensive care, everything was luxuriously catered for. Well, everything except eating disorders, but Freya was planning on addressing that.

Just not today.

Today she had this interview to get through, but there

was one good thing about last night, Freya thought—it had made a tiny email flirt seem pretty tame.

Yes, she'd get through the interview and then head back to the hotel and wait and see if lightning did strike twice.

Freya walked through the entrance into the foyer with its marble floor and pillars and stunning floral arrangements that were changed daily. A huge chandelier shed a calming light and Freya did her best to walk as if she hadn't been having torrid sex all night.

Sometimes the luxury of The Hills gnawed at Freya.

All her life, disparity had. She could remember tours of Africa with her famous parents. Seeing the utter poverty and then taking off in a luxury jet had felt so wrong. Being photographed with people who walked miles just for water and then watching her mother guzzling champagne for hours and bemoaning her menu selection later had made Freya furious.

Her questions to her parents had gone pretty much unanswered. 'Why are they hungry and we're not?' Freya had asked. 'I just don't get it.'

'We're doing our bit,' had been Aubrey's dismissive response, and her father, Michael, had had no time for his daughter's questions either.

'Freya, can you just, for five minutes, stop trying to change the world.'

James *had* listened, though, when Freya had approached him, and now things were finally getting under way.

'Hi, Freya.' Stephanie, the receptionist, smiled. 'James said to go straight through to his office.'

Freya nodded and promptly ignored Stephanie's instruction by heading for her own office. Yesterday evening James had finally sent Freya the bio for the cardiac paediatrician. He kept all staff files himself and there were no sneak peeks, even for his sister.

She wanted to read up on Zackary Carlton rather than explain to James that she was utterly unprepared for this interview. She was usually meticulous in preparation and her intention had been to read up on Zack over a leisurely breakfast this morning.

She opened up her laptop and accessed the file but looked over as there was a knock on her open door.

'Freya,' James said. 'I asked Stephanie to tell you to come straight though.'

'Happy New Year to you too.' Freya smiled at her brother. 'Stephanie did ask me to go straight in but I'm just having a quick read through.'

'I'll deal with all the medical stuff, you just need to explain the publicity side of things and get a decent bio, so we can get the word out he's on board.' James gestured for her to come to his office and Freya picked up her laptop and went with him.

'Is he on board, though?' she asked.

'He has to be. We need this guy,' James said as they arrived at his office.

Freya took a tentative seat and thanked the spanking gods he'd stopped when he had, and she started to scroll through the file as James spoke.

'I'll bring you up to speed—Zackary Carlton. Australian, drifter, arrogant bastard. He won't commit to more than three months anywhere but, God, he does magic with his hands…'

Indeed he did.

Freya looked at the résumé and very impressive bio. There was also a photo attached and, yes, she could concur, Zackary Carlton made magic with his hands.

It was Him!

The man she had thought was safely in one of the clinic's luxurious apartments reserved for visiting guests had been staying at the hotel all along.

Freya felt sick.

And doubly so when she thought of the daiquiri-laced emails she'd sent him.

It was the same man!

How could she possibly face him?

Quite simply, Freya couldn't.

'James,' Freya croaked.

'What?'

But Freya couldn't answer straight away. After all, how did she tell her brother that she'd had random sex last night with the cardiac surgeon he wanted to hire?

'Do you really need me here for this interview?' Freya attempted. 'I've got the worst hangover. I actually feel a bit sick.'

'You hardly drink.'

'Well, I did last night,' Freya lied. 'I really think I need to go home…'

'Freya, you couldn't even begin to match my hangover,' James said, and as the intercom buzzed and interrupted him, it would seem her nightmare had just arrived.

That sexy, somewhat scruffy man she'd met yesterday scrubbed up terribly well.

He was clean shaven and wearing a dark suit in a lightweight fabric. His hair was so thick that it was still a touch damp from the shower he had been in when Freya had run, and she wanted to run again now.

Absolutely she did. So much so that Zack watched her eyes dart to the door.

Poor thing, he thought.

Zack was also surprised, not that he showed it. He hadn't expected her to be on the interview panel and seeing her face pale, rather than redden, he did what he could to put her at ease.

'James.' He shook James's hand. 'It's good to meet you.' He turned then to her. 'Freya…'

She swallowed.

'I saw you in the brochure,' he explained as he took a seat, and her embarrassment turned into anger.

He knew who she was.

Which meant that he'd known who she was last night.

Zack's teeth gritted as he saw her eyes flash in anger and he realised that, far from putting her at ease, he'd made things worse.

James and his very real hangover were going through the mountain of forms that had come in about the man he would hopefully be recruiting.

'You said no to the apartment?' James checked as he caught up on some finer details. 'Was there a problem?'

'Not at all. I just prefer to stay in hotels,' Zack said.

'What about if you work here?'

'Same,' Zack answered.

James was one of the most in-demand cosmetic surgeons in Los Angeles and he looked over at Zack, who was highly in demand too, and he chose not to play games.

'Look, I'm not going to waste your time or mine with small talk. We want you on board. The Hills needs a cardiac surgeon specialising in paediatrics and we want it to be you.'

Zack gave an appreciative nod. He preferred people who cut to the chase.

'The only issue I have,' James continued, 'is that you're only prepared to commit to three months.'

'Then you have an issue,' Zack said, and Freya blinked

at his assertion. She had never met anyone so in command of themselves.

'We're going to be building your profile and reputation and for that we'd hope—' James started.

'Now there are two issues,' Zack interrupted. 'I don't need my profile or my reputation to be built, they already speak for themselves.'

'They do,' James said. 'But our partner, the Bright Hope Clinic, desperately needs funds. I see you're keen to do some pro bono work.'

'That's the main attraction.' Zack nodded. 'Working on these cases with top-level facilities is an enticing prospect.'

'How many charitable cases were you thinking of taking on?' James asked.

'One a week during my regular list and I'll also do a full pro bono list one Sunday a month.'

There was a lot of good that he could do in three months, Freya thought.

'I've brought Freya in to discuss the PR side of things.'

'I don't get involved with any of that.' Zack shook his head and looked at her and she recognised his voice. It was the one he had used on her that morning when they'd discussed the condom issue. He was now utterly engaged in work. Only Freya was scorching with embarrassment, because Zack was looking at her and talking to her exactly as if they'd never met. 'If I come on board I won't be doing interviews and happy smiley photos. I'm sure young Paulo won't mind. I hear no other surgeon wants to touch him.'

'Correct,' James said.

Paulo was five years old and had been brought to the Bright Hope Clinic from Mexico with his single mother, Maria. His complex cardiac problems meant that no surgeon would operate on him as it was very possible that he wouldn't survive surgery.

'It happens a lot.' Zack nodded. 'I take on high-risk patients that others refuse to go near.'

'I've explained that to Freya,' James said, 'and I've spoken with my colleagues. We're all agreed that we're not involving ourselves in charity to fudge figures just to make us look good. We want to do some necessary work and that involves risks.'

'I'd only operate if I thought there was a chance,' Zack said, and James nodded. 'I focus on the surgery,' Zack continued, and turned to Freya. 'That's it.'

He was arrogant, utterly immutable, and if Freya wasn't so angry that he'd known who she was all along, she could possibly have jumped on his lap and started purring.

She didn't know how she could simultaneously be embarrassed and cross while also being impossibly turned on.

'I work on short-term contracts and the patients benefit from that.' Zack further explained his stance. 'I might not be around to do the follow-up but they have my skill and attention in the operating theatre, or the OR, or whatever the terminology is you use here. In Nepal I was working in a field hospital so I can't wait to use the amazing facilities here. I am up to date with technology and I am also very hands on with the basics…'

Freya crossed her legs.

'Will you consider extending your contract?' James asked. 'If things are going well?'

'I'll speak with you after a month.' Zack conceded the smallest fraction. 'If I can commit for another three months, I'll let you know then. If I can't commit to more than that it will give you time to start looking. I am, though, going to Australia for a couple of weeks in April.'

'To visit family?' James asked, and Freya blinked as Zack simply didn't answer the question.

Yes, they were being told that what Zack did in his own time was his concern only.

And then Freya glimpsed again the joy of anonymity and the pain of it going wrong. Zack had told her in bed this very morning that he was running from stuff. Their gazes met briefly and then Zack flicked his away and she saw his neck stretch in slight discomfort.

Oh, she wanted to know this man.

'So, when could you start?' James asked.

'I just have to sort a couple of details out and then I can let you know.'

Freya's phone buzzed and James tensed. He loathed texts and Freya rolled her eyes at his familiar response. 'It's mine.'

She glanced in her bag and saw that it was Mila.

'Sorry about that,' Freya said.

'Do you have any questions for Freya?' Jack asked.

'I do but I'll speak with her later,' Zack said.

'I...' Freya was about to say she couldn't hang around but she knew she was just putting off the inevitable. 'Sure.'

'I'll send Zack through to you when we're done.'

'Thanks,' Freya said. 'It was nice meeting you, Zack.'

Her voice was pleasant and her lips smiled, but her eyes told him what a bastard he was.

She went into her office and her skin was crawling with embarrassment and she pressed her fingers into her eyes.

This was, very possibly, going to be the longest three months of her life.

'Freya?'

She turned at the sound of Stephanie's voice.

'Are you okay?'

'Just…' Freya took a breath. 'A bit dizzy,' she explained. 'It was a big night last night.'

'Sure,' Stephanie said and handed over some files and then left.

Great, Freya thought. Stephanie just loved to have her nose in everyones business.

No doubt, that Freya was dizzy, would soon work its way back to James.

Freya made the call she had just missed.

'How are you?' Mila asked.

'You really don't want to know,' Freya said.

'Oh, but I do.' They both laughed. 'I'll have to prise it out of you later.'

She'd better not! Freya thought.

'I just wondered if there was any news about that surgeon for Paulo? I've got Geoff, his cardiologist, here now and he's concerned.'

'He's in with James now. Let me…' Freya glanced up as James and Zack came to the door. 'I have to go,' Freya said hurriedly. 'I'll call you back.'

Zack noticed her cheeks redden and that Freya was flustered as she quickly ended the call.

'All okay?' James checked, because Freya was usually completely together, or did everything to appear to be.

She was behaving very oddly today.

'Of course it is,' Freya said. 'I thought you were giving Zack a tour.'

'We're going to do that at eleven. I've just got a patient that needs a quick review. If you can get started on the paperwork, and a head shot so that everything is in order, that would be great. We'll also need you to write up a press release and let the world know we've got Zack on board.'

'Sure.'

'Oh, and I'll ring the Bright Hope Clinic and see about getting the child looked at by Zack today,' James said.

'I can do that,' Freya offered.

'Do what?'

'Arrange his transfer.'

'Zack has to see the patient first.' James frowned. 'Since when did you start acting as a receptionist? I'll leave Zack with you.'

He walked out and Zack stood and watched as Freya picked up the phone.

'Could you give me a moment, please?' Freya asked.

'Sure,' Zack said, and stood there.

'I meant I'd like a moment of privacy, please,' she snapped, and Zack stared at her for a second before exiting her office, closing the door behind him.

God, this morning was a disaster, she thought as she frantically called Mila back.

'You haven't told James about me yet,' Mila said. 'Have you?'

'No,' Freya admitted. 'And he's just about to call the clinic.'

'It's fine,' Mila said. 'I don't generally man the phones. I'll have him put through to Geoff, but, Freya, he needs to know that the Bright Hope Clinic is mine.'

'I know he does and I am going to tell him.'

'If you can't do it face to face, just text him.'

'He hates texts.'

'Well, he's going to hate finding out that we're going to be working together a whole lot more.'

'Leave it with me.'

Freya ended the call, took a breath and opened the

door on her currently more overwhelming problem. Zack was leaning up against a wall outside and not looking very impressed to have been asked to step outside. 'Sorry about that! Come on through,' Freya said, and put on her bright corporate smile and stepped back to let him in. She waited till the door was safely closed for the smile to go and then she let him have it.

'You knew…'

'No.' He gave a small shake of his head.

'You weren't even surprised when you walked in. It was supposed to be one night, no names…'

'I thought you looked vaguely familiar but it only clicked this morning when I was in the shower,' Zack said. 'I just looked you up, and you were quite a wild child, it would seem.'

He thought of the photos of her collapsed and being carried out of a nightclub that he had seen, and he thought of the article he had read that spoke of drugs and alcohol and a lengthy stint in rehab.

'I'm not discussing this here,' Freya said. 'I don't bring my private life to work.'

'And neither do I,' Zack said. 'So go and get some blood work done and then tell me when I can start work.'

Where were the green eyes that had locked with hers last night? Oh, he was looking right at her but his expression was serious.

Grim.

'I'm a cardiac surgeon and this morning we had unprotected sex and it would appear you've had a habit. I'd like a little more than your word that you're not using.'

And she could only find a grudging admiration that he had the guts to address it directly.

'I've never done drugs.' She looked at him. 'I did have some tests last week and they all came back clear.'

'Has there been anyone since then?'

'Zack!'

'Freya, don't play coy. You've got all my lab results sitting on your desk, I haven't been with anyone since I had blood pulled, and I sure as hell haven't been in rehab. So I need to know the score.'

'I had some blood work for fertility issues and they ran the tests as routine. I was in rehab for an eating disorder. Happy now?'

'Well, *happy* isn't the word I'd use to find out the condom split with someone having fertility treatment, but, yep, glad to know we're both clean.'

'Well, you don't have to worry about the fertility issue. I haven't started treatment and I shot my ovaries.'

'Shot your ovaries?' Zack frowned and then got it.

Her eating disorder meant she couldn't have kids and he understood better now what she'd told him about running and trying not to.

'I'll let James know that I can start straight away, then.'

He gave her a nod and turned to go but Freya halted him. 'Zack, you won't—'

'Freya.' He turned around. 'I'd never say anything and, as you're about to find out, I'm a very different person at work.'

'Sure.'

'The only reason I am talking about last night in this office is because it's pertinent to work. What happened is not to be brought up or discussed, do you understand that?'

'Yes.'

It was the longest day.

All she wanted to do was go home and curl up with

her shame, yet, now that Zack was on board, her life had gotten busy.

His résumé was impressive on a professional level. He'd worked all over the globe, in both lavish and sparsely equipped hospitals. She looked up his hometown and her eyes widened when she read about the tiny population and how widely it was scattered.

Well, they could go with the country-boy angle, Freya thought, and then tried to picture herself suggesting that to Zack.

Ah…perhaps not.

What else could she find out?

It would seem that five years ago he'd been in Canada at an ice hockey match when a player had gone into cardiac arrest and Zack had successfully resuscitated him.

A couple of phone calls later and she was in touch with the player's own PA. Nothing was said, just a little touching base query to see if the player might be open to being flown to LA.

'He's on vacation but I'll get back to you at an *appropriate* time.'

God, no wonder people were tense, Freya thought as she realised that most of the world considered today not really a day for such calls, but at The Hills, though there were no scheduled operations, it was a work day as usual.

The staff up on the cardiac unit didn't say, *Oh, no, it's a holiday,* as they prepared the bed for Paulo to arrive.

And neither did the pilot of the luxury helicopter question it when, after examining Paulo and going through his tests at the Bright Hope Clinic, Zack called James.

'I've just spoken with Maria, his mother,' Zack said. 'I've told her that I'm still not sure if he's a candidate for surgery but I would like to run some more tests at The Hills. Their equipment is terrible.'

And so by three that afternoon a new little patient with black hair and eyes and a gappy smile was sitting in bed with his worried mother by his side.

And by five all Freya wanted was home and was struggling to hold it together when James knocked at her door.

'He's not very sociable, is he?' James rolled his eyes. 'I tried to schedule a meeting and he wants it to be held in a meeting room, rather than my office. Neutral territory, he said.'

Freya actually laughed.

'Three months in a hotel…' James shook his head. 'The guy's a well-dressed gypsy. I've asked him to come and get a security tag—can you please sort out his head shot?'

'I shall,' Freya said.

She'd sort it tomorrow.

All she wanted now was home.

CHAPTER SIX

So DISTRACTED WAS Freya that she forgot she'd booked in for another night at the hotel until she was nearly home. Freya decided to check in on Cleo and then head back, grab her stuff and just come home and sleep away the shame.

She really wanted to curl up and pull the covers over her head and hibernate till the end of March when Zack would be gone but knew that wasn't going to happen.

Freya parked and went up to her apartment, and as she opened the door she saw that her neighbour Red was just on his way out after feeding her little pug, Cleo.

'Hi.' Freya smiled.

'How are you, Freya?'

'I'm well! Thanks so much for this.'

'No problem. Are you back for the night?'

'I'm not sure,' Freya said, deciding she might just crash at the hotel. 'If I'm not here, can you let her out for me?'

'Of course.'

She had great neighbours and favours were freely given and returned. Red told her that he'd watched a movie last night with Cleo and had had a couple of beers.

Freya thanked him again and kept her smile on and wide, and only when Red had gone did she sink down onto the sofa and let her smile fade. She rested her head in her hands and just sat with the panic that had been chasing her all day since she'd worked out who Zack was.

'Oh, Cleo…'

She picked up her little, fat friend and told her all of it, well, not in specific detail, but that she'd lost her head last night to the most gorgeous of men on the promise they would never again meet.

'And now I have to work alongside him for three months. I don't know what to do.'

Cleo gave her no answers, just snuffled. The little pug was the absolute love of her life. James had bought her for Freya on her discharge from rehab and Freya had finally found a soul she could pour her heart out to.

'How can I face him?' she asked her fur baby.

Freya cuddled her for a good hour and then she carried her down for her little walk. Cleo was getting so tired and so old and Freya knew she wouldn't have her for much longer. James, because he was concerned how Freya would cope when her beloved companion died, had suggested, under the guise that it might give Cleo a new lease of life, that Freya get a puppy.

'I don't want another dog,' Freya said to Cleo as she popped her onto the sofa.

And not just because she could never love another dog as much as this one.

Freya wanted a baby. She was so over attempts at relationships and had no qualms about being a single mom.

She couldn't do a worse job than her parents had, and they'd been together till Freya was thirteen.

As she drove back to the hotel, Freya felt drained and exhausted. She'd had basically no sleep all night and the most awkward, uncomfortable of days and, joy, she had to face him again tomorrow.

She stood in the elevator and tried not to think of what had taken place such a short while ago and then she wearily swiped open her hotel door.

And there, just sitting there, drink poured, tie loose and wearing a triumphant grin, waving an envelope, was Zack. He just watched Freya groan as she remembered the room card she'd left.

'One night, no names?' Zack checked, holding up the envelope.

And when you've been truly caught, all you can really do is admit it.

'Two nights, then,' Freya said. 'I never said I didn't enjoy it.'

'Great, wasn't it?' Zack grinned. 'Well, thank you for the test results. That was actually very good of you. So good of you that I'm here to service you. Get over here.' He stamped the floor with his boot.

'I thought we were never to discuss it again.'

'At work it is never to be brought up,' Zack said. 'Out of work is a completely separate thing. So come here.'

Oh, now she understood better his stance on not answering questions.

'I can't,' Freya said. 'I'm so embarrassed.'

'Don't be.' He grinned. 'Come here.'

Freya made her way over and he pulled her onto his lap and she was just one burning blush but he was laughing.

'I really don't get involved with people I work with,' Freya said. 'Dating and—'

'Guess what,' Zack interrupted. 'I don't date.'

'Never?'

'Nope,' Zack said. 'So don't worry about awkward stuff and holding hands and all that sort of thing. Poor us, just sex.'

'Oh, no.'

'Liar, liar…' And her knickers *were* on fire because he slipped a hand up her dress.

'And you don't have to worry, no one will ever hear your secret from me.'

'Secret?' Freya frowned.

'That the uptight Freya likes a bit of no-name spanky on the down-low.'

'Zack,' she said, 'I didn't know till last night that I liked that…' She looked at him and could tell he didn't believe her. 'I'm not like that.'

'Freya, you emailed me a couple of weeks ago and said you were *very* single and not to tell James.'

'That was after a very difficult night being told by my soon-to-be-married and married friends that it would be my turn next. I'd had too much to drink and decided to live a little. Believe it or not, you're the only person I'd been with for the whole of last year.'

'Well, given we saw in the New Year downstairs, you had no one last year, Freya, so you have some catching up to do.'

'I don't think so,' Freya said, yet she was fighting not to undo the buttons on his shirt.

'I'm here for three months,' Zack said, 'and we're both as clean as whistles. Though, given we couldn't get through one night without tearing the rubber, you need to get on the Pill. I really don't want to rely on your shot ovaries, as you so fondly refer to them.'

'Zack, we can't.'

'But you know that we shall.'

Freya said nothing, he was so assured they'd be back in bed.

Sadly for her self-control, he was completely right— she was already unzipping him and taking it out.

'Don't tell James…'

CHAPTER SEVEN

ZACK REALLY WAS a master at keeping his private life separate from work.

By day he was remote, perhaps even a bit unfriendly at times. There were absolutely no shared looks, or exchanges, not even behind closed doors.

He dived straight into a very full schedule but occasionally Freya found herself back at the hotel, and, yes, the sex was amazing but they didn't talk much. She knew some stuff, but the information he shared was as generous as a waiter with the cracked pepper—there was never enough.

They lay there one morning and he was the monkey on her back, unknotting all her muscles, when he asked her something.

'Why are you avoiding James?'

'I'm not,' Freya said, and he felt her shoulders stiffen.

'Who were you speaking to on the phone the morning of my interview?'

'I can't remember.'

'You got all flustered.'

'Well, my one and only one-night stand suddenly had a name.'

'Tell me,' he said, 'were you on the phone to some guy?'

'A woman, actually,' Freya said, and he laughed.

'Do tell.'

'Nope.' The fewer people who knew about Mila and James's rocky past the better. And the fewer who knew about her and Zack's torrid present, all the better too!

'How come you stay here?' Freya asked as breakfast was served. Coffee for him, green tea and avocado smash for Freya.

'I just like it.'

'But you could have an apartment.'

'I don't want one.'

'Well, if you've got money to burn…'

'I've been sleeping under a mosquito net for six months,' Zack pointed out.

'Even so…'

Freya stayed quiet.

It wasn't money that was the issue, it was his transient existence that irked her.

Everything he had was in this room and he could check out tomorrow, Freya knew. His time in one place was only as long as his theatre list.

'Are you going to operate on Paulo?'

He didn't answer at first then he said, 'Is that PR Freya or Freya asking?'

'Freya.'

'Yes, I'm just trying to get him at optimum health first. You know his mother lost another son?'

Freya nodded.

'I don't want her losing two.'

And he watched as she cracked a very generous amount of cracked pepper on her avocado.

'My brother died nearly ten years ago. I saw what losing one kid did to my mother.'

For Freya, to hear Zack suddenly reveal such a vital

part of himself, it was like the cracker had fallen off the pepper mill.

'Zack! I'm so sorry to hear that.'

He grinned. 'Don't use your psychologist voice on me.' Then he asked her something he was curious about. She'd told him about her psychology degree and he wanted to know why she didn't use it. 'I know you're good at PR but do you really enjoy it?'

'I do,' Freya said, and she took a breath and told him her plans, wondering if he'd laugh. 'I want to start seeing clients. I wasn't ready to before.'

'Ready?'

'I just didn't know if I had any right to advise on eating disorders when I was working so hard on myself. I'm not sure I'm ready even now.'

'I'd say you're ready.' Zack smiled. 'I've spoken more to you than I have to anyone. You're very easy to talk to, Freya.'

'You're not.' She smiled back, glowing on the inside that he thought she could do it, but then she was serious. She really wanted to know more about him. 'How did your brother die?' she asked.

'How we all die,' Zack said, refusing to open up on her demand. He told only what he wanted to. 'His heart stopped beating.'

Aaagh! He was so frustrating but when he shared a part of himself it just made her want to know more.

'Head injury.' Zack relented a touch.

'Do you miss him?'

'I do,' Zack said, and he liked it that she didn't say that he must miss him. 'It's always there in the background, other times...' He shrugged, reluctant to explain it. 'My parents, though, still grieve every day.'

'That must be hard to watch.'

'Which is why I don't,' Zack said.

Subject closed.

And so she knew something but so little about him and that was proven on his second week at work as the day of Paulo's surgery neared and Freya wanted more for another press release.

'Everything you need is on my résumé,' Zack said, clearly less than impressed to be in her office.

'Well, can we go with the small-town angle?'

'It's hardly small,' Zack snapped. 'It's the size of LA.'

'I meant the population.'

'If you bring my family into this,' Zack said, 'then you'd better find a stand-in for Paulo's surgery. Oh, that's right, you won't be able to, so you can go and tell his mother why the clinic lost the only doctor prepared to operate on her son.'

'I'll take that as no!' Freya was used to difficult doctors. Putting the new brochure together had been difficult enough, but running promo on Zack took the cake. 'Can we just get a photo of you with him?'

'I don't work like that, Freya. You're not getting your cheesy photo.'

'Fine,' Freya snapped. 'What am I supposed to write?'

'That a child from the Bright Hope Clinic with a complex tetralogy of Fallot is being operated on at The Hollywood Hills Clinic and that—'

'I've already got that part, thanks.' Tough Freya wasn't working so she lodged an appeal with her eyes but he stared back coolly and dismissed her flirt. 'People like to see the human angle.'

'Then get it elsewhere,' Zack said. 'Because it's not coming from me.'

'I still need your head shot.'

'Take it, then.'

'Do you want to go and freshen up?'

'No.'

'You haven't shaved.'

'I don't shave on the week of a big operation.'

'Really?' Freya's eyes lit up. 'Zack, that's just the type of information people want to—'

'Freya,' Zack warned, 'I'm getting tired of this.'

She took out her camera. Usually she'd dab a bit of powder on the subject's face but she didn't think it would be appreciated in this case. Usually when someone was about to have their picture taken they would now be at the mirror, fixing their hair or rearranging their tie or stethoscope.

Zack just sat there and stared back.

'Can you at least smile?'

He gave her such a fake smile that Freya actually laughed. 'I'll settle for scowling.'

She got her shot and it was actually an incredibly good one.

'Can I go now?'

'Sure. Do you want to come over tonight?' she asked, but he just stood up and walked off.

Zack kept her hanging.

Oh, they'd agreed to never discuss the other side of them at work, but just some indication about where she stood might be nice.

Except she knew where she stood.

Zack had made it very clear.

He didn't come to her apartment. They played at his hotel.

Which meant she should not be sending her phone a copy of his photo and she should not be wondering, hoping, that night as she left work, if Zack was going to call.

He did.

Or rather he fired a text that night at eight to see if she wanted to meet at the bar of the hotel.

She wanted him to come to her home.

Freya fired back her answer.

Busy tonight.

She wasn't.

Well, there was always work she could catch up on but she was starting to struggle with her end of things.

No problem.

Zack's response annoyed her.

There were no questions or comment, no *I miss you*, no *Pity*. There was nothing to indicate that her response mattered to him.

It did.

Zack was actually relieved that Freya said no to coming to the hotel.

Well, not relieved in a sexual sense, just that he knew now that he would not be seeing her again socially for several days now.

They were getting too involved for his comfort. Too many times through the day he went to call her or saved something in his head to tell Freya about that night. Certainly he wasn't comfortable with the idea of going over to her home.

He didn't want a relationship.

He thought of his brother, chained till the day he'd died to a life that he hadn't wanted, and it would never happen to Zack. And yet he didn't feel chained when he was with Freya, he felt more open and honest than he ever had.

It was too much to think of now.

So, yes, he was relieved that she'd declined coming over as it meant that he didn't have to worry about his increasing feelings towards Freya for now. He would be in bed early tomorrow, preparing himself for a very long operation, and he would be living more or less between his office and Paulo's bedside for a couple of days afterwards.

If Paulo made it.

CHAPTER EIGHT

ZACK WASN'T AT work the next morning.

Freya noticed.

All night she had been fighting with herself not to change her mind and go over to his hotel but really, Freya knew, she wanted more than she was getting from Zack.

'How's it all going?' James asked as Freya dropped by.

'Very well,' Freya said. 'James, I'm just going to Bright Hope to take some posters over for them to put up.'

'Well, I don't want any posters put up here,' James said.

'I wouldn't tarnish your walls,' Freya said.

'Is everything okay?' James checked.

'Everything's fine. Why?'

'You just seem…' James shrugged.

'I'm just busy and I'm also…' Freya knew that she had to tell him. Mila's name was on the posters she was holding in her arms. If the operation was a success it was going to be all over the press and it was time that her brother found out what had been going on behind his back. 'James, we need to talk.'

'Sit down, then.'

James had always made time for her and she could see the concern in his eyes. She wished he'd stop being so protective, so ready to assume that at any moment she might slip back into ways of old.

Freya was tired of being treated like glass and didn't get why they couldn't speak openly about things.

That time in their lives hurt too much, Freya guessed.

And what she was going to say now would hurt James, she guessed too, which was why she had been avoiding it.

'You know the Bright Hope Clinic…'

'What now?' James sighed. 'Freya, my charitable cup does not runneth over. I do have patients of my own.'

'I know that. It's not about a patient, it's about the founder.' She swallowed. 'Mila Brightman…'

She watched as her brother's face paled but he said nothing at first, just sat there, but then he spoke. 'Mila wouldn't get involved in anything that has my name on it.' James shook his head. 'No way.'

'Of course she would for the sake of her patients.'

'How long have you known that she's involved in Bright Hope?'

'I've always known,' Freya said. 'We've stayed friends.'

'You stayed friends with my ex?'

'She was my friend too,' Freya said.

'And you didn't think to tell me any of this?'

'It was very easy not to, you avoid the charity stuff…'

'And Mila's the reason why I do!'

'I know that.'

'No, you don't,' James snapped. 'I thought she was overseas and all this time you two have been colluding—'

'We've been doing what we can for the patients. Come on, James, look at the amazing stuff that's happened already. Paulo's getting a chance, you've got a burns patient next—'

'Get out,' James interrupted.

'James—'

'I mean it, Freya.'

And she looked at her brother who had always been there for her, now telling her to get out.

'James,' Freya said in her most patient voice, 'let's talk about this.'

'Are you still here?' he asked. 'I'm telling you, Freya, get the hell out.'

Freya walked out his office and straight to her car. She had known that he wouldn't be pleased, but to be told to get out had been unexpected.

James couldn't choose who she was friends with.

Mila and he had been engaged, had been about to be married. Just because he had chosen not to go through with it, it didn't have to mean that she'd turn her back on Mila.

Freya was so upset that for once she didn't notice Zack walking towards her.

'Hey,' Zack said. 'Where are you off to?'

'I'm just taking some posters to the Bright Hope Clinic. I'm hoping—'

'Enough.' Zack put up his hand. 'I shouldn't have asked. I'm trying not to think about tomorrow just yet.'

'Sorry,' Freya said, and she thought of the pressure he must be under.

'About last night—'

'Not here, Freya.'

'It's a car park.' Freya pointed out. 'Look, how about tonight? I could cook something. Come over—'

'Freya, not here,' Zack said again. 'We agreed.'

'Sure.' Freya said, and walked off. She loaded all the posters into her car but before she drove off she texted Zack her address and again asked if he wanted dinner. Yes, she knew she was pushing to move things along to more than they had agreed to.

She wanted things to move along, though, Freya thought.

She hit 'send' and then headed south for the Bright Hope Clinic.

'Hi,' Mila said when she arrived, and then saw Freya's tense features. 'You told James.'

Freya nodded. 'I did.' Though it wasn't just James and their row that she was feeling so tense about. She was still waiting for Zack to respond. 'It didn't go down too well.'

'How is he?'

'Shell-shocked,' Freya said. 'I think he thought you were still overseas. He pretty much left all the research of charities to me.'

Mila was busy working and Freya put up all the posters and then left. As she stepped through the door of her apartment she had her answer to dinner and her invitation to come over in a less than effusive text.

No thanks. Zack

He hadn't even put the little exclamation mark that they jokingly used in their exchanges. Oh, Freya knew it was a tiny detail but she could feel that they were slipping away from each other and she didn't want them to.

I could come over to you.

Freya read what she'd just typed and she loathed herself for it. She looked at Cleo, who just stared back at her and told her to please not do it.

She hit 'send'.

'Sorry,' she said to Cleo.

And, rather more rapidly this time than last, she got her response.

Not tonight.
I've got a big day tomorrow.
Zack

And it was there, in that second, Freya knew, that things had changed.
Maybe not for Zack.
But for her.
It wasn't just sex for her.
Maybe it never had been.
For Freya, it felt a whole lot more than anything she had ever known.

CHAPTER NINE

THINGS HAD, IN FACT, changed for Zack.

He'd declined her invitation for dinner, when he actually wanted a quiet night in with Freya, but it moved them into uncharted territory and Zack did not have the head space to explore that now.

Instead, he hit 'send' and then walked into his office to speak with Maria, which was a very difficult conversation to have.

'You've told me all this,' Maria said. 'Many times. I understand that he might not make it…'

'Maria,' Zack said, 'listen to me. You have to hear this.' They went through it again, not just the risks of the procedure but how they would deal with Paulo tomorrow as he went under anaesthetic.

He left her crying with Sonia, a skilled PICU nurse, who would help Maria compose herself before she went back in to be with her son.

Then he got Freya's invitation to come over and sex really was the last thing on his mind and, annoyed at her persistence, he hit 'send' on a thanks, but, no, thanks text and then felt like a bastard.

She was too much, too intense, yet he liked it. Freya was complex and changeable, fragile yet strong, and he simply could not think about her now.

He lay in his hotel room, turning up the news to drown out the sound of a couple at it in the next room.

Zack couldn't face the noise and chatter of the restaurant. Instead, he ordered room service, looked at the steak he'd ordered and washed it down with a side of pasta and a couple of bottles of sparkling water. Then it was time to start thinking about tomorrow.

He knew that there was a lot riding on this operation being a success. The Bright Hope Clinic desperately needed the donations that would start to roll in if it went well.

But it wasn't that that truly daunted him. What did, was a five-year-old with a seriously messed-up heart. That was all there was space for in his head.

Zack checked in on his ego to make sure he wasn't being cavalier, and then he phoned Cale, a mentor and friend in Australia that he'd trained under, and went through his proposed procedure with him when Zack still couldn't wind down.

Then he slept a dreamless sleep, which he had trained himself to do on the night prior to a big operation, and instead of the car he'd hired he had a taxi drive him in.

He went through things with the anaesthetist and the OR team and checked in on PICU. Paulo had been admitted there last night so he would be used to it when he came around and also to have some medications administered overnight.

'Hello, you.' He smiled at his little friend.

'Zack!'

He was groggy from light sedation but Paulo smiled at his big friend. Zack looked over at Maria and could see she was about to crumble. 'Not now,' Zack warned, and Maria nodded, remembering the long talk they'd had yesterday.

'I'll see you in pre-op,' he said to Paulo, ruffled his hair and walked off.

He made his last checks and then he was told that Paulo and his mother were there and Zack went through.

'Did you just get more handsome?' Zack asked, and Paulo grinned his gappy blue-lipped grin.

'He's my handsome man,' Maria said. 'I love you, baby,' she said to her son. *'Te amo...'*

'Te amo, Mamma,' Paulo said.

Maria gave him a kiss and Zack watched as she cuddled him tight while the anaesthetist started to give the medicines and then, as Maria had tried so hard not to do, once he was safely under she broke down.

'Well done,' Zack said, and he gave her a hug. 'I will do all I can, Maria. You were wonderful with him.'

That was the hard part over with, thought Zack as he headed off to scrub.

Now came the harder part, eight hours of surgery.

He just hoped that today he didn't get to the hardest part—telling Maria that her beautiful son was dead.

The whole clinic was on tenterhooks throughout a very long day.

The estimated operating time of eight hours became nine.

Nine became ten and as it did so Freya's phone went again. She knew, even without looking, that it would be Mila.

She was right.

'I know you said you'd call with any updates but I'm going crazy here.'

'I've heard nothing,' Freya said. 'I'll be the very last to know if Zack has his way. He doesn't consider PR a high priority.'

'I know,' Mila said.

'It's been more than ten hours now. Is that good?' Freya asked.

'I hope so,' Mila sighed, and they chatted for ten as they hung out, waiting for news on Paulo. 'How are you and James doing now?'

'We're still not talking,' Freya admitted. 'He's been in, observing the operation.' Then she heard familiar footsteps and knew it was James heading for his office and Freya put the phone down on her desk and ran out.

'James?'

'I was just coming in to tell you. Paulo's in Recovery and Zack is, basically, amazing,' James said, and the animosity between him and Freya was temporarily cast aside for a moment just to breathe in the relief. 'It's still very early days, of course. I can see why no one wanted to touch that heart.' James shook his head. 'It was a mess, yet it was like watching a miracle to see him operate. Zack must have nerves of steel.'

And then he seemed to remember that they weren't talking and James gave her a nod and Freya went back to the phone.

'James said—'

'I heard,' Mila interrupted, and Freya sat silent as Mila started to cry. She truly didn't know if Mila was crying with relief over Paulo or hearing James's voice, or both.

God, James! Freya thought.

Why did you have to do what you did?

He had caused so much pain and though she loved her brother very much, it didn't take away her anger for all the hurt that he had caused to her friend. And the worst part of all was that Freya simply didn't know why James had decided to end things with Mila on their wedding day.

Freya sat there listening as her friend tried to pull things together.

'I have to go,' Mila said. 'Sorry to cry.'

'It's an emotional time.'

'Well, you've had plenty of them and yet you never cry,' Mila snapped. She knew how closed off Freya was and she could sense something was wrong. 'Freya, is everything okay? Apart from James and things.'

'Everything's...' Freya didn't even know where to start. Zack had made it very clear that the two of them were not to be discussed and she guessed there would be plenty of time for introspection once he had gone. 'I'll bring you up to speed soon enough.'

'I'm going to keep you to that,' Mila said. 'Can you keep me up to date with any news about Paulo?'

'Of course I shall.'

'What time are you going home?'

'I don't know,' Freya admitted.

It was the oddest night.

As the clock hit ten, Abi Thompson, a reconstructive surgeon who had viewed some of the operation from the gallery, stopped by for a chat.

'Zack was awesome,' Abi said. 'There was no music, no chatter. Zack just stopped for water and half a banana a couple of times. It was so intense in there, there were a couple of near misses—not that you'd have known from watching Zack.'

Oh, Zack knew *all* about the misses.

He stood at the end of Paulo's bed and checked all the charts with Sonia, the PICU nurse. He knew exactly how close Paulo had come to death and the surgery would certainly have turned that way if he hadn't had such state-of-the-art equipment.

Maybe he should put himself out there a bit more, if it meant more funds.

'He's going to be a doctor when he grows up,' Maria said, holding her son's hand. 'You wait, he's going to make you proud.'

Zack nodded. Maria didn't need to know that those were the words he dreaded, and why he didn't have pictures of smiling children lining a regular office.

He didn't want the strain on a teenager's face as their father shook Zack's hand and said a similar thing.

Paulo owed him nothing.

Not even a good life.

It was up to Paulo.

His life was his to live.

'Shouldn't you get something to eat?' Sonia broke into his thoughts. 'I could be calling on you a lot throughout the night.'

Zack nodded. 'I just rang down and asked for a meal to be left in my office.' Sonia was right, he had done all he could, and for now Paulo was critical but stable and there was a whole team starting to take over his care. 'I'm going to try and grab an hour of sleep,' he said. 'Page me for anything. Don't wait.'

'Sure.'

He headed down and just nodded to James, who was speaking with Stephanie at Reception. Zack was thankful that James understood he wasn't in the mood to speak and just gave him an appreciative nod back.

He walked past Freya's open door and she saw that but then Zack turned around.

'I'm not ignoring you,' he said. 'I just can't talk to anyone right now.'

'Fair enough.' Freya smiled. She was prickly about last night but wasn't selfish enough to address that now.

'I've spoken with Maria and she says you can release the news that he's out of Theatre.'

'Thanks.'

Still he didn't leave.

'Sorry about last night,' Zack said. 'I wouldn't have been much company.'

'That's fine.' And they looked at each other for a long time, Freya trying to bite back from saying that it didn't all have to be about sex, but well aware he didn't need her stuff now.

'For what it's worth,' Zack said, 'I regretted it.'

And Freya said nothing. She guessed more than ten hours of surgery counted for a little lapse and that he might also later regret saying what he just had.

'I'm going to get something to eat.'

'Well, whatever you ordered was just delivered to your office and, I have to say, it smells amazing. Go and have a rest,' Freya said. She had never seen someone look so wiped out.

'I'm just going to try and grab an hour and then head back up there.'

'Do you want me to come and wake you?'

'Would you?'

'Sure.'

Zack went to go and then again changed his mind. 'Freya, could you take my pager and answer it? If it's PICU come and get me straight away but if it's anyone else…'

'Sure.'

'Were you going home?' Zack checked.

'Nope.'

The food was amazing, and he ate it and then rehydrated with more water. Then he lay back on the plush couch and tried not to go over the surgery in his head. He just wanted to clear his mind.

Only he couldn't.

Twice during the surgery he'd thought he'd been wrong to take the procedure on. One hour in, he had considered closing but had pushed on. Five hours in he had been certain that the heart was too much of a mess, but it wasn't as if he'd had any choice by then but to carry on.

Watching that heart start beating when it had come off bypass, he'd heard the elation in the theatre but had said nothing.

Going in to speak to Maria, he had warned her that the next forty-eight hours were critical and had been guarded with his optimism. No matter how Zack had warned her that Paulo might not make it through surgery, that the little boy had survived was more of a miracle than Maria would ever know.

Since the operation started he had not been able to relax for a moment yet now he had to.

And Freya knew that too.

His pager buzzed and when she saw that it wasn't from PICU Freya rang the switchboard. 'He's not taking any calls unless it's PICU. If you can take a message I'll pass it on.'

'Sure,' the operator said, and Freya waited and then frowned when the operator came back on. 'It's his father calling from Australia, he says that it's urgent.'

'Okay,' Freya said. What choice did she have? 'I'll let him know.'

Freya knocked on the door to his office and went in. 'Zack,' Freya said. 'Zack!'

'Is it PICU?' He sat straight up on the second call.

'No...'

'Later, Freya.'

'It's your father,' Freya said. 'He says that it's urgent.' She handed his impatient hand the phone.

'What's going on?' Zack asked. 'Is it Mum?'

He saw Freya standing there and he glanced up, about to tell her, as she had once told him, that he'd like some privacy, given it was clearly a personal call. Then he saw the concern in her face and it wasn't intrusive.

Freya saw his glance and realised she was hovering, and tried to remember the rules, but as she went to go he caught her wrist and frowned as his father spoke on. 'Zack, I need some medical advice. Do you remember Tara?'

'Of course I remember Tara, Dad.' Zack's jaw gritted—did they think he had no soul just because he hadn't stayed? 'Is she okay?'

'Tara's doing well, it's the baby that's causing me some concern.'

'Tell me.'

'He was four weeks premature and breech but healthy, they kept him in for five days and he was discharged at birth weight.

'He's fourteen days old now and for the last couple of days Tara's been coming in. The baby seems to be doing well but…'

'Dad?' Zack frowned because his father sounded hesitant yet he was the best diagnostician Zack knew.

'He's eating, he's drinking and he's crying. I can't put my finger on it, Zack, but there's something not right. There's a big emergency north of here, only high-priority transfers…'

'What does Tara think?'

'Well, Jed—'

'Not her husband,' Zack said. 'What does Tara say?'

'She's distraught. She says that his cry has changed. I can't pick up a murmur...'

'Do you think that it's cardiac related?'

'I'm sure that it is,' his father said. 'That's why I'm calling you.'

Zack went through everything. There was some sweating but the temperatures were sky-high back home, and there was also a slight reduction in peripheral perfusion, his father felt, though that was more on instinct.

'I should get him seen but on all the guidelines he's non-urgent at this stage.'

'Dad, if he's got a ductal dependent lesion...' Zack didn't need to spell it out that these babies were all too often diagnosed at post-mortem. 'If you're worried then he needs to be seen straight away.'

'There's been a train crash and the air ambulances have to prioritise.'

'I don't think you called me for a chat,' Zack said.

'No.'

'He needs to be seen by Cale. I'll call him now and he'll put the baby's transfer as a priority.'

'There's not much to go on.'

'Yes, there is,' Zack said. 'You have forty years' experience, I'd take that any time. What's the baby's name?'

'Max,' his father answered. 'Zack, what if I'm wrong?'

'Then I'll be more than happy to wear it. I'll call you back when I've spoken with Cale. You tell them to send the air ambulance as a priority.'

Zack no longer felt tired now.

Freya sat on the couch as he rang his mentor and then called his father back.

'It's all sorted in Brisbane—they're expecting him. Cale's coming in and will be there when the baby arrives.'

'Thanks, Zack. We've got clearance for the air ambulance.'

Zack breathed out as he ended the call.

His head couldn't take it. The very thought of Tara going through what Maria had today brought it all too close to a personal level, which Zack did his best to avoid.

'That was my father...'

'I heard,' Freya said.

'Tara's my ex.' He shook his head. 'Too much?'

'No, I think it's nice that you care.' Freya really did, as the impression given by Zack was that he always walked away without a second glance.

'Well, my parents don't think that I do. They've both asked if I remember her, as if I've cut off the first eighteen years of my life. In fairness they never knew we were on together, but as if I'd forget a friend!' He was not going to spill it all out just because he was tired, and anyway PICU rang at that moment to alter some drug doses for Paulo.

'He's doing all the right things,' Zack said, leaning back. 'I'll go and review him at midnight, unless there's any change before then.' He glanced at his phone and Freya saw that he was looking at the time in Australia.

'What does your father think is wrong with the baby's heart?' Freya asked.

'Some defects aren't picked up at birth but when the ducts close at around a couple of weeks old... It might be nothing, it might be a small lesion that could have waited, but if my father's ringing me that means he's seriously worried because nothing would get that proud old bugger to call me otherwise.

'Hell, I still can't believe that he did.'

'Well, you are a cardiac surgeon.'

'Ah, but he'd prefer...'

Zack stopped and then handed her the phone. 'If PICU calls…'

'Sure.'

'Or are you going home?'

'I'm staying tonight.'

'You don't usually.'

'No.' Freya didn't know what to say—she was here because she wanted to be and Zack didn't know what to say because it was actually a help to him that she was.

He didn't like leaving his pagers with others, though he had to at times, of course.

He looked at Freya and he told her more about Paulo's operation. 'I thought twice I'd lost him,' he said, and for the first time he *told* another person what he usually put in his reports, though he gave Freya a far less comprehensive version.

'And if you put any of this in your press releases…'

'I never would,' Freya said. 'I'll email them to you first if you prefer.'

Zack nodded. It felt odd to be unloading thoughts that he usually kept in his head and he was grateful that Freya, when he was too tired to do so, drew a very firm line to ensure that nothing he said he could live to regret.

'I called a colleague last night to go through the surgery I planned and also to check that it wasn't my ego taking him to Theatre. He agreed that Paulo had a chance and that he'd proceed. It's actually the guy Tara's baby has gone to. I spent a year working on his team.'

'So the baby's in good hands.' Freya smiled.

'The best of hands,' Zack said, and then continued to talk about the surgery he'd performed. 'When I first opened him up I was just going to close him and then five hours in I actually wished that I had. I was just going through the motions for the last hours, repairing what I could, remembering all I'd been taught. When they took him off bypass and I saw that heart fill…' The adrenaline that had kept him going through surgery and again when his father had called was still surging through his veins.

'I can't switch off,' Zack admitted.

'When are your days off?' Freya asked.

'I'm not going to get out of this place for the next couple of days.'

'Do you want to come riding at the weekend?' It just popped into her head and then she realised that it might be open to misinterpretation. 'I meant horses.'

He grinned. 'I got that. Do you ride?'

'Not very well,' Freya said, 'but I love it when I do, it helps me to unwind… It was a part of my rehab.'

'Really?'

Zack was about to say no but then thought about it and, yep, a few hours on horseback to look forward to sounded like a good way of staying sane during these coming days.

Freya could see, though, that he was hesitant.

'No strings, Zack. I'm not asking you out on a date.'

She'd got his back-off message yesterday loud and clear.

'I know,' Zack said. 'Are we awkward?'

'A bit.' Freya shrugged slightly. 'But that's because I've never done this before.'

'Done what?'

'Not now,' Freya said, and shook her head. Now really wasn't the time to explain how she was struggling with her feelings for him and the inevitable ending of them. Maybe there would never be a suitable time to tell him all he was starting to mean to her, Freya realised. 'I'd better go.' Only that was the problem—she didn't want to go. She wanted to be here with him and she'd never stop wanting him.

The energy between them was undeniable.

How much easier would this all be if she could simply stand up and walk away, instead of looking down at him where he lay?

Zack broke his own 'nowhere near work' rule and his hand went to the back of her head to pull her down to his mouth. The long, slow kiss that evolved she wanted just as much he did. And it blew beyond proportion in a moment as her hand moved down. He put his hand over hers, though not to halt it, and then Freya moved her mouth back from the kiss and licked her lips as she had the night they had met.

She wanted to sink to her knees just as much and just as naturally as she had that first time, and he wanted ten minutes of pleasure to get out of his head.

'Do I stay or go?' She ran a finger along his erection.

'I thought you said you didn't like it?'

'A concession?' Freya smiled.

'Lock the door.'

She got up and did so and as she walked over he went to check in that she was okay with this, because he had pulled back from the two of them last night, Zack knew that. 'Freya—'

'I get it, Zack.'

They did not need a long discussion tonight so they got back to what they were supposed to be about—sex.

Yet this was different, because Zack never brought it to work and he never just lay there and did nothing except moan with want and relief.

And he could never have known that for Freya this was very different indeed; she had never done this before. She just knelt on the floor and lavished him, loving the pressure of his hand and how he held her hair tight. She took him first with her tongue and then deeper as her hand worked his base.

'More,' Zack moaned, just as she did on occasion, and she took him in as deep as she could and gave him the oblivion he craved.

He sank into bliss and she knelt up higher and her thighs were pressing together at the noises they made, and on the most hellish day and at a less than romantic coupling, they were possibly the closest they had ever been.

Feeling him start to come in her mouth, hearing his shout of relief, Freya came to the salty taste of him.

He made her dizzy.

Her cheek rested on his stomach and she gathered back her breath as Zack lay there. She took it as no insult that his hand slid from her head and he was already asleep.

There was one odd talent Freya had, from too many years hiding in the bathroom, and that was performing a quick tidy up. Freya dealt with all that, she popped it all back and retied his scrubs, then slunk out of his office and sat silent in her own.

And she admitted it properly then.

The life goals she'd had just a short while ago had all shifted.

She was thirty-one years old and, for the first time in her life, Freya was wondering if she was falling in love. Never could she imagine she'd have done what she just had. Zack had no idea that the thought had always made her feel ill.

Not now.

Was this love?

Very possibly, because the thought of him leaving, hurt enough for it to be.

CHAPTER TEN

'THE DONATIONS ARE pouring in,' Freya said to James early on the Saturday after a meeting about Paulo.

It was a reluctant meeting on both their parts.

James had been 'too busy' during the week to touch base, but given the publicity surrounding Paulo, James slotted in a brief catch-up.

Freya didn't want to be there either. It had been a very busy week with work, and Zack aside, the only place Freya now wanted to be was on the back of a horse and letting go some of the tension that she was carrying.

'Donations for the Bright Hope Clinic have started to take off,' Freya said. 'And the general feedback regarding The Hills is positive.'

'General feedback?' James checked.

'As to whether or not the charitable side will be maintained.' Freya pulled no punches. 'The Hills is high-end luxury and people are waiting to see if it's a gimmick.'

'We'd play with a five-year-old's life as a gimmick?'

'I've pretty much responded with that,' Freya said. 'Still, given that it was such a risky procedure, had it not paid off some people are asking if that would have been it for your foray into charitable work.'

'Well, they don't know me,' James said. 'Still, hopefully not every case will be as complicated. Maria has given her consent to Paulo being photographed, if you could get onto that now.'

'Sure. Will you be in one of the photos?'

'He's not my patient.'

'No, but I'm not going to get Zack to agree. I am working on another angle for him, though. I'm trying to get in touch with an older patient of his—perhaps he'll agree to that—but for now we'll just make it about what's so far been achieved and that's thanks to The Hills partnering with Bright Hope.'

Yes, Freya was tense.

In the absence of Zack, the best photo would be both Mila and James with Paulo, but Freya wasn't game to suggest that!

Things weren't great between them and she guessed now wasn't the time to be asking James about her starting to see her own clients, so instead they finished things up.

'Freya?' James said as she folded up her laptop.

'Yes?'

'I'm still angry.'

'I get that,' Freya snapped, 'but surely you can see that both sides benefit and I happen to care about both sides.'

'I'm not discussing that now,' James said. 'I'm just saying that, even though I'm angry, I'm still your brother and if there's a problem…'

'Problem?' Freya frowned.

'Stephanie said the other that day that you went dizzy.'

'And?' Freya rolled her eyes. 'I knew that she'd make a deal out of it. James, I'd been out all night for New Years Eve. I don't need your concern.'

'Well, like it or not, you've got it.'

'It's not necessary, James. I was ill a long time ago.' She had been seventeen! James still looked out for her, was still way too overprotective. 'Don't worry, if I need to see someone I'll be sure to ask for a referral.'

So much for leaving it! But that was Freya—once her mind was made up she could not just sit by.

He stared back at her and Freya wondered if he'd got the point she was making so she spelt it out.

'Why don't you have an eating disorder unit here?' Freya asked.

'We can't have everything.'

'Please!' Freya said. 'That's the whole point of The Hills, the patients have everything! Given that the majority of your clientele are in the public eye I'd say an eating disorder unit might be a necessity rather than a luxury. Yet you refer them elsewhere.'

'I'm trying to…' James started, but then he halted and it incensed Freya.

'Trying to watch out for me, trying to avoid hurts, trying to pretend it doesn't exist.'

'You're better now,' James said. 'Do you really need constant reminders?'

They were getting nowhere.

'I need to get on,' Freya said. 'I'll see you up there.' She walked out, collected her camera from her office and headed up to the cardiac unit, where Paulo was now being cared for.

He looked amazing.

The dusky colour of his skin on admission was now a gorgeous coffee colour and his lips were pink and he was sucking on an ice stick.

And then Zack came in with a colleague he was handing Paulo over to, to check on the boy before he headed off on a well-deserved weekend break.

'I thought you were off for the weekend!' Maria exclaimed.

'In an hour I shall be,' Zack said, and then looked at Paulo. 'I don't have to ask how you are, do I?' He glanced over and nodded to James and saw Freya and her damned camera. 'Is Maria okay with this?'

'Maria is,' Freya said.

'I'm delighted to have our picture taken if it will do some good.' Maria nodded. 'Will you be in it?'

'No, thanks.' Zack shook his head. 'I keep it up here, Maria.'

'Come on, Zack.' Maria was the one who pushed for him to join in the happy shot.

'Seriously.' Zack shook his head. 'Maria, I've got to go and see another patient now.' He was honest. 'They don't need my smiling thumbs up if it doesn't go well for them.'

It was who he was, Freya thought.

Private.

And she wanted in, though she was doing her best to hold back.

Zack went and wrote up his notes and his instructions for Paulo and his other patients while he was away.

He had a small baby on NICU that had already had more tests and procedures done than most people had in a lifetime but he had to go back up there now and order some more before he made a decision next week as to whether or not to operate.

'Hey,' Zack said, when Freya came out from the photo shoot. 'Are we still on for riding?'

'We're at work!' she reminded him.

'Sorry.' He rolled his eyes. 'I've got cabin fever. I've been here since Tuesday.'

'I've booked us for midday,' Freya said. 'We can meet there.' She gave him the address and Zack nodded.

She had meant what she'd said, Zack thought, about today having no strings attached.

Their paths had only crossed briefly since the other night.

For Zack it still felt like it had been a bit of a dream. Even when she had come in to wake him up when PICU had paged him a couple of hours later, Freya had made no reference to what had taken place.

He had brought them to work and the trouble for Zack was that he wasn't adequately troubled by it.

Even now he had asked her about riding, and there were people around.

He needed to reel things back, but it was very hard to do so when you were walking through stables and another person had come up with the very thing you needed.

It felt so good to get away and be doing something he probably wouldn't have made the time for today.

'I didn't know how experienced you were,' Freya said when he arrived. 'I said intermediate…'

Oh, no, he wasn't.

It didn't take long to establish that Zack knew his way around horses and he was given Bullet, who, Zack was assured, lived up to his name.

Freya had Camp, her usual horse, who was patient and steady and everything that she was not.

And they were off.

Together but separate and it suited Freya today. Half an hour in, Zack found a lovely flat length and went for a gallop as Freya just plodded along and looked at the stunning view, past the city and out to the Pacific Ocean.

Then she heard Zack coming back and he was all breathless and Bullet wasn't even sweating.

'I needed that,' Zack said, falling into pace with her.

'And I needed this,' Freya sighed.

After a while they stopped to eat the lunch Freya had made. It was nice to breathe in fresh air and eat but Freya was distracted. Her mind kept going over that morning and her conversation with James.

'You okay?' Zack checked.

'I will be,' Freya said. 'I had words with James.'

And they weren't anonymous strangers any more and this wasn't about Mila and James so she told him the part she felt she wanted to, even if it was rare that she spoke about it.

'James took on a lot when I was ill and now we can hardly talk about it.' She told him how he'd come and hauled her out of a nightclub and that she'd collapsed. How James had found a rehab place for her that was a bit alternative but which had suited her.

'How long were you there for?' Zack asked.

'Six months. Two of those were spent fighting.'

'Fighting?'

'Well, pretending I agreed with them while waiting for an opportunity to do another hundred sit-ups… And I loathed group discussions. Anyway, finally I saw the damage I was doing to myself, that I'd already done, and I decide to work on getting well. They didn't believe me at first. They thought I was just going through the motions to get out.'

'I'm not with you.'

'Well, I just made a decision without all the drama and crying and pouring out my fears. I just set a goal— to get well. So, yes, two months fighting, four months starting to get well and then a lifetime of keeping to it.'

'Is it a fight every day?' He was curious.

'Some days,' Freya said. 'James wants it cured, fixed, healed, and in many ways it is. I'll never go back to how I was.' Freya was sure of it. 'I know that. I just need healthier ways of dealing with tension. My parents said I was attention-seeking…'

'Were you?'

'Not at first,' Freya said. 'I was actually trying to get away from attention. My parents' divorce was everywhere, all their lovers were speaking out, and it was horrific. I know you think I'll go to any lengths for publicity but I'm nowhere close to them. They spoke not just about the rows and the money but about their sex lives, and their lovers did too.'

He said nothing and she was so glad.

'It was excruciating,' Freya admitted. 'I turned to food.' She told him about the reports about her being only a little younger and a whole lot larger than her father's latest girlfriend. 'I was a teenager and there were pictures of my stomach and thighs everywhere. I lost some weight and I lost it quickly, but instead of stopping I carried on, and then maybe I did get some attention from my mother...'

Freya thought back. 'Not for long, though. And so I'd go to clubs and drink and get into trouble and then sit at home and watch an interview my mother might be having about how hard it was to have a troubled teenager. And then I had my father, when I collapsed, on the one hand asking the press to respect the family's privacy while on the other getting off with some nineteen-year-old, knowing the press would erupt.' She still could not stand the memories. 'Everyone knew my business, or thought they did,' Freya said, 'but I had a bigger secret and I was on a mission by then—to get below a hundred pounds.'

'You met that goal?'

'I knocked that goal into the ground and kept going,' Freya sighed. 'James was beside himself. I think he was the only one in my family with any sense at that time.'

'You're usually close to your brother?'

'When we're not arguing.' Freya smiled.

They lay there for ages and then looked at the map. 'I'm going to take the long way back,' Zack said. 'And go fast.'

'I'll take the short way and go slowly.'

They met back at their cars, all dirty and smelly and worn out from the bliss of a day away from it all.

'Do you want to go and grab dinner?' Zack offered.

'No, I want to go home and shower and get changed,' Freya said. 'And then eat.' She deliberately didn't invite him this time but the very last place Freya wanted to be was back at the hotel.

She was tired of putting on the same clothes in the morning, tired of her hair smelling of the lemon ginger hotel shampoo.

It smelt fantastic on Zack, she just didn't want it on her.

Freya liked her own things and if he didn't want a part of them that was up to Zack.

'Sounds good,' Zack said. 'I'll see you there.'

And Freya did her very best as she got into her car, and drove off, not to look for a deeper meaning.

CHAPTER ELEVEN

FREYA LOST ZACK on the freeway and she stopped off at a store to get something more suitable for a tall, muscled male who had been riding than anything she had in her fridge, so he was already outside her place when she arrived.

Red was leaving the building as she got out of her car. 'Been riding?' he asked with a cheerful smile.

'Yes.' Freya smiled back. 'Red, this is Zack.'

'Hi, Red.'

Zack watched as Freya and Red chatted for a couple of moments. 'We're all getting together next Friday,' Red said. 'Are you in?'

'I'm in.' Freya nodded. 'I'll see you then.'

They walked up the stairs to her apartment and Zack was surprised when Freya opened the door and a small dog wagged her tail from the sofa and Freya went over and made a huge fuss of her.

'You have a dog?'

'I do,' Freya said. 'Her name is Cleo and she's a very old lady.'

It really was a home, Zack thought as he looked around. It was large, open-plan and very tidy, as he might have expected from Freya, but the dog he hadn't expected.

'Who lets her out when you stay with me?'

'Red or another of the neighbours…we all help out. Cleo's too old to go to a boarding kennel now.'

'You all get on?'

'We do,' Freya said. 'We try and get together once a month and have a barbecue or something.'

She had a life, a very, very nice life.

'I'm going first,' Freya said. 'Help yourself to a drink.'

'First?'

'I want a shower.'

And Zack got the hint that she wanted to shower alone and if he wanted a beer he'd better start liking the American stuff.

He sat out on a large balcony that looked towards the hills that they'd ridden in and it was actually nice to sit out on a balcony that didn't have one above and one below.

Freya rinsed off a whole day of riding and used her own shampoo and conditioner and soap.

She stepped out and, even with a steamy mirror, a very self-aware Freya frowned at her reflection.

She had spent way too much time examining her body but it was for different reasons that she examined it now.

Wiping her mirror with her towel, she saw the pink of her breasts and the swell of them.

She might be getting her occasional period, Freya thought, but then glanced at the packet of pills she had been taking since the second night in his hotel room.

And then she put it out of her mind.

It was nice to be able to open a drawer and pull on some yoga pants and a top rather than scrabble on the floor for last night's clothes.

And, she decided as she combed her hair and tied it

back, if she went to the hotel again, next time she was going to bring some things.

He might choose to live out of luggage.

Not she.

'Do you need a hand?' Zack called as she came into the kitchen.

'No, thanks.'

Freya grilled two steaks, one massive, one smaller, and she made a large salad. He watched her measuring everything out when he'd have just thrown it in.

Two spoons of oil, one of vinegar, a quarter of a teaspoon of salt.

And she could feel him watching her from the balcony but she wasn't going to change her routines for him.

She carried them out and he got the massive steak and she and Cleo shared the smaller one.

'I'm going to ache tomorrow,' Freya said. 'It's been ages since I rode. I should try and get around to it more often.'

'And me,' Zack said. 'It's been great. I'm so glad I didn't give it up.'

'Why would you give it up?'

'My brother was killed in a riding accident. You know how they say get back on the horse...'

'Zack!' Freya was appalled. 'This must bring up some—'

'Freya, it does and it doesn't. I love riding; I miss that part of home. I don't spend my life avoiding thinking about my brother. It's there every day, the same way your eating disorder is. Sometimes it's hard, sometimes not so much, but it's a part of your past that has to live with the you of today.'

It was always there, a part of her past that could never be erased.

The fattest pug he had ever seen looked up at him. 'Not a chance,' Zack said, but cut off a piece.

'Don't give it to her,' Freya said. 'She's already had some.'

'How old is she?'

'Thirteen,' Freya said. 'James got her for me when I came out of rehab.'

'Did it help?'

'Very much,' Freya said. 'I didn't have Red and a group of neighbours then and dogs don't forget meal-times…' She looked at Cleo and she could hear her heavy breathing. 'I don't think I'll have her for much longer. Still, the vet says that if she loses some weight it will help with her joints. I can't imagine my life without her.' And then she shook her head. 'Sorry.'

'For what?'

'We've been talking about you losing a brother…'

'Freya,' Zack said. 'Losing Cleo will hurt.'

'Yes,' she said. 'James thinks I should get another puppy before she dies.' She rolled her eyes.

'Are you going to tell me what's going on between you and James?'

'I told you.'

'You two haven't been talking since before this morn-ing.'

She looked at Zack and Freya was confused. She was handing over more and more of her life, yet she wanted to.

Freya trusted him, she knew nothing would go fur-ther than them.

'When we were growing up, as dysfunctional as it was, my parents were involved in a lot of overseas charities. They'd take James and me along for photoshoots and things but a lot of good was done. James pours everything into The Hills and it annoyed me that there was no charitable side to it. He avoids that sort of thing.'

'A lot of people do.'

'Not James,' Freya said. 'And last year we had a discussion and he said if I found the right charity and handled all the PR side of it, he'd implement it. Anyway, I didn't have to look far. I already knew about Bright Hope. My good friend Mila runs it.'

'I met her when I saw Paulo,' Zack said. 'Actually, there's another patient she wants me to review. She seems nice. Very dedicated.'

'She's James's ex,' Freya said.

'Oh! I see.'

'Believe me, you don't. She and I have remained friends. I just told James that Mila's the founder of Bright Hope.'

'How could he not have known?'

'Because the reason he avoids anything that combines medicine and aid work is because Mila is so heavily involved in it. She works overseas but she came back and started the foundation…'

'Was it a bad break-up?'

'The worst,' Freya said. 'He jilted her on their wedding day.'

Oh, there were so many reasons Freya didn't trust people.

She loved her brother very much but still had no idea how he could have done that to Mila, or why.

'Families!' Zack said.

'We all have them.' Freya shrugged. 'Even if we choose not to deal with them.'

He heard the slight dig.

'I'm going back in April,' Zack reminded her.

'I know. How's the baby doing?' she asked.

'He collapsed in the ambulance on the way to Brisbane. Cale said that they got to him just in time. But he's doing okay. He'll need more surgery when he's older, but fairly minor.'

'What does your dad say?'

'We haven't spoken about it.'

'You haven't spoken about it?'

'Freya…' He went to get another beer. 'Do you want one?'

'No, I just keep them there for Red if he comes to keep Cleo company.'

'Do you want—?'

'Nothing,' she said. She was actually incredibly tired but curious about Zack. 'Do you help out when you go back?'

'Help out?'

'With your father's practice.'

'I don't stay there long enough for that,' Zack admitted. 'You know how you said you couldn't stand everyone knowing your business—that's what home's like,' he explained. 'Everyone knows everything and it's great for some, but not for me. I swear I could not get out of that place fast enough. I used to come back in my breaks but it just got harder and harder to after Toby died. He'd worked in the family practice so his dying left a big hole, not just for his family.'

'On the community?'

Zack nodded.

'One they think you should fill?'

'They can't get another doctor, it all falls on my dad. As well as the fact I don't want to settle down and give them grandchildren. Toby was married and Alice wanted babies, and by now…'

'So if your brother had lived?'

'He didn't, though,' Zack said. 'But, yes, they seem to think that had he lived…' Zack didn't tell her the rest. 'Anyway, it's not the life for me.'

'What is?'

'What I've got,' Zack said. 'A few weeks here, a few months there.'

'Why can't a few months be *there* to give your father a break?'

Zack didn't answer.

'I still don't get why you'd choose a hotel over an apartment.'

'It suits me.' Zack said.

'Company on tap,' Freya said, and was cross with herself for the jealous note to her voice. She couldn't knock it as that was how they'd met after all.

Zack said nothing and Freya got up and sorted out the plates, which had Cleo wake up, suddenly interested. Freya knew why—he had saved some steak and thought she didn't notice when he sneaked it to Cleo.

'I'm going to take her for her little walk,' Freya said.

'I'll clear up.'

She was suddenly unsettled.

Freya carried Cleo down the stairs and took her for her little nightly outing and was, despite a wonderful day and one of the nicest evenings, very, very close to tears.

He didn't deny that his life was the life for him.

Zack didn't make excuses about his ways with women.

She wished, in some ways, that it had stayed at one night.

One amazing night instead of a very intense glimpse of a future that Freya now wanted but could never have.

She'd been snarky.

It had been but a few weeks and already she was counting down the days left to her, or biting her tongue to stop herself from suggesting he ditch the hotel and stay with her instead.

He'd decline, Freya knew.

And that was just as well because imagine having three months of bliss and...

Two months.

January would be over soon.

'I'm going to be without both of you soon, aren't I?' In the darkness all she could see was Cleo's pink tongue and her fur baby was out of breath from the shortest walk. 'You'd better be here when he goes,' Freya warned Cleo. 'I'm going to need you so much.' And then she picked Cleo up and buried her face in her fur. 'I'm so selfish...' Freya said, but she had to tell her friend. 'Cleo, I think I'm pregnant.'

Cleo just carried on breathing. Just kissed her face and cuddled in till Freya's panic subsided.

'I can't be,' Freya said to Cleo, who really didn't care if she was or not.

She just loved her back.

Freya carried Cleo back up the stairs and put her on the sofa with her toy. The kitchen was tidy and Freya could hear Zack in the shower and it hurt that it felt so nice to turn off the lights and get into bed and know that he'd join her.

Zack wasn't sure that he would.

Here was everything he had always avoided and possibly with good reason because it made him want more.

He should get dressed and go, Zack thought.

Cleo had got off the sofa and was crying at the bedroom door, and Zack grinned when he came out.

'I'm sleeping in her bed.'

'Yes, and she'll hate you for it, even if you did sneak her some steak. Did you have pets?'

'A few,' Zack said, and got into bed and tried not to think of home.

'I'm going to start seeing clients,' Freya said. 'I haven't told James yet, but I'm going to.'

'Good.'

'I was thinking about it while we were riding.'

'I was thinking too,' Zack said.

'About?'

He didn't answer. Zack just lay there thinking about plans that had been made and might be broken. He was tired, not physically, though. For the first time he was tired of hotels and starting over, of borrowing a horse, leasing a car, starting out, over and over again…

He wanted this but did not want it, just as he wanted home but not to be there.

Life was easier with no names.

Except *she* had one and, lying in the dark, he told Freya what he hadn't been able to over dinner.

'I stay away because I'm worried that I might end up telling them that Toby wasn't happy when he died,' Zack said.

He'd told no one.

Ever.

'We'd gone camping for a weekend,' Zack said. 'I was surprised when he suggested it but we just went out into the bush. It was great…'

Actually, no, it hadn't been. It had been revealing.

'He told me how unhappy he was,' Zack said, and Freya looked at him.

'He'd been going out with Alice since they were teen-agers and she'd stuck by him while he'd gone off and studied medicine. He said that he'd had enough and wanted to move to the city. So when I am home I get to hear how happy Toby was, what a great son, husband, doctor, and how happy he'd been there and how he'd hate how I've let them down. I dread that one day I'll tell the truth: that he was planning on getting out...'

'He was going to leave his wife?'

Zack nodded.

What a terrible secret to carry, Freya thought, to be the only one to know and be able to say nothing.

'That was why he'd asked me to go camping with him. He wanted my take on things.'

'And that was?'

'I had lots of takes on it,' Zack said, and he told her about that last night. 'Never knowing that the next day he'd be dead.'

'Was he killed outright?'

'No. At first I didn't think it was that serious,' Zack said, but then he shook his head. 'Actually, I think I did know because I activated the locator beacon and you only do that if things are dire. And then it was a matter of waiting.' The longest wait ever. 'I love the outback,' Zack said. 'You have never seen anywhere more beautiful and the remoteness is hard to comprehend, but it's a long wait if someone you love is dying.'

'How long?'

'Four hours,' Zack said. 'Well, three spent dying, one hour with him dead. I told him I'd live for both of us...'

And he had.

Zack crammed everything in.

Then he corrected himself in his head.

He had crammed everything in bar a relationship.

CHAPTER TWELVE

FREYA SLEPT WITH the windows open.

For everything Zack liked about hotels, windows that didn't open were one of the things that he didn't like. It was a cool night and the sound of rain was lulling.

Not for Freya.

She lay listening to the sound of night-time from her bed but with Zack by her side, and all in her world was shaken.

Beautifully so but scarily so.

And how could you let yourself simply enjoy something when you'd been told it couldn't last?

And what if what she had discussed earlier with Cleo turned out to be right?

'What's wrong?' Zack asked, as Freya turned to get comfortable again.

'Nothing,' she said.

'Liar.' He gave her a kiss. 'But that's okay.'

Side on they faced each other and Freya found that she was smiling. 'You smell of my soap.'

'I taste of your soap,' Zack said. 'If you need to check.' His leg hooked her in closer and he made her feel all shivery as his hand played with one tender breast. 'For someone who doesn't like it…'

'I didn't like the idea of it,' Freya said. 'I'd never done it.'

Zack frowned.

'So in my office...'

'It was my first time.'

They'd never spoken about it. Sometimes, for Zack, it almost felt like a dream, only he knew that it hadn't been. It had been the night they'd moved their relationship into work. They'd shifted the lines but in ways he hadn't even known at the time.

That should daunt him. No doubt it would soon—that something that was clearly an issue for her wasn't when she was with him. Zack had thought oral the least intimate of sex, but not now.

He slipped his hand between her legs and got the clamp of her thighs.

'I don't think I'd like it.'

'Do you want to try?'

Freya nodded.

Her mind was going at a hundred miles an hour. She wanted everything while she had him. Always she stopped him, beneath the belly button a no-go zone for that beautiful mouth and she didn't really know why.

'I'm messed up, aren't I?' Freya said.

'I told you the day I met you, that's how I want you.'

It hadn't been what he'd meant then but it made her smile now. He kissed her long and deep until her thighs were loose to his hand. And then he moved down and her breasts were so tender, and Freya was starting to know why.

Zack was oblivious, blissfully so. He just heard her fevered moans as he tasted and sucked and licked till she rolled from her side to her back.

He slid down and paid the same attention to her stomach and then he moved lower and kissed her right up her thighs, nibbling at the top inner part that she had once hated so much.

Zack made her body feel beautiful, every part of it. She had worked on herself for ever and had got to like herself enough, but he made her in love with it.

'I don't like it,' Freya said when his mouth took possession, and he ignored her and probed at the tension, tasting her deep, and then back to her clitoris. Freya closed her thighs on his head and he burrowed in deeper and her hips lifted from the bed. She resisted the pleasure, she stayed tight to his tongue, and then Zack moaned into her.

She felt the vibration, the sensual moan of his want and his turn-on. His focus was intent now and she succumbed. It was the most bliss she had known, to come to the most intimate kiss his mouth could give, to be tasted and adored.

There was no triumphant smile as his mouth lifted, Zack was the one crossing his own lines now. He came up the bed and kissed her mouth as deeply as he had her sex. He had Freya taste herself on his lips, his cheeks, and then he moaned again as he slid in. The same moan he had given earlier, and they stopped holding back because this wasn't just sex.

'I'm going to come,' Zack said, almost with regret, because he was loving her, he knew.

Freya was frantic, coming, while making this strange attempt to climb out of arms that would one day let her go. They were saying each other's names, breathing, kissing, coming and so close, so completely besotted and not fighting it now.

'Zack...' She pressed her lips together because she was going to say the wrong thing and lay there afterwards, with something else building—tears. The utter release to her body, the clearing of her mind and she was as close to crying as she dared to be.

He held her so hard afterwards. 'You can cry,' Zack said.

But she wouldn't.

He'd had everything, all of her, he had taken her right to the edge. She would not give him that.

CHAPTER THIRTEEN

'WHY DON'T YOU ditch the hotel?' Freya said.

She shouldn't have.

It was six a.m. and they lay chatting in the dark, talking about, of all things, his suits.

'How much can you get into a backpack?' Freya had asked. And then she'd found out he bought suits and that, when he moved on, he donated them.

'It's an expensive wardrobe.'

'Yeah, well, it's an up-to-date one.'

And then he'd admitted that living out of a backpack was tiring at times, and had been about to say he was actually looking forward to going home for a few weeks, when someone, namely Freya, who had to fix everything this very minute, suggested he move in.

'Freya,' he half groaned in frustration.

'I'm not asking you to move in as in live together, just…' She could have kicked herself.

Zack just lay there.

'Forget it,' Freya said. 'I was just thinking out loud.'

She simply could not stop thinking.

About them.

'I'm going to take Cleo out.'

Freya stood in her dressing gown and she was too

embarrassed to even admit to Cleo what she'd just said to Zack.

'It's not such a stupid idea,' Freya said hopefully to her friend, but then gave in.

Oh, it was such a stupid idea and, of all things, to say it on the first night that he'd come back to her apartment.

Freya was worried, though.

The clock was ticking on them and not only couldn't she imagine him gone, Freya was rather worried that there might be a more permanent reason for them to keep in touch.

She felt sick.

Not a nervous sick feeling, more there was a taste in her mouth as she came back into the apartment.

Cleo waddled into the bedroom and Zack lay there with his hands behind his head as she jumped up onto the bed.

He *was* leaving LA at the end of his three months.

He looked around the bedroom and he knew that he needed to head back to the hotel.

'Hi.' Freya came in, trying desperately to detract from the prior conversation. 'I just got an email…' Zack blinked, he was just waking up but Freya was in busy mode. 'Do you remember when you were in Canada a few years back and that hockey player went into cardiac arrest…'

Zack nodded. 'Why?'

'Well, I was just trying for a new angle. I get that you don't want to be photographed with kids, but he's here in LA and I thought we could get the two of you together.'

'Freya,' Zack said, sitting up, 'how many ways can I say it? I don't want to be a part of your publicity stunts. I'll do the surgery—'

'It's just such a great opportunity.'

'I don't get involved, Freya, they don't owe me any-thing. I do my best for them in Theatre, without obliga-tion. I don't want to be making small talk with some guy who had the misfortune to go into cardiac arrest in front of ten thousand people and now has to feel he needs to publicly thank me for doing my job.'

Freya gave a tight shrug. 'Just trying to do mine.'

'It's Sunday,' he pointed out. 'And I only get one off a month.'

'Sure.' Freya nodded. 'Do you want some breakfast? I'm just making some.'

'A coffee would be great.'

He lay back on the bed again. She'd be in soon with a needle and thread to try and hem him in.

Cleo waddled up to his chest and stared at him with her big pug eyes and he stroked her head and thought, What the hell am I doing?

He'd told her stuff last night that he could never have envisaged telling another, he had made love, and Zack had not lied with his mouth, he'd adored her.

It was all too close, and that was the very thing he avoided.

He didn't want to be tied down like his brother had been, or chained to a town as his father was. They were getting far too close and another couple of months of this and, Zack wasn't stupid, his leaving was going to hurt her.

And no hurt had ever been intended.

It was time to call it now, Zack knew, before they got in any deeper than they were.

Cleo bared her teeth.

She just stared him down and bared her teeth and it was as if she warned him, in or out?

'Cleo!' Freya threatened from the kitchen when she

heard her growl. She went to make coffee but found she had none. Coffee wasn't something she drank but she generally kept some in case of company.

She added it to the list she kept on her phone and divided the drink she'd blended into two glasses as the toast popped up. For the first time in the kitchen she was distracted. Freya had bigger problems on her mind than food for once, and instead of preparing just one plate she made two plates and smeared on some avocado she'd mashed and added a shake of black pepper.

She would go and get a pregnancy kit today and get this over and done with. Maybe when she'd found out it was a false alarm she could relax. Freya carried the tray into the bedroom. 'I was thinking, maybe today we...' And then she stopped because Zack was sitting on the edge of the bed with his jeans and boots on and he was pulling on his T-shirt.

'I need to get back to the hotel,' Zack said. 'There's some work I need—'

'It's Sunday,' Freya pointed out, just as he had.

'Yep.'

'Have some breakfast.'

'I don't generally eat breakfast, and definitely not green ones.' He was direct, he was honest and, yes, it hurt a lot. 'It's all too much, Freya.'

'Zack—'

'Freya, I made it clear. I don't want a relationship, I don't want someone making plans for my day off, I don't want to have to account—'

'You're annoyed because I suggested you move out of the hotel.'

'A bit,' Zack said. 'Do you know why I like it there, Freya?' He looked at the tray she'd prepared. 'If I ask for coffee, I get coffee. When I put the "Do not disturb" sign on the door, guess what? They don't disturb…'

They weren't talking about coffee or signs on the door, Freya knew.

Zack didn't want more than sex. He'd been upfront from the start and she had been more than willing to go along with it.

It was Freya whose wants had changed.

And he told himself that on the drive back to the hotel.

Last night had been amazing—dinner, conversation and the sex had been amazing.

More than amazing.

He wanted to turn the hired car around and go back there. He wanted to have a decent row with Freya and tell her to get out of fixing and sorting mode and get back to bed.

Zack got back to the hotel, went up in the elevator and then passed the maid with her trolley, doling out the toiletries so that five hundred guests smelt the same.

Then he stepped into the room that had been beautifully serviced and he thought about heading out for the day. Just driving into the hills, or taking a walk along the beach.

He needed a shower, he smelt of sex, or rather he smelt of Freya.

Zack did everything on his to-do list. He showered, changed and then headed for the hills, and that evening, instead of the hotel bar, he took a walk on the beach and told himself that this was the life he had chosen. And he had chosen it carefully. He never wanted to be tied down, or have people reliant on or beholden to him.

Not his patients—he fixed what he could and let them get on with their lives.

Not his family—they all knew how that had worked out.

And certainly he did not need someone who decided what he might want to eat for breakfast!

Damned cheek, Zack decided, and headed back to the hotel.

He went to the bar because it really was *that* easy, only it wasn't so easy tonight because he didn't want company.

Only his own.

Back up to his room he went and the bed had been turned down, the towels and soaps all replaced, and Zack found himself kicking his backpack across the room.

CHAPTER FOURTEEN

It hurt.

Far, far more than the end of any other relationship ever had.

Even though Zack would insist that it hadn't been a relationship because he didn't do that type of thing.

'Men!' Freya said to Cleo as they stood in the little patch of garden early one morning, more than a week after their row.

She carried her back up the stairs and, instead of driving to work, Freya decided that she would run. She hadn't run all week, she'd been huddled on the sofa at night with Cleo and busy with work by day.

It was time to get back on track with her schedules. She had a change of clothes at work so she pulled on her running gear and put in her earphones and did what she loved to do. She arrived at work all hot and sweaty and stood bent over in the stunning foyer.

'James will have you using the side entrance,' Zack said as he went past, and Freya actually laughed.

She wasn't the prettiest sight for such expensive surroundings but she felt better for a run and glad that she and Zack were almost at the point they could acknowledge each other in passing.

There was a meeting with James this morning and

Zack would be there so Freya wasn't looking forward to it one bit.

She walked into the changing rooms and they were like a luxury spa. There was soft music and fluffy towels and Freya stepped under the delicious jets of water, and then everything shifted.

Her legs started to shake and Freya went dizzy. She didn't even turn off the taps, she just stepped out and grabbed at a towel then sat on the bench with her head down.

'Freya?'

She could hear Stephanie's voice and it seemed to be coming from a long way off, except her face was right next to her ear.

'I'm okay,' Freya said.

'You're ever so white.'

'I just need a moment,' Freya said. 'Could you get me some tea?'

The waiting rooms all had oolong tea, kept warm by a candle, and little glasses and so it was just a couple of moments before Stephanie returned.

By then Freya had put on a robe and was a bit more together. 'Sorry about that,' she said.

'It's fine.' Stephanie smiled. 'I saw that you ran in. Maybe you overdid it.'

'Maybe,' Freya said, and she felt a twist of indignation because she knew the implication behind Stephanie's words. She had, in fact, underdone things this week but it was always there, the feeling that everyone was waiting for her to slide back into ways of old.

Even James, Freya thought.

They made no mention of her past, it was a subject he avoided, but she could always see the concern in his eyes.

She didn't need it.

And it was one of the things she had loved about Zack. He hadn't raised his eyes at her ways, he had let her be, and she missed him so much.

So much.

Over and over she tried to tell herself it had just been a few weeks, that you couldn't fall in love in that time, and certainly it wasn't love if it was unrequited.

'I'm fine now,' Freya said, and put down the little cup but she knew she was going to throw up. 'Honestly.'

Please, go now, she thought.

Freya walked to the toilet and closed the door and she wished Stephanie would leave as she threw up the tea as quietly as she could.

No, Freya thought, she hadn't overdone her run—the nausea and dizzy spells were for different reasons altogether.

How the hell could she ever tell Zack that she was pregnant?

Freya put on her grey dress with capped sleeves and did her hair and make-up and then she had another glass of tea and that one was nice.

Feeling a whole lot better, she arrived at the meeting room.

'Where's Zack?'

'He's talking to your good friend Mila about another patient.'

Freya ignored the dig and James got down to business and said he would, as of today, be starting to put out the feelers for a new cardiac surgeon to replace Zack. 'Already?'

'Well, if they have to give notice. I just asked Zack if he'd go on a month-to-month contract but he said no, he's out of here at the end of March.

'And it's February today.' James said.

So it was.

'Morning.' Zack came into the meeting room with no apologies for being late and she and James shared a small smile.

He was such an arrogant bastard.

Even down to the fact they were having this meeting in a meeting room when usually they'd be in James's office for such things.

Zack played second fiddle to no one.

'I can't stay long,' Zack said. 'I've got a patient that's not doing well on NICU.'

'I heard,' James said. 'Are you going to operate?'

'I don't know. I've just spoken with Mila and we're trying to schedule Bright Hope patients. I want to squeeze an ablation onto the end of the Sunday list on the fourteenth.'

'That's Valentine's Day.' James raised an eyebrow. 'Won't you want to be finishing up early?'

'Same as any other day to me,' Zack responded. 'I'm an incurable unromantic.'

James took a call and it would seem that it was a personal one because he excused himself and took it outside the office, leaving Freya bristling beside Zack.

'Can you not do that?'

'What?'

'Consistently point out…' She was so incensed. 'I get you don't do romance but your little digs are unnecessary.'

'I wasn't digging, Freya.' Zack gave a bored eye-roll at her drama. 'I've used the same line for ten years. I'm not changing *anything* for your benefit.'

That was a dig at the breakfast she'd made him.

Oh, yes, it was because there was a small smirk on his lips as she opened her mouth to argue.

Then she closed it and then, to hell with it, she said it. 'I'd run out of coffee.'

'What on earth are you talking about?' Zack asked. He knew full well!

'You overthink everything,' he said.

'No, I don't.'

They were sulking and turned on and now staring ahead as they sniped, and both wanted to be down on the floor.

He had told James with absolute certainty that he would not be staying on after March, but the certainty had been in his voice only.

'Freya.' James came back into the meeting room and his voice had them both turn around. 'That was Red.'

'Red?' Freya frowned. 'Why would he call you?'

'Because he can't get through on your phone.'

Red had James's number in case Freya was away and there was an emergency.

'He thinks you ought to go home. Cleo's not well,' James told her. 'I'll drive you.'

'I don't need you to drive me,' Freya snapped, and got up. 'I can drive myself.'

But she'd run to work this morning.

'What's going on?' Zack asked James when Freya had left, as if he didn't know, as if just last week a fat pug hadn't been asleep on his feet and then stood on his chest, baring her teeth at him.

'Her dog's not well,' James said. 'She's a vicious little thing.'

Freya or Cleo? Zack nearly said, but stopped himself. It was getting harder and harder to separate things, and he was glad when James gave up on the meeting.

'Can we do this tomorrow?' James asked.

'I'm in Theatre all day tomorrow.'

'Well, I've got a list this evening.' James was distracted and so too was Zack. 'We'll work out a time later.'

'Will she be okay?' Zack asked.

'Cleo?' James said, and Zack frowned as if he had no idea who James was talking about. 'Oh, you mean Freya. I think so, though you never really know with Freya. She always says that she's fine.'

Zack found her coming out of the changing room, where Freya had left her phone.

'You haven't got your car,' Zack said. 'Do you want me to drive you?'

'No, thank you,' Freya said. 'You're busy today. I'll get Stephanie to call for a car.'

Stephanie did so. 'Are you still not feeling well?' she enquired, and Freya wished she was more like Zack and simply didn't answer questions that she didn't want to.

'I'm much better. Thanks for all your help this morning,' Freya said. 'I just got a call and my dog's sick.'

'Cleo?'

'Yes.'

Freya knew that Red wouldn't call without good reason and she was right.

The vet was there and Cleo lay on the sofa and her little tail thumped when she saw Freya.

'She got all breathless,' Red said, and then the vet told her things weren't going to get better.

'She's comfortable. We can take her back to the clinic and put her on some diuretics...'

'No.' Freya shook her head. 'She hates being away from here.' It was why she didn't put her in boarding kennels and why she'd be grateful forever to Red because in the last year of an old dog's life she'd stayed home every night.

It was time, but not for Freya.

'Can I have a day with her?' Freya asked. 'Can you do it here?'

'I'll come by with Kathy at the end of surgery,' he said, and Freya nodded. Kathy was her favourite nurse at the vet's.

She thanked the vet and she thanked Red and saw them all out, and then she sat on the sofa with her best friend who'd seen her so far on her journey.

'I'm not getting another puppy,' Freya told her. 'I could never love it as much as you.' She buried her face in Cleo's black fur. 'And I don't think it would be very fair on the baby.' She looked into loving black eyes. 'Shall we find out?'

Poor Cleo had been listening to her rabbit on about it for days now and it didn't seem very fair that she died not knowing for sure.

And so she peed on the stick and came out a few moments later.

'I am,' she said to Cleo, and she accepted her lick and gave Cleo a kiss as the news sank in.

She was pregnant by a man who had hauled on his boots at the first sniff of commitment.

A man she was seriously head over heels about.

But more than that.

She was pregnant.

But more than that…

Freya wanted to be.

Zack knew that James had an evening theatre list and he actually drove past Freya's and wondered if he should go up.

It was odd, but when James had said that Cleo was vicious, Zack had wanted to laugh. That morning, back in her bed, he'd thought Cleo had been warning him to be nice to her mistress. Instead, it had just been a demented dog.

It was her demented dog, though, who had been with her through all the hard times. He saw Freya come down the stairs, carrying Cleo and chatting to her as she did her business and then back up the stairs they went.

And a little while later he saw a couple come down carrying a bundle in a blanket and he knew it was the vet and assistant and that Cleo had just been euthanised.

Zack, who never got close to anyone, was tearing up over a dog, or was it over Freya and how devastated she must feel right now?

This would not end up in bed, Zack told himself as he got out of the car. He was knocking on a door as a friend.

Or maybe it would end in bed, he amended, but only if she so chose.

Yet the woman who answered it didn't just surprise him—Freya shocked him.

'Yes?'

She was pale and rather angry looking but what floored Zack was that she was absolutely dry-eyed.

'I heard that your dog wasn't well…'

'And?'

'Freya?'

'What do you want, Zack?' Freya asked. 'Do you think sex is going to help?' She looked at him. 'You do, don't you?'

'I get what works for me might not for you. I'm just checking if you're okay.'

'Well, as you can see, I am.'

She slammed the door on him.

Screw you, Freya thought.

Oh, she wanted him but, more than that, she wanted Cleo tonight.

Her phone buzzed and it was a text from Mila.

James told me about Cleo.

Then it buzzed again and it was James.

Do you want me to stop by?

No, thanks, I'm fine.

How many ways could she say it?

Red came and drank all her beer and he cried and then he did all the stuff with the bowls and leads and things for her.

And finally a teary Red headed off and it left Freya alone in her apartment minus Cleo, and that had never happened before.

She'd done everything right by her, Freya told herself. Cleo had had the best possible last day.

There was only one thing about this day Freya regretted.

That Zack wasn't there.

Not for the sex, or the possible progression of them, and not because she had found out she was pregnant...

It would have helped to have him here tonight.

Just that.

CHAPTER FIFTEEN

IT WAS THE oddest week.

No Cleo to chat to.

All her routines felt shot and she didn't know how to tell Zack the news.

Beth had returned from her honeymoon and they had a girls' night in to go through the photos and videos.

The tamest girls' night in—they were all pregnant now, not that Freya let on.

She was detoxing too, she told them!

'The photos are amazing,' Beth said. 'Except these ones.'

There was Zack striding down the stairs and people turning and frowning in annoyance as he messed up the shot.

And Freya found herself laughing quietly and said that she wanted a copy.

'I can have the crowd edited out,' Beth offered.

The crowd being her friends!

'No, no,' Freya said. 'I like it.'

So much so that when they were all talking husbands she snapped a photo of it onto her phone.

After that it was a weekend for thinking. Freya knew that she had to tell Zack and she went by his office on the Monday morning but got cold feet.

'What I can do for you, Freya?' Zack said.

There were so many possible answers to that question that they even shared a smile, and Freya made up something about the Canadian hockey player. It served its purpose and diverted them back to work, and Zack got cross but it was clear the lust remained.

Freya was now swiping oolong tea every time she went past one of the waiting rooms just to keep hydrated as she was throwing up so often.

'How are you?' James stopped by her office.

Lately he seemed to be doing that a lot.

'I'm fine.'

'That doesn't mean anything with you,' James said, and finally he told her what was on his mind. 'You've lost weight.'

'James…' Freya took a breath. 'Every time I drop a couple of pounds it doesn't have to mean that I'm back to sticking my fingers down my throat.'

'I didn't say that. I asked if you were okay.'

'Well, I am.'

'Good.'

'And while we're discussing the great white elephant of my eating disorder,' Freya said, 'I'm going to start taking clients. I'm having some cards made up. If you want me to see them elsewhere…'

'Are you sure you're not taking on too much?'

'Do I ever ask you that?'

'Actually, yes,' James said. 'I've got to go. I've got interviews but I'll let the others know that you're taking on clients and if they have anyone who might benefit from a referral.' He gave a roll of his eyes. 'That's half my patient list, actually. I don't think you'll ever need to advertise.' He turned at the sound of Zack's footsteps coming down the corridor. 'I'm just about to start interviewing for your replacement.'

'Not now,' Zack clipped. 'I've got a patient to see.'

He was dreading it.

It was the last-chance saloon for this little mite and his parents knew it.

All night he had been up late, speaking with colleagues, going over and over the ultrasounds with the best brains he knew, and the response had been the same. Zack would take on more than most, which was why his stats came in low, but in this…

Zack sat with the twenty-year-old mother and the twenty-two-year-old father and he told them as best as he could that their son would die.

'Please,' Rachael begged. 'Can you at least try…?'

And he went through it all over again, how the damage was too much and that his system was collapsing.

'He'd very likely die on the operating table, or shortly post-operatively,' Zack said. 'Or he can die in your arms.'

Zack could have gone then but he stayed and spoke with them extensively and made sure they understood he wasn't simply giving up on their son.

Sometimes you didn't get a choice.

Like ten years to this day when his brother had died.

It was not a good day at the office!

Freya tried not to notice Stephanie's raised eyebrows as she came out of one of the patients' very luxurious restrooms. She hadn't been able to make it to the staff one.

Oh, no. If Stephanie mentioned to James that she'd seen Freya dash off to vomit, he'd have her back in rehab by the end of the week.

And there was Zack, handing over his pagers.

'I'm not on call tonight,' Zack said to Stephanie.

'I'll call if there's anything urgent with one of your patients—'

'I said that I'm not on call tonight.' Zack made things clear to Stephanie. 'I'm going to get blind.'

'Oh.'

He was as grey as she'd seen him and they didn't bother with small talk as they walked out to their cars.

'Freya…' he called her over as she climbed into her car.

'Yes?'

She turned and looked up at him and Zack stared back and he honestly didn't know what to say, he hadn't even meant to call out to her.

He needed her tonight.

Sex, yes, but he wanted all the rest tonight too. Hell, he'd even take the green smoothie.

Just because he didn't want to move in it didn't mean he had wanted it to end, and he was kicking himself for doing what he did best—put on his boots and get out.

'How have you been since Cleo?'

He didn't get to know that, Freya decided. 'It happens.' She went to walk off and then remembered what she'd heard. 'I heard that you lost a patient today. I'm sorry.'

'It happens,' Zack said, but it nearly killed him when it did, especially one so tiny.

Especially today.

And she looked at his eyes and he said not a word of that but she knew him, and she could feel the want between them.

And that was why she cried each night. She was crazy about this guy.

'You've lost weight,' Zack said.

'Oh, here we go. Have you been talking to James?'

'No,' Zack said. 'Is he worried?'

'James is always worried.'

'Does he have reason to be?'

'No.'

'Freya, I know I didn't end things very well.'

'There was nothing to end, Zack. It was sex, we both agreed to that and no more, and as good as it was…'

Their eyes met at the memory and Zack looked very deep into her eyes. She could not believe his gall.

Yes, his eyes were asking her for that.

'You are kidding me,' Freya said. Did he really think they were going to have sex?

She wanted to so much.

To just ignore that she was completely incapable of *not* wanting a relationship with this man and to take the good they had.

It would be too much for her heart to bear, though. She had to tell him about the baby, but she could see his anguish today so Freya chose not to now. She abruptly pulled back from telling him and got angry instead.

"You know what, Zack? We should have kept it at one night. Life was so much easier when I didn't know your name.'

Freya climbed into her car and reversed out angrily.

She wanted him—oh, my, she wanted him.

But even if they had kept it at one night, she'd still be in trouble.

Freya drove towards home and hoped she wasn't too late to let Cleo out and then she remembered that Cleo wasn't there any more.

And so instead of knowing that patient black eyes awaited her, Freya had the joy of chatting with herself on the drive home.

She had to tell Zack.

Or not.

He'd be gone in a few weeks.

And she'd been considering donor eggs and donor sperm after all.

But the donors *chose* anonymity and it would be her baby's right to know, and Zack had the right to know too.

He'd find out anyway soon.

Stephanie was gossiping, Freya knew, and she trusted Zack wouldn't just assume her eating disorder was back.

They had both messed up that first night but it wasn't a disaster. Freya had it all under control.

She was thirty-one, she'd planned to be a single mom.

Zack deserved to know and he also deserved to know that she neither needed nor expected nothing from him.

Freya took the exit and then joined the traffic heading into the city.

She left her car with the valet and walked into the hotel and went straight to the elevators. Down a familiar corridor she walked, but with a different type of anticipation knotting her stomach now as she tried to guess his reaction.

There was a 'Do not disturb' sign on the door and Freya ignored it and knocked.

'Read the sign,' came his deep, surly voice in response to her knock on the door.

'Zack, it's…' Freya started, and then she had the appalling thought that he might be in there with someone he might have met in the elevator or bar and was banging his brains out, as was clearly his chosen stress response. But then the door opened and he had on only a towel, and then she glanced over his wet, naked shoulder and saw that, no, there was no one else in his suite.

'I'm just in the middle of a phone call,' Zack said.

'Do you want me to wait outside?' Freya offered.

'No, no,' he said, and as she walked into his suite he

caught her off guard and pulled her in. 'Thank God,' Zack breathed into her ear, and then his mouth was on hers in a hungry kiss and she got a slab of wet muscle pressed into her. It took Freya a second to register that he had assumed she was taking him up on his earlier offer.

'Zack…'

'I won't be long,' Zack mouthed, and put his finger to his lips and then walked over to the bed and picked up the phone he had left there. 'Sorry, Mum, it was just the maid.'

He gave her a wink and took her right back to their first conversation and straight back to when all they had been was sex. Freya stood there, her dress damp from his freshly showered body, and she tasted him as she licked her lips. She was unsure what to do as Zack carried on the conversation and she could actually see the tension in his back as he tried to keep his patience as he spoke with his mum.

'Alice has a right to have a life…it's been ten years,' Zack said. 'She's allowed to go out on his anniversary. We don't have to sit behind the curtains to grieve.'

Oh, God, it was the anniversary of his brother's death, Freya realised as he spoke on.

On top of it all he was dealing with that today.

He went over and got out another glass and went to pour her some wine from an open bottle.

Freya shook her head and he held up some water and she nodded.

'Why don't we at least try it tomorrow?' Zack said. 'It's all set up and we can speak face to face wherever I am in the world.'

He gave Freya a smile that said, thank God he wasn't video chatting with his parents today, because the towel was lifting and Freya, who hadn't properly smiled in a long time, found that she was.

He put ice and lemon in her water and then, while dealing with this very difficult conversation, he came over and placed it down on the desk. And there was one little problem, Freya realised.

Well, there were many, many problems, but he thought she was there for sex and the sight of him naked and a taste of his tongue, and, as his hand slid around her waist, she was turned on.

Okay, sex tonight, and she'd tell him tomorrow, Freya thought, and she stood.

Or, should she just write 'I'M PREGNANT' on the little hotel pad now and pass him a note?

Zack was just finishing up the conversation as his fingers worked her breasts. Her thick nipples told him she was just on the edge of getting her period and he loved the intensity of a woman's orgasm then.

He turned off the phone and was just so relieved that call was over and especially that she was here and his response told her so.

This kiss was as fierce as their first. It was actually more so because it toppled her back onto the bed.

'Freya.' He said it like a moan. He was kissing her face, her mouth, her ears and just pressing her into the bed. Her legs were over the edge and he was roughly parting them and just tearing at her knickers but Freya was hungrily kissing him back.

She was holding his face just to keep it still enough for her mouth and then she gave in and held onto his shoulders as Zack seared inside.

His feet were on the floor and his elbows were each side of her head.

He thrust in hard and the friction they generated meant

neither would last. Her legs wrapped around him as all the hurts of past weeks were gathered into an intense peak.

Freya came, a beat before he did, and it was a come so deep that it demanded him now and Zack spilled into her.

'God, but I needed you tonight.' He really did, so much so that he had been planning to head to Freya's because living like this wasn't working. 'What made you change your mind and come over?'

He saw her rapid blink.

'Freya?'

'I came here to talk to you…'

'What?'

He replayed the events and Zack pulled out and got up and whipped a towel around his hips and looked at her as she pulled down her dress.

'I didn't force you?'

'Zack,' Freya said, 'I might not have come with the intention of sex but I was a very willing participant.'

'But you came here to talk?'

'Yes.'

He was still going over it in his head. 'For a moment there I thought…'

'Thought what?'

'It doesn't matter,' Zack said. 'What did you want to talk about?'

'I'm pregnant.' It came out faster than she'd intended. It just came out.

He hadn't had even a hint that she was and there was no lead in, no warning, she just hit him right with it.

'You choose your moments, don't you?' Zack said.

'I thought I'd tell you when you weren't working…'

'I lost a six-week-old today, I've got my parents on the phone, crying about St Toby and all the grandchildren they haven't got. Should I ring them back and tell them I'm going to be a father?' He went on, 'But do you know what, Freya? I wouldn't do that to them on a day like today!'

'I didn't know it was the anniversary of your brother,' Freya said. 'We don't know enough about each other to do specific dates.'

'I lost a six-week-old today!' Zack said. 'How's that for a specific day because his parents will remember it for ever!'

'Zack?'

'You know for a moment there, I thought…'

'What?'

He shook his head. He had honestly, for a moment there, thought that Freya had got him.

That the woman he had first met had come to his room and that they were back to the beginning but with history and understanding now.

That maybe, just maybe he'd met someone who things might work out with, but he had only just been starting to think like that and now Freya had her voice on.

'Now, I know it's a lot to take in, Zack, but—'

'Don't do your psychologist voice with me,' he warned. 'Don't tell me it's a major life-changing event, but that soon I'll—'

'It doesn't have to mean a major life change.'

He looked at her.

'Er…do I have a say here?' Zack checked, but there was still a warning note to his voice. Was she popping by to tell him she was on her way to get a termination?

'That's why I'm here, Zack.'

'Stop calling me Zack in that voice,' he hissed. Freya was using her patient and reasonable and very together voice and it was driving him insane.

'I'm not having a termination.'

Zack looked at her as she told him how things would be, as Freya, because it was Freya, dealt with all the current things on her to-do list.

'I was already looking into fertility treatments and donors—'

'Oh, so I've done my job, then.'

'You're being petulant.'

'I feel petulant,' Zack said.

'I'm just saying that I've thought this through and there's no need for you to get worked up. I can more than cope with single motherhood.'

'That's good to know,' Zack said, but with an edge. 'And do I get to see my child in this plan you've made?'

'If you choose to, then I'm sure we can sort that out.'

'You've really thought this through.'

'I have,' Freya said. 'So when I have your thoughts we can make plans or not.'

'Are you worried, upset?' Zack checked. 'You were just getting back into psychology.'

'I don't see that one has to exclude the other.'

'Are you—?'

'Zack, I'm thirty-one,' Freya interrupted his questions. 'I was already planning on single parenthood. I'm not going to fall in a heap.'

'You don't like it when the tables are turned, do you?' Zack said. 'You want my thoughts, yet you refuse to give yours.'

'Ask away,' Freya said.

'Okay, what about us?'

'You've made it clear that it's just sex you want from me.' Freya put her nose in the air as if she disapproved.

'You don't want sex?' Zack asked, and she didn't answer. 'Well,' he said.

Freya pressed her lips together. She didn't know this mood. He was arrogant and angry yet there was this twist of a smile on his face that she didn't get.

Zack carried on. 'With all this sexual attraction do Mommy and Daddy do it when you drop the baby off?'

'I don't know where this is leading, Zack.'

Oh, my God, Zack thought, she'd just used that voice again.

'Well, you've been so busy sorting it out I just wondered if that was covered already. Curious…' Freya could see that black smile was there and it wasn't the news he seemed annoyed with but her.

Freya.

The woman, Freya knew, that he didn't want to have a relationship with.

'What about the two of us?'

'No,' Freya said. 'I lived through my parents' unhappy marriage. I'm not inflicting it on my child.'

'You jump straight to marriage.' His grin was incredulous now!

'I'm saying that I don't want a marriage, I want to do this on my own. Of course you'll be entitled to access.'

'Do you know what I like about you, Freya?' Zack said. 'You've got it all worked out.'

Freya looked at him.

'Do you know what I don't like about you, Freya? That you've got it all worked out without me.'

'I don't understand.'

'That's okay.' Zack shrugged. 'I'm not in the mood for explaining. Well, thank you for dropping by.'

He stood and went to the door.

'Are you asking me to leave?'

'Yes.' Zack said. 'Pay attention to the sign next time. If it says don't disturb, don't disturb.'

'But we need to talk.'

'We already have.'

'I need your thoughts.'

'Well, you can't have them yet.'

He didn't have a clue what they were.

CHAPTER SIXTEEN

HIS HANGOVER WAS impressive and instead of going to The Hills, where no doubt Freya would be tapping her feet, waiting for him to snap to her snappy tune, he took the morning off and in the afternoon he drove into South LA and to the Bright Hope Clinic.

'Mila's not here today,' Geoff said.

'I know. I'm just dropping by to see how things are going.'

'Well, we're taking delivery of an MRI machine tomorrow,' Geoff told him, 'and I've just ordered a state-of-the-art ultrasound that might mean we can have intelligent conversations…'

It had been frustrating. Knowing that The Hill's equipment would give clearer answers, there had been a lot of doubling up. Zack wanted state of the art, so nearly every test Geoff had done had been repeated.

'It's great news about Paulo.'

'I think he'll be going home soon,' Zack said.

They went through the patients and Geoff said he'd like to come and watch the scheduled ablation.

'On a Sunday?' Zack checked. 'And it's Valentine's Day.'

'My wife is very understanding.'

Zack saw a few patients and then drove back to the

hotel and lay on the bed with his hands behind his head and tried to make some sense of his thoughts.

He took out his laptop and typed in a few things, and found out that their baby, assuming it had been conceived on the first night, was due on September twenty-fourth.

He stared at that date for ages and then he texted Freya.

Are you okay?

She took less than a minute to respond.

I've told you I'm fine with it.

He fired back another text.

Such a well thought-out response!

Then he deleted it, unsent, and wrote another.

Let me know if you need anything.

She wouldn't.

That much Zack knew.

He still couldn't get over how she'd been the night Cleo had died. Even he had teared up but not Freya. It was like she kept all her emotions inside and yet he had glimpsed them.

The things she'd told him, Zack knew, only he knew.

And it worked both ways. Freya knew stuff he would never discuss with anyone else.

She had pushed too hard and too soon, though, Zack thought, but then he smiled as he did so because that was Freya.

They were so good together and she had wanted more,

and he could see now that she'd probably known she was pregnant and starting to stress.

His head was a mess and there was no one he could talk to, or was it that there was no one he would talk to?

His alarm went off and Zack remembered that his mother had reluctantly agreed to try video-chatting.

Zack sat up and picked up the laptop.

This should be fun!

Not.

After a few goes, there was his mum and she had make-up on, when she only wore it at Christmas or on birthdays.

'How are you?' Zack smiled when he saw her.

'Sorry about yesterday.'

It had been a very tense phone call, which was why Zack could not have been more relieved when Freya had arrived.

'It's fine,' Zack said. 'Yesterday was a tough one.'

'You're right,' Judy said. 'Alice deserves to be happy.'

'So do you guys,' Zack said. 'Where's Dad?'

'He's in with a patient. Max is here for a check-up.'

'How is he doing?'

'Very well,' Judy said. 'I was thinking when you come home in April…'

And that was the trouble with communicating like this. Judy saw Zack close his eyes.

'You've changed your mind?'

'No,' Zack said, but how did he tell his mother that things here in LA had suddenly got very complicated? They didn't speak about such things.

Could they?

'I've got some stuff going on at the moment…'

'Another patient who needs you?'

'Isn't Dad the same?' Zack challenged, and Judy smiled.

'I guess.'

'Anyway, it isn't work that's complicated,' Zack said. 'I like someone.'

His mother said nothing.

'A lot.'

'You can tell me, Zack.'

'I'm trying to.'

'Times are changing.' Judy sat very composed and Zack looked at her, and then his face went right up to the screen.

'Do you think I'm gay?'

He could not believe it.

'You've never had a lady friend,' Judy said. 'Tara had a thing for you and you never did anything about it…'

He'd been trying to keep Tara's dad from knowing! 'Mum, just because I don't discuss my sex life with you it doesn't mean that I don't have one.'

'I'm talking about relationships. You've never spoken about anyone special and I was worried that you felt you couldn't tell me.'

'There hasn't really been anyone special,' Zack said. 'Till now.'

'And you said that there would never be grandchildren.'

'Because I could never see myself as a parent or tied down.' And he sat there in silence, with his mum doing the same, and it wasn't a strained silence this time. He didn't feel tied down with Freya. That morning when she'd suggested he move in had jolted the hell out of him but he could laugh about that now. That was Freya. It was who she was.

'I need to work a few things out,' he said.

'Well, I think that's a very good reason not to come home,' Judy said. 'Does *she* have a name?'

He was about to say 'Fred' but realised his mum maybe wouldn't get his joke. 'Freya.'

And he named her.

He named the woman who, wherever they were headed, was in his life.

Freya and Zack.

'I might have a glass of sherry tonight,' Judy said, and Zack laughed.

'I am coming home soon,' he told her, and he thought about what Freya had said. 'Maybe for two or three months. I could help out properly and give you and Dad a break.'

'That would be wonderful.' Judy smiled. 'But sort yourself out first and while you're at it, get a haircut.'

And the relationship that had always been difficult was being worked on and it felt good that it was.

'There's your dad. I'll let him say bye to Tara and then go and fetch him.'

'Can I see Max?'

He wanted to see the little guy.

After a little bit of drama getting them all on the sofa and the computer in place, there was Tara and they shared a smile.

'Thank you,' Tara said.

He looked at his ex and the feelings were only of friendship, both knew that, but all these years on and, without talking, this friendship remained a good one.

It wouldn't have.

Both knew that had they stayed together and made promises that the other could not keep, they would have been fighting and, yep, a divorce statistic now. And he thought of Toby and Alice. It had been such a hard secret to carry but Freya knew it now and that helped.

'This is Max,' Tara said. 'The cause of all this drama.'

'He looks fantastic. Cale told me that the surgery went really well.'

'It did,' Tara said. 'But apparently we got there just in time. He collapsed in the air ambulance.'

Jed, Tara's husband, spoke then. 'We're very grateful to the surgeon and to you and Dr Carlton. You made a great team.'

Even if they'd only managed to work as a team that once, it was a great result. Max was healthy and starting to cry and Tara tried to quiet him with her finger as Jed spoke on. 'I was saying to Tara it's hard to imagine now but in a few years he'll be bringing in the cows...'

And Zack looked at a very little infant that would probably be as strapping as his father one day and there were all the assumptions there, but then Tara spoke.

'Max gets a chance to be anything he wants to be now.'

It was a little message between her and Zack.

'He does,' Zack agreed.

'Thanks, Zack.' Tara smiled. 'You'll be sure to stop by when you're home?'

'I shall.'

They stood and walked off and left Zack with his dad. No doubt his mum was leading them through to the kitchen where she would have some cake ready. It was never just a visit for some patients.

Zack could remember most days getting in from school and the lounge would be full with patients, or families of patients.

'I've been tough on you, Zack,' his father said.

'And I get why you have been,' Zack said. 'I hate that

it all falls down to you. And I do worry about you retiring and what's going to happen but—'

'You've got your life.' His father said it without malice now.

'I'm good at what I do,' Zack said. 'I need to stick with it. In the same way you stuck with general practice when it was tempting to go to the city.'

He was about to tell his dad his plans to come back, maybe at Christmas so that he and his mother could have a break, maybe take a holiday, but then Zack smiled to himself. If things worked out, and he hoped that they would, there was no way his parents would be heading off on a holiday the next time their son came home.

Whatever happened between him and Freya there would, God willing, be a grandchild for them to get to know.

Now he just had to sort things out with the person who thought she had it all sorted out—Miss Freya.

CHAPTER SEVENTEEN

HE WAS OVER at Bright Hope the next day and made no effort to contact her. His lack of response to the issue drove Freya insane.

And then, when he finally did rock up at The Hills, at ten the next day, he gave absolutely no indication as to his thoughts or feelings.

He kept her on the boil all week and she made an excuse to have to be there on Saturday afternoon, just because she knew he was passing through.

Zack had brought cake.

A great big white chocolate cake piled with fresh raspberries and the staff all oohed and ahhed and Freya sat there in the staffroom, trying to fathom its meaning.

For a clue.

And she was still searching for the secret sign when he came down and sat opposite her, having cut a large slice. He crossed his long legs and gave her a smile.

'How are you, Freya?'

'I'm very well, thank you.'

'I don't usually see you here at the weekends.'

'I've got a consulting room for my future clients that I'm setting up,' Freya said, which was true, but she was hardly grappling with an Allen key. This was The Hills after all. Her consulting room was gorgeous. It was attached to her office and Freya had chosen the artwork and rugs to ensure that it was an oasis of calm.

'Did James mention that I might have a client for you?' Zack checked, and Freya shook her head.

'I haven't seen James today.'

'Her name's Emily, she's nineteen years old. I'm seeing her sister. Her mother mentioned some of the issues that she was having with her daughter. I gave her your card to give to Emily if the time was right.'

'Thank you.'

Stephanie stood up. 'Thanks for the cake, Zack, it was a lovely gesture.'

'No problem.'

She walked off and Freya sat there facing him.

'Cake?' Freya asked.

'Do you want some?' Zack pretended that he didn't know what she meant.

'No!' She wanted to know what the hell he was thinking. The only change in him she could see was that he'd brought in a cake and was sitting there with almost a smile on his face.

'Why cake?'

'Because I was pretty off the other day, with Stephanie and a couple of others, when the baby died, and I thought I'd apologise to the staff.' He stood. 'It's not all about you, Freya.'

'We need to talk.'

'When I'm ready,' Zack said. 'Anyway, what's the rush? You've already got it all worked out.'

She closed her eyes in frustration.

'And we've got months to sort things out,' Zack reminded her, and Freya shushed him.

'I want this sorted. I want to know what your plans are.'

'When I've decided I'll be sure to let you know.'

'You're the most annoying—'

'Why?' Zack said. 'I only jump into bed, Freya, not to your tune, and *my* thoughts are measured.'

'Meaning?'

'Just that,' Zack said. 'No deeper meaning. Do you want to go out for dinner tonight?'

She stared at him and she hated that, yes, she tried to search for a deeper meaning to his offer.

'Yes.'

'I'll pick you up at six.'

'Six?' Freya said. 'Are we going to check out the children's menu for future reference?'

He resisted laughing. 'I'm operating early tomorrow, I need to be in bed at a reasonable hour.'

And he still had that smile and she was still, still searching for deeper meaning in every word he said.

He set her on fire.

Just that.

She was squirming on the inside and wondering if it was dinner and bed together, or bed alone, if it was talking or what the hell went on in that beautiful head.

He gave her no clue.

Zack cut himself another slice of cake and walked out.

CHAPTER EIGHTEEN

'Hi…'

Freya had just put the final touches to the consulting room and was about to dash home for a quick shower and change before her very early dinner with Zack when the phone in her office rang.

She was about to let it go to the machine but at the last minute changed her mind and was very glad she had when she heard the nervous young voice.

'My name's Emily…' the young woman said, and then she started to cry. 'I've just done it again.'

'It's okay,' Freya said. Whatever Emily had done, it wasn't the point right now, but that she'd called was so, so important that Freya wasn't going to waste time questioning her for details. 'It's okay,' Freya said, and gradually the sobbing stopped.

Freya just listened as Emily told her that she'd had a massive binge and purge and her mother, who was already worried sick about her sister, had found her and was now upstairs, crying.

'She doesn't need this,' Emily sobbed.

And Freya thought of James, who had tried so hard to be a parent for her, and the anguish she had caused him, and how relieved he'd been when she had accepted help.

'Are you going to tell her that you've called me?'

'Yes.'

'Well, I think she'll be very relieved to know that you're talking to someone about it. So that might be something you can tell her when we've finished chatting.' They spoke for a few moments until Emily had calmed down. 'Why don't you go to bed now?' Freya said, knowing how drained Emily would be. 'Tell your mom that you're coming in to see me tomorrow at nine. Would that be okay?'

'It's a Sunday.'

'That's okay,' Freya said.

They spoke a little more, but Emily really was exhausted and Freya was glad that her plan for her to tell her mom and meet tomorrow seemed to have given her some measure of relief.

'I'll see you in the morning, Emily,' Freya said, and then the oddest smile came to her lips as she realised Zack was right and she had her *voice,* as he called it, on. 'I'm looking forward to meeting you,' Freya said, more normally. 'Go and speak to your mom and then get some rest.'

Of course Freya did some major overthinking on the drive to her apartment, wondering if she should have seen Emily straight away, but there was no real point speaking at length with Emily tonight.

And she wasn't going to be available every time her clients had a binge.

Emily needed to rest and recover and get some fluid into her…

Tomorrow.

They would start this journey tomorrow. She just hoped that Emily didn't cancel, because that first reaching out was the hardest, Freya knew.

She had fifteen minutes to get ready when she had

hoped to have thirty and Freya quickly peeled off her clothes as she turned on the shower, and then everything stopped.

There was a flash of blood in her knickers and when she saw it, Freya was convinced she was losing her baby.

Everything in her world just stopped and the panic that hit had her frantic. She felt like a cat with its tail on fire and yet she was crouched, kneeling on the bathroom floor, and, she was sure, losing her baby.

'No...'

And it was all her fault, for not eating, for running, for riding and for believing for a second that she could be a mother. She felt as if she was back to being seventeen and being told her bones would one day crumble and she'd never be able to have babies. Freya was sobbing so violently she couldn't breathe.

She could hear someone knocking at the door and then they started to knock louder.

Realising that it must be Zack, Freya pulled a towel from the rail and, barely covered, wrenched open the door. Zack saw her red face and angry eyes and this time there *were* tears streaming down, and because she was scared she hit out with words.

'Panic over!'

She never cried, never, ever, but they were pouring out now. 'I've lost it,' she shouted to him, 'so panic over.'

'Freya...' He was so calm that it angered her further. 'I'm not panicking.'

'Because you don't care!' she screamed. 'You didn't want it anyway.'

'Tell me what's happened.' His voice was normal and it made hers sound all the more mad. 'Are you bleeding?'

She was holding up a towel and Zack looked down at her legs and there was no blood that he could see.

'Yes, I'm bleeding!'

'Come on.' He led her to the bedroom.

'I knew I'd never be able to have children, after all I've done to myself, I don't deserve them, you don't want them…'

And he remembered her 'I shot my ovaries' comment and knew that all the loathing was aimed at herself.

'How much are you bleeding?'

He was still so completely calm, like a doctor, only he wasn't the doctor, he was the father, and she hit out at him but he caught her wrist.

'Freya.'

She'd lost her towel on the way to the bedroom and Zack sat her on the bed. 'How much bleeding is there?'

He looked at her and she seemed fine and he heard the shower and went in and the relief that hit when he saw the tiny amount in her knickers was something he kept to himself.

She was a mess.

He looked out towards the bedroom where Freya was sobbing and curled up in a ball on the bed. Whatever he had intended to say over dinner would just have to wait now. He turned off the taps in the shower and went back into the bedroom.

'Have you got any cramping?'

'No.'

'Everything might well be fine…'

She couldn't believe it.

He tried to unfold her tight body but she wouldn't relax and he got onto the bed beside her and brought her cold body against his warm one. 'Match my breathing,' he said. It was like he was breathing for her, and she tried to get hers as slow and as deep, and then he spoke.

'Freya, a lot of women get bleeding. You're eight weeks pregnant—'

'Six.'

'Eight,' he corrected her, and smiled because sometimes he forgot she had studied brains, not bodies. 'You add two weeks.'

How was he smiling and talking, all calm and normally? It wasn't because he didn't care, she knew that because he was lying on the bed beside her and she was curled into him.

'Did you lose anything in the shower?'

'I didn't get into the shower,' Freya said. 'I just saw the blood and I freaked...'

'I know,' Zack said. 'Well, I don't exactly.'

How was she, Freya wondered, breathing and calming and starting to believe that it might be okay? And then she remembered how she had lashed out before. She had utterly lost it and it was something she had fought all her life not to do.

'Turn over,' Zack said.

'I can't,' Freya admitted. She had screamed, she had hit at him, she had shown her worst self and all her fears, so how could she turn around?

'We can go now and do an ultrasound,' Zack said.

'No.' Freya shook her head. 'I don't want anyone at The Hills knowing.'

'They won't. I can—'

'No.'

'Have you got an OB?'

Freya nodded. 'I'm seeing someone for fertility so I already had an appointment for next week.'

'Do you want to call her and see if I can drive you in?'

'On a Saturday night?'

'Yes,' Zack said, and then he realised she might be stalling. 'Do you want to see someone?'

'I don't want to find out,' Freya said. 'I just want one more night where I might be pregnant. I don't want to know yet if I've lost it. Zack, I've wanted a baby for years, I honestly thought I couldn't have one. I wasn't using you.'

'I know that.' Zack said. 'Who told you that you couldn't have children?'

'In rehab,' Freya said. 'I had stopped menstruating and they said I was a shoe-in for infertility, osteoporosis…'

'Whoever said what they did was trying to scare you into eating.' He could only guess the damage of knowing for years that you'd blown your chances. 'They were clearly talking rubbish.'

She turned around in his arms and he gave her such a nice smile.

'Do you really think that I might still be pregnant?'

'Well, I haven't been anywhere near that field for many years but, yes, a little show, no cramping. I think it happens a lot.'

And from hell she entered calmer waters.

'I'm sorry you saw me like that.'

'I'm very glad that I saw you like that,' Zack said, and Freya closed her eyes.

She knew she'd blown any chance for them now.

They lay for a while, Freya becoming calmer, Zack thinking.

'You've got surgery tomorrow,' Freya said, remembering he'd said he needed an early night.

'I do.' Zack nodded. 'I'll go and make something to eat.'

Zack got out of bed and went into the kitchen. He bypassed all the little measuring cups and returned to the room with two bowls of lovely creamy pasta.

'We'll go and get you checked tomorrow. I'll call work and have them reschedule.'

'No.' Freya shook her head. It was his Sunday list and there were so many people relying on him. 'Unless things get worse, you ought to go in. I've got to go in as well—I've got that young girl coming in. It would be awful for her if I cancelled.'

'Okay.'

His calm control seeped into her.

They ate pasta and she found out he could cook and they lay in bed and watched a movie. Zack noticed something on the bedside table and asked what it was.

'Cleo's ashes.'

'No way!' Zack said, and he wasn't Mr Nice now. He took them straight out to the lounge room. 'I can't sleep with them next to me.'

'Are you staying?'

'Freya?' Zack checked. 'You really think I'd leave you now?'

'You want an early night.'

'And you need one!'

He got into bed.

'You're not keeping the ashes, are you?'

'I don't know.' She looked at him. 'Are they freaking you?'

'A bit.'

'I didn't think anything freaked you.'

'I'm a mystery,' Zack said.

He turned out the light and he was back in her bed when she had never thought he would be.

'I really am a mystery,' Zack said. 'It turns out that my mother thought I was gay.'

Freya laughed and she told him about the hotel events coordinator checking him out when he'd checked in.

It was nice to lie in the dark, talking and then falling quiet.

'So, is this what parenthood looks like?' Zack said when she was feeling a little calmer. 'Knot in your chest and no sex?'

'I think so.'

He rolled over and put his hand on her stomach and then he said the nicest thing.

'I want you to be pregnant,' he said. 'I want the baby.'

And, because it was Zack, she knew he meant it.

'So hang in there, little one.'

CHAPTER NINETEEN

ZACK WOKE TO the mechanical sound of a blender.

Get used to it, Zack, he told himself, because he might well be waking to it for the rest of his life.

And so, as Freya pulped broccoli and blueberries and did what she had to do to keep her place on this planet in order, she watched as a dishevelled, barely dressed, sexy Australian came out of the bedroom and walked out of her apartment.

And there was no feeling of dread when he left this time.

A few moments later he walked back in with a tin of coffee, which kept his part of the planet in better order, and they shared a smile.

'Why do you have coffee in your car?' Freya asked.

'Because I like coffee in the morning and I know you don't have any.'

'Oh, so were you intending on staying last night.'

'Yep,' Zack said. 'Well, I was hoping to.'

And she opened a cupboard and showed him that she had indeed bought some coffee since he'd walked out.

He wrapped his arms around her and Freya let herself be wrapped in them.

'Any bleeding?' he asked.

'None.'

'How do you feel?'

'Better,' Freya said.

She couldn't give a completely honest answer—that the world felt safer just for the fact that he was next to her now. Freya knew she pushed too hard, pressed for too much, and so she held it back.

Last night he had taken such precious care of her and she let herself be grateful for that.

And so, getting into separate cars, they both waved to Red and then headed into work.

Today would be a day that Freya found out how strong she was. Maybe pregnant, maybe not, and with her love life in shreds because Zack was probably thinking what hell was he going to have to co-parent with after her outburst last night.

And yet she could put it aside.

Not too far aside, because her issues came with her, and they were needed today.

For a long time Freya had doubted if she was the right person for this role, whether she had healed herself enough to offer advice to someone going through what once she had.

Now, though, she knew it was a lifelong journey and she had learned so much on this path.

'Thank you for seeing me,' Emily said.

They sat in her new consulting room and Freya told Emily she was her first client and then she told her a bit about herself. Emily said nothing at first, but when Freya mentioned her food diaries Emily got out her phone and Freya looked through it.

It was like looking back on her own life.

The exercise, the obsessions with food, the waiting till someone left the room so you could do a hundred more sit-ups. The agony of a cruel disease. Emily wasn't dangerously thin but, Freya knew, the real battle was in her mind.

They went way over time and Emily laughed at the end when Freya said, 'You're far more honest than I was.'

'There's no point lying any more,' Emily said. 'I just want to get well.'

Emily would do well, Freya was sure.

They made another appointment for Thursday.

'Just to let you know,' Freya said, 'that I might be having a small procedure during the week, so if I have to reschedule, that's why.'

'I'm sorry to have messed up your Sunday.'

'You didn't,' Freya answered. 'It's good to get things under way.'

Emily left and Freya knew that she felt better and so too did she. It had been right to come in today and it was time to get something else under way. Freya was ready to know now if she was pregnant or not so she called Hilary.

'Hi, Freya.'

'Sorry to call on a Sunday,' Freya said.

'I doubt you would without reason,' Hilary said. 'What's happening?'

'I got a positive pregnancy test, I think I'm eight weeks,' Freya said, 'but then last night I bled.'

'Are you still bleeding?'

'No.'

'Any pain?'

'No.'

And Hilary asked some more questions just as calmly as Zack had. 'Do you want to come in today?' she offered.

'On a Sunday?'

'Babies keep their own schedules,' Hilary said. 'I tend

to write off uninterrupted weekends, that's why my vacations are taken overseas.'

As Freya walked out she stopped at James's office. He was a complete workaholic and catching up on some files.

'Hi,' Freya said.

'Freya.' He gave her a nod. 'How was your first client?'

'It went well,' Freya said. 'It was helpful to me too. Thank you, James, for all you did for me back then.'

'I'm your brother,' James said. 'Freya, are you okay?'

'I am,' Freya said.

She was.

However it all unfolded, Freya knew now she would be okay.

'Are we talking?' Freya checked.

'Not really,' James said.

But he was still her brother.

He gave her a smile and Freya headed off, alone, to find out about the baby.

She loved Zack and however he felt about her, or them, she could handle it. That he wanted the baby meant the world. If they got the chance to be, they would be good parents. Possibly unconventional ones, with a father who drifted, but when he was there, Freya knew that he'd be the best dad in the world.

Freya sat in her car for a moment before going in and when tears came she shed them.

She just let them happen for the first time as she acknowledged she wanted *this* baby so much.

This father.

This miracle.

This life and this world.

And so in she went.

Hilary didn't care a jot about Freya's leaking eyes, she was more than used to them.

And then, just as Freya thought she had everything a little more under control, the most appalling thing happened, and she found out she *really* had no control.

'I feel sick,' Freya admitted, as her green breakfast rose in her stomach, and her eyes scanned the room for an exit, because, in her head, no one could see her do that.

'Are you going to throw up?' Hilary asked.

Absolutely she was.

In front of another person!

And there was no chance of being tidy and hidden any more.

'Feel better now?' Hilary asked a few minutes later as she calmly took away the little dish she kept for these moments.

Freya did.

She had cried, she had thrown up, she'd had a cuddle from Zack and had seen her first client, and she was being open and honest and vulnerable.

It was the oddest of days, the scariest of days, but it felt like the nicest too.

'I'm nervous to find out.'

'I know,' Hilary said. 'Have you had a lot of vomiting?'

'Loads,' Freya said. 'And I got dizzy after my run. Should I have run?'

'Do you run regularly?'

'Yes.'

'Then that's fine. Just keep hydrated. You know your body.'

'Sex?' Freya asked.

'Well, that's how babies get there in the first place!'

They talked. Hilary knew already about Freya's past

medical history and after answering some of Freya's questions Hilary had a few of her own.

'I admit that I'm confused. I'm looking at your notes and we were talking sperm and egg donors the last time I saw you.'

That seemed like such a long time ago.

'Do you know who the father is?' Hilary asked, and Freya laughed at the directness of the question.

'I nearly didn't,' she admitted. 'It was supposed to be no-name sex.'

'Ha-ha.'

Oh, and the world was so much better when you were honest.

'He's amazing,' Freya admitted.

'Does he know about the pregnancy?'

'Yes,' Freya said. 'He knows and we both want the baby. It's just a bit too soon to know if we want the other…' Then she looked at Hilary and a doctor's office doubled as a very nice confessional. 'Well, it's not too soon for me to know but I'm trying not to push and crowd him and just see where we go…'

And it was time to see where this pregnancy was going.

She lay on an examination table and Hilary had a feel of her flat stomach and squirted some jelly onto it.

'I guess you might not see much,' Freya said, 'given it's so early and…' She chatted to keep herself busy. 'I haven't got a full bladder, so you probably can't—'

'Freya,' Hilary asked, 'how often do you menstruate?'

'Every six months or so.'

'Okay.'

And she was going to be told, no, Freya knew, that maybe in six months or so's time that she could try again.

'Well, when your ovaries zap, they really zap,' Hilary said, and she turned the screen. 'What do you see?'

A map of the moon, Freya thought, and then she looked again and there was a tiny person, a little bean with a head and a flicker that was a heart.

'Oh…' Freya said, because she was still pregnant.

'And over here,' Hilary said, and Freya's eyes wandered to another little bean and another tiny flicker that was a heart.

'Beautiful embryos,' Hilary said. 'Their position is perfect and their heartbeats are strong and a very good rate…'

'Their?' Freya checked.

'Twins,' Hilary said. 'So get used to throwing up for a few more weeks. Double everything, including the fun.'

'What about the bleeding?'

'It happens,' Hilary said.

'Do I have to be careful?'

'I tend to find they stay put or not whatever a woman does,' Hilary said, 'and these two look to me like they're staying put.'

It was overwhelming, completely, and then she thought about telling Zack that they were having twins and she blew out a breath.

Oh!

Drifter Zack the father of twins.

Freya had blood taken and then thanked Hilary and walked out to her car. She sat there for ages and then drove home and collected Cleo's ashes, feeling so glad she'd told her about the baby before she had died.

Babies!

'Thank you,' Freya said, as she scattered her friend's ashes into the huge ocean that separated the US and Australia. It was a place Cleo had loved in younger days and she was so glad of the gift James had given her at a time she had been so fragile.

Not any more.

Oh, it was a sad and happy day and she watched the sun go down and thought of Cleo. Her phone rang and when she saw it was Zack she answered it.

'Hi,' Freya said.

'You've been crying?'

'Yes, I scattered Cleo's ashes. And don't you dare suggest I get another dog.'

'How was your client?'

'It went well,' Freya said. 'How was surgery?'

'Long,' Zack said. 'Have you had any more bleeding?'

'No.'

'That's good.'

'It is,' Freya said. She didn't want to tell him the news over the phone and decided she'd wait till a more suitable time than the last time she'd dropped a bombshell on him.

'Freya, can I ask a favour? I'm going to be here all night and I'm supposed to be speaking to my parents. They're driving me mad with video chats. Can you stop by the hotel and bring my adaptor?'

'Adaptor?'

'I don't have US appliances and I need to charge my laptop.'

'Oh.'

Well, what chance did they have? Freya thought as she let herself into his hotel room. Even their plugs were wired differently.

Freya lay on the bed in a room that had seen an awful lot of their goings-on and she smiled and decided to pinch a shirt of Zack's while she was there.

And if he found out, so what?

It wasn't a crime to be in lust, she would tell him, and just leave the love part out.

She drove to The Hills and there was Stephanie and her beady eyes at Reception, mentally weighing Freya as she walked in.

'Hi, Freya.'

'Hi.' Freya smiled but didn't stop for conversation. Thanks to Stephanie, rumours were flying but because of her past everyone was assuming her eating disorder was back with a vengeance, rather than that she had a baby on board.

Two babies.

Yikes!

She knocked on his office door and waited.

'Come in,' Zack called, and as she stepped in it dawned on Freya the possible real reason she was here.

The room was in darkness and, as memory served, Zack liked to unwind after Theatre.

'Did you get me here to give you…?' And then she stopped because there was a table and two places laid and it was lit by a candle.

'Valentine's Day,' Zack said.

Oh, so it was.

'What did you get me?' Zack asked.

'You don't do Valentine's Day,' Freya said. She had truly forgotten. 'Actually, I've never done Valentine's Day either.'

She sat at the table and as lovely as it all was it was dark.

'I can't see you,' Freya said, and he laughed and put the lights on.

'Better?' Zack said, and now that she could see him it was. 'I got you a present.'

'Are you trying to make me feel extra-awkward for forgetting?'

'I am.' Zack nodded.

'And then I'd have been accused of being over the top,' Freya said.

'You are over the top, Freya,' Zack said, and he went behind his desk and very carefully carried over a very large box.

Oh, no, Freya thought as he gingerly put it down, and she watched for movement and saw all the little holes punched in the box so it could breathe.

He'd got her a puppy.

And she didn't want one.

'Zack...'

'Just open it.'

'I don't want it.'

'You might when you see it.'

Twins and a dog, Freya thought. Well, there goes any chance of freedom for the next two decades. And what about dog jealousy? And yet of course she was going to love her new puppy, it had come from Zack after all and it beat stealing a shirt from his wardrobe.

Freya pulled back the lid, waiting for a wet nose to peek out, but it didn't.

The box was empty, except for one thing.

A ring.

'Where's my puppy?' Freya croaked.

'A puppy is a big commitment and you have to be very sure,' Zack said. 'Pretty much the same with this. Freya, marry me.'

'Oh, Zack.' Freya shook her head. 'It's way too soon...'

'Not for me.'

'You're marrying me because I'm pregnant.'

'Freya! One, we don't even know if you're pregnant.

Two, I don't marry women because they're pregnant. In fact, usually I'd be running out of the door the same way you did the morning after we met.'

'Really?'

'I'd have had morning sickness just at the thought,' Zack said, 'but I don't feel like that with you. I am in love with you. You're the most difficult, grating person I have ever had the fortune to get to know, and I want to get to know more of you, every day.'

He gave her a smile, a self-satisfied one. 'You'll never be able to top that,' Zack said. 'Even with all your PR skills, you have to concede that I have organised the best Valentine's Day and you, Freya, didn't even get me a card.'

'Of course I did,' Freya said, and she went into her bag and handed him a card, well, a photo of her ultrasound.

'Top that,' Freya said, and she watched his mouth open as he realised that, yes, Freya was pregnant and, because he could read ultrasounds far more easily than Freya, he saw straight away that it was twins.

He laughed.

He had everything he'd dreaded having for so long, but everything had changed—he wanted it all now. With Her.

They had arms and legs and heads and they were so much more than hers or his, they were theirs.

Then Freya watched as his laughter died and tears pooled in his complex eyes.

He wanted his brother to have had this moment.

Zack wanted his brother to this day and for ever he would.

'If we have a boy, can we call him Toby?'

'Yes.'

'He was so unhappy…'

'Not all of him was unhappy and he had someone

he could speak to,' Freya said. 'His last night was spent under the stars, drinking and being honest with you. That's a very nice last night to have had on this earth. I know that I'd take it.'

She turned his world around.

The last night of his brother's life had always been an agonising memory.

Not now.

Zack could now, without reservations, remember their laughter and two brothers talking and just a night where you put the world to rights.

Now they had put their worlds to rights.

'I don't want to tell people yet,' Freya said. 'I am the happiest ever but I want some time to get used to the idea and—' she rolled her eyes '—don't get me started on my parents.'

'Okay, we shan't tell anyone, though you'll start to show fairly soon.'

'No.' Freya shook her head. 'I meant all of it. I meant I need to get used to the idea of us.'

'The idea?' Zack checked.

'That you love me.'

'Get used to it,' Zack said. 'But I get it.'

It was like being handed a prized package and being told to sign for it, the start of a life he had never imagined.

'I'm such a difficult person,' Freya said. 'Don't say I didn't warn you.'

'Freya, I'm so glad I saw you raw the other night. I don't care how much you try to change, or control me, or rush me with my thoughts. You can't.' He smiled. 'You can keep on being you and I'm just going to keep on being me.'

'You're sure?'

'Completely.'

Zack took on the hardest hearts. Ones that others shied away from. But the hardest hearts gave the sweetest rewards and ones that were just so unexpected, because, for all she wanted to keep them quiet for now, on a night that should be just about them, Freya offered to share the happiness around.

'Tell your parents,' Freya said, 'when you video with them.'

'I'm not speaking to them tonight. That was just a ruse to get you here.'

'Tell them,' Freya said.

'Now?' Zack raised an eyebrow. 'I set up a romantic dinner and you want me to speak to my parents?'

Life changes.

Zack rang them and told them to get on the computer and they did.

'Here's the reason I didn't think I could come home in April,' Zack said, and he pulled Freya onto his knee.

'Hi, Freya!' they both shouted.

'They know about me?'

'I told them that there was someone special in my life,' Zack said.

That he had told them about her told Freya that this was real.

'Freya and I shall be home for Christmas, and hopefully with twins.'

'Zack!'

Oh, there was an exclamation mark at the end of his name for a reason.

Freya held up the ultrasound and watched his father put his glasses on, and it was such a precious moment.

'He's having twins,' Zack's father said to his wife and then recovered. 'I mean you are, Freya. I just don't know what to say.'

'We thought he was gay,' Judy confessed.

'Well, I'm pleased to say he's not.' Freya laughed and realised that must have been his mother's reaction when he'd told them about her.

It was a very nice meet-the-parents and after a few moments Zack told them that, unlike in Australia, it was still Valentine's Day in LA, and he was getting back to his.

'Thanks for that,' Zack said, and as he closed the laptop she remained on his knee. 'Well, I guess we've both made it a special Valentine's Day, even if you forgot.'

'I didn't,' Freya lied. 'And I do have something for you.'

She opened up her phone and found a photo and they both smiled as they looked upon the night their world had changed.

A perfect shot.

Almost.

Save a man coming down the stairs and walking over everyone just to be by her side.

'I'm going to love you for ever,' Zack said, and it wasn't a revelation.

They knew.

'I'm going to be busy doing the same,' Freya said.

This was love.

* * * * *

FALLING
FOR THE
SINGLE DAD

EMILY FORBES

For Amanda, Ali and Sarah.

Thank you all for an amazing thirty-plus years of friendship. Together we somehow survived our teenage years, the fashions of the eighties, cross-country moves, marriages, babies and now our own teenagers! As we begin to celebrate another round of milestone birthdays I've been thinking about the incredible memories we've created along the way and how lucky I am to have such "old" friends.

With love xx

CHAPTER ONE

THE HOLLYWOOD SIGN flashed intermittently into Abi's peripheral vision as she wound her way up into the Hollywood Hills. Her heart rate accelerated as she drew closer to her destination and she felt her palms go clammy as her nervousness increased a notch or two. She tightened her grip on the steering wheel, not wanting her hands to slip as she fought back the wave of panic that threatened to overwhelm her. She hadn't expected to feel quite so terrified today. She'd rehearsed this, she'd prepared for this. She could do this.

She had debated about catching a cab for her first day but had decided that if she could drum up the courage to drive that would give her the freedom that waiting for a taxi wouldn't, and in order to prepare she'd done a trial run yesterday with Jonty. She'd needed to know where she was going and she'd needed to make sure it was safe. Bringing Jonty yesterday had given her courage and confidence but today she was travelling solo.

One more corner to go and then she was able to turn off the steep, winding road into the staff parking area for The Hollywood Hills Clinic. The iconic Hollywood sign loomed large above her again, its fresh white paint stark against the dull green and brown of the hillside and the shrubby flora that sprouted there. She swiped her card at the gate and waited nervously for it to open. The staff car park was secure, fenced and gated, and she was relieved to see the addition of good lighting and CCTV cameras. She breathed a sigh of relief as she squeezed her second-hand, two-door, soft-top 4x4 between two immaculately shiny sports cars.

She took a moment to sit quietly in her car as she summoned up the nerve to get out of the vehicle. It had taken all her courage to get into her car this morning and now that she was here she needed to find some more. Starting a new job and meeting new colleagues was going to test her limits. She was in the rebuilding phase, trying to cope with the stress of life, and anything unexpected could, and often still did, unsettle her. She needed to find the strength to get out of her car. She closed her eyes and rehearsed the process her psychologist had taught her. She imagined herself walking—no, not walking, *striding*—confidently into the building and introducing herself to her new colleagues. It would be fine. She could do this. This was a safe environment. She had a plan and she had to believe things would go accordingly.

She gathered her bag, took a deep breath and opened her door very carefully, mindful of the pristine paintwork of the car beside her. She'd made it this far this morning, she'd found the strength to negotiate the LA traffic and now she was here. She held a conversation with herself in her head as she stepped out into the morning sun and followed the sign to the clinic. A short path took her to the front of the building and as she rounded the corner the vista took her breath away.

The view was incredible. The crisp, blue February

sky was clear of smog, just one of the bonuses of winter, and she could see over Los Angeles out to the coast where the Pacific Ocean shimmered in the morning sun. She turned her attention to the building itself. It was long and low, sleek and white. A massive wall of windows, shiny and gleaming, faced west, taking in the stunning view, and a semicircular driveway swept around in front of the glass separated from the building by a wide plaza bordered by sculpted, orderly, perfectly manicured gardens and hedges.

There was a low, unobtrusive sign of silver lettering on a white background that read 'The Hollywood Hills Clinic' in front of the building. Despite its name, the overall impression that she got was that she was about to step into a five-star resort, not a medical clinic. The sign didn't need to be large. Everyone who arrived here knew exactly where they were. No one's arrival at the clinic would be unplanned or unscheduled.

Her job interview had been conducted by phone and although she'd been on the internet and done her homework on the clinic and its management, nothing had prepared her for the reality. The first impression, from the exterior of the building alone, was definitely one of privilege, wealth and exclusivity.

Abi could see her reflection in the glass facade as she approached the front entrance and she self-consciously straightened her navy jacket and made sure her shirt was tucked into her pencil skirt. Her civilian clothes felt unfamiliar. The fabric was slippery and light compared to the thicker, more robust fabric of her army uniform and tended not to stay in place quite so firmly. Her low heels clicked on the pavers as she crossed the plaza area and she wondered if she was underdressed. If the luxury cars parked in the staff car park were any indication, she suspected her colleagues were going to be a hell of a lot more sophisticated than her. She suddenly felt like a country bumpkin on her first day in the big city.

You grew up in LA, she reminded herself. *You can do this. You are an excellent doctor, you will be a valuable member of staff.*

She didn't have to fit in; she just had to do a good job. She needed a job, this job, as her money wasn't going to last for ever and her psychologist had suggested, rather strongly, that it was time for her to start testing her reserves and her limits.

As the glass doors slid open Abi noticed a helicopter landing pad positioned at the far end of the building. It wasn't on the roof, neither was it tucked away discreetly out of sight, but instead it sat out the front, making a bold declaration that this was a place for the privileged and wealthy. Were people planning on making a statement as they arrived? That wouldn't surprise her given the sensational appearance of the clinic itself. The building alone certainly looked as though it was out to make a statement. Time would tell her what that statement was.

An expansive, modern foyer greeted her. A reception desk stood at one end in front of a wide window that looked out to the city below and on the opposite side of the foyer was a large courtyard with a central water feature and several oversized sculptures. More sculptures were displayed in the foyer itself and artworks hung from the walls. The look was reminiscent of a contemporary art gallery that had been merged with a very expensive and exclusive hotel. The artworks were beautifully lit and the foyer was sleek and modern.

She approached the reception desk, which was a long slab of marble. An enormous flower arrangement was positioned at one end and two chandeliers hung above it. The more Abi saw, the more the clinic looked like a five-star hotel—six-star, even, if there was such a thing. There wasn't much to indicate it was a medical facility. Even the woman behind the desk looked as if she had stepped out of a fashion magazine. Her hair was styled in a neat bob and her make-up had been expertly applied, and Abi felt more and more like the country cousin who expected to be evicted for not being glamorous enough.

She tried to ignore her misgivings as she introduced herself to the receptionist and explained that Freya Rothsberg was expecting her. Abi knew the clinic was owned by Freya and her brother, James. James was a world-renowned reconstructive surgeon who specialised in cosmetic surgery, and, from what Abi had discerned, Freya was responsible for the PR side of things. Freya had interviewed Abi over the phone but they were yet to meet.

'Welcome!' a woman called out loudly from several feet away. This must be Freya. She was about Abi's age, thirty or thereabouts, and of similar height, but that was about the extent of any resemblance. The closer Freya got the more the differences between them multiplied. Freya gave the immediate impression of someone who belonged here in the sun-kissed glamour of LA and the Hollywood Hills. She had a mane of dark hair that fell over her shoulders in natural surfer-chick waves. Her blue eyes were shining and her skin had a light tan, even at the end of winter. She had the typical LA cheerleader look—fit, trim and toned—and Abi doubted anything would have ever gone wrong in Freya Rothsberg's life.

In contrast to Freya's glowing Californian beauty Abi felt like a pale imitation of an LA woman, even though she had been born and bred here. Her dark brown hair with mahogany lights was cut just below her chin and had been softly feathered to frame her oval face. Her porcelain skin always looked like it had never seen the sun and Abi had never felt particularly pretty or noticeable. Her best, most striking feature were her eyes and she noted Freya's double-take when their eyes met as they introduced themselves. Abi was used to that reaction from people. Her eyes were a deep, rich amber, much like the glass eyes often found on a child's teddy bear. They were an unusual colour and she knew that was what people remembered about her.

'Hello, I'm Freya Rothsberg,' she said as she shook Abi's hand firmly. 'It's so nice to meet you! I hope you'll love it here at The Hills. Hold on one moment,' she said, 'there's someone I want to introduce you to.' A man entered the foyer and Freya called out to him. 'Damien!'

The man started walking towards them and Abi's first thought was that he was absolutely divine to look at. There was no other word to describe him. Was there no end to the beauty in this place?

He had designer stubble, brown eyes, so dark they were almost black, and a full head of black hair, short and spiky. He was tall, lean and looked like a model. His black suit might have been tailor-made for him rather than off the rack. No tie, open-collar shirt. Incredibly smooth, unlined skin.

'Abi,' Freya said as he reached them, 'this is Damien Moore, chief of reconstructive surgery.'

Abi recognised his name. This gorgeous man was her new boss. She found herself looking for telltale signs of plastic surgery and hoping not to find any, hoping it was just good genes because, despite working in the industry, she didn't find narcissistic men attractive. Not that she should care about what Damien Moore did with his body or his spare time.

'Damien, this is Abi Thompson, the new addition to your surgical team.'

'Dr Thompson.' He greeted her with a slight nod of his handsome head. Everything about him was dark and intense. Serious. He sounded totally controlled or was he just underwhelmed? Abi's lack of confidence made her question his expression before she could tell herself to relax. There was no reason for him to be un-impressed. He extended his hand but as Abi took it she felt a sharp shock as if there was a massive amount of static electricity between them. She felt as if her hand had been burnt and she withdrew it quickly, almost snatching it away, and resisted the temptation to check her palm for redness.

'You're a reconstructive and plastic surgeon?' he asked, apparently oblivious to the shock. Had he not felt it? 'Fully qualified?' he added, and Abi felt her-self bristling.

What the hell did he mean by that?

'Of course,' she replied.

'Your résumé is very extensive.'

Was he accusing her of lying about her experience? Abi met his chilly stare head on and felt some of her old fire returning. 'If you'd like to fetch my application I'll wait and then we can compare notes.' She could feel the steam coming out of her ears and knew her amber eyes would be flashing angrily, but if she thought that would scare him into apologising she was mistaken. So she carried on. 'I have spent the past two years in Afghanistan, working in a CASH unit, putting soldiers back together. Making sure they have viable stumps for prosthetic limbs, repairing hands, sewing fingers back on that have been blown or shot off, holding chest walls together on the side of the road while under fire, so I think I'll be able to handle working here. I'm sure your facilities and your clients won't trouble me too much.' A combat support hospital may not be the equivalent of the five-star set-up currently surrounding her but Abi knew the surroundings were irrelevant. She was good at her job, very good, and she refused to let someone denigrate her skills.

Abi was aware that Freya was grinning and trying to suppress laughter but her cellphone rang before she could comment.

Freya glanced at the screen and apologised to them. 'It's Mila. I'm sorry but I have to take this. We have to finalise the plans for the function this weekend. Damien, would you mind giving Abi a quick tour of the clinic? I was going to do it but I'll catch up with you at morning tea instead.'

Abi hesitated as a slight sense of panic crept up on her. 'I don't mind waiting,' she said. It seemed a better option than going with Damien, who clearly wasn't impressed by her and who was putting her on edge. She didn't need to be stressed. Not on her first day. But Freya had already turned away to answer her phone, leaving Abi and Damien standing in silence, staring at each other.

'Looks like you're stuck with me.' The prospect

didn't seem to bother him. 'Come on, it'll give us a chance to get acquainted. To see if we'll be able to work well together.'

Not an overly pleasing prospect. Abi was feeling increasingly nervous about the decision she'd made to take the Hollywood Hills job. Perhaps it had been a mistake not to have had a face-to-face interview and checked out not only the facilities but her new colleagues too.

She needed to calm down, employ some of the coping strategies she'd been working on.

She took a deep breath and fought for composure. She needed to present a professional, controlled demeanour. It wouldn't do to fall to pieces in front of her new boss in the first five minutes of her first day.

'How much of the clinic did you see when you had your interview?' Damien asked her.

'This is the first time I've been here. My interview was conducted over the phone, that's why you read my résumé and why we haven't met.'

'I see. I've been on leave, I assumed this was all finalised while I was away. Didn't you want to see where you'd be working?'

'I know the clinic's reputation. That was enough for me.' In reality it was the closeted, safe and secure environment that she was most attracted to. She wasn't ready for a large public hospital. She didn't want to fight for funding or waste hours in meetings. She wasn't ready to deal with emergencies and chaos and shift work. She needed regular patterns and habits. She needed regular sleep too if she was to get her life back on track. Well-mannered, exclusive and polite was what she wanted and she hoped that this job would be a peaceful environment compared to public-hospital and defence-force work.

Damien showed her to her new office, which had light oak furniture, leather chairs and large picture windows with one-way blinds that looked out over Los Angeles. His office was beside hers and they shared a secretary who managed their appointment diary and theatre bookings. Damien introduced her to Jennifer and Abi expected that he would palm her off onto the secretary, but he surprised her by continuing her tour himself. Abi wasn't sure what to make of that. Was he being polite or was he going to use this as an opportunity to cross-examine her further about her experience?

Let him interrogate her, she decided. She'd answer any question he put to her.

He showed her through the rehabilitation area, which included a gym and hydrotherapy pools used by the physical therapists on staff, before taking her into the operating theatres. The facility was amazing. Absolutely no expense had been spared and Abi couldn't help but be impressed.

'Different from what you are used to?' Damien asked as he pushed open the swing door that led into an operating suite.

'We have state-of-the art equipment in the defence forces but those facilities don't extend past the medical necessities. The army certainly doesn't waste money on modern art and marble floors.'

'The Hills patients have high expectations,' he said with a light shrug of his designer-clad shoulders, 'not only of our expertise but of the service. They're LA's wealthy and they are used to having every whim catered for, and they have the same expectations when they walk through our doors as when they walk into a hotel or restaurant. They expect to be well looked after.'

Abi didn't care about the patients' expectations. The demands these patients would put on her would be nothing compared to what she'd put upon herself. In the army people got what they got, they had no expectations, the most important things were to keep them alive and maintain their function, but her expectations of her own skills was high. She knew she'd be able to handle the patients here. Operating on a millionaire would have to be less stressful than operating under fire. What she was interested in was a job that wasn't dangerous. She wanted peaceful. She *needed* peaceful. She knew she was going to get demanding but she was confident that she could cope. Stress presented in different ways and the pressure that she expected to encounter here, in civilised luxury, would be entirely different from the high stress in Afghanistan.

She was interested in a low-stress environment and one factor in keeping her stress levels down was knowing that the people she worked with were capable. It was time to ask Damien some questions of her own. 'How long have you worked here?'

'Two years.' He didn't volunteer anything further as he led the way out of the theatre suites. 'Our definitive observation unit is through there and the patient suites are around this way.'

They were six feet along the corridor when there was a crackle over the ceiling intercom.

'Code blue, room five. Repeat, code blue, room five.'

Damien took off. One minute he was next to her, the next he was gone, his long legs eating up the metres of the corridor and leaving Abi staring after him.

CHAPTER TWO

ABI LOOKED AT his retreating figure before she came to her senses and followed in his wake as the voice continued through the loudspeaker. 'Code blue, room five.'

Damien sprinted past the next two rooms before he shouldered open a door and Abi followed him into what was possibly the largest private hospital room she had ever seen. In the centre of the wall in front of them was an oversized hospital bed. A nurse was kneeling on the bed, delivering cardiac compressions to a young woman wearing pale pink silk pyjamas.

'She's in cardiac arrest. Unresponsive, not breathing, no pulse,' she told them as she continued with the compressions. She was doing a good job, delivering regular hard, deep compressions. The patient's shirt had been opened at the front and Abi was astounded at how underweight the woman was. She was so thin Abi could see each and every rib.

'Ellen, this is Dr Thompson,' Damien said, as he reached behind the bed and pushed on the wall. A small door that was set flush into the panelling popped open and he pulled a defibrillator from the alcove. And that was it by way of introductions. There was no time for anything more as he quickly tore open the packets and

Ellen sat back, stopping CPR, as Damien applied the adhesive electrodes to the patient's chest wall.

Abi watched as he connected the wires, flicked the machine on and pressed the 'analyse' button. The patient's heart rhythm appeared on the screen. She could see the disorganised pattern of ventricular fibrillation indicating that the brain was sending chaotic impulses to the heart that the heart couldn't interpret. This meant the heart couldn't fire a proper beat and it lost its rhythm and was unable to pump blood. The brain would be starved of oxygen, causing the patient to lose consciousness, and if the heart rhythm wasn't corrected the patient would die. Defibrillation to restore regular rhythm and normal contractions was the best way to stop ventricular fibrillation, and that was exactly what Damien was instigating.

The machine issued instructions in its automated voice.

Stop CPR, analysing.

Shock advised.

Abi could hear the whine as the power built up in the defibrillator unit.

Stand clear.

'Clear.' Damien repeated the machine's instructions to Abi and Ellen and checked to make sure they were well away from the patient before pressing the flashing red button. The machine delivered its first shock but there was no change in the rhythm of the heart.

Continue CPR.

'Ellen, can you get an IV line in, oxygen monitor and an Ambu bag,' Damien instructed, as he lowered the bed before continuing chest compressions.

Abi kicked off her shoes and stepped forward, ready

to help. She hitched her skirt up to give her room to move, wondering why on earth she'd thought it was a good idea to wear a suit, and climbed up on the bed. She tipped the patient's head back, opening her airway. She was ready to breathe for her the moment Damien paused in his compressions. They worked at a steady rate for two minutes until the AED machine interrupted them.

Stop CPR, analysing.

Shock advised.

'Clear.' Damien repeated the process to deliver a second shock.

Their patient was pale and clammy and she was starting to go a little blue around the mouth and jaw. Abi and Damien continued another round of CPR but this time Abi used the Ambu bag, squeezing air into the patient's lungs after each set of thirty compressions. Another two minutes passed.

Stop CPR, analysing.

Shock advised.

They stood clear again as once more Damien pressed the red flashing button and this time a normal heart rhythm was restored.

Abi's shoulders sagged as she slid off the bed and all three of them breathed a collective sigh of relief as they watched the heartbeat on the little screen.

Ellen removed the electrodes of the AED and replaced them with ECG leads as a second team, who Abi could only assume were the resus team, moved further into the room. Abi hadn't noticed their arrival in all the chaos and they departed as swiftly and silently as they had arrived. Accompanied by Ellen, they wheeled the patient out of the room, no doubt taking her to the definitive observation unit, and Abi was left alone with Damien.

Now that the drama was over she didn't know where to look or what to do. She stood in the middle of the room and tried to avoid looking at Damien. She studied her surroundings instead. The oversized hospital bed was gone but the room was far from empty. In front of a large window that overlooked a courtyard was a carpeted lounge area complete with a leather sofa, an armchair upholstered in a rich cream fabric and a marble-topped coffee table. She wandered over to the window, the carpet thick and plush under her stockinged feet, and took in the view over the courtyard. It offered complete privacy but even so the glass was tinted. Abi could see out but no one could see in. An en-suite bathroom was tucked into the far corner of the room and Abi could just glimpse a marble vanity in the mirrored reflection. The medical equipment was all tucked away discreetly, Abi assumed into purpose-built storage, and the room looked and felt like a hotel suite. The surroundings might be very different to what she was used to but the patients were the same. They all had lives that needed to be improved, or even saved, and that was her job. It didn't matter if they were civilian or military, she just had to do what she was trained for.

'Thanks for your help.' Damien was standing beside her. 'It was a good outcome,' he added with a slight nod of his head.

Was that all the acknowledgement she was going to get?

She supposed she was only doing her job, she didn't need to be congratulated for that, but she felt a little short-changed that he wasn't more effusive, particularly after his previous criticism and questions relating to her medical qualifications. Surely she'd put some of his doubts to rest now?

She was pleased with how she'd coped. She hadn't panicked, hadn't felt stressed, she'd simply just clicked into gear. Her medical skills were as precise as ever. It was like riding a bike and she was thrilled to know that she hadn't lost her touch in that regard. Her personal life might be a disaster, her self-belief might have taken a pounding and she might be struggling to cope out in the big wide world, but in the familiar environment of a hospital it seemed she'd lost none of her confidence. It was a reassuring discovery but it didn't take away the disappointment that Damien didn't seem quite so impressed.

'I'd like to retract my earlier comment,' he added.

'What?'

'When I questioned your qualifications. I jumped to conclusions and I'm sorry for that.'

'Thank you.' That was all she'd wanted. Some recognition of a job well done. Her day had just got a little bit brighter.

She could do this.

'It's obvious you can think on your feet and cope under pressure. Your defence-force experience means that you are undoubtedly qualified to cope with anything we can throw at you, as you've capably demonstrated, and I apologise,' he said, and then he smiled.

Abi's knees went weak. She sat down hard on the sofa as she tried to pretend that it was the adrenalin from the resuscitation that was flooding her system and making her knees wobble but she knew it was Damien's smile. Suddenly he lost his serious, intense expression.

His smile transformed his face and now he looked like a man who knew how to have a good time, who knew how to laugh.

'Come on,' he said, 'let's grab a coffee and catch our breath. We can finish the tour later.'

He extended his hand to help her up from the sofa and the touch of his palm as Abi placed her hand in his created a current of electricity so strong that it couldn't be contained and it shot out of her to ignite the air surrounding them until it seemed to glow. She could feel the air around them moving. It crackled and swirled like a living, breathing entity, creating a fire that sucked the air from her lungs and made it impossible to breathe. She pulled herself up on wobbly legs. Her vision was blurred around the edges and she felt dizzy and light headed. She couldn't seem to catch her breath.

'Are you okay?' Damien asked as he let go of her hand.

Released from his hold, abruptly disconnected from him, she found she was able to breathe again. 'I'm fine,' she said, as she smoothed down the front of her skirt and stepped into her shoes. She closed her eyes briefly and took a quick deep breath to make sure she really was all right before she followed him out of the room. As they walked along the corridor she made sure she kept a couple of feet between them. Touching him again was out of the question.

Damien drank his coffee as quickly as possible without being impolite. He had taken Abi into the staff kitchen to make coffee but the room felt too small for both of them. He was having trouble breathing and it had nothing to do with the emergency he'd just averted and everything to do with a slim brunette who sat opposite him. He'd been dismissive of her without cause earlier and he felt badly about that, but now he was having trouble remembering exactly what his issue had been.

He could smell fresh peaches and he knew that was her fragrance he was inhaling. Was it any wonder he was having difficulty breathing? Every breath was like inhaling the essence of Abi and it was sweet torture. She made him think of the golden days of summer. Her amber eyes glowed like the late afternoon sun and she shimmered as if there was an energy within her that was too big to contain, although a sixth sense told him that something had happened that had diminished her glow. Something had damaged her, something had given her an air of fragility. She was only a waif of a girl but it wasn't just about her size and he wondered what had happened in her past. But he didn't have the time or energy to worry about her psyche; he had enough of his own issues to deal with. He didn't have time for distractions and that was what she was.

He needed to breathe, he needed to leave.

He drained the dregs of his coffee, pushed his chair back and stood. 'Will you be able to find your way back to your office? I need to speak to Freya.' He knew he was making excuses but he needed to get away. He needed to break the spell he could feel her casting over him.

His departure was abrupt, and he could see from Abi's puzzled expression that she thought so too but she didn't complain or argue. She just nodded silently. It appeared she wasn't much of a talker.

He did genuinely want to speak to Freya—he felt she needed to know about Clementine Jones, though he knew she would have heard the alarm and the code-blue call—but he suffered a moment of guilt over his hasty exit. He pushed those thoughts to one side as he knocked on Freya's door and then brought her up to speed on the emergency.

'Clementine was booked in for a breast enlargement but she has a long-standing eating disorder that probably triggered her cardiac arrest. She's in the DOU under Geoff's care now, but she needs counselling. I know you're only taking on a handful of clients but this girl needs to be included on your list. She's playing Russian roulette at the moment. It's only a matter of time before she's a statistic instead of a person. If she won't see you then she needs to see another psychologist. James is her admitting surgeon but I'm sure he'll agree.'

Freya nodded. 'I'll take care of it.' She tilted her head to one side. 'So you were first on the scene?'

'With Abi.' He had to give credit where it was due.

'You resuscitated her together?'

Damien nodded.

'Now do you think she can handle the job?'

He needed Abi to pull her weight. He'd fought to have an extra surgeon on staff to ease some of his caseload but his first impressions had worried him. He hadn't thought her old enough or strong enough to help him but he had to admit he had revised his opinion. He would give her the benefit of the doubt now after the composure she had displayed during the emergency. 'I'll agree I'm more confident now,' he replied.

'Good.' Freya nodded. 'Because James wants her to assist you in Theatre tomorrow. That will give her a feel for how the clinic runs and also give you a chance to assess her skills. Once you're happy we'll start to give her patients of her own, which will free up some of your time.'

Damien was happy with that. He was exhausted and had far too much on his plate. There were far too many things fighting for his attention. He had too much else to think about at the moment. He was virtually a single parent, raising a young daughter, and he had more work than he could handle. He couldn't work twenty-four-seven—it wasn't feasible and it was not what he wanted. Abi's appointment needed to be successful. She had to work out and if she didn't she'd have to go. It was as simple as that.

Abi's head was spinning as she pulled her 4x4 into the driveway and hit the button for the automatic garage door. She needed time to think about her day and what had happened. What she'd seen, what she'd done, who she'd met. She would collect Jonty and they'd go for a walk. That would give her time to sort through her thoughts on the clinic, on Freya and on Damien.

The motor of the garage door made a distinctive whine as it kicked into gear and Abi could see Jonty racing across the lawn to greet her as she eased her car forward. A wave of guilt washed over her as she saw how eager he was to welcome her home. This was the first day that she and Jonty had been parted. She wondered if his day had been less eventful than hers. Was this how working mothers felt? At least she'd organised company for him. He shouldn't have been lonely but she still hoped he'd missed her.

She closed the door and made a beeline for her landlords' bungalow at the front of the property. Her landlords, George and Irma, were a retired couple in their late sixties and Abi rented their converted garage apartment. She had moved in about six weeks ago and had since found herself adopted by George and Irma as part of the family. She didn't mind; she was enjoying feeling like she was part of a family. They had adopted her dog too, offering to keep him company while Abi returned to work. She wished she'd been able to take Jonty with her, for her sake more than his, but the clinic was no place for a large, hairy, golden retriever.

'How did your first day go?' Irma asked as Abi stepped onto the back porch. 'Not quite what I expected,' she replied. 'But I'm sure it will be okay.' She still needed time to process the day's events. The Hills was different from what she was used to, very different, and even if she wasn't sure that she would be suited to working there she suspected it would be interesting, albeit slightly more routine than the army. But perhaps that was just what she needed—ordinary and routine, excluding the odd cardiac arrest, of course.

'I've made an extra-large pot of chilli beef. Would you like to eat with us tonight? You must be tired.'

Abi was more than happy to be looked after by Irma. She knew her fridge was bare and dinner at her place was likely to be toast and maybe a packet soup. But more than the dinners it was the feeling that someone was interested in her and cared enough to make sure she was fed. She'd never experienced that on a regular basis. Growing up, her family life had been erratic, to say the least. Swings and roundabouts. Her mother had done her best at times but she really hadn't coped with the real world and Abi didn't remember her father. And army life, while she'd been looked after, she suspected was also very different to normal family life. George and Irma missed the company of their children and Abi enjoyed filling that void. It was nice to feel normal.

'That sounds delicious. Have I got time to take Jonty for a quick walk first?'

'Of course.'

Above the garage George had added a bedroom, small bathroom and a kitchen/living area that opened out onto a deck that overlooked a small park. Jonty loved exploring the park but Abi avoided it once the sun had set. She needed milk for her morning coffee so she changed quickly into a pair of black exercise leggings, a long-sleeved black T-shirt and a bright pink, puffy, padded, insulated vest. She wrapped an orange scarf around her neck, shoved her phone and some coins into her pocket and clipped Jonty's lead to his collar. They'd make a quick dash to the mini-mart two blocks away. She let Jonty go to the toilet before they left as once he had his coat on he would know not to stop unless she directed him to. She fastened his coat around his body and headed out to the street.

Jonty had been assigned to Abi on her return from Afghanistan, on her psychologist's recommendation. According to Caroline, many of her patients who had been diagnosed with post-traumatic stress disorder found that an assistance dog brought enormous benefits, and Abi had to admit that she was grateful for Jonty's companionship. She'd never had a dog, she'd never had any pets before, but she had very quickly grown attached to Jonty. She was a dog person, she'd decided.

Jonty had been assigned to help calm her and to increase her confidence in her ability to cope with the outside world, but nervousness still made her heart rate increase as they approached the supermarket. Ever since the incident in Afghanistan she had been exceedingly nervous in new or crowded environments until she'd had a chance to check out the lie of the land.

She quickly scanned the interior of the shop and only when she could see that it was relatively quiet, with few customers, did she step inside, taking Jonty with her. He was allowed to accompany her so long as he was wearing the coat that identified him as an assistance dog. They headed to the milk fridge at the back of the store, Abi wishing, not for the first time, that the shop-keeper would keep the milk near the front. Having to go to the far corner of the store always bothered her, even though she knew where the emergency exit was.

A dark-haired man stood in front of the open fridge door. He was reaching for the same milk that Abi wanted. She thought about asking him to grab one for her too but that would mean initiating a conversation with a stranger. Even with Jonty beside her she wasn't comfortable doing that. She waited as the man closed the fridge door and turned around.

'Dr Thompson!'

Abi's heart skipped a beat as a voice that had become almost familiar in just one day uttered her name. She lifted her eyes.

He was tall and lean. His thick black hair was expertly styled to look effortlessly casual and a day's worth of stubble darkened his square jaw and contrasted with the smooth olive skin of his forehead and cheeks. He was watching her with eyes so dark they were almost black. He was gorgeous.

Damien.

His serious expression vanished, to be replaced by

his wide smile, showcasing perfect white teeth. Did this man have any physical flaws?

'You need milk?' he asked.

'For my coffee,' she replied, as if he'd care why she needed it.

He took a second carton from the fridge and passed it to her, not checking which one she wanted. 'Do you live near here?'

'A couple of blocks that way,' she said, pointing east.

'We're two blocks south.'

She wondered who 'we' meant. Was he married? He didn't wear a wedding ring.

She glanced at his left hand, double-checking, but she knew she was right. What she didn't know was when she'd noticed and why. Not that it mattered. Lots of surgeons didn't wear rings and his marital status was of no concern to her.

'Is this your dog?'

She nodded. 'This is Jonty.'

'An assistance dog?'

'It's a project I'm involved with,' she said. She didn't see any need to mention that the project was personal and involved trying to fix her fragile psyche. There was no need to mention that her psychologist had recommended the programme. She didn't intend to share tales about her private life with her new boss.

Finding out he was practically her neighbour was enough to deal with. He didn't need to know anything more about her. She was used to mixing her work and her social life, there wasn't another option in the military really, but things had changed recently. She had changed. She had become more reserved, more introverted, and that was part of the reason that Caroline had suggested Jonty. She'd hoped it would help to restore Abi's confidence and alleviate some of her fears about the world. Bad things weren't always going to happen. Abi needed to experience the world and remember the good things.

Damien insisted on paying for her milk, along with his own, and they left the shop together. As they stepped onto the pavement he pulled a set of keys from his pocket and pressed a button. Abi heard the sound of doors unlocking and saw the lights flash on a black, luxury SUV that was parked out the front of the shop. 'Can I give you a lift?' he offered.

It seemed he had the charming personality to match his very appealing features. But Abi knew how dangerous a weapon charm could be in a good-looking man. She looked at his car. There was not a speck of dirt or a scratch or dent on it. Its paintwork was immaculate and it suited him. It was shiny, sleek perfection and so different from her old soft-top. She couldn't imagine hopping into something so tidy, let alone putting her hairy, thirty-kilogram companion in there too. Had he forgotten about Jonty?

'No, thank you. We need the exercise.' And she needed more time to think.

He was good-looking and charming, there was no denying that, but that was no reason to let him drive her home. She'd had good-looking, charming bosses before and things hadn't turned out so well for her the last time. In fact, things had gone terribly pear-shaped and she was still recovering. She needed time to herself, time to heal. There was no room in her life or in her head for anything other than surviving. Her goal was to achieve emotional stability and financial security. She didn't need any complications and she knew all too well how complicated men could make things. Besides, he was part of a 'we' and that was all she needed to know about him to ensure she kept her distance. Single men were one thing but men with other commitments were definitely off her list. That was one path she knew she would avoid at all costs. Being pleasant at work was one thing, mixing socially was another, but men with baggage were a definite no.

CHAPTER THREE

ABI ARRIVED AT The Hills on her second day wearing her smartest dress, a simple black jersey wrap, and nude-colored heels. She had a thin gold chain around her neck but she still wasn't sure if she was dressed smartly enough. Freya had arranged a morning tea yesterday to introduce Abi to everyone and all the staff she had met had seemed extraordinarily beautiful and impressively well-dressed.

She supposed it made sense given that the clinic serviced the wealthy and elite of Los Angeles society but she wasn't sure how, or if, she measured up by comparison. She suspected both her wardrobe and her looks were severely lacking and decided she'd have to wow them with her medical talents instead.

She found her way to her office, where she was greeted by Jennifer, the secretary who took care of her and Damien, and the news that Damien had requested an eight-thirty meeting.

A white doctor's coat was hanging behind her office door. Still unsure about her outfit, she took the coat off the hook and slipped it over her clothes. She would feel more comfortable and in control if she was already in scrubs but this would have to do. Perhaps she could engineer her diary to ensure she spent most of her time in Theatre—she felt at home in that environment and in that uniform. She checked her reflection in the mirror on the wall and saw that the coat had The Hills' intertwined double H logo monogrammed on the breast pocket. Like everything else in the clinic, even the coats had been taken to the next level.

Damien's door was open. She took a moment to check him out before she knocked. He was wearing a different suit today, dark navy with a pale blue shirt and a red silk tie embroidered with blue fleurs-de-lis, but he still looked as if he'd stepped out of the pages of a fashion magazine. Abi pulled the white coat more firmly around her as she knocked and entered. Her whole outfit had cost no more than a hundred dollars; Damien's tie alone had probably cost twice that.

There was a coffee waiting for her and Damien slid it across his desk as she sank into the leather seat by the window. His office was identical to hers in size and also looked out onto an internal courtyard complete with a bubbling water feature that had a stunning metal sculpture as its centrepiece. Everything about this place was slick and professional and for the first time since the previous day Abi relaxed slightly. It would be nice to be associated with this clinic. This move could turn out to be a good decision and having something work out right for her would be a pleasant change.

'Milk?' he asked, making a reference to their unexpected meeting last night. His voice was deep but it lightened when he smiled. She'd noticed how it changed with his mood, from serious surgeon to friendly colleague to charming shopper, and she wondered which one was the real Damien.

She nodded but Damien was already adding it for her. 'Do you know how our patient from yesterday is? Clementine?' she queried. She'd been worried all night about the young woman who'd gone into cardiac arrest.

'She's in a stable condition. I just spoke to Geoff, our cardiologist. He's monitoring her closely but he's happy. She wasn't physically strong enough to undergo surgery so, in a way, this is not a bad outcome. She's had a long-standing eating disorder that her parents thought was being managed but it appears not. Clementine needs to agree to get more help,' Damien replied.

'What was she booked in for?'

'A breast enlargement,' Damien explained. 'James had been delaying her operation, telling her she had to put on weight because her body wouldn't cope with an anaesthetic, but I have no idea if this episode will make any difference. From what I understand, she's had intervention and therapy many times before. Freya is going to see her with her psychologist's hat on— she has a special interest in patients who have eating disorders—but if Clementine isn't receptive she'll be transferred to another facility. Apparently Clementine wants to stay here and her parents have agreed so that will be the carrot Freya dangles.'

James Rothsberg was the head of the clinic and also a reconstructive and plastic surgeon, and Abi was re-lieved to hear that he had put the patient's well-being first but surprised to hear that Clementine had been scheduled for a breast enlargement. 'Do you do a lot of cosmetic surgery here?'

'We are in Hollywood.'

'I realise that.'

'It's not all we do,' Damien continued, 'but you're

assisting me in Theatre today and it's what's on our list
and what I wanted to talk to you about.'

'We're doing cosmetic surgery? That's not what I expected.' She was a specialist in the field of plastic and
reconstructive surgery but her experience was in the
reconstructive side of things. Cosmetic surgery wasn't
her forte.

'It's awards season in Hollywood,' Damien said as
he shrugged his shoulders in his bespoke suit jacket.
'The film industry awards are only twelve days away,
which makes this our busiest time of the year. Everyone wants something done without anyone knowing
about it. James can't possibly keep up with the demand
so I lend a hand.

'Don't worry, no one will know you've relaxed your
ethics,' he added, making her wonder if he'd had another look at her résumé and refreshed his knowledge
of her background. 'The celebrities don't want anyone
to know they've had surgical assistance to look their
best on awards night. We have a lot of rather wealthy
and sometimes reclusive patients who demand privacy
and anonymity. They won't mention your name and they
expect the same consideration from you.'

He smiled again and Abi's breath caught in her
throat. 'All your recognition will come from your reconstructive work and there will be plenty of that. We
have an arrangement with the Bright Hope Clinic to do
some charitable work for the underprivileged children
who are treated there and that, along with the other
external referrals that come to us for reconstructive
surgery, will keep you occupied most of the time. But
this cosmetic work on the celebrities and their partners,
and the Hollywood heavy hitters and their mistresses,

wives and girlfriends, and the cash they are prepared to part with for the best medical care and for our discretion means that we are able to do that charity work, and I suspect that will appeal to you.

'You will get paid for any charity work that you do but The Hills, by which I mean James, absorbs those expenses. We are strong believers in giving back to the community. It's a win-win situation. So, does that make you feel better about today's list?'

Abi nodded. She hadn't really thought about the ramifications of the clinic's location on the client base but Damien's explanation did ease her conscience. Besides, the surgical procedures were the same no matter what you called them. Although the surgeries were performed for different reasons, aesthetics or function, the actual operations were similar and giving them labels such as cosmetic or reconstructive was really just semantics.

'Okay,' Damien continued, 'on today's list we have two blepharoplasties, one neck lift, two liposuctions, a breast lift and an arm lift. I have to warn you, a couple of our patients are men. One is a very well-known actor who has decided to treat himself to a neck lift and the other patient has recently left his wife and is planning on unveiling his much younger girlfriend at the awards and he wants to take a few years off his face with an eyelid lift. But remember, discretion is something we guarantee at The Hills and I know it's been written into your contract but I need to know that you can rock a poker face. It doesn't matter what we think about cosmetic surgery, these patients have their reasons for undergoing this work and we need to be discreet and respectful.'

Abi had plenty of her own insecurities. While she

didn't think she'd ever resort to cosmetic surgery, as her insecurities weren't really physical, she could understand people's need to change or to make a better version of themselves to boost their confidence, and she wasn't going to judge them for their choices. She understood that different things worked for different people and she certainly wouldn't criticise a patient's decision, although, given the opportunity, she thought she might try to dissuade some of the people some of the time.

She wondered what the clinic's policy on that was. Was honesty considered the best policy or was the bottom line the main consideration? But she wasn't going to ask that question on her second day. She would toe the line for the moment, there would be time to find out later just how much she was expected to keep her opinion to herself.

'Don't worry about me,' she said as she finished her coffee. 'I understand how this works.'

The day ran smoothly and the time passed quickly, as it always seemed to when she was immersed in surgery. She was impressed with Damien's skill but also with the way he related to the theatre staff. He treated everyone with respect and she could tell that the nurses adored him. She had done a large percentage of each of the surgeries under Damien's watchful eye and he'd been encouraging and complimentary about her skills. As far as she could tell, there was not a vast difference between cosmetic surgery and regular reconstructive surgery, although it was perhaps *always* important to make sure the stitches were as tiny and neat as possible, and preferably hidden, in all cosmetic procedures. But neat stitching was one thing she had always prided herself on.

They were finishing off the second blepharoplasty and there was one more surgery still to come when the theatre phone rang. The blepharoplasty was something different for Abi. She was used to repairing eyelids, stitching eye injuries and even, on one occasion, making a new eyelid, but to do an eyelid lift purely to make someone look younger was novel.

The scrub nurse had answered the phone and Abi could see her looking at Damien. 'Dr Moore, it's for you, it's your daughter's school. Apparently no one has come to collect her.'

He had a daughter?

She didn't know why she was so surprised. She knew he was a 'we' but a daughter was more than she'd expected.

'Can you finish up for me, Dr Thompson?' Damien asked as he tied off the last stitch. Abi glanced at the clock on the theatre wall. It was already after four in the afternoon and she wondered what he was planning on doing. 'She needs ointment applied to her eyelids before they are bandaged,' he continued.

'I can do it,' the theatre nurse offered. Abi wasn't sure if she was offering because she saw Abi's vague expression and took pity on her or whether she was trying to get into Damien's good graces, but Abi wasn't about to let her take over. She could do this.

'I've got it,' she said.

She listened in to Damien's conversation as she applied the ointment. He could have taken the call on another phone but he seemed quite happy to have the conversation in front of the staff.

'This is Dr Moore,' Damien said, as the scrub nurse held the phone to his ear. He could feel the pressure building in his chest as anger rose in him. What was Brooke up to now? She was supposed to be collecting Summer from school. Had she forgotten again? What was the point of making arrangements with her if she was so unreliable? He worked hard to accommodate his ex-wife, he wanted to make sure that their daughter got to spend time with both of them, but sometimes Brooke made it impossible.

'Summer hasn't been collected,' the woman on the end of the phone told him. 'She has been sent to after-school care and I need to notify you. I need to make sure she is picked up by six o'clock.'

'I've been in surgery all day, I'm *still* in surgery and I won't be finished by then.' Damien was aware that all the theatre staff could hear his conversation quite clearly but it was too late for secrets now. Abi was busy bandaging their patient's eyes but he could sense by her posture that she was listening just as intently as all the others, but he couldn't worry about them. Summer was his priority, now and always. 'Have you contacted her mother? She was supposed to collect her.'

'Of course, but she is in New York.'

'What? She's *where*?' God, that woman was unbelievable. What the hell was she doing in New York?

'She told me she contacted you.'

'What? No, she hasn't,' he said, but he knew what she would have done. She would have left a message on his cellphone. No matter how many times he told her he didn't check his cell if he was in Theatre, she never listened. Brooke always danced to her own tune; other people's lives were of no consequence to her, she didn't make allowances or exceptions for any of them, not even her own daughter. Once again, Damien would have to pick up the pieces left by Brooke's selfishness. 'Can you give me five minutes?' he asked the woman on the phone. 'I'll make some arrangements and call you back.'

He nodded to the scrub nurse to hang up the phone and let out another expletive.

'What's going on?' the theatre nurse asked.

'Summer hasn't been collected from school,' he replied. He had another couple of hours left in Theatre and just five minutes to work out a solution. He wouldn't be finished before six so he wouldn't be finished in time to collect Summer.

His eyes roamed the room as he tried to figure out what to do. Abi taped the last bandage in place and looked up just as his gaze settled on her. She might just be the answer to his problem.

'Abi, do you think you could do me a favour?' he asked.

Damien looked worried, stressed, and Abi thought it was probably best that he didn't operate while in this state. 'Sure,' she replied without hesitation, expecting he was going to ask her to start his final surgery, but his question when he asked it was completely unexpected.

'Would you collect Summer for me?'

'What?' Was he crazy? Surely he was kidding. 'I've never met your daughter,' she retorted, but even in her flustered state she realised there was something he hadn't considered. 'I doubt the school would send her home with a complete stranger. Why don't you go and I'll start the last case?'

'The last case is a breast lift.'

Abi knew that, she was supposed to assist for that surgery too.

'How many of those have you done?' he asked, and judging by his tone she knew he already knew the answer.

Exactly none. She stared at Damien and her silence was all the answer he needed.

'That's what I thought. I need to finish off here. Would you please collect her?'

'Why doesn't Summer's mother pick her up?'

'That's a good question,' he replied with a sigh. 'She was supposed to but apparently she is on her way to New York.'

Apparently? 'New York? Didn't you know?' Had it just slipped his mind that his wife was away and he was supposed to be picking up his daughter? Was it something he forgot on a regular basis and now he was trying to make it her problem?

Abi didn't think so. It didn't seem to fit with his character and he seemed to be genuinely upset and to be struggling for solutions. She believed this had come out of the blue for him too.

Damien shook his head. 'Brooke told the school that she told me I would have to make arrangements but I haven't heard from her. This is the third time she has done this.'

'What did you do the other times?' she asked, as the anaesthetist began to reverse the anaesthetic.

'Once I collected her and another time she went home with a friend. But school finished forty-five minutes ago so those mothers would have left, and I don't have any of their numbers. Please, Abi, I wouldn't ask you if I had any other options. My daughter is five years old. You remember being five, don't you? I don't want her to feel abandoned.'

That word cut Abi to the core. *Abandoned* was the one word to use if he wanted her sympathy and co-operation. But he couldn't have known that. That would be impossible. It had just been a comment. But of course she remembered being five.

She also remembered having no one to pick her up. Day after day she would get herself home from school. On a good day it had been because her mother had been working, but on a bad day her mother would be passed out on the sofa, hungover or drunk.

Abi had had no one to rely on when she'd been five or seven or nine. She'd had no one until she'd joined the army at seventeen and had gone to medical school. She'd had no one really until she'd met Mark and even then she'd still ended up alone. There had never been anyone she could rely on. She knew exactly what Damien was talking about.

She started to cave in. 'I'd do it but I really don't think the school would let me.'

Damien had an answer for that. 'I'll ring them and I'll get Freya to email your staff ID photo to the office. You'll just have to show some ID when you get there. Please? I don't know what else to do. The school is ten minutes from home. If you could just pick her up and I'll collect her from your place as soon as I'm done here.'

He knew she lived in his neighbourhood, which would put her home close to the school. His plan made sense but Abi didn't know if she could do it, although it was hard to refuse when he was looking so distressed and imploring her with his dark, dark eyes. If she acquiesced she knew it would be stressful. Could she handle it?

But she remembered what it felt like to be five years

old and know that no one was coming for you, knowing that you were on your own. She'd hated that feeling and she knew she couldn't put someone else in that position.

She sighed and said, 'Let me make a call.' She threw her gloves and mask into the bin as Damien signed the surgical notes. She was careful not to agree to his crazy plan just yet. She still didn't know if she was capable of agreeing to his suggestion. She needed a second opinion. She needed to run it past her psychologist but that wasn't a conversation she was prepared to have in public. She pushed open the door into the scrub room and went to fetch her cellphone.

She dialled the emergency number, the one Caroline had promised to always answer. Abi wasn't sure what Caroline termed an *emergency* exactly but, for her, going unprepared into a new environment that was not only large but filled with people and knowing she would have to introduce herself to strangers without time for any research or reconnaissance definitely fell into the *emergency assistance* category. Abi had no idea how she was going to manage this and she needed Caroline to give her some contingencies to help her cope.

Caroline answered on the third ring and Abi explained the situation.

'I assume,' Caroline said, after listening to Abi's predicament, 'that you would actually like to do this favour for your boss?'

Would she? Part of her worried that if she agreed she would be setting a precedent and part of her also worried that she was letting him take advantage of her. But she could also remember what it was like to be left to find her own way home because her mother was incapable, again. Back then nobody had noticed if you weren't collected from school, lots of kids made their own way home, but not many primary school children had that freedom now. They were bundled off to after-school care before anything untoward could happen to them. Abi remembered all too well that feeling of abandonment and if she could help by collecting Summer she would. It didn't matter that Summer didn't know her; she imagined just knowing her dad had sent someone would be better than being forgotten. Abi wasn't doing this for Damien.

'I'm not doing this for my boss, I'm doing it for his daughter,' she explained. 'She was expecting her mother to collect her and I don't want her to feel that she's not important.' Abi knew that Caroline understood her reasons and where they stemmed from. They'd been over a lot of old, and new, ground together and Abi didn't have many secrets left that Caroline hadn't heard. Damien, however, was a new topic and not one they'd discussed, and neither did she intend to. Abi felt it was best, safest to leave him in the category of work colleague. There was no reason to go into any detail about him, he was of no consequence. 'But I have never met Summer, I don't know the school, I don't know the staff and they don't know me. It's making me nervous.'

'The school is close to your house, though?' Caroline asked.

'Yes.'

'Why don't you go home and collect Jonty?' the psychologist suggested. 'Take him with you. You'll feel better and if Summer likes dogs it will break the ice with her too.'

Abi took a deep breath. She could do this. 'That's a good idea. Thanks.'

She felt better when she ended the call, far more confident. This might just work.

Abi pulled her 4x4 into the school car park. The building was long and low and stretched out before her, but fortunately the car park was virtually empty and she was able to put her car two places from the front entrance. She took a moment to survey her surroundings, not that she really expected any danger but it was a habit she had formed over the past six months and it was proving hard to shake. There was no one around and she could see nothing suspicious. She was in the middle of suburban LA, she reminded herself. It wasn't Kabul and she was unlikely to encounter a suicide bomber here. But her paranoia still got the better of her and she reached across to her right and opened the passenger door, letting Jonty jump out first. He sniffed the air and once she was certain he was showing no signs of distress she took a deep breath and stepped out of the car.

She showed her ID at the office and was taken to the after-school-hours area, where about two dozen kids were engaged in various activities. She spotted Summer straight away. Three girls were jumping rope and one of the girls turning the rope was a miniature, female version of Damien. Dressed in pink she had her dark hair tied in two short pigtails that stuck out from the sides of her head but there was no mistaking that gene pool.

'Summer,' the school secretary called to her, getting her attention. 'This is Dr Thompson. She works with your father and she's come to collect you.'

'Please, call me Abi. And this is Jonty.'

'A dog! You brought a dog in.' All three girls, Summer and her two friends, immediately surrounded Abi.

Jonty lapped up the attention. Caroline's advice to bring him had been spot on.

Abi took a closer look at Summer as the girls patted Jonty. She had the same oval face, the same dark eyes and the same smile as her father. She was as cute as a button.

She seemed to have no qualms going home with Abi. She skipped along beside Jonty and was far from the forlorn, lonely figure Abi had been expecting. If she knew her father had forgotten to collect her, it didn't seem to bother her. What Abi saw was a confident, happy five-year-old who was very comfortable with strangers. Summer was not at all what she had envisaged.

Abi opened the car door and tilted the passenger seat forward. Jonty jumped in and Abi reset the seat and waited for Summer to climb up into the passenger seat, but she was standing still, her head tilted to one side, as she seemed to be considering something.

'Are you going to get in?' Abi asked her.

'Are you sure you're a doctor?' Summer replied.

'I'm positive. Why?'

'You have a very old car.'

If Summer had visited The Hills and seen the cars driven by the doctors who worked there, Abi could understand the question. She didn't have that kind of money. Not yet. While money did motivate her, she had grown up poor and didn't plan on staying poor; she couldn't, however, imagine spending a small fortune on a car. She had other priorities. She wanted to have the security of her own house and some investments, and a brand-new car was not on that list, but she wasn't about to explain all that to a five-year-old.

'It's just me and Jonty,' she said. 'He's very hairy and sometimes very dirty. I don't have to worry about him messing up this car.'

'Oh, okay. Does the top come off?' she asked, as she climbed in and continued to chatter away, keeping up an almost one-sided conversation for the short drive to Abi's house. Summer certainly wasn't shy, but despite the fact that there didn't appear to be any need for Abi to have left work to rush over here to rescue a child who didn't need her she didn't mind. Summer was delightful and it was nice to have some two-legged company.

But, of course, Abi hadn't factored in the after-school snack. She had no food in her apartment other than an apple that was more than likely past its use-by date and a box of breakfast cereal. She couldn't recall the last time she'd done a proper grocery shop. She was not all that conscious about food as she didn't have a big appetite. Growing up, there had never been enough to eat in her house and therefore food had never been a focus. Before she'd joined the army she couldn't ever recall eating three meals a day.

She decided the best course of action would be to take Summer over to her landlords. Irma always had something sweet to eat, usually fresh from her oven, and today was no exception. Abi let Irma fuss over them and feed them both, and once Summer's hunger pains had been satisfied the little girl asked, with her mouth full of one of Irma's cookies, 'Can we take Jonty for a walk?'

'Just a short one,' Abi told her, 'before it gets dark.'

Irma pressed a couple of extra cookies into Summer's hand to take with her as Abi clipped Jonty's lead on.

'I'd like a dog,' Summer announced, as they hit the footpath. 'Or a little brother.'

'A dog might be better,' Abi replied. 'Little brothers can be annoying.'

'Do you have a brother?' Summer asked.

Abi shook her head. 'No, nor a sister.'

'How do you know they're annoying, then?'

Abi laughed. Summer made a fair point. 'Good question. I'm just guessing, I suppose.'

'It'll have to be a dog. Mum doesn't want any more children. She says she didn't even want me.'

Abi had no idea what the right response to this statement was. Her experience with children was limited at best. Should she make a big deal of Summer's comment? Tell her she must be mistaken? But she couldn't do that, she didn't know the facts. For all she knew, Summer could be speaking the truth. Why would she make something like that up? What child would think like that unless they'd heard those words uttered? Abi felt as though her heart was breaking. No one deserved to hear that from their mother. Abi's mother had loved her, she just hadn't been able to care for her properly. Her addictions and her circumstances had made that impossible, but what was Summer's mother's excuse? And what was Damien's role in all this?

Abi could feel herself getting angry but she couldn't lose her temper. That wasn't going to help Summer.

She was completely out of her depth, maybe a change of topic would work best she thought as she launched into a discussion about what breed of dog would suit Summer best. Abi had no idea what Damien's thoughts were on dog ownership but right now she didn't care. If he got asked a few curly questions about getting a puppy, that wasn't her problem. The way she saw it, he owed her a favour or two after today.

Summer was lying on the floor, playing with Jonty, when Abi heard Damien's car pull into her driveway. She went out onto the first-floor deck to direct him upstairs. The moment she heard his voice Summer jumped up from the floor and threw herself into her father's arms, and narrowly avoided crushing a bunch of irises that Damien clutched in his hands.

'Daddy, Daddy, Abi has a dog. Come and see.'

'Hang on one second, gorgeous girl, I need to put these down first.'

He lowered Summer to the floor and handed the irises to Abi. 'These are for you,' he said.

'What for?' Abi asked.

'To say thank you.'

'You didn't need to do that.'

'Yes, I did,' he insisted. 'You saved my bacon and I didn't want you to think I didn't appreciate it.'

Her apartment was small and Damien was standing awfully close to her. He smelt fresh and clean—he must have showered quickly after surgery—and his proximity was making her flustered. She was far too aware of him.

'I'll just put these into a vase,' she said, inventing a reason to move away from him. She stepped backwards into her narrow galley kitchen that ran along the back wall of the living space and separated her bedroom from the rest of the apartment. She opened a couple of cupboards hopefully. She didn't think she actually owned a vase. She'd never needed one, no one had ever given her flowers before. Her ex-boyfriend, Mark, had showered her with expensive jewellery that had never really suited her—she'd always felt it had been too sophisticated or mature for her—and looking now at this simple bunch of irises she knew which gift she preferred.

At the back of one of the cupboards she found an old china jug that she assumed belonged to Irma. That would do. She filled it with water, arranged the flowers in it and displayed them on the kitchen counter. The irises were a rich, deep blue with yellow centres and looked surprisingly cheery on the bench. She'd never put much store in the power of a bunch of beautiful flowers but that was because she'd never received any. Being given flowers was so much nicer than picking up a bunch at the weekend market for herself. It shouldn't make any difference, especially given the circumstances, but Abi was touched by Damien's gesture.

She swallowed hard to dislodge the lump that had formed in her throat as Damien pulled out one of the stools at her kitchen counter and took a seat. Abi stayed on the opposite side of the bench, a safe distance away.

'Dad, can we have pizza for dinner?' Summer climbed up onto the stool next to Damien and Abi was struck again by the strong family resemblance now that they were side by side.

'I'll pick one up on the way home.'

'I want to go out for pizza and I want Abi and Jonty to come.'

'Would you like to come with us?' Damien asked her. 'My shout.'

Abi shook her head. 'No, thank you.' She really wasn't up to going out. She'd had enough stressful situations to cope with today and, while sharing a pizza with Damien and Summer sounded appealing, tackling another unknown and unsecured location didn't.

'Please come, Abi, please.' Summer was begging but Abi couldn't do it.

'Sorry, you've probably already got plans,' Damien said, misunderstanding her refusal of his invitation. 'We've taken up enough of your time, we'll get going. Summer, get your things and say goodbye, please.'

'No, it's not that,' Abi said. She didn't want to be alone. She knew the house was going to feel quiet and empty when they left. 'I don't want to leave Jonty,' she told him. 'What about if we got pizza delivered?'

'Are you sure?' Damien asked, as Summer jumped about excitedly, happy to have had her wish granted.

Abi nodded. 'Positive.'

'It's still my shout,' he said, as Summer returned to Jonty's side and Abi pulled a delivery menu off the fridge.

She wasn't about to argue and as she phoned their order through Damien added, 'I'm not sure if I should be letting Summer get away with it. I'm sure she's milking the fact that I didn't pick her up from school. She's playing on my guilt.'

'Really?' Abi wasn't so sure. 'She can manipulate you like that at her age?'

'You'd better believe it. She knows exactly how to play me. I think she gets that from her mother. She's an actress and Summer has definitely inherited the dramatic gene from her.'

'She's an actress?'

'Yes. And quite a good one.'

'Is that why she's gone to New York?' Presented with the opportunity, Abi couldn't resist asking some questions but she busied herself looking for napkins and plates so that Damien hopefully didn't feel as though he was being interrogated.

Damien was nodding. 'She got called in for an audition for a television series and, as usual, she didn't worry about any pre-existing commitments, just dropped everything and went.'

'Have you heard from her?'

'Not directly. There was a message on my phone, asking me to collect Summer, but of course I was in Theatre so I didn't see it. She's never understood that I can't monitor my emails or even check my phone constantly throughout the day. Brooke exists in her own world and has never made an attempt to put herself in someone else's shoes. This isn't the first time she's changed plans without consulting me, but her world is all about her and she refuses to consider others, even her own daughter.'

Abi felt her sympathy for Summer strengthen. She knew what it was like to have a mother who did not have her children as a priority. Whether it was because they couldn't or wouldn't cope wasn't the point. Either way it left the children feeling neglected and unloved and that was no way for any child to grow up.

'Did she say when she'd be back?'

'No. She wouldn't consider that I would need to know that.'

'But what about Summer?'

'Brooke will expect me to handle it.'

Abi found the whole situation incredible. It was obvious that Damien and Brooke had some issues with their channels of communication but that wasn't really any of her business—unless Damien made it a habit to involve her. At this stage she couldn't get involved but that didn't stop her from wanting to know more about their situation. She knew she shouldn't care but Summer was so sweet and Damien was so gorgeous and she had to admit she was wondering what sort of woman would catch his eye. If Summer's mother was an actress she was probably beautiful. There must be something special about her if Damien was letting her get away with treating him so disrespectfully, but in Abi's eyes that didn't excuse her behaviour, particularly towards Summer. Damien said it wasn't the first time Summer hadn't been collected. Why did he let her get away with it?

Damien had only talked about 'Summer's mother', he hadn't mentioned a wife. Were they divorced? Never married? What was the state of their relationship? Now and previously. Abi's curiosity was piqued but she couldn't ask those questions.

'You didn't ask?' Abi wanted to know more but Damien wasn't answering. He was watching Summer and Abi guessed he didn't want the conversation to be overheard.

'Summer, would you like to brush Jonty while we wait for our pizza?' she suggested, knowing that Summer wouldn't refuse.

'She's been asking for a dog but I really don't think we have the time to devote to one,' Damien said as his daughter headed downstairs to the utility room to look for Jonty's brush.

'I know. She told me,' Abi replied.

Damien shot a glance Abi's way, a worried look in his dark eyes. 'What else did she tell you?'

'Actually, she did tell me one thing that I think you should hear.' Abi moved around the kitchen bench to take a seat at the counter beside Damien. She needed to tell him what Summer had said but she felt she needed to be closer. What she was about to say felt a bit like spilling a secret and she couldn't do it from across the kitchen bench. It needed to be said quietly, as if saying it loudly would make it real. Although Abi had a suspicion that what Summer had told her was true.

'She told me that her mother didn't want her.' Even repeating Summer's words made Abi's heart ache and seeing Damien's expression just made it worse. He looked sad and resigned but not surprised, and Abi realised that her suspicion was correct. Summer had been telling the truth.

Damien was nodding his head. 'I know. Brooke never made any secret of the fact that her career was going to come before anything else and we weren't planning on having kids when she fell pregnant, but I always hoped that she'd embrace motherhood once the baby arrived. But Brooke has never bonded with Summer. She enjoys dressing her up and taking her out but she seems to think of her as an accessory rather than her daughter. A child takes a lot of time and energy and Brooke prefers to spend that time and energy on herself. I knew she didn't want children but I still can't believe that she's told Summer that.'

In Abi's opinion Brooke sounded nothing like the kind of woman she imagined Damien to have chosen.

'What if she gets this job in New York?'

Damien shrugged. 'I'll worry about that then.'

He tried to sound relaxed and unconcerned but the reality was the idea terrified him. If Brooke got the offer of a permanent gig on the other side of the country, how would that affect him and, more importantly, Summer?

But Abi voiced his concern. 'What if she wants to take Summer?'

'I can't imagine she'd want to do that. She really doesn't have one maternal bone in her body.' That had become perfectly clear in the demise of their marriage. 'She has no time for Summer and Summer is definitely not Brooke's priority. Unfortunately she doesn't even try to pretend otherwise. But I will always do what's best for Summer and I would fight tooth and nail to keep her with me.'

Damien hated the fact that he'd been unable to make his marriage work. He hated being a failure, even though he knew that he and Brooke were both to blame. But it was irrelevant now. Marriage was not something he intended to try again. His focus was elsewhere. Summer was his number one priority, followed by his career.

Summer was yawning as Damien finished off the last slice of pizza. He wiped his hands on his napkin and said, 'It's getting late. We'd better go.'

Abi and Damien stood up from the kitchen bench at the same time. They were inches apart and Abi could feel the air crackling around them, surrounding them in a field of electricity.

She could feel herself being drawn in by his eyes, so dark it was impossible to fathom what was going on behind them. She could see the shadow of the day's growth of his beard, dark on his jaw and chin, and along with the strong straight line of his nose there was something totally masculine about him. He looked powerful yet she'd seen how gentle and kind he was with Summer. He projected strength but also sensitivity and he was utterly gorgeous to boot.

She forgot all her rules, all her reasons why she was single and staying that way. Damien had captured her imagination and she wanted to know more about him. Where he had come from, why he had married, what had attracted him to his wife and what was the state of his relationship with her. She wanted to know what he tasted like. What he felt like and what it would feel like to have his lips brush across hers.

She could feel herself leaning towards him. Perhaps the field was magnetic, not electric, but it was almost too powerful to resist. Was it her imagination or was he leaning towards her too?

Abi felt pressure against her leg, a knock, a bump. She looked down. Summer had squeezed herself between them and wrapped herself around Damien's leg, breaking the spell, releasing the tension that surrounded them.

Damien bent down, scooped his daughter into his arms and stepped back. He picked up her school bag and Abi stood at the top of the stairs and watched them leave. She had to force herself not to follow.

What would that achieve? Why would she want to?

She had to keep her distance. Yes, he was an attractive man, gorgeous even, and he was wonderful with Summer, but he was also a colleague and she couldn't go there again. This time she knew his life was complicated. This time she would have no excuses. It sounded as though his relationship with Summer's mother was extremely difficult and she had vowed that her next relationship would be simple, straightforward. Next time she was going in with her eyes open.

Next time! Next relationship! Why was she even thinking like that? She was in no hurry to go there again and when she was ready a man like Damien would not be on her list. A complicated man with baggage who she also had to work with—she couldn't afford to even think about that.

CHAPTER FOUR

THERE WAS A light knock on Damien's open office door and he looked up in anticipation, hoping to see Abi. Disappointment lodged in the back of his throat when he saw Freya standing there instead. He should have known it wasn't Abi as her scent, already familiar to him, always preceded her.

She smelt of fresh peaches and sunshine, she smelt like the month of July, of summer, and her amber eyes blazed with warmth in contrast to her cool, pale skin. He wondered if she tasted of peaches as well and for a moment last night he'd thought about finding out. He'd been tempted to kiss her. Caught up in a moment of madness, he'd been tempted to press his lips to hers and taste her.

For one crazy moment he'd forgotten about his daughter, he'd forgotten about his issues with his ex-wife—all he'd been aware of was Abi. He'd been drawn to her. There was something between them, a connection that he hadn't felt with anyone for a long time. He didn't think he was imagining it, he was certain she felt it too. He was certain he'd seen desire in her golden eyes and he'd definitely seen her lean towards him—or had he leaned towards her?—but then reality had forced its way between them in the form of an impatient five-year-old. Although that was probably just as well. He couldn't jump in, despite wanting to. All his energy was directed at his work and his daughter, and he had no room in his life for anything else.

But he couldn't keep thoughts of Abi out of his head. So much about her was already familiar and he was still trying to process how that could be after only a few days. How was it that she had worked her way into his subconscious so swiftly? There was something ethereal and mystical about her. She was weaving her magic over him, casting a spell.

'Are you okay?' Freya asked, and Damien was aware only then that his thoughts were drifting.

He shook his head to clear it. 'Yes, I'm fine. What can I do for you?'

'I just wanted to check on how Abi's first day went. Did you have any problems? Is there anything I need to know about?'

'No, everything's good.' Everything except his equilibrium but that wasn't Freya's department.

'What do you think of her?'

'Is this where you want me to say, "You were right"?' he asked, but Freya didn't reply, just smiled at him and raised an eyebrow. Damien decided he wasn't going to give her the satisfaction of the truth. 'You chose well, she's extremely competent,' he said.

'Oh, I know that,' Freya responded. 'I meant what do you think of her as a person? She's cute, isn't she?'

'I hadn't noticed,' he lied. He didn't want to notice cute women. He had enough going on in his life without complicating things by adding women into the mix. But his brain was defying instructions and he was spending far too much time contemplating Abi Thompson. He couldn't admit the truth, not to Freya. He knew she would want to meddle. She was happy in her new relationship with Zack and Damien knew she thought everyone around her should be so lucky. He didn't need her interference.

'Really?'

'Really.'

He was happy on his own. He didn't need, or want, a woman at this point in his life. He'd made a mess of his marriage and he knew it had made him gun-shy. He'd got so many things wrong, starting with his judgement of Brooke's character. He'd been badly burned and he hated the knowledge that his marriage had failed; he hated not making a success of things. His focus now was on his daughter and that was how things should be. That was how things had to be.

'So, if you'll excuse me I have a meeting with Mila shortly and I need to get a few things ready.'

Freya didn't argue but she did give him a look that implied she hadn't believed a word he'd said. That didn't bother him. She could believe what she liked. It didn't mean she was right.

Abi had struggled to get out of bed that morning. She'd lain awake for hours, tossing and turning, willing herself to sleep, but her mind had been buzzing with thoughts of Damien. When she had slept she'd been so wired that the extra adrenalin had given nightmares permission to intensify. Several times she'd been woken by dreams that had seemed even more vivid and real and dreadful than normal. She'd thought she was getting used to these dreams, she thought she'd learned what to expect, but last night had been particularly horrific and she was exhausted as a consequence.

When she arrived at the office, bleary-eyed and fuzzy-headed, she was informed by Jennifer that her day's schedule had been slightly revised and Damien wanted to see her.

Walking into his office, Abi saw a very attractive woman sitting in the chair by the window. In the chair Abi had sat in just yesterday. She stood as Abi entered the room.

She was about Abi's height with hazel eyes and amazing hair, thick, long and dark with mahogany highlights. She looked very 'together', sensible, calm, unflustered, serene and rich. She looked like old money and Abi fancied that she even smelt like money.

Damien looked as neat and tidy as always and the two of them made a striking pair.

'This is Dr Mila Brightman from the Bright Hope Clinic,' Damien introduced her. 'Do you remember I mentioned the joint venture that Freya has been working on?' he said as Mila shook Abi's hand.

Abi nodded. Freya had also talked about this and she remembered some basic information. The Bright Hope Clinic was located in Southern LA, demographically an area that was the polar opposite of The Hollywood Hills. It had been established to provide medical services to underprivileged children, both in LA and abroad, and Freya had recently established a project allowing the Bright Hope Clinic to access The Hills' facilities and staff on a pro bono basis. The first joint patient had been operated on just recently, a little boy who had undergone complicated heart surgery. Abi had heard all about Paulo and the success of the surgery.

Freya had been hugely excited and was planning a function to celebrate the partnership between the clinics and to garner some good publicity. She intended to promote The Hills and attract sponsorship for the Bright Hope Clinic at the same time.

'I heard about Paulo. That was quite a success story,' she commented, but she didn't mention the forthcoming party—she had no intention of attending that if she could possibly avoid it.

Mila was beaming. 'It was incredible! He is an amazing little boy with quite a spark, and to have such a great result was brilliant. You know no one expected him to survive the surgery? No one would touch him and to think he not only survived but is thriving is fantastic. Just imagine the amazing things we might be able to achieve together.'

'The Bright Hope Clinic is Mila's project,' Damien explained. 'She established it, it's her baby, and she has another patient who needs our assistance.'

Abi was keen to hear more.

'I was hoping you could help,' Mila said, as Abi took a seat. 'Damien tells me you've had a lot of experience with burns victims?'

'Unfortunately, yes. In Afghanistan.'

'We have a patient, a seven-year-old boy with third-degree burns to his arms and chest, sustained in a house fire. Dylan tried to put the fire out but was trapped and received extensive burns before the fire brigade could retrieve him.'

'When did this happen?'

'Four days ago. His mother was referred to us with an enquiry about skin-graft surgery. They don't have any medical insurance but I don't have any doctors who are skilled in this area. I am hoping that it is something you might be able to do here.'

From what Abi had been briefly told this would be exactly the type of case that Freya was keen to support and Abi was happy to help if she could. 'I've had lots of experience with burns victims but they've been adults,' she told Mila.

'The principle is the same surely?'

Abi nodded. The only issue she could envisage was dependent on the size of the area that needed grafts and whether or not a seven-year-old would have enough skin for donation, but she wouldn't know that until she'd examined the patient. 'When can I see him?' she asked.

Damien answered. 'He's being transferred by ambulance as we speak,' he said.

Abi looked at him quizzically and he shrugged his shoulders in reply. His tailored jacket lifted and then fell again to hang perfectly from his broad shoulders. 'I thought it might be a case you'd be interested in taking on,' he explained. 'It's not cosmetic surgery. As such, it's more along your lines, and I was pretty sure you'd agree to Mila's proposal.' He smiled at her and she knew that he wouldn't have much trouble getting her to agree to a good number of things.

But he was right. She'd enjoyed being in Theatre yesterday but this type of case, as opposed to cosmetic surgery, was exactly what she would prefer to be doing. A successful outcome would not only be a huge thing for the patient but it would cement her place at The Hills. It would be a challenge but one she was ready for. But she wasn't going to commit that easily and certainly not just because he'd smiled at her.

'I need to assess him first. I need to see whether there is anything I can do before I agree to take him on.'

'Of course,' Mila said as she stood. 'A consultation is all I'm asking for at this stage. Shall we go and meet the ambulance?'

Abi and Mila left Damien's office together, leaving him behind. That was a good thing. She needed to focus, to concentrate on this new case and if Damien had chosen to come with them she knew he would only distract her. But she would swear she could feel his dark-eyed gaze following her out of the room, although she knew she was being completely fanciful. Why would he follow her movements when he could watch Mila instead? Mila was far more glamorous.

'Thank you for agreeing to see Dylan,' Mila said as they stepped into the main corridor and headed for the ambulance bay. 'My clinic is important to me. I want to be able to provide medical care for people who can't afford it but it's an expensive exercise and there will always be some things we just can't do, but with Freya's help and with the support of The Hills we will be able to achieve more.'

Mila might come from a wealthier background than her but Abi sensed that despite that difference they had one thing in common—wanting the best for their patients. It was a common thread among those in the medical profession—patients came first—and Abi had seen it already at The Hills.

As they headed for the ambulance bay Abi could see James Rothsberg—head of The Hills and also Freya's brother and Abi's new boss—walking towards them. Abi felt Mila tense at her side as he approached them and Mila's pace slowed, not enough to stop her movement altogether but Abi got the sense that if the corridor hadn't been long and straight but had presented Mila with an alternate route to take, she would have taken it. She got the feeling that Mila was looking for an escape.

Abi saw James's eyes widen in surprise as they approached him and he stopped short a few steps before he reached them.

'Mila! What are you doing here?' He looked uncomfortable and appeared to be unsure how to greet her. He didn't seem to notice Abi at all. He certainly didn't acknowledge her, having eyes for Mila only.

'I needed to discuss a patient,' she said, as Abi tried to blend into the background. 'I have another patient that I'm hoping can use your services.'

'Already?'

Abi could hear the note of surprise in James's voice, or was it cynicism?

Mila obviously heard it too as her reply was frosty. 'I wasn't aware there was a time limit. Freya assured me you were okay with the collaboration.'

'Of course.'

He didn't sound okay. Abi could sense the tension between them. It was almost palpable and Abi could visualise the sparks snapping backwards and forwards between them. She wondered if she should give them some privacy but she was expecting the ambulance to arrive at any moment with Dylan, and she wanted Mila with her when they greeted their young patient.

In her peripheral vision she saw an ambulance pulling to a stop. James saw it too.

'Well, I guess I'll leave you to it,' he said as he stepped away. 'It was good to see you,' he added, but Abi wasn't at all sure that he meant it.

Mila also seemed a bit unsettled and looked a little lost when James walked away. She was no longer quite so unflustered and serene. Abi wondered what the story was—she was positive there was one.

Mila was still watching as James walked away. The rear doors of the ambulance were being opened and Abi started to move towards the exit. Her movement drew Mila's attention back to the matter at hand and Abi forgot all about Damien and the Bright Hope Clinic and the tension between Mila and James as she focused on her young patient.

'How did Dylan's skin grafts go?' Damien asked as he stuck his head into Abi's office.

Abi had performed the surgery the previous day but this was the first chance Damien had had to follow up the case with her. She swivelled her chair around to face him and stretched her legs out. She was wearing one of The Hills' white coats over a cream silky blouse and a black skirt that finished just above her knees. Her legs were amazing and Damien had to remind himself to keep his eyes fixed on her face and not to ogle her slim calves.

'The procedure went well. Now it's just a matter of waiting to see if the grafts take and keeping my fingers crossed that Dylan doesn't get an infection.'

She looked pleased with herself and so she should. Mila had observed the surgery and Damien had heard from her how impressed she had been with Abi's ability. It seemed as though Freya's decision to offer Abi a position at The Hills had been a good one. She was a competent surgeon, more than competent, and he was enjoying the development of their professional relationship, but he couldn't pretend he hadn't noticed her other attributes. She was beautiful in a fragile, delicate way but he sensed an underlying strength and he was keen to find out more about her, which brought him to the other reason for his visit.

Freya's party was only a day away but, according to Freya, Abi was making excuses to avoid attending Saturday night's function. Damien hadn't been particularly keen on attending either but when Freya had made it clear that she expected all senior staff to make an appearance at the publicity event he'd decided that one way to make the evening more appealing would be to have Abi there too.

He knew he should attend, it could be good for business, but since he and Brooke had split he'd avoided as many of these social gatherings as he could. He'd had enough of dressing up and parading around and chatting to people who didn't really interest him. He much preferred to spend his weekend nights lying on the couch, watching a movie and sharing a bowl of popcorn with Summer.

But that revelation had given him a brief glimpse into the future and he hadn't liked what he'd seen. He was in danger of becoming a sad, lonely old man. While, if anyone asked, he would tell them he wasn't interested in dating he didn't really want to end up old and alone. Summer wouldn't be with him for ever and he knew he should make more of an effort but there wasn't normally much incentive to do so. Women were trouble. Until now.

Until Abi had come into his world he would have been quite happy to remain a hermit but now the thought of being able to escort her to the function appealed to him and therefore so did the function. Now he had some incentive.

'Dylan's case was an interesting one for you?' he asked, posing the question while he tried to think of a way to segue into his proposition.

She nodded and her unusual amber eyes glowed.

'Do you feel like celebrating a successful first week on the job?' he asked.

'I won't know how successful I've been until Dylan's bandages come off next week.'

'Freya has organised this cocktail party for tomorrow night. It's part promotion, part celebration and we are all expected to attend, but I'd rather poke myself in the eye with a sharp stick. She tells me you feel much the same.'

Abi nodded. 'Having to mingle with a room full of strangers is my idea of purgatory,' she said.

'In that case, I have a suggestion.' He took a deep breath as an unfamiliar burst of nerves made his heart jump in his chest. 'Seeing as this party is supposed to be spotlighting the joint venture between The Hills and the Bright Hope Clinic and you've just had your very first joint-venture patient, I think that if I have to go, you should come with me.' He shouldn't be doing this but he was. He wanted to find out what made her tick. She was intriguing, a mixture of strength and fragility, a complicated combination—her army background combined with her delicate looks. Was she made of steel or spun silk like a spider web? Whichever it was, a mesh or a web, he was ensnared. 'I'll pick you up and I promise we'll just make a brief appearance and then we can escape. I'm going to use the babysitter excuse.'

'You have an excuse worked out already?'

'It pays to be prepared.' He grinned and was relieved to see an answering smile from Abi. 'And if you let me give you a lift, you'll have an excuse to leave too.'

She laughed and Damien felt the warm glow spread further through his body. He hadn't heard her laugh before and the sound burst from her, rich and joyous and completely unexpected. She sounded confident and full of life. Her laugh had wiped out all traces of fragility, leaving a sense of excitement and anticipation, and he knew he was going to do everything he could to make her laugh again.

'I've run out of excuses,' she said once she stopped laughing. 'I even tried telling Freya I have nothing to wear but then she offered to lend me a dress. So I think I will use your excuse. I would love a lift, thank you.'

Abi hesitated in the entrance and fiddled with the small diamond studs in her ears. She had sold all the jewellery Mark had given her during their ill-fated relationship when she'd discovered his deception. She'd only ever liked it because he'd given it to her but it hadn't really been her style— it was too ostentatious for her. She had simpler tastes and once she'd discovered the truth about Mark the jewellery had made her feel cheap and naive. She'd used the proceeds to buy herself a simple pair of diamond studs. They were the only decent jewellery she owned.

'Are you coming in?' Damien asked.

She hadn't been sure if accepting Damien's offer of a lift had been a wise decision. She still wasn't sure but after discussing the facts with her psychologist she had decided not to rescind his invitation. Caroline had convinced her that she needed to start socialising and she had suggested that this cocktail event would provide a perfect opportunity. It was in a safe, familiar location with a large number of people she already knew and there was no need for her to stay for hours. She could make an appearance and once she'd had enough she could leave. Abi wasn't totally convinced but she had agreed to give it a go, though she had known she wouldn't have the courage to arrive on her own. Damien's invitation had seemed like the lesser of two evils.

'Shall we?' Damien asked.

He was still waiting patiently for her. She needed to get moving, they couldn't stand outside all night. She ran her hands down the front of her dress, Freya's dress, in a self-conscious, nervous gesture.

'Don't worry, you look gorgeous,' he said.

'Really?'

Abi had been worried about this dress. She'd never owned or worn anything like it but she had no option. It was a simple sheath with thin spaghetti straps but its simplicity belied its eye-catching silhouette. The dress was made of gold sequins that matched her eyes and it shimmered and sparkled as she moved. It looked expensive and it was. There would be no hiding in the corner in this one. She had draped a black wrap over her shoulders in an attempt to tone the outfit down but she still felt very conspicuous. 'I was worried it might be too much. It's not too revealing?'

Damien shook his head. 'It's perfect.'

'Thank you.' His compliment sent a thrill of pleasure through her and boosted her confidence. She wanted to tell him that he looked amazing too but she couldn't summon the courage. He was in a black evening suit, single breasted, cut to his slim frame, drawing attention to the blackness of his hair and eyes. She wasn't a girl who was taken in by a man in uniform, years of army life had made her immune to that, but a man in a dinner suit with a crisp white shirt and a bow tie that had been tied on, not clipped, was a different story. Especially when it was carried off as well as Damien did. He could have stepped off the cover of a magazine.

He placed a hand in the small of her back and ushered her towards the door. A security guard was stationed there and Abi felt herself relax, knowing no unexpected guests would have gained entry.

Together they stepped into the clinic foyer, where Abi stopped and looked around her in awe. The foyer was normally spectacular, reminding her of a modern art gallery, but Freya had outdone herself tonight. Chandeliers had been hung from the ceiling, enormous crystal vases held oversized flower arrangements, a string quartet played in the corner and young, beautiful waiters, whom Abi suspected would be models or actors, served French champagne.

The party spilled from the reception area into the internal courtyard, although the room was not yet crowded. Abi was relieved to see that she and Damien were among the first to arrive. She wasn't brave enough to walk into a room full of people, it was far better if the room filled up around her.

Freya had timed the party to begin at sunset and the view of the city sparkling below them as the lights began to come on was spectacular. Freya was greeting guests just inside the door. Abi knew it wasn't technically Freya's party but that was how she thought of it. She had talked of nothing but work and the party all week and even though the party was a publicity event for The Hills and for the Bright Hope Clinic, Abi couldn't help but associate it with Freya.

Even the guests looked as if they could all be Freya's friends. Everyone looked rich—some looked like new money, others like old, but Abi was neither. She had grown up poor, something she doubted any of these people were familiar with. Although she looked the part tonight she still felt a great divide between her and everyone else. There wasn't anything she could do about it but she didn't like it and she worried that the guests would see through her smoke-and-mirrors dress to the girl who had grown up poor, raised by an alcoholic single mother.

'Abi, let me check your wrap.' Damien's voice interrupted her thoughts. His hands were on her arms and she could feel the warmth of his fingers spreading through her body as he started to slip the wrap from her shoulders.

She wanted to go with him to the coat check. She didn't want to wander unaccompanied among the other guests, and she didn't want to introduce herself to strangers. She was about to follow him when Mila appeared by her side.

'Good, you're here,' Mila greeted her. 'Come with me, there's someone I want you to meet.'

'I'll catch up with you later,' Damien said, as Mila tucked her arm into Abi's almost as if she was afraid Abi would run away if she didn't keep hold of her.

As Mila led her through the crowd Abi felt as though she'd been dropped into a movie set, a glamorous, old-school Hollywood movie. It was good in a way as it didn't feel like real life. Perhaps if she could pretend it was make-believe she would be able to relax and enjoy the evening.

Mila stopped next to a solid, muscular man with cropped dirty blond hair and brown eyes and introduced her. 'Here she is. Abi, this is Tyler Richardson, my boyfriend.'

Abi was taken by surprise. After witnessing the exchange, and the tension, between Mila and James earlier in the week she realised she hadn't expected Mila to have a boyfriend. Maybe Tyler was the source of the tension she had felt.

'It's good to meet you.' Tyler took her hand and shook it hard. He seemed laid back and relaxed but she couldn't figure out why he'd want to meet her. 'I wanted to thank you,' he continued.

'Thank me? For what?'

'For taking on Dylan's care.'

Abi frowned, unsure what connection Tyler had with her patient.

'I'm a fireman,' he explained, as Mila excused herself to visit the bathroom. 'I was in the crew that went to the scene of Dylan's accident. I pulled him out of the house.'

'Oh, I see. Is that how he ended up at the Bright Hope Clinic? Through you?'

'I called in at the hospital to see how he was doing and spoke to his mum and mentioned that Mila's clinic might be able to help. How did the surgery go? How is he?'

'I'm not sure how much I can tell you without breaking confidentiality,' Abi replied.

'That's okay. It's just that when we are able to save someone it's nice to know how they're doing. Sometimes we never hear anything. We rescue someone and then…' he spread his hands wide '…nothing. The nurses in the public hospitals will often give us a bit of an update. Hearing that someone survived and is doing well helps make our job worthwhile, it helps to make up for the ones that don't go so well. But once he was moved out of there it was almost impossible to find out anything.'

Abi could understand that. Tyler wasn't so different from her, trying to make a difference, trying to save lives. Hearing good news always lifted spirits. What could she tell him? She was happy with Dylan's progress but it was early days. The bandages wouldn't be removed for another couple of days so it was impossible to tell how successful the grafts had been. The only positives at this stage were that she'd been able to do the grafts and that Dylan's temperature was normal, indicating the absence of infection. She compromised. 'It's still early but I'm happy at this point. He'll be with us for another week. Do you want me to ask his mum if you can visit?'

Tyler nodded. 'I'd like that, thank you.'

Abi smiled at him. She knew exactly where he stood, and she was still smiling when James approached them.

James Rothsberg was a handsome man, tall and fair-haired with blue eyes and great bone structure— Abi always noticed bone structure, she was trained to do that—but although he was good-looking and of a similar build to Damien, he wasn't nearly as striking. Damien was sleeker and leaner but their contrasting colouring made her think of positives and negatives, and Damien was the positive. She couldn't ignore Damien and even now her eyes searched the crowd, looking for his familiar figure. There was something about Damien that captured her attention, something that went beyond the fact that he was tall, dark and handsome. She'd have to be careful and keep her guard up around him if she didn't want to make a fool of herself.

'Abi, one week gone. How are you settling in?' her new boss asked.

'More smoothly than I expected,' she said. She'd been busy. The film industry awards were a week away, which had bolstered her patient list, and Dylan's case had kept her on her toes, but she'd enjoyed her first week.

But James barely listened to her reply before offering his hand to Tyler. It seemed she wasn't the only one whose mind was wandering.

'Did you come with Abi?' he asked Tyler.

'No, Tyler is with me.' Mila had reappeared and answered before Tyler had a chance.

Abi could tell from James's expression that Mila's answer wasn't the one he'd been hoping for. Although the air around them was chilly at the moment, it was obvious that at some point these two had been more than acquaintances.

James made polite small talk for a few minutes but Abi noticed that when Mila headed to the opposite end of the room to prepare for the speeches, James's eyes followed her.

The string quartet finished their set and lapsed into silence as Mila and Freya stepped up onto a raised platform that had been positioned in front of the reception desk. As the speeches began Abi felt Damien's presence at her side. The air stirred whenever he was near;

it seemed to move differently around him. She turned to her right.

'Are you okay?' he asked. 'Having a good time?'

She wasn't really. She still felt uncomfortable and out of place, although she was better when Damien was near. Her world seemed to make more sense and her doubts and fears lessened, even though she still felt off balance, but she knew that was because of the effect he had on her rather than her own uncertainties and insecurities. But she nodded, trying to project confidence as she listened to the speeches.

Mila took the microphone first. She spoke passionately about the aims of the Bright Hope Clinic and about Paulo, who had been the first joint-venture patient between the two clinics. After the success of the first operation Freya had plans to ramp up the cooperation between the two clinics but she needed funding. Her speech emphasised the success of the first surgery and encouraged the wealthy LA guests to contribute to the charitable organisation she and James were establishing. That would give Mila access to the funds she needed, as well as bring good publicity for The Hills.

Both of them spoke very well about their vision for the partnership but Abi knew it was easy to talk in public when you were invested in and knowledgeable about your topic, and while she was interested in the project she could listen to Freya without watching. There were other things that had caught her attention, like what was going on between Mila and James. James's eyes were still glued to Mila. It was easy to see why, she was a beautiful woman, but Abi could feel that it was more than that.

'Ready to go?' Damien asked, as the speeches wrapped up.

He had his car keys in his hand. Abi could hear them jingling in his fist. They had agreed to leave as soon as possible after the speeches. Abi had known she would have had enough of the crowd by then, and Damien wanted to get home at a reasonable time to relieve the babysitter. Abi also wanted to get home to Jonty. Irma and George were away for the weekend, visiting their daughter, so Jonty was home alone.

She nodded. 'Give me a minute to grab my wrap.'

'I'll get it for you, I have the ticket.' Damien pulled the stub from his pocket. The storeroom behind the reception desk had been doing double duty as a coat check for the evening, manned by their regular receptionist, Stephanie, and Abi could see James making his way towards the desk and to Mila, who had just stepped off the platform at the conclusion of the speeches.

Curiosity got the better of her. 'It's okay,' she said as she took the ticket from his fingers. 'I'll only be a second.' She wanted another opportunity to examine Mila and James.

She headed for the coat check. James and Mila stood at one end of the reception desk, looking tense. Freya had disappeared into the crowd before James had crossed the room, leaving Mila and James alone. Not wanting to disturb them, she approached the desk from the opposite end but their conversation carried to her.

'Mila, can I talk to you?' James reached out a hand but Mila stepped back.

'It's not really a good time,' she replied, and again Abi got the sense that if there was somewhere that Mila could run and hide she would do so.

Abi handed Stephanie her ticket. She kept her face averted from Mila and James as she waited for Stephanie to fetch her wrap but it didn't stop her from being able to overhear their conversation. She didn't like to think of it as eavesdropping but she was fascinated by the tension between them.

'I'm sorry for everything,' James said, but he didn't elaborate on what 'everything' was and Mila didn't question him; she obviously knew what he was talking about.

'You want to apologise but you don't want to explain?' she said.

'I can't.'

'Can't or won't?'

Mila waited for an answer but James was mute. Stephanie returned with Abi's wrap as Mila said, 'It doesn't matter any more anyway. It's ancient history.' She brushed past James as she added, 'Tyler is waiting for me. I have to go.'

Mila's path took her within a couple of feet of Abi but she didn't look at her. Abi thought she could see tears in her eyes.

Abi glanced at James. She couldn't help herself. She wanted to see his reaction. He wasn't looking at her either so Abi followed the line of his gaze. His eyes were on Tyler, who was on the other side of the room, chatting with Freya's boyfriend, Zack. It didn't look as if Tyler was waiting for Mila. Why had she made that excuse? And what was James apologising for? There was definite history between them but from James's expression Abi was guessing that he didn't want it to be history. He'd looked jealous.

'Do you know if everything is okay between Mila

and James?' she couldn't resist asking Damien as she
sank into the soft leather of his car seat as he wound
his way down through the Hollywood Hills and back
to Pacific Palisades.

'Mila and *James*?' he queried. 'Why?'

'There just seemed to be a bit of tension between
them and I wondered what it was all about. Whether
there is an issue with the joint venture?' She added a
reason in case Damien thought she was being too in-
quisitive.

'The joint venture was Freya's idea but as far as I
know James is behind it. They're both very conscious
of giving back to the community, even though Freya is
the one driving it. I'm not aware of any issues.'

That didn't mean there weren't issues, it just meant
that, as a man, Damien possibly hadn't noticed anything.

But her own fabricated question made her wonder
if she was mistaken. Perhaps it was simply a conflict
over the joint venture. Perhaps it wasn't jealousy but a
financial issue. Not love but money?

Damien pulled into her driveway and as he killed
the engine Abi could hear Jonty barking. She frowned.
He wasn't a noisy dog usually. He hadn't barked when
she'd come home from work this week but then he'd
had George and Irma there. Perhaps he recognised the
sound of Damien's car and was excited to think he finally had company.

'Is that Jonty?' Damien asked, as he got out of the
car and came around to open Abi's door.

Abi nodded and as she stepped out onto the driveway
Jonty came tearing around the corner of the converted
garage and skidded to a halt by her side.

Abi scratched behind his ears. 'Hello, boy. What's got into you? Did you miss me?'

Damien walked Abi around to her door which was on the side of the garage and opened up to lead onto the internal stairway. Jonty was barking again as Abi pulled her keys from her handbag. 'Shush,' she said as she pushed the doggy door with her foot, thinking that perhaps once Jonty was inside he'd stop barking, but the doggy door didn't swing open.

'That's strange,' she said.

'What is?'

'The doggy door is locked. I'm certain I wouldn't have locked him out.' Jonty had stopped barking but he was pacing and whining at her feet as she slid her key into the lock.

'Wait.' Damien put his hand on her wrist and her skin thrummed with the heat of his touch. As she turned to look at him she heard a noise upstairs in her apartment. The sound of something falling over.

There was somebody in her apartment.

CHAPTER FIVE

ABI FROZE. SHE COULDN'T have moved if she'd wanted to. This feeling was familiar to her. This sense of feeling helpless, useless and most of all vulnerable. Knowing she should be doing something but unable to make her body function.

Her brain shut down. It was unable to issue instructions. Normally she was a quick, decisive person, years of training in medicine and in the armed forces had instilled that in her, but since returning from Afghanistan she had lost that ability to make a swift decision under pressure, unless it was in a medical context. The slightest bit of stress or anxiety outside work rendered her incapable. And the thought that she was vulnerable in those situations terrified her even more, which only served to worsen her predicament.

Damien showed no such hesitation. He stepped in front of her as she remained standing, rooted to the spot. He unlocked the door and Jonty raced past him as it opened and tore up the stairs, barking madly once more when he was thwarted again by another closed door that led into the apartment.

Damien followed Jonty. He made no attempt to climb the stairs quietly but, Abi supposed, there was no need for stealth. Her dog had well and truly announced their arrival.

He reached for the handle. She wanted to tell him not to open it, to be careful, but the words lodged in her throat and although she opened her mouth she couldn't get the words to come out. Fear rendered her speechless but she had recovered control of her limbs and was able to follow him up the stairs. Even that was driven by fear. She was more afraid of being left alone at the bottom of the stairs than confronting whatever was at the top. She needed to stay close to Damien, even if it meant closing the gap between her and danger.

As he turned the handle and pushed the door open Abi heard the sound of glass breaking. His back blocked her view so she craned her neck and stood on her toes to look past his shoulder, just in time to see a figure disappearing through her balcony doors and onto her deck.

Jonty dashed across the room and Damien followed, crossing the floor in four strides. Abi was close behind him, her heels crunching through the fragments of broken glass that had fallen out of the balcony doors as they had been slammed open and which now lay strewn across the deck.

The balcony was empty. Abi's heart was beating at a million miles an hour but she breathed a sigh of relief when she realised they were too late. She hadn't stopped to think about what might happen if they confronted the intruder but, thank God, they weren't about to find out.

Whoever had been in Abi's house had leapt over the railing of the deck and dropped eight feet to the lawn below. All they saw was a figure in dark clothing land awkwardly and run across George and Irma's lawn at a fast limp.

Damien had both hands on the top of the railing as he watched the retreating figure hobble away. 'He must have twisted his ankle when he landed. Shall I go after him?'

This time it was Abi's hand on Damien's arm as a precautionary gesture. 'No!'

'But I can catch him.'

'And then what? What if he has a knife? Or a gun?' Abi could feel herself shaking as adrenalin flooded her system. Her heart was racing again. She couldn't put Damien in danger. It was better just to let the man go. She wanted to avoid danger and minimise harm at all costs. 'He wouldn't have found anything worth stealing, I have nothing of any value. Let him go, it's not worth the risk.'

Her wrap had slipped off her shoulders and caught in the crook of her elbows and Damien reached over and lifted it back around her. The touch of his fingers made her tremble even more.

'Are you okay?' he asked.

She had no idea.

Damien insisted on checking the rest of the apartment to make sure there was no accomplice and Abi insisted on going with him. Even though her apartment was small with very few hiding places and wouldn't take long to search she didn't want to be left on her own. There was safety in numbers. There was safety with Damien.

She and Jonty followed behind him as he cleared the upstairs, a task that didn't take long as besides the kitchen and living area there was only Abi's bedroom and the bathroom. Coming out of the bathroom, Abi noticed that Jonty was protecting his front paw. She was torn between sticking close to Damien or checking the dog, but once they had finished investigating the upstairs Abi decided to tend to Jonty, letting Damien check the garage and utility room downstairs alone. There had been no more noises. It appeared that the intruder hadn't had company and she felt it was safe to stay upstairs.

She knelt on the kitchen floor and picked a piece of glass from Jonty's paw. It took her a while as her hands were shaking but once she was confident it was out she retrieved some first-aid supplies from the bathroom cabinet and washed his foot clean with antiseptic solution. She didn't bother to bandage it. Now that the glass was out it didn't appear to be worrying him and she knew he'd only gnaw at the bandage until it came off.

Damien reappeared from downstairs. 'There's a broken window in the garage,' he said. 'He must have come in that way and then locked Jonty out. Do you want to see if anything is missing? You might want to make a police report.'

Abi was certain that nothing would be missing and if there was she doubted it would matter to her, but some of the items in the apartment belonged to George and Irma. She'd have to let them know. 'I'll do it tomorrow when I've spoken to George and Irma,' she said as she folded her arms in a vain attempt to stop her body from shaking.

'Are you cold?'

Her apartment was warm and she had closed the drapes over the balcony doors to keep the draught out. She shook her head. She wasn't cold, just shaken up and probably in shock.

'Do you have any whisky?' Damien asked, as he

opened cupboards and searched the contents. He couldn't seem to stand still. Was he on edge too?

'No.'

When the search of her kitchen cupboards proved fruitless he wandered back over to the balcony doors. He opened the drapes and inspected the damage. 'Would George have anything I could use to board up these windows to make them secure overnight?'

'I'm sure he would. He has a whole shed full of carpentry stuff.'

'Would he mind if I took a look? Should I wake him up?'

'He and Irma have gone away for the weekend but I have the key to his shed.' Abi opened a kitchen drawer and pulled out a bunch of keys and handed it to Damien. Her fingers brushed his and the keys jangled as her hand shook.

'Are you going to be okay in here while I check the shed?'

'I'm fine.' She was far from okay but she was coping. Her heart rate had been settling now that she knew the house was clear but the briefest of touches from Damien made it skyrocket again. Two different triggers, one pleasant, one definitely not, but both had the power to set her heart racing. She doubted she'd be able to sleep tonight so a glass of whisky sounded like a good idea, but she'd worry about that later.

Damien disappeared again but within a few minutes Abi could hear him hammering downstairs and then he went to work on the balcony doors, using some bits of plywood he'd found in George's shed to fashion a makeshift repair job.

'I've managed to weatherproof your apartment but

it's not terribly secure. I was going to suggest that you stay over at George and Irma's but if they are away I think you should come home with me. I don't think you should stay here alone.'

'I'm not alone, I have Jonty. I can't leave him.'

'Bring him too. You can have Summer's bed and I'll put Summer in with me.'

Abi hesitated before answering and Damien mistook her hesitation for apprehension.

'Do you want to call someone and let them know you're staying with me?' he offered, realising she may have reservations about going home with him but she had no one to call. She was totally alone.

'Freya can vouch for my character,' he added. Abi had no doubt Freya would approve but if she did accept Damien's offer she wasn't sure that she wanted anyone else to know. Besides, it wasn't the fact that she was considering going home with a virtual stranger that was making her hesitate, she actually felt safe with Damien, but the fact that she was even considering the idea at all was what worried her. The fact that she *should* have reservations when she didn't was the concern. She barely knew Damien. Was it wrong to trust him so quickly?

'I don't want to put Summer out of her bed.'

Damien grinned at her and Abi was transfixed by the smile lines that appeared in the corners of his eyes. It was the only time his perfect features looked real. 'It's my bed or Summer's,' he said, 'they're the only options.'

Abi swallowed. She hadn't meant to imply anything untoward but Damien settled her nerves.

'Don't worry about Summer. She ends up in my bed most nights anyway and I'm really not going to leave you here on your own in an unsecured house. Grab what you need and come with me.'

Abi didn't need further convincing. The idea of staying in the apartment by herself made her jittery. She knew she wouldn't sleep and the idea of having company, of knowing there was someone just a room away, was far more reassuring. She had thought the apartment was secure and safe but after tonight's events she wasn't so certain. Perhaps if she still had a weapon she might have felt more comfortable but she'd returned her army-issued handgun when she'd gone on leave and she hadn't wanted to replace it. She hadn't wanted a weapon. She'd seen the damage they could do, and even now she knew she wouldn't want that responsibility or that temptation. She would rather stay at Damien's than pick up a gun.

She collected Jonty's essentials—his water bowl, lead and the large cushion that he slept on at the foot of her bed—and carried them downstairs to where Damien was loading her dog into his car. She remembered refusing Damien's invitation of a lift earlier in the week. She'd been worried then about Jonty messing up the pristine interior but she had no such qualms tonight, and neither, it seemed, did Jonty, who was more than happy to leap into the car.

Damien felt as if he'd only just drifted off to sleep when he was woken by the sound of a dog whining. He sat up in bed, disoriented, until he realised it was Jonty. What was wrong now?

He got out of bed, careful not to disturb Summer, and as he stepped into the hallway he saw the light come on in Summer's room. It shone under the door. Abi must be awake. But that didn't explain why Jonty was whining.

He should check to make sure everything was okay, but as he stretched out his hand to knock on the door the noise stopped. Should he still intrude? He had no idea. He didn't want to disturb Abi or frighten her or make a nuisance of himself, but what sort of host would he be if she needed something and he didn't offer assistance.

'Abi?' He knocked lightly and spoke through the door. 'Is everything okay?'

He opened the door and the scent of peaches wrapped around him. Abi's scent.

She was still asleep. Jonty was standing beside the bed, pushing his nose against her cheek. Did he want to go out?

But if Abi was still asleep who had turned the light on? He frowned. He was certain he had seen the light go on.

He was still standing in the doorway, trying to decide what to do, when Abi opened her eyes. He saw her jump when she registered his presence and he realised how it must look to her—an unfamiliar man appearing in her room in the middle of the night. He could see she was frightened. Her amber eyes were wide and unblinking. She reminded him of a deer caught in a spotlight and he felt like the hunter.

'Sorry, I didn't mean to frighten you.'

'Damien?'

Her cheeks were wet with tears and she was breathing heavily as if she'd been running but he knew that was impossible. There was a sheen of sweat on her brow and her hair was damp. This wasn't about Jonty needing to go outside.

'I heard Jonty whining. What's the matter?'

She sat up in bed. She was wearing one of his T-shirts

and it slipped off her shoulder to reveal a pale, creamy expanse of soft, smooth skin. They hadn't thought to grab any clothes for her, she'd been busy getting Jonty's stuff together and he hadn't given it a thought, so he'd lent her one of his T-shirts. It suited her, even though it swamped her tiny frame. With her messy hair and startled eyes she looked about twenty, although he knew she was ten years older than that. She pulled the damp T-shirt away from her body but it fell back as she let it go, clinging to her skin and drawing his attention to her nipples, which jutted against the fabric.

She was trembling.

Damien didn't hesitate any longer. In two strides he was next to the bed. In the next second he was sitting beside her. In one more second she was wrapped in his arms.

He hugged her tightly to him as he tried to stop her shaking. He had gone to her without thinking. A reflex action triggered by her fragile appearance had made him react impulsively. It seemed perfectly natural to take her in his arms and she didn't resist, didn't protest.

It *felt* perfectly natural. She was small and slight and fitted into the crook of his elbow and the curve of his shoulder as if they were designed just for her. Her head rested on his bare chest and he could feel her tears damp against his skin.

'What's wrong?'

'I had a nightmare. Jonty is trained to wake me.'

'Really? He can do that?' He made sure to keep his eyes focused on her face. The T-shirt he'd lent her was old and he hadn't realised it was quite so thin.

Abi nodded. 'He's an assistance dog. It's one of his many talents.'

'And the light? I swear I saw the light turn on when I was in the hall.'

He wasn't sure how to explain that but Abi seemed to know what he was talking about. She looked up at him. 'Jonty can flick switches.'

'You're kidding me.'

'No.'

'Is he going to make breakfast for us in the morning too?'

She smiled at him and he felt absurdly pleased that he'd managed to elicit a smile from her. 'Only for me. He's *my* assistance dog.'

'So this project you said you were involved with? You're not just training him or taking care of him? It's more personal than that?'

'Yes.'

'He's been assigned to you?'

Abi nodded.

'For nightmares?' He was trying to make sense of what was happening.

She nodded again.

'Do you have lots?' he asked.

'Only since Afghanistan.'

'Is there anything I can do?'

'Now or in general?'

'Now, for starters. Can I make you a hot chocolate? It's what I would do for Summer.'

She'd stopped shaking but she still felt cold.

'That sounds lovely but I don't need it. I'd rather you stayed here.'

He didn't need to be asked twice. It felt good to have her in his arms and he wasn't going to pretend otherwise.

He leant back against the bedhead and swung his

legs up on top of the quilt, stretching them out in front of him. Abi stayed curled against his chest and he kept his arm around her shoulders as he felt the steady, rhythmical rise and fall of her breathing. She seemed calmer now but he wasn't surprised to hear that she had nightmares. He could only imagine what she would have seen in Afghanistan. What she would have been through. What he didn't know was whether it would help to talk about her dreams or if it was best to ignore the horrors of the past in the hope that she could put it behind her. Would talking about it make it better or worse?

He couldn't remember much from his psychology studies. What would be the recommended practice today?

He decided to try talking about it. If she didn't want to talk to him she'd soon tell him. She didn't seem to have a problem with telling him if she thought he had overstepped the mark or was wrong. She'd put him back in his place a couple of times already this week.

'Is it always the same dream?' he asked.

'Pretty much.'

Silence fell and he thought that was it. If she didn't want to talk about it he wasn't going to force the issue.

She shifted her position, turning her head so she was looking at the ceiling. Had that been a protective movement designed so that he couldn't see her face? So he couldn't feel the dampness of her tears?

She started talking. 'In the dream I'm in Kabul. It's always Kabul, even if sometimes it doesn't look like it. Sometimes it looks like LA or Phoenix but I still know I'm in Kabul. It's hot and dusty, crowded and chaotic. There are people shouting and jostling. Traffic noise, car horns, brakes, engines revving, sirens.

Big-city noises and big-city smells—diesel fumes and garbage. I always have the impression of Kabul as loud and kind of manic but then the mania goes up a notch. One minute it's just regular bedlam, and then an explosion rips through the crowd, showering everyone with debris, intensifying the chaos. I can feel the force of the blast. It knocks me off my feet and for a moment everything is silent. In my dream I know instantly that a bomb has exploded but it wasn't like that at the time.'

At the time? This dream was real? Or rather the events in the dream were real? No wonder she had woken up in a cold sweat.

'The beginning of the dream is always the same,' she continued, 'but the actual explosion takes me by surprise every time. After the bomb explodes the dream varies. I can never change the beginning, the bomb always goes off, but what happens next changes, although it's always bad, just different degrees of terrible, and I can't control it.'

'What happens next?' he asked, not sure he was prepared for the answer, but if she needed to talk he would listen.

'My commanding officer is there too. He's injured and I try to help him. In my dream I crawl across the ground. I can feel glass and stones and metal cutting into my hands and knees but all I can see is Mark lying on the ground. He's not moving and I don't know if he's breathing. I keep crawling but this bit varies. Sometimes I reach him and sometimes I feel like I'm just crawling for minute after minute, never getting any closer. Sometimes Mark dies before I can reach him and sometimes I get there while he's still alive. He has a wife and daughters, sometimes they are in my dream too, but they do nothing, just stand and watch and ask me why I'm not saving him. Why aren't I doing more? I don't have anything to tell them except that I am trying, but the end is always the same. Mark dies and I wake up crying.'

'You were actually caught up in a situation like that? This was real?'

She nodded. 'We had gone into Kabul for a meeting, me, my commanding officer, Mark, and another captain. We were leaving the meeting to head back to the base. It was around lunchtime, the streets were busy as they always were, crowded with cars, trucks, motorbikes and pedestrians. Our driver was waiting on the street to collect us. He was out of the truck, holding the back door open for Mark, when there was an explosion. There was no warning, although I don't know why I would have expected one. One minute I was rounding the back of the truck and the next I was knocked off my feet.'

'Were you hurt?'

She shook her head and her hair brushed across his chest. 'Not critically. When a bomb explodes there're degrees of injury—dead, critically injured, non-life-threatening injuries and okay. Some of the blood was mine but I wasn't badly injured. My ears were ringing but other than that I could hear nothing else for what seemed like minutes but was probably only seconds. The air was thick with dust and smoke. I was disorientated but I had worked out what had happened. A bomb had been detonated, but I didn't know what sort or where. Not that it mattered. It had succeeded in creating the damage it had been designed for. I can remember lying there, fighting to breathe but being unable to move because I had no air. When I did catch my breath my throat and tongue were coated with dust. I inhaled and I could smell burnt flesh and the metallic tang of blood but I didn't realise some of it was mine.

'When I got up my leg gave way beneath me. I had shrapnel embedded in my thigh but I hadn't realised it. My leg wouldn't support my weight, which was probably lucky. It was a stupid idea to try to stand up. It would be safer to stay low but I wasn't thinking clearly.'

Damien could scarcely believe what he was hearing. He'd seen images from Afghanistan but he'd never really spent much time thinking about the people who were caught up in the war. It had all seemed to be so remote. Until now. Until he was listening to Abi's recount and feeling her tremble in his arms and seeing the fear and confusion in her eyes.

'I could see the other captain lying on the ground ahead of me. He had already walked around to the far side of the vehicle, which had sheltered him from the force of the blast. He was groggy and probably concussed but otherwise uninjured. I thought we'd been lucky. I thought we'd escaped any real damage but it turned out that wasn't the case. I dragged myself around to the other side of the truck, looking for the others— my CO and the driver. People were screaming now and crying. Running. Falling. It was complete chaos, there was no sense of order, just panic.

'We needed to get out of there but when I got around the vehicle I found that our driver was dead. And he wasn't the only one. There were plenty of dead and injured. My commanding officer had been hit. He was bleeding from his side, frothing blood from his lips. He must have thrown his arms up when the bomb exploded. It would have been a reflex reaction but it meant that he'd exposed the area under his arm, a gap in his flak jacket, and shrapnel had ripped through his chest wall. He'd sustained serious chest wounds and I knew I was unlikely to be able to save him but I had to try. There were others I could have tried to help but I didn't. Mark was my priority, my responsibility.

'I was kneeling in the middle of the road, trying to plug the wound in his chest with my hands. It was hopeless. There was a first-aid kit in the truck, a good one, a combat one, but I needed a hospital. There was nothing I could do in that environment. It wasn't safe. We had to get out of there. We had no idea what would happen next.

'The other captain helped me to lift Mark into the truck and then we had to load the body of our driver as well, we couldn't leave him. Everything had happened so quickly there was no time really to think, only to react. We had to get away but I still think about all those injured Afghans we left behind, even though I know my duty of care was to my own team. That was my priority.

'All the way back to the base I fought to keep Mark alive. The first-aid kit was substantial. I had bags of saline and bandages but what I needed was units of blood and an operating theatre. I knew he was unlikely to make it but I had to try. He was dead before we reached the base.'

'It sounds like you did everything you could. Even if there had been a whole team working on him, it sounds like the outcome would have been the same.'

'I know that, but it was the first time I couldn't save someone I knew well, and that's a hard thing to let go of. I think that's why I keep replaying the day in my dreams, hoping that it ends differently, but it never does.

It always ends the same way. With people dying. I feel guilty that I couldn't save him, I feel guilty sometimes that I survived when so many others didn't. I've never met Mark's wife and daughters but they turn up in my dream as my guilty subconscious.'

'Have you spoken to someone about this?'

'Officially?'

Damien nodded.

'I have. I've been diagnosed with PTSD and the military medical corps insist on therapy for all personnel even while on leave.'

'You're on leave? I thought you'd left?'

'I can't apply for a discharge from the army, it has to be recommended.'

'Do you think you should be working? Shouldn't you be taking some time to recover?'

'I need to stay busy. Work gives me something else to focus on. Without that I have nothing and I can't sit around with just my thoughts for company. I've been assessed as being fit to work but not fit for active duty. I can't work in a combat support unit but a hospital that's not in a war zone is fine. And I feel safe at work.'

'You don't feel safe generally?'

'I get nervous in unfamiliar, noisy or crowded environments so I try to avoid them if possible, but sometimes I can't, which is why Jonty was assigned to me, to help prevent panic attacks.'

'Should I have brought Summer to stay at your house? Has being in a strange place triggered your nightmare?' Damien felt terrible, as if this was somehow his fault.

'Maybe,' she said, making him feel even worse. 'But

I think it was more likely to be an after-effect of the shock of the break-in.'

The break-in had threatened her safety, Damien realised, and that thought eased his conscience slightly, although not completely. He needed to fix this.

'What can I do? How can I help?'

'Would you stay with me? Just until I fall asleep? I'm scared I'll have another dream.' Her voice was quiet and it sounded almost as if she expected him to refuse.

How could he refuse? He didn't want to. 'Sure.'

He half lay in the bed, with his shoulders propped against the headboard and Abi's head resting on his chest. Summer's bed was narrow and Abi had to lie on her side to fit. She curled herself against him and he wrapped his arm around her shoulders to keep her in the bed. He doubted whether either of them were going to go back to sleep and he wasn't planning on leaving her here alone if she did succumb.

He reached across and switched off the bedside light. He could feel Abi's eyelashes fluttering against his bare skin and each tiny puff of air as she exhaled. He usually slept naked but because he'd had to share his bed with Summer he'd put a pair of boxer shorts on so at least he was semi-decent. Although he didn't think thin boxer shorts were going to be enough of a shield against the touch of Abi's fingers and the smell of her hair.

Her fingers rested lightly on his chest and her head was tucked under his chin. He definitely wasn't going to be able to go back to sleep now.

The hall light was still on, taking the edge off the darkness, and he lay in the shadows and stared at the ceiling and thought about the enigma that was Abi.

She intrigued him. She'd been in his life for less

than a week but something told him she was going to leave a lasting effect. There was something fascinating about her. She was fragile and damaged but he sensed an underlying strength of character that suggested she would not be easily defeated. Where had that strength come from?

Her breathing slowed and she drifted off and he could feel his resistance weaken as she slept in his arms. He had vowed not to get involved with a woman again, he didn't have the time or the energy, but Abi was making him revise his thinking.

She was an anomaly, a mixture of courage and strength, fragility and insecurity, and she stirred a mixture of emotions in him. He wanted to know more about her. He'd never met anyone quite like her and he wanted to make the time to find out what made her tick.

In recent times his world had revolved around his daughter and his work. He didn't socialise and even when he had it had been with Brooke and her actor friends. He had never really understood them, never been sure what was real and what was fake, but Abi felt real. He was drawn to her. She was interesting and gorgeous, smart and strong, and yet he sensed some self-doubt in her. Had she always had that or was it the lasting effect of her CO's death?

He had noticed her hesitation when they had walked into the party last night. He hadn't expected that. Brooke had always been self-confident, she would have walked into a party and stopped and waited until everyone had looked at her. She would have arrived late so that she could ensure there were people there to notice her arrival. She'd had the behaviour of a celebrity even before she'd become one.

Abi was so confident in a work situation that he'd expected the same generally, and her reluctance, her lack of confidence, had surprised him. Had something else happened to her? The story she'd told about the bomb didn't explain it. She'd acted quickly, selflessly and bravely, she hadn't acted like a person lacking in self-confidence. He was certain there was more to her story and he was keen to find out what it was.

He wanted to know the answers, all the answers.

He turned his head and watched her sleep until fatigue overcame him too.

When he woke in the morning he'd been dreaming of sunshine, of peaches ripening in the summer sun.

Abi was still curled against him. Her breasts were squashed against his chest and her hand rested on his stomach. He was still shirtless. He should have gone back to his bed once she'd fallen asleep but he hadn't wanted to leave her alone. If he was completely honest he was enjoying the feeling of a woman, this woman, in his arms and he hadn't wanted to let her go. One of Abi's thighs was tucked between his, slight and warm. His hand had moved south from her shoulders and was resting on her hip. He could feel his erection, swollen, throbbing, pleading for release. Her hair smelled like peaches and her skin was the colour of vanilla ice cream. She was soft and sweet and delicious. It had been a while since he'd had anyone quite as delightful in his bed and he wasn't averse to the idea of exploring her attractions.

The quilt had slipped off her leg and from beneath the hem of her T-shirt, *his* T-shirt, he could see the shrapnel scars on her thigh. He replayed the story she'd told him in the night and remembered she was tougher than she looked. He ran his fingers lightly over the scars. They were raised and darker than her skin, reminiscent of a raspberry swirl in vanilla ice cream. A legacy of her past and a reminder that she was a survivor.

Abi stirred at his touch. Her eyelashes fluttered and her amber eyes opened. He could see her taking a moment to work out where she was.

He didn't want her to panic. She brought out all his protective instincts, which were never far from the surface anyway. He knew he had a habit of wanting to look after women, to protect them, a desire that stemmed from his upbringing. His mother suffered from debilitating rheumatoid arthritis and his father had been her primary source of care and support and that sense of protectiveness was strongly instilled in him. There was something vulnerable about Abi and he didn't want any more harm to come to her, not if it was in his power to prevent that.

'You're okay, Abi,' he told her. 'You're in Summer's bed.'

She woke properly and he could tell she was embarrassed to find herself draped across him. Not that he was complaining. She moved away from him, pulling her thigh out from between his legs and lifting her hand from his stomach, leaving a palm-sized patch of skin that felt cooler now she was gone.

Her eyes ran over his body, making his erection stand to attention even more than before. Her gaze moved from his bare chest down over his abdominals and further south. There was no way to disguise his reaction to her and he didn't want to. As far as he was concerned, there was nothing wrong with letting her see what effect she had on him.

He saw her swallow and when she looked up at him there was a question in the golden depths of her eyes.

She pulled farther away and he resisted the urge to hold her close. He didn't want to let her go but he didn't want to frighten her either. He relaxed his arm around her shoulders, giving her space.

'We didn't, did we?'

He shook his head. 'No. That would always be your decision.' His words were more of a question than a statement. It was obvious to both of them that he was keen but he would never make a presumption about sex. Both parties had to be willing and he was curious to know her thoughts but she gave a tiny shake of her head.

'I can't.'

That was more hopeful than a 'no' and better than an 'I don't want to' but it wasn't a 'yes'.

'Can't or won't?' he asked.

'Can't,' she clarified. 'We can't. Summer is in the house. This is her room. What if she comes in?'

She had a point but her answer gave him hope. He suspected she might be just as willing as he was in different circumstances but he wasn't going to push her, he wasn't going to take advantage. He would bide his time, certain that it would come in the not-too-distant future.

He wasn't sure exactly when he'd changed his mind, when he'd begun to feel like he wanted to pursue her, when he'd begun to think that women *weren't* too much trouble, well, one woman in particular. Had it been last night, when she'd curled into his side, or the night of the party when he'd given her a lift and his car had been filled with the scent of fresh peaches, or the afternoon that she had collected Summer from school and he'd so badly wanted to kiss her?

He knew this attraction was fraught with danger. He knew there were all sorts of reasons why he should keep his distance—they were colleagues, she had issues, he had baggage, he was a single dad with a difficult ex-wife and his priorities should be on Summer—but it was hard to ignore the stirring of desire when he'd held her in his arms. It had felt good. It had reminded him that he was a man.

The throbbing in his groin was another strong indicator that all his manly bits were working but he'd have to relieve the tension himself. He would do well to remember to focus on other aspects and keep a lid on his attraction to Abi. He wasn't planning on ignoring it altogether but he needed to slow things down. He couldn't jump in, he didn't know how she felt and he wasn't sure if he was ready. There were lots of complicating factors. It would be a different story perhaps if they'd met in a bar or at a conference, if she didn't already know Summer, if they didn't work together, if she hadn't spent the night in his arms.

'Just so I know, in case we ever find ourselves in this position again, how would Jonty react? Is he trained to attack?' His question lightened the mood, as he'd hoped it would. It let Abi back out of this situation but also made his intentions clear. He would slow things down but he wouldn't give up completely.

'Does he look like he's about to attack?' she countered, and Damien glanced over to where the dog lay, fast asleep, on his cushion, completely oblivious to what was going on around him.

'People who need assistance dogs often need them

for things like panic attacks, PTSD or epilepsy,' she explained. 'They might need help from paramedics or the public so it wouldn't be useful if the dogs were trained to protect their owners and not let people close.'

'Good to know.' He smiled and stood up, disentangling himself from Abi. 'But I guess it's time for me to shower and take care of some business.' His erection was plainly obvious in his boxer shorts and he still made no attempt to hide it. He left her lying in the bed and hoped he was giving her plenty to think about.

Abi stretched lazily as she watched Damien walk out of the room. She'd slept soundly and had woken up feeling relaxed and comfortable for the first time in months. It was amazing the difference having a warm, hard body in the bed with her had made. She had felt safe, and feeling safe had allowed her to sleep peacefully. She hadn't had a recurrence of the nightmare, she hadn't dreamt of Mark, but perhaps that wasn't surprising given that a half-naked Damien had lain beside her.

He moved gracefully on his long legs and she wondered if he was a good dancer. He looked fluid and she could imagine him on the dance floor, could imagine herself in his arms. She felt a blush steal across her cheeks. Thank God he had his back to her and couldn't see her devouring him with her eyes. His black boxer shorts left very little to her imagination. His body was lean and muscular, and she knew exactly how it had felt under her fingers, warm and firm. Her hand had been spread across his stomach, her fingers resting on the ridges of his abdominals. She was mortified to think that she'd been draped across him when she'd woken up but relieved to know that nothing more sexual had happened. It was clear that he wouldn't have minded. Should she be flattered by that or nervous?

She felt both flattered and nervous but she was also hesitant.

She had ignored his obvious erection, or had tried to, but her hesitation had had nothing to do with the fact that his young daughter was in the house. Summer had been a factor but not the ultimate deciding factor. Abi had made a promise to herself. No more colleagues. No more men with baggage.

Summer's presence was a reason but she hadn't been the problem. The problem was Abi herself.

She was damaged.

She was still recovering.

But most of all she was afraid.

CHAPTER SIX

ABI WAS AFRAID of lots of things. Of getting hurt. Of getting involved. Of jumping in before she'd tested the water. But she couldn't tell Damien that.

Ironic, considering all the things she'd told him last night, but in the reality of the morning she was embarrassed about confiding in him. She wished she hadn't said anything but she couldn't take it back now.

Her psychologist had been encouraging her to talk to others about her experiences and feelings but Abi had no one to confide in. She had no one to spend time with, no family and no friends, she had lost touch with any friends who were not in the army and in the wake of Mark's death she certainly didn't want to spend time with army acquaintances. Which left her with no one.

She had to admit that it had been a relief of sorts to talk to Damien about her experience but she wasn't quite sure what had prompted her to do so. Had he caught her at a moment of weakness when she hadn't been thinking straight, or had she downloaded because she felt safe?

She'd been thrown by the break-in and then by being in a strange bed. Her nightmare had unsettled her further, as had waking up in Damien's arms. At first she'd thought she was dreaming but that dream had been much nicer than her recurring nightmare.

Abi wondered what it meant that she had been prepared to tell him about her experience, about the circumstances of Mark's death, but that she still hadn't told him everything. She hadn't told him she and Mark had been lovers and she knew it was because she didn't want him to think badly of her. Neither did she want him to see her as someone who had affairs with married men, even though she hadn't known that Mark had been married until he'd died. She'd known he'd had two daughters but he'd told her he was divorced. It had only been at his funeral that she'd discovered he'd lied to her. But would Damien think that was a suitable defence? She hadn't known Mark was married but she still felt guilty and she wasn't prepared to expose herself to Damien in case he judged her. Why did his opinion matter so much? Why had she confided in him?

Could she behave as if nothing had happened?

She'd have to, she thought as he came back into the room.

He had showered and was dressed in jeans and a T-shirt, and he held a cup of coffee in one hand and a pile of clothes in the other.

He passed her the coffee and put the clothes on the end of the bed. 'You didn't bring any clothes with you and I wasn't sure if you wanted to eat breakfast in your evening gown. You might be more comfortable in something from this pile.'

'Thank you,' she said, as she surveyed the pile. He'd brought a pair of his track pants with a drawstring waist, an old university sweater and a white towelling dressing gown. Everything would be miles too big for her, except maybe the dressing gown. She wondered who it belonged to but wasn't about to ask.

The bedroom door opened and Summer wandered in, rubbing the sleep from her eyes. 'Good morning, sunshine,' Damien greeted her, but she wasn't interested in her father. She only had eyes for Abi.

'Abi? Why are you in my bed?'

Abi hadn't given any thought to what they would tell Summer but fortunately Damien had an answer ready.

'Abi's house was damaged.'

'How?'

'A raccoon got inside and broke a window.'

Abi choked back a laugh. She was pleased Damien hadn't told Summer the real story—that wasn't something a five-year-old needed to hear—but she hadn't expected him to be quite so elaborate with his story-telling. 'I was worried about the rain getting in so Abi stayed here.'

Summer happily accepted Damien's embellishment of the truth. Abi guessed at her age she still believed in fairytales and Damien's tale was almost believable.

'Okay, let's give Abi some privacy. You can come and help me make the pancakes.' He turned to Abi. 'That's our Sunday morning tradition. Why don't you get dressed and join us?'

Abi showered and wrapped the dressing gown around herself. She had debated wearing Damien's clothes, but despite the fact that she'd worn his T-shirt last night—she'd been too distressed to think clearly then—now that she'd calmed down she decided it would have felt odd to step into Damien's clothes. It would feel far too intimate.

More intimate than sharing a bed? she questioned herself. Under the circumstances, she decided it would.

She could smell pancakes. She belted the gown tightly at the waist and followed her nose. Summer was feeding Jonty a pancake when she wandered into the kitchen. She checked Jonty's paw, relieved to find that he didn't appear to be suffering any after-effects from the glass fragment getting stuck in his foot, nothing that a pancake breakfast wouldn't fix anyway.

Damien had another coffee waiting for her on the kitchen bench, plus juice, maple syrup for the pancakes and a bowl of oranges. He had a tea towel tucked into the back pocket of his jeans and he looked at home in the kitchen. Abi was a terrible cook. She didn't have a big appetite and there was no point cooking for one, and in the army she'd always had meals prepared for her so there had been no need to learn. She could get used to having Damien cook for her but she kept that thought to herself.

She was on her second pancake—they were delicious, light and fluffy—and for some reason this morning her appetite was flourishing, when Damien spoke to Summer.

'Okay, sunshine, what would you like to do today?' Summer had finished her breakfast and had a computer tablet booted up on the kitchen bench. 'Have you checked the weather?' Damien asked as she swiped her finger across the screen. 'Is there any rain?'

'Nope.'

'Outdoors, then.'

'Can Abi choose?'

'Choose what?' Abi asked.

'Sunday is our day to explore LA,' Damien told her. 'Summer usually chooses the activity and I'll work out where we can go.'

'You could choose somewhere, Abi, and then you could come with us,' Summer added.

'I'm not really dressed for a day out. I need to go home and make arrangements to fix the "raccoon" damage.' She made her excuses, sure Damien didn't need or want her tagging along with them. This sounded like father-daughter time that she didn't need to intrude into.

'You could borrow my mum's clothes.' Summer's statement was very matter-of-fact, as if she saw nothing unusual in other women helping themselves to her mother's wardrobe.

'Your mum's clothes?'

Summer was nodding. 'She has heaps of clothes.'

'Summer, why don't you take Jonty out into the garden for a minute?' Damien suggested. Had he noticed Abi's expression?

She waited until Summer left the room before asking the question. 'I was under the impression that you and Summer's mother weren't together?'

'We're not.'

'But her things are here?'

'Some of her things.'

Did that mean she was still here or did she come and go as she pleased? What if she arrived now and found Abi sitting at her kitchen bench? Abi had assumed from Damien's comments that he was single but had she chosen to believe that? Wanted to believe that? Had he encouraged her to think that?

'Whose robe am I wearing?'

'Not hers.'

She didn't want to ask the next question. If it wasn't Brooke's, who did it belong too? She didn't want to know. She had already been told more than she wanted to hear.

'Does she still have a key?'

'Yes.'

'How could you bring me here if she still has access? What if she walks in?' Even though nothing had happened between them Abi felt completely stupid. She should have stuck to her guns, not just fallen in with Damien's wishes. Why hadn't she resisted him? What had happened to the Abi who'd used to be so independent minded and strong? Since Afghanistan it seemed as if her reason and logic had deserted her. Had Mark's lies and deceit shaken her confidence so much that now she didn't trust herself to make good choices? Was she so eager for company, so lonely that she would forsake her principles and blindly follow where someone else led?

She needed to consider her motives. Why had she agreed to come home with him? Was it because she hadn't felt safe to stay home alone or was it because she found him attractive? Had she been thinking with her hormones or her head? She couldn't afford to think with her hormones. Danger lay down that path. It had got her into trouble before. She needed to be calm, methodical, rational. She needed to make measured decisions and sound judgements. She couldn't jump into something without consideration of her own motives or his. She didn't want to get into the middle of something.

'Abi, Brooke is in New York, she's not about to walk in and find you here, and this isn't her house anymore.

She doesn't live here.' His voice was calm and patient. 'She's just storing some of her stuff here. She has far too many clothes and hasn't been able to take them all with her. They're in the spare room. She's my ex-wife, we're divorced. What I do is none of her business as long as it's not hurting Summer.'

'Well, I'm still not wearing her clothes.'

'Fair enough. I didn't suggest that you should.'

He was right. It had been Summer's suggestion. She had bitten his head off for no reason. But was it for no reason? She only had his word for what the situation was. How did she know he was telling the truth? She didn't have a good track record when it came to picking trustworthy men. Once again, this could just be a case of a man telling her what he thought she wanted to hear.

She wasn't sure but did it matter?

It shouldn't matter to her what the situation was between Damien and his ex-wife. She hadn't done anything to regret yet but she wouldn't apologise, just in case. And she wouldn't spend the day with them. It would be best if she put some distance between her and them. She couldn't afford to get involved.

She took her empty plate to the sink. 'I'll call a cab,' she said. 'I need to go home.'

'I'll take you. It's only two blocks. Summer and I can wait for you to get changed and then you're welcome to spend the day with us if you'd like to.'

'No, I can't. I really do need to go home and organise to get my windows fixed.'

'I'll take care of that,' he offered. 'I'd like your company.'

Abi hesitated.

'Say yes because if you don't *you* can tell Summer

why you're not joining us,' Damien added as his daughter opened the back door to step inside.

'What are we going to do?' Summer asked.

Abi looked at Damien. She could see the challenge in his eyes, daring her to join them. But she didn't know if she could.

'You get to choose where we go,' he told her, and his voice was quiet, reassuring. 'You can choose somewhere you'll feel comfortable.'

Could she do this?

She realised with surprise that she wanted to. What was the harm in making a spontaneous decision? She used to do that all the time but since Mark's death she'd felt constrained by her fear. She had to remember that bad things didn't always happen, things didn't always go wrong. But where should they go?

Somewhere outside, she thought. Being winter, an outside venue was unlikely to be crowded, especially if they went early. 'Maybe we could walk to the Santa Monica Pier,' she suggested.

'Walk to the pier? Nobody walks in LA,' Damien teased.

Abi relaxed as Damien messed about. It felt good not to over think things for a change, not to worry about every decision. She took a deep breath; she could do this.

'The exercise will do us good,' she said, hoping that Damien didn't suggest that she walk and he'd meet her there. She really didn't want to walk to the pier on her own. She had set walks that she took Jonty on, streets she knew, past houses she was familiar with. And she didn't want to walk to the pier without Damien. He made her feel safe. She was pretty sure that Summer would choose to go with Jonty, which meant that Damien would choose to go with Summer. At least, she hoped she would.

'Can I hold Jonty's lead?' Summer asked.

'Of course.'

Abi smiled at Damien, pleased to get her own way, and he laughed. 'Why did I bother arguing against two women?'

'We'll compromise,' Abi said. 'Let's drive down past the Beach House and walk half the distance to the pier. That's only about a mile each way.'

Damien and Summer drove Abi home and while he waited for her to change he organised a glazier to do the repair work later in the day. Abi was used to managing on her own but she had to admit she liked the feeling of having someone else to look out for her. She didn't feel as if she'd been doing such a great job of taking care of herself of late.

Damien drove them to the Annenberg Beach House, where they piled out of the car to walk to the pier. Summer walked next to Abi, holding Jonty's lead with one hand and Abi's hand with the other. Her hand was tiny and warm and Abi could feel herself becoming more enthralled with Summer and the idea of motherhood. That was something she'd always had mixed feelings about because of her own childhood. She wasn't sure if she had the right genetic make-up for parenthood. Both of her parents were screw-ups and while she would love a chance to have a family of her own, one that wouldn't leave her, she had always had a fear that maybe she wouldn't cope either, just like her parents hadn't. But Summer was gorgeous and Abi could feel a tug on her heartstrings as the little girl skipped along beside her, keeping up a one-way conversation with Jonty.

Even walking at the pace of a five-year-old and with a dog who liked to stop and sniff everything in his path, they still made it to the pier just as it opened, which meant, to Abi's relief, that they had beaten the crowds.

'Where to first?' Damien asked.

'The carousel,' Summer shouted.

The carousel was indoors and as they entered the building Abi immediately scoped out all the exits. It was a habit she had formed in the past six months. She needed to know the quickest way out of a building or a potentially dangerous situation. Summer hopped up onto one of the carousel horses as Abi got her bearings then chose to sit in the sleigh, which allowed Jonty to come onto the carousel with her but it also left room for Damien.

He sat beside her as that position allowed him to keep an eye on Summer. The sleigh was narrow, the seat just big enough for two. Jonty sat at Abi's feet but Abi was aware of Damien's thigh pressing against hers, the heat radiating from his body burning through her exercise pants.

Going on the carousel had been a mistake. Not only did it put her too close to Damien but the high sides and back restricted her view. As the music began to play Abi could feel her anxiety level building. She felt hemmed in, trapped, and as the carousel started to turn, panic really set in. She was losing sight of the exits, her sense of direction was being compromised by the rotation of the carousel, and the noise and repetition of the music was making it hard to concentrate. She reached down to stroke Jonty's coat as she tried to calm herself. Her eyes darted back and forth as she tried to keep an exit in sight. Her breaths were becoming more rapid; she could hear herself panting.

'Are you okay?' Damien asked, but Abi couldn't answer. She opened her mouth but she couldn't form the words. She didn't know the answer.

'You'll be all right,' he said, putting his hand on her knee. 'You're safe.'

But Abi knew that wasn't necessarily true. Bad things could and did happen unexpectedly, despite what she'd told herself earlier.

Damien lifted his hand from her leg and covered her hand with his. 'Focus on me,' he said, but now all she could think about was the sensation of her hand in his. Perhaps that was his point. She looked down, focusing on their fingers and the way his had wrapped around hers. His hand warmed hers and distracted her.

'Look at me,' he told her, and she lifted her eyes.

She looked into his eyes. They were dark and intense and everything around her blurred and disappeared until all that was left was Damien. The building and the ride merged into blank surroundings, indistinguishable from each other. Even the carousel music seemed muted. Only Damien was in sharp relief.

'I'll keep you safe. Trust me,' he said. 'Do you trust me?'

She wanted to trust him but she'd been let down too many times in the past. 'I have trouble with trust.'

'The ride is nearly over.' His voice was quiet and sure. 'You're okay. You're safe.'

The ride slowed and the music ceased and the building came back into focus. Abi looked around. She was safe, she could see no immediate threats, but she needed to get outside; needed to escape these four walls. She stood up, eager to get off the carousel. Her legs were shaky but Damien kept hold of her hand, steadying her.

Summer was already down off her horse. 'Can I have another turn?' she asked, but Abi barely heard her.

'Not right now.'

Abi was itching to make a run for it but Damien hadn't let go of her hand. She tried taking some deep breaths, focusing on the connection with Damien. Letting his strength anchor her, allowing him to stop her from taking flight. She had Jonty's lead in one hand, Damien in the other. She should be okay.

'But I want to ride on the bunny rabbit,' Summer insisted.

'Jonty needs some fresh air,' Damien told her, and that was the end of the discussion. Summer didn't bother to argue further. At the moment, whatever Jonty needed he got. He was Summer's number-one priority. Abi forced her legs to move towards the exit as she wondered if she should suggest that Damien get Summer a dog of her own. It would be good company for her if she was destined to be an only child. Abi knew how much Jonty's company had come to mean to her and she could imagine how much she would have loved a dog growing up. She saw a lot of similarities between her own childhood and Summer's situation, though with one big difference. Summer had a father who adored her but that didn't necessarily mean he had the time to devote to her. A dog would be a distraction, a responsibility and a companion for her.

Summer skipped ahead of them and if she noticed Damien and Abi holding hands she didn't comment. Abi pulled her hand from Damien's as they followed

Summer outside. As nice as it felt, it also made her feel uncomfortable.

Summer was heading towards the Beach Bounce, a trampoline and bungee harness contraption that allowed children, or adults, to jump and twist and turn without the danger of falling. 'What about this?' she asked. 'Can I try it?'

Damien turned to Abi. 'Will you be okay here?' he asked.

Abi needed to be where she could keep an eye on the situation, where she would be able to see what was coming her way. The Beach Bounce was on the edge of the pier. She could stand on the far side of the trampoline so that her back was to the water as she faced the pier. No one could come up behind her. She nodded and made her way around the trampoline.

Damien paid for Summer's ticket, put her into the queue and then came to stand with Abi.

'Shouldn't you wait with Summer?' Abi asked. Her anxiety was still in hyper-drive.

'I can watch her from here. It will be her turn in a few minutes.'

Abi kept her back to the water and let her eyes roam over the pier. Jonty sat on her right and Damien stood to her left. He was turned slightly sideways, shielding her a little, his posture protective, and she felt quite safe.

'She hasn't been on this before?' Abi asked as she watched Summer, who had been strapped into the harness and was now turning somersaults and bouncing higher and higher as her confidence built.

'No. I don't remember this being here last time we came to the pier or perhaps she was too small. Lots of the rides have a height restriction.'

'Why are you spending your Sundays out exploring LA?' she asked.

'I'm from San Francisco originally but we moved here two years ago. Brooke pushed for the move to further her career. I admit I resisted the idea but when it became clear that she would go with or without me I realised I had to move, for Summer's sake.'

So he had moved for his family, for Brooke, and now she had taken off again, this time to New York. Abi wondered whether he would follow Brooke again, for Summer's sake. She would do well to remember that he was a man who came with baggage.

'Do you miss San Francisco?'

Damien nodded. 'I do. It's taken me a while to feel like I belong here, I'm still not sure that I do. I love working at The Hills but LA is a completely different type of city and we're still finding our feet. What about you? Where did you grow up?'

'Here.'

'Here? You're a native?'

'We do exist, you know.'

'I know, it's just that almost everyone I've met has moved here from somewhere else.'

'That's the movie business, no doubt.'

'I guess so. So you'd be the perfect tour guide for me and Summer, then. You could show us all your favourite childhood haunts.'

'I think my childhood might have been different from the one you're imagining. It would certainly be different from the one you'd be dreaming of for Summer.'

'What do you mean by that?'

Abi wasn't sure how to answer. She found it odd that

Damien wanted to know about her. She wasn't used to talking about herself—in fact, she usually tried to avoid it unless it was in a controlled environment, like with her therapist.

'I didn't have the idyllic childhood you might be picturing. I never knew my father, he abandoned us shortly after I was born, and my mother...' Abi paused. Even after thirty years she always hesitated when it came to describing her mother. She'd loved Abi in the best way she'd known how but she'd suffered from depression, which had manifested into substance abuse, mostly alcohol, and there had been plenty of times when Abi had just had to manage as best she could. Despite Summer's mother's failing in the child-raising department, she doubted it would match those of her own mother. 'Let's say she struggled to cope with raising me on her own. We didn't spend weekends at the pier or at theme parks.' Abi had spent a lot of her childhood alone.

'Is your mum still in LA?'

Abi shook her head. 'She's dead.'

'I'm sorry. Was it recent?'

'No. She died in a car accident just after I turned eighteen.' Abi had been alone for almost half her life. Long enough to be used to it, and to know she didn't like it, but not long enough to get over the guilt.

She had left home at seventeen to join the army. She'd been unable to continue to live with her mother, she couldn't be responsible for her any more, but she had always blamed herself a bit for the accident. She wondered if it would have made a difference if she hadn't left but she'd known she'd had to get away. Her home life had been toxic. She had never known whether her mother had suffered from depression before her father had left them. She could have had post-natal depression which had perhaps been exacerbated by Abi's father's abandonment, but, whatever the cause or the reason, her mother had turned to alcohol as her crutch and one day she had crashed her car into a tree. Abi had wondered if it had been suicide but had never been sure. She'd just been so relieved that no one else had been hurt.

She still carried the guilt. For her mother's death, among other things. Her therapist had told her time and again that she was not responsible for her mother's accident or her father's abandonment or Mark's death, but Abi found it difficult to move on. She had carried so much guilt for so long that she didn't know how to let it go.

Caroline had also told her she needed to talk about these things, that it didn't help to bottle things up and let them fester. She had suggested that if she talked about them she took away the power they had to hurt her, that it would make the problems smaller, but Abi didn't know how to do that.

Summer's turn on the Beach Bounce finished and Abi was happy to let her take over the conversation and distract her from her thoughts by leading them around the pier. They followed her past numerous rides and sideshows before she stopped at the basketball hoops and insisted that Damien have a turn.

He shrugged out of his jacket and asked Abi to hold it for him. He slung it around her shoulders when she agreed. It was warm and comforting, a bit like being wrapped in his arms again. It felt safe.

Removing his jacket had left him standing before her in his shirtsleeves. His arms were muscular and he could pick up the basketball in one hand with his long fingers. She watched as he transferred the ball from his left hand to his right before throwing it. He was quick and accurate and it wasn't until the game was finished that Abi realised she had forgotten to be nervous, she'd been too busy admiring Damien's skill and physique.

He had scored enough points to win a soft toy for Summer and she chose a seahorse covered in pink and silver sequins layered like scales. Abi wasn't certain that seahorses actually had scales but she supposed it didn't matter—a soft toy didn't need to be a perfect replica of the real thing. Come to think of it, seahorses probably weren't pink and silver either. But not everything in the world had to be perfect. Sometimes it was okay to have some imagination and succumb to fantasies. Summer was reminding Abi of what it was like to be a child, to believe that good things could happen, how to have fun.

'You have to have another turn, Daddy,'

'I think one toy is enough, Summer, especially as I know I'll end up carrying it *and* you.'

'It's not for me. Abi needs a toy too.'

Damien looked at Abi. 'In that case…' he said, and Abi felt warmth flow through her. To think he was doing this for her.

Summer wriggled her way between Abi and Jonty as Damien tossed balls through the hoop. Summer was rubbing Jonty's head with one hand but Abi felt her other hand slide into her own as they watched. It was tiny and warm and the contact melted Abi's heart.

'What takes your fancy, ma'am?' he asked as he turned around at the end of the game, victorious once more. He was smiling broadly and Abi sensed he was enjoying the day as much as she was. She was pretty sure she wasn't projecting her feelings. This was the best day she'd had in a long time.

She smiled back, feeling relaxed. For a few minutes she'd forgotten to be self-conscious, forgotten to be nervous, forgotten to be worried. It felt good not to worry. She wasn't over-thinking things, she wasn't creating concerns. Despite the fact that the crowds were building up, her earlier nerves had eased. She felt safe with Damien. He seemed to have the ability to create a wall that surrounded the three of them and Jonty and didn't allow the outside world to intrude.

'Get the tiger,' Summer instructed, before Abi could answer.

'Why the tiger?' Damien asked.

'It's got the same eyes as Abi.'

He looked back at Abi then asked to see the toy. He took the tiger with its amber glass eyes and held it beside Abi's head, looking from the glass eyes into hers.

'So it does,' Damien agreed as he held her gaze, and Abi felt the rest of the world dissolve into a haze around her as his dark eyes looked deep inside her. Could he see her reaction? Could he see how happy she was? How confused?

She dropped her gaze and reached for the toy and tucked it under her arm. She couldn't continue to stare at him, afraid she would say or do something she'd regret, like step forward to touch him.

'Thank you,' she said, but her words seemed inadequate to express her feelings. She would remember this day for ever and she knew that if she had nothing else, this tiger would always remind her of today. The first day in six months where she'd felt able to breathe, to relax, to forget her worries. It would remind her of the person she could be; it would inspire her to get over the past, to recover; and it would remind her of Damien and Summer long after they were gone from her life.

She couldn't imagine being part of them for ever. They didn't need her but she was starting to think she needed them. They were saving her, making her feel safe, whole and normal.

She was staring at him with her incredible amber eyes and he knew he would never forget this day.

'It was my pleasure,' he replied.

She was still wearing his jacket. It swamped her tiny frame and made her look vulnerable. She was beautiful but damaged and brought out all his protective instincts. She put out a distress call that he had to answer. He was a sucker for anyone who needed protection. Having someone to protect or care for, like his father had done for his mother, was what it was all about. It made him feel strong, valuable and worthy, and he liked those feelings. He liked feeling needed.

CHAPTER SEVEN

ABI WAS PLEASED to get to work on Monday. She was feeling overwhelmed, not physically but emotionally. Her emotions were swamping her and her head was full of conflicting thoughts about Damien. She wanted to trust him but she knew it was because she was attracted to him, and she really couldn't afford to be. It broke all her rules.

But she had to admit she had enjoyed the day at the pier. She'd felt self-conscious at first about spending the day with Damien, but he and Summer had relaxed her and entertained her to the point that she'd forgotten to be worried, forgotten to be nervous about the crowds. It had felt like the type of Sunday thousands of normal families might enjoy and she had liked that feeling. It was something she'd never had. She had almost been able to pretend they were one of those families.

But they were not.

Perhaps she needed to think of any time spent with Damien and Summer as therapy. It had certainly made her feel good yesterday. She'd felt confident, she'd felt safe and she had coped with situations that she'd never imagined she would be able to face again. She had enjoyed herself. But Damien was still a colleague. It would be prudent to be careful.

She needed to be at work so she was forced to think about other things, things that mattered, like her patients.

She headed for Dylan's room. He was due to have his dressings changed for the first time following the skin grafts to his arms so she needed to be there. She needed a dose of reality. This was her life. Her work. And work was something she could handle. She was trained for this and it didn't require anything extra of her personally. She could cope with work but she couldn't cope with her feelings for Damien or his daughter.

The pull towards them was strong. They were magnetic. Hypnotising. Was it them or was it the idea of them? A family unit but not quite? Something was missing for them, she could feel it. She recognised it because something was missing for her too, but was she living in a fantasy world? Was she kidding herself if she thought she could be the answer for them and vice versa? Why would they need her? No one ever had.

She gloved and gowned and straightened her shoulders as she tied a mask over her nose and mouth before entering Dylan's room. Ellen had been nursing Dylan and she had everything ready and waiting for Abi.

She greeted Dylan's mother, who was pacing at his bedside, waiting anxiously and hoping for good news. 'Morning, Julie,' she said, doing her best to project confidence.

Abi had one eye on the monitors as she picked up Dylan's chart and flicked through it. 'How's he doing?' she asked Ellen, as Dylan dozed. He'd been kept sedated since the surgery as it was important to keep him as still as possible to protect his arms from rubbing or pressure.

'He's doing well. Obs are all good. Temperature normal,' Ellen replied.

A normal temperature was encouraging.

'All right, let's take a look.'

Ellen pushed the trolley closer to the bed as Abi spoke to Dylan's mum. 'We'll change the dressings on his arms this morning. You're welcome to stay while we do this but don't expect the skin on his arms to look normal. Even though I have transplanted normal, healthy skin, it needs time to attach and for the blood supply to be restored.'

Abi and Ellen worked together to remove the bandages. Most came away easily and there was only one small section that required a little soaking. Abi felt positive. The skin she was revealing was red, indicating that the blood vessels were functioning.

'Vascularisation has started,' she commented, pleased with the outcome. 'It's looking good.'

'What about his thighs?' Julie queried.

'The dressings on the donor site will remain on for another few days. His thighs are likely to be more uncomfortable due to the exposed nerve endings, but I will start to lighten his sedation.' She turned to address Ellen. 'Keep the antibiotics running for now.'

'When do you think he might be able to come home?' Julie asked.

'Do you have somewhere to live?' Abi realised she had no idea how badly their house had been damaged in the fire.

'He'll have to share a bedroom with his younger brother but the house is liveable.'

'You should expect him to stay with us for another week but I'll review that in a few days' time and give you a more definite answer then.'

'Will I need anything special when he does come home?'

'We will go through all of that with you before he's discharged. He will need physical therapy but I will get Grace Watson, she's our resident physio, to speak to you before Dylan leaves and she or I will also organise a visit for you from a nurse or occupational therapist to organise any aids he might need. We've got time. The main thing is that he rests, stays relatively still and has time to heal,' Abi explained, as she signed off on Dylan's notes before returning to her office to get the rest of her day under way. She was consulting today. She had four new patients and she wanted a chance to read through their referrals before the appointments.

She sat at her desk, booted up her computer and scanned the list of names in her diary. One jumped off the screen at her. It was the first name on the list but that wasn't what had caught her attention. She recognised this name.

Nicolette Farrington.

It couldn't be.

The name was familiar but surely it couldn't be her.

Abi's heart was racing and she could feel a lump lodge in her throat, but she wasn't quite sure what the lump was. It could be so many things. Fear. Apprehension. Panic.

Nicolette Farrington.

Mark had been a Farrington. He'd had two daughters— Nikki and Natasha.

Abi closed her eyes and took a deep breath as she

tried to stem the rising tide of panic. The words that had been printed on his memorial card flashed across the back of her eyelids.

Devoted husband of Tanya.
Loving father of Nikki and Natasha.

How many Nicolette Farringtons could there be in California? In LA?

She clicked on the patient details, almost reluctant to see what information had been entered. Did she really want to know?

Nicolette's date of birth would make her twenty, which would make her the right age to be Mark's daughter.

Abi was having trouble breathing. Her chest was tight and she could feel a sharp pain between her ribs as she tried to inhale. Apprehension had been replaced by guilt, which joined together with fear and panic. She fought down a wave of nausea as she tried to figure out what to do.

She buzzed her secretary to ask if Nicolette could be moved to Damien's list. She hoped Jennifer wouldn't ask why because what could Abi say?

I have a conflict of interest. She might be the daughter of my ex-lover. My married ex-lover. My dead ex-lover.

But of course Jennifer did ask why. 'Why? Her mother phoned and specifically asked to see you,' she said.

Why would she ask for her by name? Abi wondered. What was going on? What did she know?

'Anyway,' Jennifer continued when Abi stayed mute,

'Damien is in surgery and Nicolette and her mother are already here. They're waiting for you,' she said, as if that ended the issue.

But Abi knew it was far from over. It was only just beginning. Unless it was a different Nicolette Farrington? That was her only hope.

She read through the referral letter on the screen, forcing herself to focus on the important facts and the patient's history as she tried to ignore her nerves. The patient had sustained facial injuries in a motor-vehicle accident three months ago. She had fractured her eye socket, cheekbone, nose and jaw. She had been put back together but the initial focus had been on making sure she survived, not making sure she looked the same as before. And apparently she didn't. This was a reconstructive surgery case and one that Abi would normally be excited about, but it was difficult to be excited when she felt like vomiting.

Still hopeful that she was panicking over nothing, she knew there was only one way to find out. She stood up from her desk, crossed the floor and opened the door.

It was her. *Them.*

There was no mistaking mother and daughter. She recognised them both, even though she had only seen them once before, at Mark's funeral. But they were regular visitors in her dreams and the real-life versions looked identical to her guilt-induced, night-time visions.

They looked up as they heard the door open and Abi felt her heart stop as Mark's pale blue eyes looked directly at her. Nikki's eyes were identical to her father's, the same shape and exactly the same shade, pale blue framed by thick dark lashes. It was like looking at Mark all over again, except a younger, damaged version. Abi hoped her own shock wasn't written all over her face. She wasn't shocked at the damage to Nikki's bone structure but Nikki wouldn't know that. She didn't want her potential patient to think she was shocked by her appearance.

But the surprise of seeing Mark's eyes looking back at her rendered her immobile for a few seconds before she came to her senses. Before she was able to ignore the colour of Nikki's eyes, to ignore the fact that she had dark hair like her father's, although his had been sprinkled with salt and pepper, before she was able to look at the whole person.

This wasn't the girl Abi remembered from the funeral. There were few similarities between this girl and the one she recalled. She had been a pretty girl but the right side of her face looked completely different now. Her facial injuries must have been extensive or perhaps she had simply been badly managed. There was no correlation between the two halves of her face, between right and left. It was as if two different people had been put together to make one. Her face was lopsided, her nose was crooked, her right cheekbone was depressed and her right eye drooped.

Abi began to examine Nikki from a distance, looking at her face shape and bone structure and working out how she could fix her. She forgot about Mark. She forgot about his connection to this young woman. All she saw before her now was a girl who needed her help.

She swallowed her nerves and worries. Her professional mask slipped into place, hiding her own fears and insecurities. 'Nicolette? I'm Dr Thompson. Would you like to come through?'

Abi managed to get through the beginning of the

consultation by sticking to the script. She introduced herself to Nikki's mother, Tanya, Mark's widow, terrified she was going to start making accusations, but Tanya didn't mention Mark and Abi relaxed. She got Nikki's history and made an effort to focus on her; she couldn't afford to dwell on Mark. The sins of the father were not Nikki's fault or her problem.

She made notes about Nikki's medical and surgical management post-accident, listing the issues Nikki reported—difficulty with eating and talking—and her concerns about her appearance. She listened to her say she just wanted to be normal. Abi could relate to that. Some people had external scars, others internal, but in the end everyone just wanted to be accepted, and for a young woman appearance was important. Abi got that and she would do her best to help.

Abi typed Nikki's information into her computer, aware that Tanya was watching her closely. 'Have we met?' she asked.

'No,' Abi answered quickly, almost abruptly, and hoped Tanya didn't hear the strain in her voice. She wasn't telling a lie. Abi had seen them at Mark's funeral but his betrayal had stunned her and she had avoided them. She had left as soon as she'd realised, not wanting to stay until the end, not wanting to make any accidental eye contact with Mark's widow. She'd been terrified her guilt and shame and anger would have been written across her face for anyone to see.

The fear that she'd managed to put to one side after seeing Nikki's name on her list returned with Tanya's question. How had Tanya ended up here, in her consulting room? How had she found her? Was it a simple coincidence or was there more to it? Did she know something she wasn't telling Abi? Was she deliberately stirring the pot?

Abi couldn't ask—to do so would admit she'd known Mark and invite a whole lot of questions she wasn't prepared, or probably equipped, to answer. It was better to feign ignorance. She could treat Nikki without ever having to reveal her connection, her history, with Nikki's father and Tanya's husband.

Did that make her as deceitful as Mark?

No, it didn't. It couldn't. Mark's lies had destroyed Abi but that didn't mean she wanted to do the same to his family. There was no point in saying anything now. There was nothing to be gained. To speak up would only hurt people. Keeping quiet was the best option, the only option, in Abi's mind.

She was aware of Tanya still watching her, studying her closely, and it made her feel uncomfortable. In an attempt to distract her, she moved on to discuss the process for the surgery.

'I will need some time to plan the surgery. I'll need to take measurements and photos of Nikki's face and if you have some photos of Nikki from before the accident that would be helpful. Did my secretary ask you for those when you booked the appointment?'

Tanya nodded and hoisted her handbag onto her lap and pulled out a large envelope. 'I brought some with us.' She passed the envelope to Abi, who shook the photos out onto her desk.

She felt herself go pale as she picked up the first picture. It was a family photo, a snapshot of Tanya, her two daughters and her husband. The resemblance between Nicolette and her father was even more obvious in this picture.

Mark had turned fifty when they had been in Afghanistan. Abi could remember the long weekend they'd had on leave shortly after, the weekend they had spent in Prague, celebrating. This picture must have been taken around the same time, some time in the past twelve months at least. Mark looked just as she remembered him. His dark hair had been greying slightly, starting at the temples where it had turned silver. He had carried a bit of extra weight but had been in great shape. He had looked vital, alive, robust. He didn't look like the Mark she saw in her dreams. This wasn't the Mark who had lain on the ground in the middle of a panicking crowd, bleeding onto the street, or the man whose life had drained out of him while she had tried in vain to save him.

In this photograph, taken when he'd been smiling and his pale blue eyes crinkled at the corners, he looked like a man you would trust. But it just showed that looks could be deceptive, for in reality he had also been a liar and a cheat.

But all that was in the past now. There was no way of bringing him back and she knew she wouldn't want him back now, even if that had been an option. She was done with him. Now she just needed to get his family out of her life too.

She should be able to reconstruct Nicolette's face without too much trouble. Despite everything, she could remember the shape and feel of Mark's face under her fingers. She would be able to restore his daughter's face.

She put the photo down and flicked through the others. Had she spent too long looking at that one? Too long looking at Mark's face instead of at Nikki's? Had she seemed distracted, inattentive, vague? She moved to the other photos—Nikki dressed for a school prom, her yearbook photo, a birthday party, a close-up head shot of her with her sister.

'Can I keep these photos?' she asked.

'What are you going to do with them?'

'I'll make enlarged copies. The more information I can gather, the better the outcome of surgery.'

Tanya nodded. 'So you think you can help?'

'Yes.' Abi's voice was strong, confident.

She printed off a diagram of a face and measured Nikki's features, jotting figures onto the paper record. She was relieved to find that her hands didn't tremble as she measured the width of Nikki's face, the distance between her eyes, the height of her philtrum, and took more photos.

'What happens next?' Nikki asked, as Abi put the camera down.

Now she needed some time. 'I will see you again in a couple of days to go through the plan for the surgery in more detail once I've worked out the best approach, and if you want to go ahead we should be able to schedule the surgery for next week. I'll get my secretary to make a follow-up appointment.'

Abi asked Jennifer to pencil the surgery into her diary and make sure that Damien would be free to assist her before she said goodbye. She could feel a headache starting and would really have liked to lie down somewhere quiet and pull the covers over her head. She needed Jonty's company, or Damien's. Either of them would help to settle her nerves and fears, relieve the tension she could feel building inside her, but she didn't have either of them. And she couldn't seek Damien out. She wouldn't be able to explain her problem. She didn't want to discuss it with him so she stretched her neck and shoulders, took two paracetamol tablets and got on with her day.

Abi had expected to have a few days to pull herself together before she saw Tanya again but it happened sooner than she expected. She was waiting for Damien as they had a meeting scheduled to discuss Nikki's surgery further when Jennifer buzzed her office.

'Mrs Farrington is here,' Jennifer said.

'Nikki's appointment isn't until tomorrow,' Abi replied.

'She knows that. Nikki isn't with her. Mrs Farrington wants to know if she can have a minute of your time. She has some more photos for you.'

Nikki's surgery was scheduled for next week. She didn't need to see Tanya, there was absolutely no reason to see her, but she found herself saying yes.

She carried a fistful of photos in with her. Photos Abi assumed were of Nikki, and she wondered why she couldn't have left them with Jennifer, but as Tanya marched across to her desk and fanned the pictures out across the surface, Abi realised why. These weren't photos of Nikki. They were photos of Mark.

And Abi.

'I knew I'd seen you before,' Tanya said.

Abi clenched her fists at her sides to stop herself from reaching out and picking up the pictures. 'I worked with your husband,' she replied. Her heart was hammering in her chest and it made her voice jump in her throat.

Tanya spread the photos out further, shuffling through the assortment until she found the one she wanted. She pulled out a shot that showed Mark with his arm around Abi's shoulders. She was beaming up at him, looking like a woman in love. It had been taken on their weekend's leave in Prague, a belated celebration of Mark's fiftieth birthday. At the time Abi had thought it was the most beautiful city, the most beautiful place, in the world but it had all been lies. Abi couldn't believe that woman in the photo was her. It had only been taken nine months ago but she had been so naive back then. She had grown up a lot since and now she didn't even recognise this woman.

'Let's be honest, shall we?' Tanya said. 'This was more than a working relationship. A lot more.'

'Where did you get these?' Abi's voice was wobbling and her hands were shaking. She kept them clenched at her sides but now it was in an attempt to stop the tremors.

'They were sent to me with Mark's things. All neatly boxed up. Photos of my husband with another woman.'

Of course, Abi realised, his personal effects would have been sent to his next of kin. His wife. The one Abi hadn't known anything about.

Why had she insisted on printing these photos and giving them to Mark?

She knew why. She'd wanted him to put them in his office or his room but he never had. She'd wanted to feel like they were a proper couple, like she was going to be part of his life when they returned to the States. After all, that was what he had promised her, and she had believed him. Despite the fact that he'd insisted on keeping their relationship secret—he'd told her that, because of his position as her CO, he didn't think it was right to parade their relationship, and she had agreed. She'd had the future to look forward to so she could wait. But then she'd found out his promises had been empty ones. At the funeral she'd realised why he had wanted secrecy.

After he had died she hadn't thought about looking for the photos, destroying them. She'd been too upset to consider things like that. She'd had her own copies and she hadn't considered that Mark's personal belongings would be sent back to his family. She hadn't thought he'd had a wife. Daughters, yes, but he'd told her he was divorced. And she had believed him. She'd had no reason not to.

'Were you having an affair with my husband?' Tanya asked.

Abi didn't know what to say. 'We were having a relationship,' she admitted. It seemed pointless to deny that under the circumstances. 'But I didn't know he was married. I didn't know it was an affair. I didn't know about you until his funeral.'

Abi had seen Tanya and her daughters at the front of the church but had still assumed that Tanya was the ex-wife. Until she had opened the memorial card and seen what it so clearly stated.

Devoted husband of Tanya.
Loving father of Nikki and Natasha.

Mark hadn't been divorced. Mark hadn't been planning on making a life with her. He had still been married.

She had left the funeral before it had finished. She had fled almost before it had started. She would never have attended in the first place if she had known. She'd felt embarrassed, humiliated and ashamed.

Abi picked up the photo of her and Mark in Prague. Looking at her picture, it would be obvious to anyone how she felt about Mark but Mark, other than the fact he had an arm around her shoulder, looked completely unaffected. Abi could just be a silly colleague. What had made Tanya suspicious?

'How did you know?' she asked.

'You're in all these photos. And I know Mark. You weren't the first and I would guess you wouldn't have been the last,' she continued. 'I knew Mark had affairs.'

'You knew?'

'I didn't know about you specifically, you were just another in a long line, I expect, and I had learnt to turn a blind eye.'

'Didn't it bother you?'

Tanya shrugged. 'As far as I was aware, his affairs were always conducted when he was away from home. I figured as long as it didn't affect the girls I could put up with it. I could have asked for a divorce but I didn't, for the sake of the girls. It was easier just to get on with my life and ignore what he got up to when he was away. He always came home to us and I always let him. That was my choice.'

Tanya didn't sound angry or upset. If Abi had to describe how she sounded, she would have said resigned, but it was Abi who was surprised. Of everything she had expected, imagined, this sense of resignation wasn't it.

'Only this time he didn't come home.' The words were out of Abi's mouth before she could stop them. Harsh words, she spoke the truth, but she hadn't meant to voice her opinion.

'He should have been more careful.' Tanya reached

out her hand and her fingers traced the line of Mark's face in one of the photos that lay on the desk. 'I guess he didn't expect to die over there.'

Abi didn't tell her that he *would* have expected that. They all had. Tanya didn't need to hear that. She had loved her husband—that was clearly obvious. She didn't need to hear the details.

'I couldn't save him,' Abi said in reply. 'I'm sorry.'

'You were there?'

She nodded.

'What happened?'

'What did the army tell you?' Abi wasn't sure if she could bear to vocalise the truth of that fateful day. Talking to Damien was one thing but it was something quite different to tell Mark's widow the cold, hard facts. She didn't want her to have the same nightmares she had. Someone who was emotionally invested in Mark didn't need to hear the details. She didn't need the truth.

'Not much,' Tanya replied. 'They said it was a bomb and that he died instantly. But if you were there…' Her voice trailed off and Abi knew what she was thinking. She was wondering how Abi had survived.

Abi knew the army would have been as kind as they could when they'd informed Mark's family of his death. She agreed there was no need to go into the details of his suffering—to tell Tanya that Mark had died in her arms, that he'd been unable to speak and unable to breathe. That she had listened to his last breath, had seen it bubble out of his chest and leave his lips. She nodded. 'That's what happened.'

'But you were all right?'

Did Tanya think that was unfair? Abi couldn't blame her but she couldn't argue with the facts. Abi had survived, although not without scars, both physical and emotional. 'I was injured but not badly. Mark was nearer to the explosion.'

Tanya sat on the chair in front of Abi's desk and Abi could almost see the strength seeping out of her. She had obviously been fighting to hold it all together. Was it still for the sake of her daughters or was it her way of coping? Abi didn't know but that made her think of the reason Tanya was even in her office in the first place. Nicolette.

Considering how things stood now, would they still choose her as Nicolette's surgeon? She imagined this might be enough to persuade them otherwise. How would she explain that to Damien? He had agreed to assist her with the surgery—how could she tell him that the surgery wouldn't be going ahead because she'd had an affair with the patient's father?

Her first concern wasn't how she would explain this to James and Freya, how she would tell them that she had lost them business, but how she would break the news to Damien. What would he think?

'Do you want me to find someone else to do Nikki's surgery?' Abi asked. There was no delicate way of asking that question.

'*Can* you do it?'

'Yes.'

'Will your feelings about Mark or me or Nikki affect your process?'

Abi's only feelings towards Mark now were anger and betrayal. She knew she needed to let that go and she was in the process of doing so, but she would make sure her feelings would not affect Nikki's care. She was a professional, an expert. At least in a surgical sense she was, even if all other areas of her life were a shambles, this was something she knew she could do and do well. Medicine was all she had. 'Not at all,' she said. 'I always give one hundred per cent. What happened between Mark and me has nothing to do with Nikki. She will get the best possible care and outcome I can give her.' This would be her way of making amends.

Tanya was nodding. 'Good. I don't want to find someone else. Nikki liked you. She felt comfortable and you were recommended to us. We are still struggling to come to terms with Mark's death and Nikki's accident has just made matters worse. I'm used to being on my own and taking care of the girls, but there's a lot more going on than normal.

'Things have changed. In the past I always knew that Mark would come home or I could pick up the phone and discuss issues with him. I can't do that any more. I have to be able to manage on my own. If I can get one thing back on track, perhaps it will help us to feel as if we will be okay. This is important to Nikki. I don't think she will cope with another setback. The girls are all I have left. Everything I do, everything I have ever done has been for them.'

Tanya had straightened her shoulders as she'd spoken, as she prepared herself to fight on her daughter's behalf, and listening to her made Abi wish she'd had someone who would have fought like that for her.

'I'll do my best for her,' Abi promised.

Tanya was a strong woman and, ironically, Abi thought she could probably take a leaf out of her book. She could learn to stare adversity in the face, to not back down, to not be afraid.

But, then, Tanya had something to fight for. She had her daughters.

What did *she* have?

Abi saw Tanya out of her office. She opened the door and found Damien poised on the threshold. In the shock of Tanya's disclosure Abi had forgotten about their meeting. She turned around and Damien followed. To her dismay, the first thing she saw when she turned were Tanya's photos spread across her desk. She hadn't thought to pack them away, she hadn't known what to do with them. She didn't want to keep them, she didn't even want to look at them, but to sweep them off her desk and into a drawer would only draw Damien's attention to them. She would have to stack them in a pile and get rid of them later, but before she could gather them together Damien had reached over and picked one up. It was one of Abi in uniform.

Abi held her breath while he looked it over.

He pointed at Mark. 'Who's this?'

'Mark Farrington.'

'Your commanding officer?'

Abi nodded.

'You were in a relationship with him?'

Abi felt the colour drain from her face. Was it obvious to everyone?

She nodded again.

'So Nicolette Farrington is a relative?'

'His daughter.'

'You know her?'

'No. I'd never met her until two days ago. The referral is just a coincidence. I don't know his family. They don't know me.'

'His family?' Nicolette's file was on Abi's desk.

Damien flicked it open and picked up another photo. The family photo. It clearly showed Mark and Tanya's hands. Their wedding rings. 'He's married?'

'Seems he was,' Abi replied. 'Not that he shared that information with me.'

'You didn't know?'

She shook her head. 'I found out at his funeral.' She tried to explain. 'Finding out that I'd been in a relationship with someone else's husband compounded my PTSD. The guilt over Mark's death and the affair in addition to the stress from the bombing incident was the last straw.' Abi wasn't sure if Damien would believe her but it was suddenly extremely important to her that he did. She wanted, needed, him to trust in her.

Damien put the photos back on her desk. He turned the one with her in it face down, very slowly and very deliberately. What was he thinking? Did he believe her or was he going to torture her over the affair?

'Does his wife know?' he asked.

Abi nodded. 'She gave me the photos.'

'Do you still think it's a good idea to take Nikki on as a patient?'

'Yes. I can do this and I think it will be amazing. We can transform Nikki physically, improve her function and her aesthetics and restore her confidence. I know what it's like to have your confidence completely destroyed. Mark's lies did that to me.'

'Will you be able to put that behind you when you operate on his daughter?'

Abi nodded. 'I'm angry with Mark for taking advantage of me and angry with myself for being so gullible, but I'm not angry with Nikki. This is my chance to make amends for what I did, albeit unknowingly, but it's a form of redemption. I'll feel better if I can make up for my mistakes.'

'Are you doing this for Nikki or for yourself?'

'For both of us.' Her own self-confidence had been seriously dented by Mark's lies but even if her personal life was a wreck, at least she had her work and despite Mark's behaviour she would do her best for his daughter. 'I have no intention of failing to do my best for any of my patients, and that includes Nikki. But I need your help.'

'Are you sure you can do this?'

Abi nodded.

In Damien's opinion that was a big statement to make and he wasn't convinced that he believed her but, despite that, he could feel himself wanting to help her. But he hesitated before he committed himself to her cause. He needed to examine why he felt this urge to help. Was it because he felt she would need support? There was no doubt she was qualified to perform the surgery but did he think she was emotionally capable? Did he want to help because he thought he might need to pick up the pieces?

He knew she had been taken advantage of. She'd been mistreated, abused, emotionally if not physically. His protective instincts were strong at the best of times but something about Abi made them even more reactive. Abi wasn't manipulative, like his ex. She was altruistic and because he could sense the goodness in her he knew he would give her anything she asked for. Including this.

'All right,' he told her. 'I will help you.'

'Hi, have you got a minute?'

Damien was standing in her doorway. She was getting used to him popping in and out on a regular basis. She was getting used to his dark good looks, the shine in the depths of his dark eyes and the spontaneous smile that was often so unexpected but always made her spirits lift.

'Sure.'

'How are you coping?' he asked.

'I'm good,' she replied, and realised that she spoke the truth. She was feeling good with herself for the first time in months. Guilt about the affair had compounded her PTSD and exacerbated her symptoms, but finding out that Tanya knew about Mark's behaviour and that Abi hadn't been his only dalliance had lessened her guilt. Her conscience had eased and so had her stress.

'Are you busy on Sunday afternoon?'

'Sunday? No.' She'd assumed Damien's question would have been work-related but she had no plans. She never had plans. 'Why?'

'I've been invited to the film industry awards.'

'Wow! Really? By whom?' He really did live a different life from her. She couldn't believe she had even dared imagine after their day at the pier that she could be a part of it.

'One of my patients has been nominated for Best Supporting Actor. He had oral cancer, a squamous cell carcinoma with secondaries in his jaw. I reconstructed his mandible and he was able to return to acting, and he's invited me on Sunday as a thank-you.'

'Would you like me to look after Summer for you?'

'Summer?' Damien shook his head. 'No. I wanted to know if you would like to come with me.'

'To the awards ceremony? Me? Why would you want to take me?'

'Who else would you suggest?' He was laughing now, the little creases in the corners of his eyes bringing life to the smooth planes of his face.

Freya, Mila. She couldn't think of any single girls. And if she could have, would she want him to choose them over her?

'I want to take you,' he said, making Abi wish everything in life was that simple. 'I thought you might enjoy it. I know you said you're coping with the pressure of operating on Nikki and I know you want to go ahead with that and I accept that is your choice—' Abi knew he had reservations about the surgery. He had told her he was worried that it would increase her stress levels and possibly exacerbate her PTSD, but Abi had insisted she could manage. Work was the one thing in her life that she felt she had some control over. '—but you've seemed a bit quiet, a bit preoccupied, and I thought this would get your mind off things. Off Mark. So, if you're going to insist on operating on Nikki and taking on all the stress that is going along with that, I'm going to insist that you have some down time. And the film industry awards are it.'

She would admit, but only to herself, that she had been thinking more about Mark over the past few days, because of Nikki, but she felt she was coping. And undertaking a complicated surgery seemed less stressful to her than negotiating LA crowds.

'Thank you, it's a lovely idea and I'm sure it would be amazing but I don't know if I can do it.'

'I know you're not busy.'

'It's not that. It's the crowds I'm worried about. They're always huge.'

'It's okay. I've checked it out, I'll organise a limou-

sine, we'll get dropped at the red carpet. Don't worry,'
he added when he saw her expression, 'we'll be there
way before the celebrities. We have to be early, but it
will be safe—security is always tight. I won't let anything happen to you.'

Abi emerged from the bathroom after reapplying her
lipstick. She wanted to pinch herself. She couldn't believe she had just been to the film industry awards and
was now at an awards after-party, rubbing shoulders
with celebrities and stars that she'd watched on screen
for years. Despite Damien insisting she would be safe,
she had been terribly nervous when they had arrived
at the theatre. She'd opened and closed her fingers repeatedly, searching for the reassuring feel of Jonty's fur,
but he hadn't been beside her. But Damien had been,
and he'd sensed her nervousness and taken her hand as
they'd walked the red carpet, but that had only led to a
whole different level of nervousness.

His touch had sent her hormones into overdrive but
at least she'd forgotten to worry about her safety. All
she'd been able to think of had been Damien, and once
seated in the darkened theatre, still hand in hand, she'd
been able to ignore the size of the audience by focusing
on him. He anchored her and made her feel safe and
eventually she'd relaxed, but she was even better now
that they were in a smaller crowd and a private setting.

She saw Damien across the room. He was talking
to Tony, his patient who had invited them to the ceremony and who had walked away with the award for
Best Supporting Actor. In a room full of beautiful people Damien was still noticeable. Tall, dark and movie-

star handsome, he was turning heads in a space that was crammed with stunning people.

He saw her and waved her over and she picked her way carefully through the crowd.

'Okay, pretty lady, photo time.' Tony's voice was raspy from years of smoking. Which he said was fortunate as the surgery had made it even raspier but no one really noticed. It was his trademark.

He held his prized statuette in his hand and offered it to Abi as he manoeuvred her between Damien and himself. 'You hold it. It'll make a great pic for your social media posts.'

Abi wasn't on social media but she wasn't about to admit that. She was sure that no one here would understand her reasons. She knew that many of the stars saw social media as a source of free publicity and that publicity was their life blood, but social media didn't have the same appeal to her.

She took the little gold statue from Tony, surprised he was willing to let it go just hours after receiving it, but she wasn't going to argue. This was a once-in-a-lifetime opportunity for her.

Damien pulled his mobile phone from his suit pocket and handed it to a passing celebrity. Abi couldn't believe that this young actress who had been nominated for an award was taking her picture.

Tony was on her right, Damien on her left as she posed for the photo, and the statuette glowed golden against the emerald-green silk of the dress she'd borrowed from Freya.

Damien wrapped his arm around her waist and the heat of his hand burned through the fabric of her dress. The dress was cut low at the back and she could feel his forearm against her spine, skin on skin. The award was heavy in her hand, her knees were weak and her heart fluttered in her chest.

The instant the photo had been taken she returned the statuette to Tony, afraid she would drop it.

Tony checked the photo. Although he was almost thirty years older than Abi, approaching sixty, he had a reputation as a heart-throb and once again Abi was conscious of the fact that these people made a living as much out of their looks as their talent. She was self-conscious about her own appearance so his comment caught her by surprise. 'You look gorgeous, Abigail. If Damien hadn't already snatched you up I'd invite you to—'

Abi opened her mouth to correct his assumption, to tell him she and Damien weren't a couple, when she felt Damien's hand on her arm and she stopped.

'She's off limits, Tony. Besides, you've got your prize already tonight.'

'True, very true.' Tony laughed. 'Point taken. Go and have some fun.' He kissed Abi's cheek and said, 'Enjoy the party.'

'We will,' Damien said, as he snared them both a glass of French champagne from a passing waitress.

'Why did you let him think we were a couple?' Abi asked as Damien handed her a glass.

'Tony is a notorious charmer,' he said. 'No one is off limits and I didn't think you'd want to be subjected to that. I didn't think he was your type.'

What was her type? She didn't know.

They sipped champagne and watched the crowd. It was an incredible evening to be a part of, even if she did feel like an outsider. Even though she didn't believe in them, it felt a little bit like a fairytale. She could pretend she was playing a part in a movie—only as an extra, but it was a fun feeling being able to reinvent herself. Tonight she could be carefree, happy, loved. Tonight she could be anything she wanted.

The band began playing an old Frank Sinatra song. 'Shall we dance?' Damien asked.

He guided her around the dance floor with his hand on her back and his lips in her hair. She'd imagined he would be a fabulous dancer and she wasn't disappointed. They danced chest to chest and Abi closed her eyes and pretended that she belonged at the party, pretended that she belonged in his arms as she continued with her fantasy of reinvention. Tonight she was a girl who could have anything her heart desired.

His hand moved lower to rest in the small of her back. She could feel each fingertip against her skin and his breath was soft on her ear. She let the occasion and the company seduce her as she imagined Damien kissing her. Tried to imagine how he would taste.

She was in a bubble, their own small world. Nothing existed except the two of them. Her senses had shut down, other than the most basic. All she could think about was sex, desire, want and need. And Damien.

Tonight she was a girl who could have anything her heart desired. And she desired Damien.

CHAPTER EIGHT

She sat beside him in the limousine. Their thighs were touching and the heat from his body scorched her skin and warmed her insides.

A bottle of champagne was chilling in an ice bucket. Damien reached for it and poured them each a glass. The champagne was cold and the sharp contrast between the coldness of the drink and the temperature of her body made her catch her breath.

Damien sipped his drink, drawing her attention to his lips. She imagined leaning forward, pressing her lips to his, tasting him, as she'd been longing to do all evening, but before she could decide whether to take that chance the driver had turned into her driveway and pulled up behind Damien's car, which was where he had left it after dropping Summer off with Irma and George for a sleepover.

He took her glass from her hand and put it down in the limousine. He picked up the bottle as the driver opened Abi's door.

'Do you have champagne flutes?' he asked.

She had been wondering if she was brave enough to invite him in when he took the initiative. Had he read her mind or seen the question, the desire, in her eyes?

She swallowed. 'I'm sure I can find something appropriate,' she said. She had no idea what was in her cupboards but did it matter if she didn't have champagne flutes? She would drink out of jam jars if it meant prolonging the evening.

Damien followed her inside and she could sense his eyes watching the tightening of her butt as she climbed the stairs. She searched the kitchen cupboards and found two fluted glasses. Damien filled them before proposing a toast.

'Here's to golden nights,' he said.

She closed her eyes as she sipped her drink. She could picture the waves of desire that surrounded her to form a kaleidoscope of colour. She could smell the bubbles, as well as Damien's fresh citrus scent. It enveloped her, surrounded her, cushioned her and kept her safe.

She opened her eyes to find him watching her. His gaze was unwavering and she could see desire in the dark depths of his eyes. She felt her temperature rise as a flush stole over her cheeks and anticipation burned brightly inside her. She couldn't breathe. His gaze was so intense it felt as if the room lacked oxygen, as if it was being burnt up in his gaze. She parted her lips to take a breath. Her lips were dry so she licked them with the tip of her tongue.

Damien groaned, giving in to his desire, giving in to hers. He wrapped an arm around her back, pulled her to him and kissed her hard. He tasted of champagne, of late nights and silent promises.

She waited for her nerves to raise the alarm, to ask her what she thought she was doing, but the anxiety didn't come, the alarm didn't sound. She wanted this, she needed this. There was no fear. In Damien's arms she felt safe. Beautiful. Special. Desirable.

Nothing else mattered.

There was nothing else.

She reached one hand behind his head, holding him to her as she kissed him back. His tongue was warm in her mouth. His hands were warm on her skin. Every inch of her was on fire, consumed with desire. She felt his fingers on her arm, could feel them tracing a line up to her shoulder, across her collarbone to the hollow at the base of her throat, where she felt his thumb dip into the little dimple. She couldn't breathe, she'd forgotten how.

Abi needed to breathe.

She pulled away and he lifted his hand, releasing her from his touch. She almost begged him not to as she didn't want him to let her go.

'Are you okay?' he asked.

She nodded, unable to speak.

His dark gaze moved lower, over her breasts. How could such dark eyes hold such heat? Such intensity? She held her breath, trying to stop the rise and fall of her breasts, but still her nipples peaked in response to his gaze burning through the thin fabric of her dress. She could feel the moisture between her legs as her body responded to his gaze devouring her. He wasn't laying a finger on her now and yet she felt ready to self-combust. A look, a glance, a smile was all it would take for her to melt under him.

'Do you want to stop?'

'No.' Her voice was breathless. 'I want you to make love to me.'

She didn't need to ask twice. With one arm he

scooped her up and held her against his chest, pressing her to him, as he carried her into her bedroom.

He lowered her to the bed before shrugging out of his jacket. He tugged at one end of his bow tie, pulling it undone and tossing it onto the chair at her bedside. He eased himself over her, supporting himself on his elbows. She reached up and ran her hands over his biceps, feeling his strength, marvelling at the firmness within him. His breath was coming fast now, she could hear it and feel it as it hit the bare skin of her shoulders and neck, but he didn't move. How could he hold himself so still? He was poised to move forward, to take this to the next level, but somehow he held his position. He was in no hurry. How could he be so calm when desire threatened to consume her?

The waiting was exquisite agony. A delicious sense of anticipation battled with the desire to have him take her now, right now. She arched her hips up towards him, pushing herself against his groin, and was rewarded when she felt his matching desire, hard and firm, straining against his trousers.

She breathed out on a sigh as she let her knees fall open and wrapped her legs around him, pulling him closer, pulling him down against her. She heard him groan and he lowered his body until it covered the length of her. She wanted this. She wanted to feel his weight on her, she needed to know this was real.

Every cell of her body tingled, she could feel each one straining, alive with the possibilities of what was to come. Her expectations were almost painful, her reaction intense.

He reached for her, ending her suspense. His lips were on her ear lobe, soft and warm, his breath in her ear. He kissed her neck and then his lips covered hers and she melted into him and let him consume her.

His fingers skimmed over her nipples, hard and peaked. He swept the strap of her dress from her shoulder and exposed her left breast to the cool air. His thumb brushed over her nipple, teasing, tantalising. She cried out as a wave of desire washed over her and a bolt of heat scorched through her, sweeping from her nipple to her groin in a searing flash.

His lips left a trail of hot spots from her lips to her throat and collarbone until finally he took her breast in his mouth, rolling his tongue over the taut flesh until Abi thought she might come then and there. But she didn't want it to end. Not yet. Maybe not ever. She wanted to feel him, to touch him, to arouse him too.

Her fingers found the buttons of his shirt and she undid them, one by one, until she could run her hand over his chest. His warm skin was firm but soft under her fingertips. She pulled his shirt from his body as his mouth continued to tease her nipple, sucking and licking. He cupped her breast in his hand and ran his thumb over the peaked bud, making her moan. She arched her back, offering herself to him, and he took one breast in his mouth again, sucking hard, and she almost exploded in his arms.

She ran her index finger from his sternum down along the line separating his abdominal muscles, following the line of dark hair that led below his waistband. She concentrated on him, wanting to extend the pleasure, wanting to share the delight. She unbuckled his belt and snapped open the button on his trousers, unzipping his fly and pushing his trousers low on his hips. His erection strained against the fabric of his boxer shorts. She pushed them out of the way and ran her hand over his shaft, which was strong and thick, and she felt it rise to meet her. He groaned and the sound of his arousal urged her on.

His hand ran up her thigh and the soft folds of her dress fell away with his touch. His fingers met the elastic of her underwear and slid under the lace. Abi let her legs fall apart again, opening herself to him, giving herself to him, and she bit back a cry of desire as his fingers slid inside her. She was slick and wet, throbbing. His thumb found her centre and she gasped as his touch took her to the edge.

But she didn't want it this way. She wanted to share the experience. She wanted all of him and she wanted him to have all of her. She let go of him to quickly pull her dress over her head, and now she lay naked before him. His dark eyes roamed over her body, setting her on fire with his gaze.

She wanted to feel him inside her. She wanted them to be joined together. She lifted her hips and reached behind him, holding his hips, cupping his buttocks, to pull him close. Her knees were bent and she arched her back as she fitted him to her like pieces of a jigsaw.

She gave herself to him and he claimed all of her.

She sighed as he thrust into her, filling her, consuming her as they became one.

This was dangerous, *she* was dangerous, Damien thought as he felt himself losing control. Everything else in his life was forgotten as Abi took over his senses. He wanted to go slowly, he wanted to savour the moment, he wanted time to commit it all to memory, but he couldn't resist her. He couldn't fight it. He was only a man, a powerless man, and he could feel himself being swept away. The world ceased to exist except for Abi.

There was nothing else.

Nothing else that mattered.

He felt her hand on his chest, felt it brush over one nipple, felt another surge of blood to his groin. He breathed her name and that was the last coherent thought he had. Her legs wrapped around his waist, pinning him to her. She pushed her hips against his and his resistance crumbled.

She tilted her hips and fitted him to her. He heard his own guttural moan as he thrust into her, filling her, claiming her for his own. He couldn't hold back, he couldn't resist, and when he heard her call his name it pushed him further.

There was nothing gentle in their lovemaking. It was fuelled by pure desire. Desperate, all-consuming desire.

He thrust into her again. Up and down he moved, faster and faster, harder and stronger, and she met each thrust. She arched her back and held him close with her legs, opening herself to him, offering herself to him.

He buried himself deep inside her and when he felt her shudder and come undone he came with her. They climaxed together and when they were completely spent he gathered her to him, holding her close, reluctant to let her go as he savoured this next moment, as they lay in each other's arms, slick with sweat and breathing hard.

She had blown his mind. She was bold and confident. *This* was the Abi who had been hiding, the one he had known was in there somewhere, the one who had been swamped by trauma and stress. He was finally piecing her together. Bit by bit he was getting to know her and he knew now he could bring her back, resurrect her, restore her. All she needed was love, a connection, someone to nourish her. He could be that man.

He wanted to be that man.

Abi woke to the smell of fresh coffee. She had slept well, without nightmares. She couldn't remember the last time she had slept soundly all night. Actually, she could. It had been last week when she'd fallen asleep in Damien's arms. She'd had two good nights' sleep in the past six months since Mark had died and both of those nights she had spent with Damien.

He was standing by her bed, holding a mug of hot coffee. She could get used to waking up like this.

'Good morning,' he said, as he put the coffee beside her bed and kissed her.

She could definitely get used to this.

'Good morning.' She smiled.

'Do you mind if I have a shower here? I need to collect Summer from Irma and George and it will save me some time if I don't have to go and come back.'

'Of course. There are fresh towels in the bathroom cupboard,' she replied. She rolled lazily over onto her stomach and watched as he disappeared into the bathroom.

He showered and returned bare-chested with one of her fluffy white towels wrapped around his waist. He dropped the towel and grinned when her eyes went straight to his groin. He was certainly impressive, lacking nothing she needed in that department, and she was disappointed to know there was no time to take advantage of his attributes.

'Another time, my lady,' he said, as he bent to pick up his trousers.

Like her when she had slept at his house, he only had yesterday's clothes to wear but there was not the same sense of shame for a man to put on yesterday's clothes. Without the jacket and bow tie his suit became just a pair of trousers and a shirt, and once he got to work and put a white coat over the top no one would be any the wiser.

She was happy to lie in bed and watch him get ready. It felt comfortable, easy; it didn't feel as if they'd only spent one night together but before they could talk about what happened next he was gone. Off to collect Summer and get on with his day, and Abi had no idea what he was thinking.

A fortnight went past in the blink of an eye. It was amazing how quickly time flew when every minute was filled. Between work and spending time with Damien and Summer, Abi had never been as busy, exhausted or happy.

Nikki's operation had gone well and Dylan had been discharged following his skin-graft surgery. She was pleased with the results of Nikki's op, even though it was early days. Her face was still swollen but Abi could already see the improvement made by the repaired bone structure. Nikki had some hip pain from where they had taken the bone graft but that was to be expected and Abi felt confident that everything had gone according to plan.

Damien's attentions were also helping to restore her confidence. Spending time with him was helping to make her whole again and she was feeling more positive than she had in a long time. She could see light at the end of the dark tunnel now, thanks to Damien.

They spent the weekends together, with Summer as their chaperone. Abi played tour guide but when Summer went to bed they got their adult time. Life was good and the sex was amazing but there had been no discussion about where they were headed. Damien hadn't raised the topic and Abi wasn't about to instigate it. She didn't want to formalise their liaison, afraid of jeopardising her happiness. Every relationship she'd ever had had ended badly, and she was superstitious and fearful enough not to want to have that discussion. She didn't want to legitimise what they had for fear that something would go wrong. She didn't want to be the one to cause the bubble to burst. She didn't want to risk ruining the fairytale she had only just started to believe could exist.

She desperately wanted to give her heart away, she wanted to find someone who might want to look after it, but she was terrified of the consequences. She was terrified that she would end up with a bruised and damaged heart and that some tragedy would befall Damien. It was better to keep things uncomplicated. It was better to just keep quiet.

But despite her reservations she was looking forward to another weekend. Their weekdays were hectic, between their work commitments, taking care of Jonty, her appointments with her psychologist and Damien's hands-on role as single dad to Summer, it didn't leave them with much time for romance and Abi had already learned to hold out for Friday night. She was enjoying having someone to share her time with, someone to spend weekends with, and she smiled to herself as she and Jonty walked up to Damien's front door.

But the smile was quickly wiped from her face when

her knock was answered not by Damien but by a woman. A rather striking, glamorous woman dressed in skinny jeans, sky-high stilettos and a figure-hugging top with a plunging neckline that revealed plenty of cleavage between gravity-defying breasts. Who the hell was she?

'Can I help you?' the woman asked as she struck a pose in the doorway, jutting one hip forward as she flicked shiny, sleek hair over her shoulder.

Abi glanced around, thinking she'd perhaps knocked on a neighbour's door by mistake, but this was definitely Damien's house.

'If you're going door to door, selling something, I'm not interested,' the woman said, as Abi stood mute, trying to work out what was going on.

The door was starting to close as Abi regained her senses. 'No, I'm here to see Damien.'

'And you are?'

'I'm Abi, I work with him.' Why had she said that? She wasn't here in a work capacity. She was here because she and Damien had made plans to take Summer out for pizza. And why was anything she did any of this woman's business? But she was too stunned to think of a better retort.

'He's in the shower,' the woman said, as she continued to stand in the doorway. She made no attempt to get out of the way and Abi was certain she was about to shut the door in her face. She certainly didn't appear about to invite her in.

Abi could see Damien over the woman's shoulder. He was dressed in jeans and a shirt but the buttons were open and his feet were bare. He looked half-dressed. His hair was damp from the shower and he was buttoning his shirt as he came towards her, glancing anxiously from her to the woman and back again. He looked surprised to see her, almost as if he'd forgotten about their arrangement, and from the expression on his face she was certain he hadn't been expecting her. But she couldn't blame him. This woman would certainly be more than enough to distract most men. But that still didn't explain who she was.

'Abi! You've met Brooke.'

Abi could feel the blood drain from her face and her hand automatically reached down to pat Jonty's head. She needed the comforting, familiar feel of his warm, soft fur under her icy-cold fingers. She felt as if all the blood was draining from her body.

This stunning, self-assured woman was Brooke!

She looked at her again. She couldn't help but compare herself to the ex-Mrs Moore.

She glowed golden. Her brown hair had been expertly highlighted and straightened and hung in a shiny curtain halfway down her back. Her face was smooth, unlined and her skin was lightly tanned. Abi's trained eye had noted that Brooke's nose was perfect for her face, symmetrical, small and narrow, and her legs were long and slim. Abi felt herself pale in comparison. She felt she was lacking something. She knew she was pretty enough in a young way, she could pass for a teenager some days, and that was the difference. Brooke was all woman. Confident and beautiful and self-satisfied.

'I'll go and finish getting ready,' Brooke said as she shot Abi a smug look that implied she'd won and Abi had no doubt that Damien was the prize.

As she turned on her heel Abi wondered what it was she was getting ready for.

'What is she doing here?' Abi asked, when Damien made no move to invite her inside either.

'I don't know.'

That was a very unsatisfactory answer but Abi let it go for now. 'Are we still going out for pizza?'

Damien shook his head. 'I'm sorry, I can't. I need to find out what Brooke wants.'

So this was how it was going to be, Abi thought. She was going to be shown the door in favour of his ex. She'd wondered where she fitted into the scheme of things, into his life, and now she knew. She could handle coming after his daughter and his career but she didn't want to come after his wife, ex or not. She'd been in that position before and it had ended badly. She wouldn't willingly put herself in that position again.

'Why didn't you call me to cancel?' she asked. She wouldn't have turned up if she'd known. She'd had no desire to meet or even see Brooke. Not without some warning. She wasn't prepared for this.

'I didn't know she was coming. She turned up without warning.'

'What for?'

'I don't know yet. I haven't had time to find out.'

Abi's first response was to panic. She didn't want to confront Damien's past—if that was what Brooke was. What *was* she doing here and what did it mean for Damien and Summer? What did it mean for *her*?

She knew what it meant. She only had to look at Brooke to know.

It meant the fairytale was over. She didn't get to live happily ever after. She didn't get the prince.

'I'll leave you alone, then, to enjoy your evening,' she said. There was no discussion between her fight and flight responses. Her flight response took over and she turned around and walked down the path, wanting to get away before she dissolved into tears, wanting to run and hide as humiliation crashed over her, shattering her ridiculous dreams into millions of tiny fragments that fell around her.

CHAPTER NINE

Damien stood and watched her leave. He was torn, caught between a rock and a hard place. He wanted to go after her, he knew he should go after her, but he didn't trust Brooke. He didn't know why she was there and he had a bad feeling about her reasons.

In the shock accompanying Brooke's unannounced arrival he'd completely forgotten the plans he'd made with Abi. If he'd remembered he would have called her to postpone. The last thing he'd wanted had been for the two of them to meet and the only thing that could make matters worse was if they'd met without him present. He had no idea what had transpired between them but he could only assume Brooke wouldn't have been particularly welcoming. She had a jealous, possessive nature and even though she didn't want him, he had no doubt that she wouldn't want to know that someone else did.

He didn't want Brooke to know about Abi, he didn't want her to start asking questions, so he definitely would have made other arrangements. Not that he could have explained what was going on. He really didn't know what Brooke was doing there but there was sure to be a reason. It would be more than just a visit to see Summer. There was always an ulterior motive as far as his manipulative, scheming ex-wife was concerned. Sure, she did it with charm, using her feminine wiles and acting skills to her advantage, but that didn't change the fact that there was always something to be gained for her. But, at the moment, he hadn't worked out what it was and until he knew the details he wasn't about to leave her alone.

Abi, for all her issues, was far less complicated, far more trusting. There'd be time to sort things out later with her, time to explain, so he let her go. He needed to conserve his energy to deal with Brooke. No doubt there was bound to be some drama or demand, and now it was time to face her music.

Abi had checked her phone a thousand times on Friday night after she'd run from Damien's but he hadn't called once. She'd worked herself up into a fever of indignation, shame and anger and had eventually switched her phone off. She didn't want to be mocked by its silence. She spent the rest of the night imagining all the sorts of things Damien and Brooke might be doing. She knew she was jumping to conclusions but he'd looked so awkward and uncomfortable when she'd appeared on his doorstep, so guilty, that of course her imagination had gone into overdrive.

It appeared she did have a type after all—good-looking, charming men who were only interested in getting her into bed. Did she deliberately choose men who would treat her badly? A psychiatrist would probably tell her it was all connected to issues with her father.

What would Caroline tell her? She knew her psychologist would berate her for thinking unkind thoughts about Damien when he'd done nothing to deserve them, but in Abi's eyes, choosing not to come after her, choosing not to explain, meant that he'd chosen Brooke over her. She couldn't blame him, Brooke was Summer's mother after all, but it hurt that, with everything he'd told her, when the chips were down he hadn't chosen her.

She needed to toughen up, needed to learn from her experiences, her mistakes, and stop being so gullible.

Abi lay in bed all Saturday morning. Her phone showed no missed calls and she couldn't face the thought of getting up and facing the day. She had Jonty and the amber-eyed tiger from the pier for company but neither of them had much to say. Which was fine with her because she didn't feel like talking. She felt like crying.

Jonty seemed to sense her mood. He lay on his stomach on his pillow, looking mournful. He rested his head on his front paws and every now and then he lifted his head as if to check on her before sighing and putting his head down again. She was positive she could read sympathy in his brown eyes but perhaps he was just bored and waiting patiently for a walk.

Eventually she gave in and got out of bed and pulled on her exercise gear. Last night she'd decided she needed to toughen up, she wasn't going to fall apart because a man had changed his mind.

Jonty raced down the stairs eagerly the moment Abi tied the laces of her sneakers, and to make up for her lazy, self-indulgent morning she intended to take him for a long walk.

It was getting dark as she turned into her driveway later and she was startled to find a man leaning against her garage door. She panicked briefly until she recognised him.

Tall and dark, lean and gorgeous.

Damien.

Her heart rate continued to accelerate at the sight of him. 'What are you doing here?'

'I wanted to see you. I need to talk to you and you didn't answer your phone.'

She'd left her phone behind for the walk. There hadn't seemed to be any point in carrying a phone that never rang. 'I thought you were busy with your wife and family.'

'Ex-wife,' he corrected. 'Have you got a minute? I need your advice.'

He looked so desperate it was almost impossible to stay mad at him. Her heart wasn't built to resist him. 'You'd better come in,' she sighed.

She made coffee and let Damien talk while she listened.

'I'm sorry I didn't let you know Brooke was in town. She honestly just appeared without warning. It took me by surprise and with Brooke the surprises are generally not pleasant. This time was no exception.'

'What is she doing here?' Abi asked, although what she really wanted to ask was, *Where did she stay last night and what have you been doing?*

'She's been offered a permanent role in the sitcom. She came to tell me she's staying in New York.'

'What does that mean for you and Summer?' With one question Abi had got to the heart of the problem.

'I don't know. That's what I wanted to talk to you about. I need to work out what my options are but I need to base my decisions on what is best for Summer. She is my priority and you are the person who knows us best. I need your opinion. I've always said I would do what's best for Summer but it turns out I don't know what that is,' he admitted. 'Is keeping her away from her mother the best thing? Or should I move to New York?'

Abi didn't want to answer that question. She knew she couldn't answer it without bias. She knew Damien had moved to LA because of Brooke and she'd been afraid that he would move again to keep his family together, but surely there had to come a time where he wouldn't be manipulated by Brooke?

Abi knew she was thinking of her own interests as well when she answered but did that matter when she also believed she was thinking of what was best for Summer too? 'Does Summer want to go?'

'No.' He shook his head and continued, 'But she is five, she doesn't get to decide.'

'Has Brooke asked for Summer to go to New York?'

'No.'

'Then there's absolutely nothing wrong with keeping Summer with you. Brooke has made no secret of the fact she doesn't want a child. You're not obliged to send Summer or to move you both. Let Summer visit her in New York. Better yet, make Brooke come here.'

'We'll have to come to some sort of official agreement if we're living on opposite sides of the country. I'm not sure if the courts will give me sole custody.'

'Well, then, you'll just have to find out about all the hoops you'll need to jump through to keep her and be prepared to start jumping. Child care will be the big thing but I imagine Brooke's hours are as inconsistent as yours so as long as you make good arrangements for that you might be okay. You can afford child care but you'll need something more permanent than sending Summer to Irma's. After-school care only covers you for so long. It's not a bad option, it gives Summer some interaction with other kids, but perhaps it's not ideal every day. You'll need a nanny or some organised care.'

'Do you think I can manage on my own? Do you think that's fair to Summer?'

'Trust me, having one parent who loves her and puts her first is all she will need.' Abi knew that she was speaking the truth this time, she had plenty of experience in that department. 'You're doing a fabulous job with her. You can do this.'

She knew she should have sent him on his way when she'd discovered him on her doorstep but she hadn't been able to resist him. He still looked a bit overwhelmed by the situation but Abi knew he would work it out. He was an intelligent, sensible man and she hoped he made an intelligent, sensible decision.

She could forgive him for the past twenty-four hours, she could forgive him for putting Summer first. She could give him forgiveness but what did she get?

She wasn't sure yet.

She was on tenterhooks for the next few days, waiting to hear what his decision was, but everything was quiet.

Every time there was a knock on her office door she found herself hoping that it would be Damien, bringing her the news she was desperate to hear, but each time she was disappointed.

And this latest interruption was no exception. There was a knock on the door and it opened to reveal Brooke. She was still in sky-high stilettos but she'd swapped the skinny jeans for a figure-hugging dress.

'I'm sorry,' she said. 'I thought this was Damien's office. I'm meeting him for lunch.'

Brooke was the last person Abi wanted to see. She'd been hoping for the news that Brooke had returned to New York but clearly that wasn't the case. 'He's next door,' Abi said, hoping to move her on, but instead she stepped into the room.

From her deliberate action and calm and measured manner Abi suspected she hadn't mixed up the offices at all. She suspected that Brooke had orchestrated this meeting but what she wanted to know was why. Had she won the battle over Damien? The battle Abi hadn't even realised they were having?

She wasn't kept in suspense for long.

'Seeing as you're so close to Damien and Summer, I expect you've heard the news?' Brooke said as she arched one finely plucked and expertly made-up eyebrow.

'What news?' Abi said, wishing as the words came out of her mouth that she'd kept quiet. She didn't want to know any news that Brooke might want to impart. A sixth sense told her it could only mean bad news for her.

'Damien and I are reconciling. He's moving to New York.'

Abi's stomach lurched. Too late she wished she'd pretended to be busy and sent Brooke on her way. Each word had felt like a punch she would never recover from. She felt ridiculous, naive, used and stupid. She'd given him her advice and her body. He'd asked her for advice but he hadn't listened. She'd given herself to him but he hadn't been honest with her. All she wanted was honesty.

She liked to think she was clever but she obviously

wasn't smart. Not worldly-wise. She was pathetic. When would she learn?

'No, I hadn't heard that.' She wondered if Brooke was expecting her to congratulate her. If she was, she was going to be disappointed. Abi summoned up all her reserves and said, 'If you'll excuse me, I have patients to see. You'll find Damien next door.' She forced the words out and prayed that Brooke would go away and leave her alone.

She sank into her chair and watched Brooke leave, knowing she couldn't compete. All she'd wanted was for Damien to find her attractive, but now that she'd met Brooke she realised there was no way she could measure up if Brooke was the type of woman he desired. Abi was far too different.

She put her head in her hands and let the tears flow. She was a fool. When would she learn?

'Abi? Is everything okay?'

She looked up at the sound of her name to find Mila in her doorway.

'What's happened?'

Abi reached for a tissue and wiped her eyes. The tissue came away streaked with mascara.

'It's nothing,' she said, as she threw the tissue in the trash.

Mila closed the office door. Was nobody going to leave her alone today? She wanted to lick her wounds in private but that wasn't being terribly professional. Mila must have come to see her about Dylan. She hoped everything was all right.

'Did you need to see me?'

'I was in the clinic so I thought I'd just give you an

update on Dylan but that can wait. Why don't you tell me what's wrong?'

'It's nothing, really. I just got some news that's upset me but I'll be fine. I just need a moment to get my head together.'

'Is it Damien?'

'Why do you say that?'

'At our age it's always men,' she said, as she came and sat by Abi's desk. 'What's he done?'

'He hasn't done anything yet but I think he's about to break my heart.' She sniffed and reached for another tissue. 'It's my own fault. Neither of us were ready for a proper relationship. I got ahead of myself.'

'What do you mean?'

'I had all these romantic notions but it seems he didn't share them.' They may not have talked about it but she had been building a fantasy in her head. A happily-ever-after where she and Damien got to spend the rest of their lives together, along with Summer and children of their own. It was a fantasy that had taken hold on the day they'd spent at the pier and she didn't want to let it go. But it seemed she might have to. 'Apparently he's planning on moving to New York with his ex-wife.'

'Really? He's just told you this?'

Abi shook her head. 'His ex has just paid me a visit. She told me.'

'And you believe her?'

'Why would she lie to me?'

'I don't know but I take it you don't want to let him go?'

'No.'

'Does he know how you feel?'

'No.' Abi loved him but she was terrified of telling him. She was terrified that it would jinx everything, even though it seemed that everything was already ruined. She wasn't about to humiliate herself further by telling him how she felt. 'I can't tell him I've fallen in love with him. I couldn't bear to hear that he doesn't love me.'

'So you're prepared to give him up?'

'No.'

'Then you have to tell him how you feel. You have to take the chance that his ex was lying to you. You have to take the chance that he feels the same way you do. You can't let him go without questions. You'll always wonder "what if." Trust me, I'm speaking from experience.'

'You've had your heart broken?'

Mia nodded. 'In the worst possible way.'

'Was it James?' Abi knew instinctively that it was. It would explain all that tension she had felt between the two of them.

Mila nodded again. 'James left me standing at the altar without an explanation and I have never found out why.'

'You didn't ask?'

'I didn't want to know at first but not knowing has stopped me from moving on.'

'Why don't you take your own advice? Why don't you ask him now?'

'It's too late. There is no point in raking up the past. But it's not too late for you. Don't let him go without a fight. Don't let him go without an explanation. You need to hear it from Damien's lips.'

Mila was right. Abi felt betrayed and she deserved some answers. She deserved some honesty.

She waited until the end of the day to confront him. She didn't want to run into Brooke again and she definitely didn't want to run into Damien and Brooke together.

'Can I speak to you?' she asked, as she stepped into his office and closed the door. 'I bumped into Brooke today. She told me you are getting back together.' Abi didn't give him an opportunity to speak. She needed to keep going, she needed to get her feelings out in the open before she lost her nerve. She paced up and down in front of his desk. 'How can you be having that conversation with her and sleeping with me at the same time? You know how Mark's lies and deception hurt me, you know what that did to me, and yet you've been sleeping with me and making plans with your wife behind my back.'

'Ex-wife. She's my *ex*-wife.' Damien stood up and ushered Abi to a chair.

'How could you do that to me? Do I matter so little?'

'Abi, listen to me. I haven't done anything that you're accusing me of. When did you speak to Brooke?'

'She came into my office before she met you for lunch.'

He frowned. 'We didn't have lunch. I haven't seen her today.'

'Do you think I'm making this up?' Abi wasn't sure who to believe, Damien or Brooke. She desperately wanted to believe Damien but she didn't know if she should.

'Of course I don't.'

'She was here,' Abi insisted.

'But she wasn't here to see me. And we are *not* getting back together.'

'You're not?'

'No. Why would you think that?'

'You have moved before for Summer. You told me you moved here from San Francisco for that very reason. I thought you might have decided that it was best for Summer.'

'I did it once before and it was a mistake. But do you think I would make this decision and not tell you myself?'

'Brooke was very convincing.'

'I don't doubt that, she's a very good actress,' he said as he sat down opposite Abi. 'She's fooled me more than once. When I met her she was a drama student sporting a black eye. She told me she and another student had collided heads when they'd been rehearsing a fight scene. Then later she told me that it was actually from her boyfriend, that he'd hit her. She'd worked out by then that I had protective instincts. She told me he was abusing her and of course I believed her and came to her rescue.

'The truth was that she saw me as someone who would be able to provide her with financial security while she pursued her career. I was a better bet than the actor she was dating plus I would be able to keep her looking good. Brooke is self-centred and narcissistic. Everything is about her. She doesn't want to be a wife and mother, she wants to be a successful actress, and she has used me to get herself there.'

'I thought you might not be able to resist Brooke. After seeing her, I couldn't blame you.'

'You're kidding, aren't you? What is under the surface is far more important. Believe me when I tell you there is absolutely nothing attractive about her.'

'Why was she here today if it wasn't to see you?'

'She came to see James for some minor cosmetic surgery.'

'James? Not you?'

Damien shook his head. 'Not me. I won't perform any more procedures on her.'

'You've done some in the past?'

He nodded. 'She's had her nose narrowed,' he said, and Abi felt a twinge of satisfaction. She'd been sure Brooke's nose was too perfect to be natural. 'She's also had her lips enlarged and after she had Summer she wanted her breasts reshaped and enlarged. I did all that but I refused to do any more surgery once Summer turned three.'

'Why?'

'Summer was old enough then to be aware of changes to Brooke's appearance. I didn't want her asking why her mother was always changing her looks. I didn't want her asking why *I* was changing Brooke's appearance. Hollywood is a superficial place, I didn't want to perpetuate the idea of physical beauty being the pinnacle of success to my own daughter, and that was the danger if I continued to operate on her mother. So I stopped.'

'But why would she lie to me? What was the point?'

'Think of it from her point of view. It's always about Brooke. She wants to be the centre of attention. Summer has been talking about you and Brooke doesn't want her attention on anyone else. She doesn't want us but she craves attention. You have to trust me when I say Brooke is not part of my life. I moved on a long time ago.'

'But that's the point,' Abi argued. 'You might think you've moved on but she will always be part of your life because of Summer. You can't cut her out but you need to decide how you want this to work. I can't invest myself in us until you've worked out what you want. I want honesty and I'm not prepared to play Brooke's games.' She wasn't sure she could handle her games or the additional stress.

Damien reached for Abi's hands and pulled her out of the chair. He wrapped her in his arms as he said, 'I have never lied to you and I promise I will work this out. I don't want you to worry about Brooke. Leave her to me.'

Abi relaxed slightly but she doubted it was going to be as easy to deal with Brooke as he would have her believe. But she would give him some time and space to sort things out. She had to make sure he had done that before she could invest in the relationship; she had to be able to trust him.

Damien grabbed his car keys and headed for the door. He had some letters to dictate but he'd have to come back later and finish those—there were things that couldn't wait. He was furious but he knew how to handle Brooke. She would have an agenda and he'd bet his last dollar that he knew what it was.

Brooke was lying on the sofa with an icepack on her forehead—the aftermath of her visit to James—when Damien got home, but at least she had collected Summer from school. He sent Summer to her room while he spoke to Brooke. He was still furious and he didn't want Summer to hear this conversation.

'What did you think you were doing at the clinic?'

Brooke lifted the ice pack from her forehead but didn't sit up. Her unlined face was a picture of innocence as she asked. 'What are you talking about?'

'Did you think Abi wouldn't tell me what you said? What game are you playing?'

'It's not a game. I want Summer with me and I didn't think you'd let her go without you. Therefore, that means you will move to New York.'

'I am not moving to New York and neither is our daughter.' He knew she was just trying to make him angry so he would give her what she really wanted. He just had to find out what that was. 'You don't want us. You definitely don't want me. I don't think you ever did. Tell me what you really want. You know I'll give it to you.'

He suddenly realised what she was after. Money and fame. It shouldn't surprise him. That was always what it was about with Brooke. Nothing had changed. She wanted Summer with her so that Damien would fund her lifestyle. Two could play that game. 'I won't give you Summer. She is staying with me but she can visit. If you agree that Summer can stay here, I am prepared to help you with your rent. I want you to have somewhere nice when Summer comes to stay.'

He took a chance that appealing to Brooke's avaricious nature would pay off. They would need to make some arrangements but he would do whatever was needed to ensure that Brooke didn't cause more complications, and then he could work out how to fix things with Abi.

CHAPTER TEN

THREE DAYS LATER Abi pulled her car to the kerb behind
a moving truck that was parked in front of Damien's
house. She locked her car and dodged around dozens
of packing boxes that were stacked on the pavement.
The boxes were all marked 'New York City'. Abi's heart
plummeted and she thought she was going to be sick.

Damien had asked her to call past after work. Had he
made his decision? Had he been lying to her all along?
Was he taking Summer and moving to New York?

Two men were loading the boxes into the truck. Abi
stopped when she noticed Brooke's name on one. She
glanced at the other boxes. They were all addressed to
Brooke.

She walked through the open front door.

Summer was playing on the floor but jumped up
when she walked in. 'Abi, I haven't seen you for ages.'

Abi had been avoiding everyone, not just Damien.
She'd avoided Mila, Irma and George and even Summer.

Summer ran to Abi and hugged her, wrapping her
arms around Abi's legs. She picked her up to hug her
properly and let her tuck her warm little body against
her side. She felt so soft and sweet and innocent. Abi's

eyes brimmed with tears as she gently put the little girl down. She had missed Summer almost as much as she'd missed Damien.

And thinking of the devil, there he was in all his dark handsomeness. Dressed casually in jeans that hugged his thighs and a black sweater that made his eyes gleam, he crossed the room and reached for her. She knew he was going to kiss her but she wasn't sure if she was ready for that. She needed to know the state of play. When she folded her arms protectively across her chest, he backed away.

More packing boxes lined the hallway and were stacked against the wall of the lounge. 'What's going on?' she asked.

'Thank you for coming. I wanted you to see this,' Damien said, as he gestured at more boxes that lined the passageway and led her out of the lounge and into the kitchen, out of earshot of Summer. 'These are all Brooke's things,' he said, as they walked through the house. 'She is officially out of here.'

'She's gone?'

'She left this morning.' He pulled a key from the pocket of his jeans and held it up triumphantly. 'She's even returned her key.'

'How did that happen?'

'I made her an offer she couldn't refuse.'

'What was it?'

'I will contribute to her rent in New York to make sure that she has somewhere decent to live when Summer visits.'

'Visits? Does that mean you're staying here?'

Damien grinned. 'It does. Brooke gets what she's wanted all along—financial security and the freedom to follow her dream—and hopefully that means that we can all get what we want.'

'We?'

'You were right. Brooke will always be a part of my life because of Summer, but that's all. There is nothing between us, there hasn't been for a long time, and if you'll let me I want to make it up to you.' He took hold of her hand and pressed his house key into her palm before closing her fist and wrapping his hand around hers. 'I want you to have this key.'

The sharp edges of the key dug into her palm. It was uncomfortable and didn't feel right. She wasn't sure about this. She wanted to be a part of Damien's life, of Summer's life, but she wasn't sure if they were thinking of it in the same vein.

She opened her palm and looked at the key. 'Can I think about it?' she asked.

'That wasn't the answer I was hoping for.'

It wasn't the offer Abi had been hoping for either but she didn't tell him that. She wasn't about to put words into his mouth. This was a start but it wasn't enough. It told her that Brooke was as good as gone but she didn't know where that left her.

Abi didn't want a key to the castle—she wanted the key to the prince's heart. What she felt for Damien and Summer was real. She didn't want a casual relationship, she didn't want a key so she could come and go. She wanted it all; she wanted the fairytale.

Abi remembered her discussion with Mila. She had to talk about her feelings. She needed to know exactly what he wanted from her and she had to tell him how she felt. She had to know she'd given everything she had to Damien and to pursuing her dream. At least then if she failed she'd know she'd done everything possible.

'I'm not sure I want a key to your house,' she said, and she lifted the key out of her palm and returned it to him. 'I appreciate the gesture but I want to be more than someone who leaves a toothbrush in your bathroom and stays over for the weekend. I have a different vision.'

Damien took the key but it sat heavy in his hand, just like his heart sat heavy in his chest.

He hadn't expected his offer to be rejected but he wasn't prepared to let go of his dream. He had a vision too, a vision of his future, and Abi was part of that. There was no way he was going to risk losing her.

'This is more than a key to my house,' he explained. 'This is a key to *our* house.'

'Our house?'

He nodded. 'You told me to work out what I wanted. I know exactly what I want. I want to start a new life with you. This is your key to our house. I want you to move in with us.'

'You want me to move in?'

'I want to show you that I am serious about us, that I'm committed to you. I'm giving you this key because I want you in my life. This isn't a spur-of-the-moment decision. My life is complete when you are there and I want to keep you in it. I've fallen in love with you and I want to see where this will lead.'

'You love me?' Abi was watching him solemnly but at least she was listening.

'I do. This key is just the beginning. I wasn't much good at being married,' he continued. 'I'm not sure if I know how to have a good marriage, a happy one, and I wasn't prepared to ever give it another shot, but you make me want to consider it and I'm hoping you will consider it too. I want you to be part of my life and of Summer's. I want you to feel safe with us, I want you to trust me. I'll give you all the time you need but I want you here. With us.' He held the key between his thumb and forefinger, offering it to her again. 'I love you, Abi. Please say you'll take a chance on me.'

She smiled and her amber eyes shone with fire as she reached out and took the key from his fingers. 'I will,' she said.

'You will?'

'Yes,' she answered him with a smile. 'I want this too. I want a future with you and Summer, a chance to build a life together, to be a family. I want *you*.' Abi leant in and kissed him. 'I love you too.'

The kiss was soft and tender. It wasn't crazy with desire, it was gentle with love, and it released his trapped and heavy heart. He took her in his arms as his heart soared in his chest and filled with love.

'Welcome home,' he said.

* * * * *